To Shirley
   a wonderful friend who
inspired me to get this book
out of my computer —
      Love
       Pam

# Tour Of Italy

PAMELA CLARK WRIGHT

ISBN-10: 149128899X
ISBN-13: 9781491288993
Library of Congress Control Number: 2013914877
CreateSpace Independent Publishing Platform
North Charleston, South Carolina

*Dedicated to Allen*

# ANA

I

I sat in the darkening room, staring out of the window. I really wasn't looking at anything specifically but thinking that this time of day, as dusk was
slowly creeping in, was the saddest time of the loneliest day of the week,
Sunday. Maybe it was just lonely for widows, I thought. I don't remember
it being so sad before. Maybe everyone felt like this to some degree on
Sundays, because they have to go to work on Mondays.

I became aware that the phone was ringing. Damn, the last thing I want
to do is talk on the phone. But I got up and made it to the receiver before the
answering machine chimed in.

"Ana, what took you so long to answer?" asked my best friend, Lena
Capello

"I don't know. I didn't hear it ringing at first. What's up?"

Suddenly, Lena became animated. "Are you very busy? Can I come over
right now?"

"Now?" I said, surprised. "I guess so. Sure. You sound very excited. I've
been home all day...you could have come over hours ago."

"I haven't had time, with one thing after another. Sara wanted to go to the mall for some new jeans, and Mama had three church ladies in for lunch, and I had to make nice with them and clean up dishes and all that. This is absolutely the first minute I have had, and I need to talk to you about something. No, I need to ask you something. Promise me that you won't say no."

"Oh, Lena, there you go again—what have you gotten yourself into this time?"

"For your information, I haven't gotten myself into anything!" Lena replied indignantly. "But can I come over right now? This can't wait. I'll bring wine. Remember, I want you to keep an open mind, so don't say no immediately."

"Well, I must say I am intrigued," I responded. "I haven't heard you this excited in a long, long time. Yup, come on over. I'm not doing anything that can't wait."

I was intrigued. Lena has been my best friend since we were ten years old, when my family had moved next door to the Capellos. There was Neva, Lena's mother, her two brothers, Tony and Alphonso, and Mr.Capello. Lena had never met a stranger and came over immediately, even before the moving van arrived, and soon we were playing as if we had known each other forever. And that's the way it has always been. Lena's brothers became her brothers and took up for her whenever there was trouble at school or in the neighborhood. Neva became her second mother, and she practically lived at the Capello house.

Some people actually thought we were sisters, even though Lena is small with big, brown Italian eyes and a mass of curly brown hair, and while I am tall and thin, with straight brown hair and hazel eyes. We shared all secrets and remained friends even when I went off to college, married Mark, and took a job teaching at a nearby university. Lena had no desire to go to college, although she could have. She was smart and always made excellent grades. What she loved was doing everyone's hair, so she became a beautician and now owns two salons and is opening a third.

Lena never married. She had numerous relationships, but most didn't last long. She always said that there was no one out there that she wanted to wake up with every morning. She said most men got ugly after two months, so she usually dumped them after a few dates. Sara was the result of one of those liaisons. This was the one thing Lena had never revealed to her: who Sara's father was.

"I can't talk about it right now," was what she always said, and eventually it just wasn't important. "Let's just say I got more than a little careless, but Sara is worth the price."

"But Lena," I asked her once, "doesn't her father want to be a part of her life?"

Her only reply was swift and adamant. "He doesn't know that she exists. He will never know, and Sara does not need or want him in her life. He is a loser with a capital L. The only good thing I can say about him is that he was very good-looking, and Sara got those genes. Case closed."

Case closed. I never said another word. Lena would tell me one day what happened. I know that. We might be seventy and gray-haired, but I would not die without knowing. What is true is that Sara is a little beauty, but she could have gotten that from Lena. Sara, now ten, is not her mother's spitting image but looks like all the Capellos in one way or another.

Sara is my godchild and will be the closest now that I will ever come to having a child. She has been the only thing that has given me any pleasure since Mark died. I have been drifting through life since that horrendous day that he was killed. It was a Sunday just like today.

I had asked him not to go running so late. It was getting dark, but he insisted that there was still a good hour of daylight left, and he would be all right. When the two police officers showed up at my door two hours later, I was already frantic with worry.

I took one look at them and knew the worst.

"Mrs. Douglas?" one of them said. I automatically corrected them. "Dr. Douglas."

"We have been combing the neighborhood looking for information on a young man, in his midthirties who is a runner. Several of your neighbors said that your husband runs."

"Oh my God, what has happened to Mark? Please tell me. Please."

One of the officers took my arm and steered me gently inside. "We are sorry to tell you that a man fitting your husband's description was hit by a car on Olde Irone Road this afternoon about four thirty. We need you to come with us to make an identification. Is there someone you want us to call to come with you?"

I remember falling to my knees and saying Mark's name over and over. I must have given them the Capellos' number. My parents had moved to Florida when my father retired two years before. Before I knew it, Tony, Alphonso, and Lena were standing at my door. We all went to the morgue together.

Tony and Alphonso went in first to see if it was really Mark. Alphonso came out with tears streaming down his face. One look at them, and I knew it was Mark.

"Oh my God, no, no, no…" was all I could say. They said I fainted.

When I went into the little room, I was struck by the fact that it did not look anything like morgues look on TV. It wasn't a huge, sterile, stainless-steel room. And it had some kind of strong institutional chemical smell. The room was small and brown, and Mark seemed to fill the room. As long as I live, I will never forget seeing him on that slab of metal. He was still in his T-shirt and shorts. One shoe was missing. I remember asking where his other shoe was. One of the policemen said that it must have come off when he was hit by the car and sailed through the air somewhere. They had not been able to find it, because it was dark.

Mark looked like Mark. It's not true that dead people look asleep. He looked dead, lifeless. He was gone and would never be back. I knew that instantly. My beautiful, wonderful, generous, funny Mark was gone forever. In a moment, he was gone. All our dreams and hopes for the future were null and void.

The next days and weeks were a blur of people calling, the funeral, the numbness afterward, and people tiptoeing around being quiet and careful, solicitous of my well-being. I hardly remember any of it. They still have never found the driver who hit Mark. Maybe that is why I can't let go of the grief.

His shoe was found the next spring by another runner. A neighbor. "Ana, this is John Spangler. I live on the street over from you. I don't know if you remember me, but I used to run with Mark sometimes, or we would often see each other running."

"John, yes, I do remember you. Of course. Do you still run?"

"Yes," said John, "That's why I am calling you. I was running today on Olde Irone Road. It's the first time I have actually gone that route since Mark…well, I'm calling because—and I really didn't know what to do about this—I think I found Mark's shoe. You know. the one he had on when…" His voice drifted off. "Marie, my wife, said you might want it."

I was stunned. "His shoe. Oh, Jesus. Yes, please, John, I do want it. Thank you so much. You will never know how much this means to me."

"Ana, I will bring it over just as I found it. But I need to warn you that it's pretty messed up. You know, it's been outside in the elements for months now, and it's pretty dirty. I'm pretty sure it was Mark's, because we wore the same brand, and we used to make comments about what good running shoes they were."

John was so sweet. His hands were trembling when he delivered the shoe in a shoe box of the same brand (one of his, no doubt) lying on a clean white towel. I was so touched that I started crying the moment I saw it. It was the last earthly thing I had of Mark's. I still have it at the back of the closet that Mark used.

A few days later Marie called. "Ana, this is Marie Spangler."

"Marie, hello. How nice of you to call. I am so grateful to John, and I apologize for falling apart when he was so kind to bring me Mark's shoe."

"That's why I'm calling, Ana. I just wanted to see if you are all right. I know it must have been a blow for you."

"It was, but as crazy as it sounds, the shoe means everything to me."

"We weren't sure it was the right thing to do, but when John came home with the shoe in his hand, he said that he knew it was Mark's and wondered if he should call you. Ana, John and Mark had a runners' friendship. They only saw each other running, warming up, or cooling off, but it's a guy thing, I guess. John felt strangely close to Mark. When he came home from your house, he broke down. He still misses Mark."

I was so surprised that someone else could miss Mark. How stupid and selfish of me. "Thank you, Marie. It means the world to me to hear that."

"Ana," Marie said hesitantly, "I am here any time you want to talk—or just come over. Or need anything. Just call."

But I never did. I just kept it bottled up.

I used to have such rage at the driver of the car. How could he have not stopped? They told me that Mark died instantly, on impact. But how can they be truly certain of that? It made sense that the car was probably speeding as it rounded the curve, and I was sure that it was a male driver. For a long time, I thought it must have been someone who had been drinking, but even a drunk person must have heard a thud or seen something, even if they thought it was a deer. Wouldn't a normal person have stopped? But this wasn't a normal person. This was a murderer. This wasn't an accidental death.

In the past year or so, especially on Sundays like this one, I have had different thoughts about this person. Maybe it was a teenage girl, an inexperienced driver, who panicked or had the music turned up too loud or was talking on her phone or doing all of that and in an instant panicked and drove on. This is a person who will have my husband's death on her hands and in her thoughts forever. How would this person ever resolve what they had done to another human being? They had killed someone in a careless moment.

I look at my young students and think that any one of them could have been that person. Would I hate them forever if I knew that? How do I resolve my own anger and hatred and pain and bitterness and get on with my life? I have been stuck in grief for six years.

Thank God for my job and those students. They were, and still are, my saving grace. I would have gone mad without them. I feel that I am moving into a different emotional space now. It is not forgiveness. I am not sure that I can identify it yet. I think about Mark and what he would say, how we would have talked through this. I have prayed to him for guidance.

"Please Mark," I have asked so many times, "help me deal with your death. I can't do this anymore. Give me something…a sign…a symbol. I need to know you are not in pain and are OK." Mark would have laughed at this. "Death is death. This is it, babe," he would have said. "You can have all the spiritual hooey in the world. There are no signs from the beyond."

I don't believe this. But I have had no reason to dispute it. There have been no signs.

# II

"Ana, open the door!" The doorbell was shrieking one long, loud ring.

"I'm coming, I'm coming. Hold your horses," I yelled back.

When the door opened, Lena peered into the dark house and screamed, "For God's sake, turn on some lights. Its pitch dark in here. How do you ever see your way around?"

She was right. The house was completely dark, and I had never noticed. I had become skilled at walking through a dark house. It seemed to be symbolic of my life. There was no light in my life. After I turned on all the lamps, we went into the kitchen. Lena was laden with a huge picnic basket and two bottles of wine. "Good grief, how much are we going to drink?" I asked.

"You know Mama. When she heard I was coming over here, she loaded me up."

The most heavenly Italian odors came wafting out of the basket, and I suddenly realized I was actually hungry.

"I think we have ravioli and some roasted chicken, besides bread, cheeses, olives, and God knows what else...Oh, yeah, cannoli. We have cannoli. But first a big glass of montepulciano."

This was a delicious red wine that we both loved. "OK, let's get it open so that you can tell me what all this mystery is about."

"Not yet," said Lena. "Mama said no talking until we have eaten, because she said you probably have had nothing but coffee all day."

Neva knew me all too well. I don't eat much anymore, and there are days when I don't know if I have eaten or not, so I just don't eat. I don't seem to have much of an appetite, because nothing really tastes good most of the time. The one exception has been Neva's cooking.

"OK, get the plates out. I have to admit, it does smell delicious. Does Neva know what you are going to ask me?"

"Absolutely. And she said that I cannot take no for an answer."

Halfway through our meal, after lots of really meaningless small talk and three glasses of wine, I finally had had enough. "OK, Lena, I am full, I am drunk, and I know more about the people who get their hair done in your shops than any one human being needs to ever know. What are you going to ask me? I can't stand it any longer. Tell me right now."

"Make us some coffee. I'll get the cannoli, and then I will get into it," said Lena.

Fifteen minutes later, we were settled in. Lena looked at me and took a deep breath. "Ana, you know, when Papa was dying, he made us promise, the three of us, that we would take Mama to Italy before she died to see the homeland and all the relatives. Mama writes to a lot of these relatives each month. Well, Zia Lucilla has been diagnosed with heart disease of some kind, and she wants Mama to come over now while she is still fairly healthy, and Mama wants to go. But she doesn't want to go by herself. She wants me to go with her."

"That's wonderful, Lena," I said, so pleased for them. "What a great trip. I know what you want to ask me. You want Sara to stay with me. Of course she can stay here. You know how much I love her. It would give us time together. When are you leaving?"

"No, Ana, that's not it at all! Sara is going with us, because Mama wants the Italian relatives to see her. You know she has taught Sara Italian, and she is very good in the language. Mama is so proud of her and wants to show her off. Alphonso and Tony can't go. They just can't leave the car dealership." The boys had inherited Papa Capellos' business when he died. They had worked there from the time they were young teenagers, knowing that one day it would be their business, as well. "Ana, Mama wants you to go with us."

"What?" I choked on my coffee. "Are you nuts? I have a full class schedule. I can't go to Italy." I said the last part, Italy, like it was another planet.

"Not now, Ana," said Lena. "We aren't going until next May. Just before school is out, so that Sara won't miss but the last couple of weeks."

"Have you forgotten that I am going to be on sabbatical next semester? I'll be researching material for my book. The university has been very lenient with me, but I have to get moving on this." "We know that, but this will be at the end of the semester, and besides, you teach European history, and we will be in Europe. You can do some research in Italy and use it as a tax write-off."

"Lena," I began in my most patient professorial voice. "My research has nothing to do with Italian history. I need material from Germany and will be going to the university in Tubingen in February. I'll be there for over a month. How could I possibly go to Italy?"

"Ana," Lena pleaded. "I asked you to be open-minded. This is very important to me, to Mama, and to Sara that you go with us. You are part of our family. We have always been there for each other. Mama is seventy-five now. And who knows better than you what blows life can deal? Her time is shorter than ours, and this is the one thing she has ever asked of you."

It was true. Mama Neva had never asked one thing of me. She just gave and gave. When Mark died, I think she sent over food for a year. Sometimes she just came over and straightened up my house or sat with me. She always made sure that there were groceries in the house—at least the staples: milk, eggs, bread, and cheese.

"But Lena," I replied. "How can I manage this? I really do have to use this time to get all my research done and to at least begin writing the book. You know the academic world—publish or perish. I have to keep this job."

"That is why I am talking to you now. It's the end of October, so there is time to start organizing and preparing. Don't you think you could really get a lot done by May and then treat yourself to a great vacation? And don't forget, Ana, I have two shops that I have to have everything in order so that I can go. Alphonso is going to oversee the bookkeeping, and I do have capable assistants, but I am leaving two businesses with a third due to open next fall."

"That's true," I agreed. "I don't know. It's so out of the blue, and I haven't done anything since Mark died but just try to get through each day without folding. All of a sudden, there are these two major things within weeks of each other, and both include flying to a foreign country."

"It is a shame that they both are occurring at basically the same time," Lena said, "but sometimes things happen that way."

"So—I am not saying I'll do it, but—how many days are you talking about?" asked Ana.

"OK, Ana, here is the part that I want you be open-minded about. Mama and I have talked about this a lot because it will be her first and only time to Italy, and we decided we needed to do everything that we want to do there and see all the sights that are important to us. Plus we want to have some flexibility to go off on our own. All of our relatives come from the area around Todi in Umbria, so Mama wants to spend some days with them. I want to visit some of the hair salons in a few of the major cities. That way I can write some of the trip off for business purposes…so we are thinking of three and a half weeks."

"What!" I yelled. "You must really be crazy! There is no way I can be gone that long. No way!"

"Ana, you can do this, and you need to do this," said Lena quietly. "Your semester will be over just before the tour begins. Please don't be angry with me, but I need to say this. We are both forty-two now. Life is marching on. Your life stopped when Mark died."

"Wait a minute," I interrupted, getting a little heated.

Lena put her hand up to stop me. "Let me finish, Ana. I don't mean to hurt you or be cruel. Look around here." She waved her arm around, taking in the kitchen, but the gesture also included the entire house. "In six years nothing has changed, except there is literally no life or light in your house, your life, or your future. You have dragged through each day in a complete fog. You live in shadows. You need a change. You need to shake up your life. You even dress brown—that's the color of your life."

Now, I was mad. "You have no right to say that. Except for a few weeks off after Mark died, I went back to work and have worked every day since then. I haven't even taken a vacation."

"That, my dear friend, is the point!" Lena replied. "Think about it, Ana. Is there anything that excites you? I bet you can teach your classes by rote."

I interrupted again, still quite angry. How dare she! "Are you aware, my dear friend," I responded sarcastically, "that I have been voted for five consecutive years as one of the most popular professors on campus? I think that might indicate that I have been living some kind of life."

"Ana, I know you are a wonderful teacher," Lena responded in a conciliatory tone, "and I know the students love you. But think about it. What have you done for yourself personally? When was the last time you actually went on a shopping spree or done something just for fun? You haven't even changed your hairstyle in what…ten years now."

I said nothing. It was true, whether I wanted to admit it to myself or not. My life had been empty for six years. Nothing excited me.

Lena continued, "Do you realize that in eight short years we will be fifty? Do you want the next eight years to look like the last six years?"

"No," I admitted. "No, I guess not." I started crying. "Am I really so drab, Lena?"

"Truthfully, since you asked, I think you could spruce up your life a little, and you could start with a different hairstyle and some color. Do you realize that you have a lot of gray showing now?"

I was shocked. I had not even noticed. "I have a lot of gray hair?"

"Ana, we have all been afraid to say anything to you about anything. We didn't want to rock your very fragile boat. Mama has been so worried about you."

"She has? But why? I am doing just fine."

Lena laughed, "No, I would never say you are doing just fine. More like you're getting through each day."

She was right again. But I couldn't go to Italy. The timing was absolutely wrong.

"OK," I said. "You are right about a lot of things. I will concede that I haven't been a ball of fire in the past few years, and I will make an appointment to do something about my hair—will you do it?"

Lena nodded and said, "What about the trip, Ana? Will you go with us? Isn't there anything about doing this that appeals to you?"

"Well, of course," I responded halfheartedly. "If it were any other time, it could be very appealing. The timing is just so wrong. I'm already feeling overwhelmed about going to Germany and trying to get a book together. I feel stressed about it even now."

"Can I at least tell you about the trip?" Lena asked.

"Of course." I did want to hear what they would be doing. "You know that I'm very happy that Mama Neva is getting this chance and for Sara to have this opportunity. Italy through a child's eyes. She will never forget this."

Lena reached into her big tote bag and brought out all kinds of brochures on different regions in Italy. "We have given this a lot of thought, Ana. It is not a fly-by-night idea. We have actually been planning it since last summer. Where we want to go, how long to stay in any one place, how we will travel over there—rent a car or go by train and maybe even fly to different regions. We have talked to several travel agents looking for the best deals. Ana, it has been so much fun, and I have wanted to talk to you about it for so long, but I knew your reaction would be exactly what I have heard tonight, so I put it off. It was Mama who kept saying, "Talk to Ana, she must come with us. Where does she want to go?"

I was touched. I do not have one drop of Italian blood in me, but I am so connected to this family. Much more than my own family. My parents have always been so insular. The Capellos have been my family.

"So," Lena said "after endless discussions, we have decided to go with a very flexible planned tour that takes us everywhere we want to go and allows Mama to leave the tour in Umbria and rejoin us in Florence."

"A tour?" I asked. "I would have never believed it. Why?"

"It was never our first, second, or even third thought, I have to admit," said Lena. "It was one of the travel agents who brought it to our attention as she was helping me sketch out an itinerary. At first we rejected it as too rigid, but she assured me that this is a tour where you can do your own thing in any city. You can go on the planned tours, or you can have the time to yourself. The tour is very accommodating, and since I want to visit salons in Rome, Florence, and Milan, it became the best plan as time evolved. It also feels like the safest way to travel."

"It sounds like you are going everywhere in Italy," I said.

"No, not everywhere, but we will get to see a lot. We fly into Rome and get on a bus to Sorrento, but we stop in Pompeii on the way. Sara is beside herself, she is so excited! She has been reading everything she can find on the ruins and the volcano. We will spend a few days on the Amalfi coast, with the opportunity to go to Capri and Positano. Then back to Rome for a few days, followed by the hill towns of Umbria, where we will stay in Orvieto and go on side trips. After that, we travel to Siena, Florence, Venice and, finally, Milan, where we will leave for home. "That is an incredible trip," I said quietly. Lena was so excited and animated.

"Ana, I am going to leave all the information and the itinerary. Please think about this. I promise you, this will be incredible. The trip of a lifetime. I have to have a final answer by the end of this week. The tour only takes thirty people."

"I will think about it, Lena, but don't get your hopes up."

She gave me a good-night hug. I felt drained but also unexpectedly hopeful. I haven't had this feeling in so long. What if I did go? It was overwhelming, and I just couldn't think about it anymore tonight.

# III

Over the next three days, I didn't hear one word from Lena. I was surprised. I thought she would hound me, but she didn't. I couldn't get the trip out of my mind. I had looked at the brochures several times. The thought of going to Italy became larger than life. I kept thinking about it in classes, in faculty meetings, when I woke up, when I went to sleep at night. I had dreams about Italy. But more than anything, I forgot to think about Mark every waking and sleeping moment of my life. I felt guilty about that.

If I got all my ducks in a row, did a lot of preliminary research before I went to Germany, and got my outline for the book together, there was a strong possibility that I could do it all—my research and the trip to Italy. I would only be in Germany five weeks. I could do a lot before I went and a lot there, maybe even start writing the book over there. I had always been organized. My problem was that I had not given the book much thought. I only knew that I had to publish something this year. My topic was going to be on medieval Europe, but I had not narrowed it down yet.

On Thursday I came home from work, made myself a sandwich, and started thinking of a focal point for my book. I began a rudimentary outline. I worked on it for the next four hours. I had to admit to myself that I was getting a little bit excited about actually doing something more academically challenging than just teaching. I enjoyed original research, and that was what the trip to Germany entailed. My German was rusty, but I could read it better than speak it; therefore, I wasn't anticipating major problems. I felt like I could remember enough conversational German to get by for my few weeks there.

Every night before I turned out the lights to go to sleep, I read the brochures on the trip to Italy. I had never particularly thought about going to Italy, but I knew some Italian from hanging around the Capellos, and I loved their Italian lives. They were my true family, and I loved every one of them. How could I not go with them? I knew I could get a solid format for a book done, and there was no real reason not to go to Italy. I really wanted to go with them, and I had not wanted to do something in so long that the excitement that I was feeling was almost a foreign emotion to me.

On Friday morning, I called Lena. "I have nothing to wear."

"What are you talking about?"

"To Italy. I have nothing to wear to Italy."

"To Italy?" I could almost see through the telephone as the light began to dawn on her. "You're going, Ana?" Then I heard her shout to her mother and Sara. "Ana is going with us to Italy. Ana is going to Italy."

I heard Neva in the background. "Tell Ana to come over after work tonight. She must eat with us. We have a lot to talk about." Everyone was shouting and laughing at once.

"Ana, are you still there?" Lena asked. "Mama wants you to come over tonight for supper."

"I heard her. I will be there as soon as my last class is over," I said as I hung up. Excitement was building in me. I kept repeating to myself, "I am going to Italy, I am going to Italy, I am going to Italy."

# KATHRYN

# I

I was exhausted. My two grandsons— Chapin, six, and Eli, three—had worn me out, and now I had a splitting headache. Chapin was a handful and getting more aggressive every day. He constantly hit and picked on his younger brother. Eli was no match for the more robust older brother and had bruises up one side of his body and down the other. Today, Chapin had bitten Eli and left a very ugly mark on his arm.

Thank God, I thought, only one more hour to go before Sammy picks them up. I have the weekend free. At just that moment the telephone rang.

"Mom?" said Sammy. "I just wanted you to know that Jenn and I will be a little late tonight. We thought since it was Friday, we would have a bite out and pick the boys up later. Mom? Are you there?"

"I'm here, Sammy, but I need for you and Jenn to come right from work. I am very tired. The boys have exhausted me, and my head is splitting. Chapin has been particularly bad today. He bit Eli."

"Oh, Mom, boys will be boys. Chapin doesn't mean anything by it. He is all boy," said Sammy smugly. That was a definite cut at Eli who, I knew, Sammy wished were more of a fighter.

"No, Sammy, it's more than that. The school called me again today. I gave them both yours and Jenn's numbers."

"I know, Mom, they called, but I was in a meeting. They are just whining again. Mom, listen," Sammy said impatiently. "I have to go; Jenn and I won't be very late. Just give the boys a peanut butter and jelly sandwich. They will be fine. See you later."

"Wait, Sammy." But he was gone. He didn't hear one thing I said about how tired I was or that I needed them to come now, I thought. This can't go on. I just can't keep these boys any longer. It's just too much for me.

"Grandma?" said Eli tearfully. "Can I sit with you? Chapin hit me again. He scares me, Grandma. Can I live with you?"

"Oh darling boy, your Mommy and Daddy would miss you very much if you lived with me. But you can sit with me. Let's read a book, but first, let me see what Chapin is doing."

"Chapin, where are you? Chapin, come here this instant."

Chapin stuck his head around the corner. "Here I am, Grandma. Come in the kitchen. I am cooking."

"What?" I yelled. "I told you never to touch the stove."

"I didn't, Grandma, I made cookies without cooking on the stove, "he said proudly.

I went in the kitchen, and a disaster hit me in the face. There was sugar, sprinkles, flour, water, and some kind of paste concoction everywhere I turned. On a cookie sheet were little globs of flour balls. The floor was sticky with something I couldn't identify.

"Oh my God, oh my God," I said stunned. It was a complete and utter mess, and my pounding headache just got ten times worse.

"Chapin, whatever possessed you to do this?" I asked, stricken.

"Grandma, I wanted to make you something. Do you love me, Grandma?" Chapin asked, looking defeated. "Are you mad at me?"

I was actually nauseated; not only by my headache, but also by the time it was going to take me to clean up the kitchen. I knew that I had to answer this question carefully: "Chapin, I love you lots and lots. Making cookies was very thoughtful. But remember me telling you once that we have to do things in the kitchen together, because there are too many dangerous things in kitchens, like knives, stoves, poisons? Do you remember that?"

"Grandma, do you hate me?"

"Of course not, my little darling, but I do have a very bad headache today, and it is making me cross."

From another room, Eli called in a small voice, "Grandma, Grandma. Are you going to read to me?"

"Shut up, you baby," yelled Chapin, "Grandma is making cookies with me."

"Chapin, don't say 'shut up' to your brother. I want you to sit in the chair while I start cleaning up the kitchen. I will get Eli to help us, and then we will read the book together."

"No," yelled Chapin angrily. "I don't want Eli. He's a baby."

"I am not a baby," said Eli as he came into the kitchen. "Grandma, Chapin made a big mess. He is a bad boy."

Chapin jumped off the chair, pushed Eli on the floor, and started hitting him, yelling, "Baby, baby, baby. Little baby boy."

"Boys, stop it. Stop it this minute. Both of you sit down and don't get up until I tell you to. Chapin, not another word from you. Not one word. You are too big to be picking on your brother like that."

I placed each of them in a chair on opposite sides of the table, after wiping away Eli's tears. He was going to have another bruise on his face where Chapin had hit him. I cannot control him, I thought. His anger is out of control.

It took quite a while to get the kitchen back into some kind of order. I decided to feed the children, because it was close to seven o'clock, and obviously Sammy and Jenn decided that, despite my needs, theirs came first.

I got the boys settled down and gave them a bath. They were tired and asking constantly when they were going home. Both fell asleep in the family room. At ten o'clock, Sammy called. "Mom, I know it's late, so we decided just to let the boys sleep over, and we will pick them up tomorrow."

I was livid, and my headache had not gotten better. "Sammy, did you not hear me this afternoon? I said I was tired and had a pounding headache and needed you to come pick the boys up on time today."

"I know Mom, but—"

"There are no buts, Sammy, you and Jenn simply disregarded me. Please come get the boys now."

"Mom, its ten o'clock!"

"I know exactly what time it is, Sammy, and if you don't come, I will bring them myself. I have had your children since six thirty this morning. My house is a disaster. Chapin is out of control. I can't do this anymore."

"Mom, listen. I apologize. I didn't realize how bad you were feeling today. I will be over first thing tomorrow morning to get the boys."

"No, Sammy, tonight. I know how your first thing usually runs. It will be afternoon before you get here. I simply cannot baby-sit tomorrow. I am worn out. I want you and Jenn to find another baby-sitter."

"Mom, why don't you go to bed, and we will talk about this tomorrow. You had a bad day today with the boys. Things will be a lot better tomorrow."

"Sammy, you are not hearing me, are you? I will bring the boys home myself, tonight. I need tomorrow and Sunday off."

"No, Mom, don't do that. It's just too late. I don't want you out driving. You said you had a bad headache. It's not safe. Are the boys asleep now?"

"Yes, they are, but they can be awakened."

"Mom, please don't do that," said Sammy. "The truth is, Jenn and I have a couple of errands we need to do tomorrow. You know how hard we work. We thought it would be nice for us to sleep in. We will be there to get the boys right after breakfast."

I was so angry, I couldn't speak. "No, Sammy, this discussion has ended. I will wake the boys up and bring them now. Good-bye!"

I hung up on him. This is a first, I thought. They can deal with cranky boys tomorrow and take them on errands as other parents do. True to my word, I woke the boys up, put coats over their pajamas, got them into the car, put a blanket on them, and drove the twenty-five minutes to my son's house.

Both Sammy and Jenn were astonished. It was almost worth the whole thing just to see the expressions on their faces. "Mom, I can't believe this," Sammy said when he saw me.

"Both boys are sound asleep, so you will have to lift them out of the car yourself." Then I addressed Jenn. "Jenn, please look at the bite that Eli got today from Chapin to make sure it's not infected. He may have to have medical treatment. He also has new bruises. Your son needs extra attention. I will talk to you later this weekend about getting other child-care help." And with that I turned and left.

I heard Sammy calling me, but I didn't look back. I drove home, took a hot, soothing bath, and got in bed thinking I would fall dead asleep, but I didn't. My thoughts took over.

This is a mess, I thought, but I am as much responsible for it as Sammy and Jenn. Chapin was born five months after Gary's death, and I was so grief-stricken that taking care of that precious little infant was a godsend. It was only supposed to be a temporary arrangement until Jenn and Sammy could find someone permanent, but as the weeks evolved into months, it was no longer an issue. I loved having that baby in my arms.

Chapin was a demanding child from moment one, but we did well together until Eli was born. Jenn only stayed home three weeks before she returned to work. I had forgotten how much energy it took with two children, one a baby and the other barely out of toddlerhood. Chapin hated Eli from the start. He was spoiled and wanted nothing to divert attention away from him. Looking back, it was easy to see that was the beginning of the problems that I was dealing with now. Jenn and Sammy absolved themselves from parenthood, and I let them.

They began to pick the children up later and would go away for "their weekends" more often. Most Saturdays, I baby-sat most of the day so that they could sleep late and run errands at their leisure. As it stood now, they had their children for a few hours during the week and thirty-six hours on the weekends at the most. The reality of this situation is that I am raising the boys and not doing a very good job at it.

Another reality check is that, at sixty-two, I did not have the energy to do this another eighteen years.

I also had not had a vacation for six years or hardly two consecutive days off in that time. No wonder I was burned out. It was time to make changes. I wanted to go somewhere.

And then there was Laura. My daughter has been so angry that I've let Jenn and Sammy take advantage of me that she was hardly speaking to me any longer. She stopped coming home for the holidays, and she never initiated calls. When I called, if she picked up, the conversation was short and strained. If I left a message, she didn't call back very often.

I knew virtually nothing about Laura and her life in California. I thought there was someone special in her life. She loved her job at Universal, but I was not sure exactly what she was doing there. In previous times when she called, we couldn't talk because the kids were always getting into something. She got fed up and stopped calling.

The last time she visited, when Eli was about a year old, she said, "This is like being in a zoo. Mom, do you realize we have hardly had one moment together the entire time I have been here? Even when we tried to go out to dinner, Jenn and Sammy wanted to go to but had no one to baby-sit, so the three of us went out, and you baby-sat."

"But," I protested, "I wanted you to spend some time with your brother."

"And I wanted to spend time with my mother, but I can see that is not going to happen. Call me, Mom, when or if you decide to quit being a free nanny for Sammy." And she left the next day to go back to California. That was two years ago.

After a restless night of little sleep and a lot of tossing and turning, I decided that I would go over to Sammy's house and thrash this out once and for all, so that we could start making some changes.

# II

Jenn answered the door. "Kathryn, I am surprised to see you today. Sammy is at the health club, but come in."

"Grandma, Grandma," said Eli, running into my arms. "Are you coming to take me to your house?"

"No, Eli, I need to talk to your mommy and daddy for a few minutes. How is your bite today?" He held out his little arm, which was turning purple and yellow around the bite site. It was a little swollen. "Does it hurt, sweetie?"

He nodded his head and put his thumb in his mouth. There were tears in his eyes.

"Kathryn, please don't make a big deal over this," said Jenn. "It makes it worse. It is just a little bite."

"Eli, you are a very brave boy, and I think your arm will be ever so much better if you just prop it up on your pillow and rest on your bed with your teddy. Can you do that? I will come check on you in a few minutes."

He nodded again and didn't say a word but went to his room.

"Jenn, his arm is swollen. He needs an ice pack on it. When do you expect Sammy back?"

"Probably within the next thirty minutes," she said.

"Good," I said. "That gives us some time together."

Jenn looked uncomfortable. "Is there something I can do for you, Kathryn?"

Jenn was a very accomplished young woman. At thirty-five, she was a corporate executive, and her career seemed to be going straight up. Both she and Sammy had chosen excellent careers. Sammy was an engineer and doing extremely well. Their professional lives were exemplary. Their personal lives, particularly as parents, were a mess. They were not attentive parents, despite the fact they loved their sons. They just didn't parent their children, and I blamed myself.

"Yes, Jenn. You can do something for me. You can listen to what I have to say. I need for you and Sammy to start looking for a new baby-sitter. I am suggesting a nanny. Someone who can live here with you, does housework, and oversees the boys."

She looked shocked. "The boys would be devastated without you."

"I would still be in their lives like an ordinary grandmother. Like your mother, Jenn." Linda Parker was no grandmother, but I couldn't resist. Linda was "too nervous" to ever baby-sit, but she was not too nervous to play bridge with her girlfriends, go shopping several times per week, or play golf or tennis weekly. The children never went to her house, because she just couldn't bear the mess they made.

"I have no intention of abandoning them, Jenn, but I do realize that I do not have the energy to raise them."

31

Jenn suddenly flared up. "We certainly aren't asking you to raise them, just watch them a few hours a week. You know what crazy people are out there. We couldn't leave them with just anyone."

"That is why I am suggesting that you think about a nanny from an agency with references. If you are worried, you could even install one of those nanny-cam things you see on TV."

Just at that moment, Sammy burst in the door. "Mom, what are you doing here?"

"Your mother is tired of the children, Sammy. She wants us to get a stranger to take care of them," said an outraged Jenn.

"Mom!"

"That is not exactly what I said, Sammy, so let me begin again. I love my grandchildren dearly, but I am just too old and tired to be a good babysitter any longer."

"Mom, you are not old…"

"Please don't interrupt me, Sammy. I need to say this to both of you. I cannot control Chapin's behavior. I am sickened by his brutality toward Eli."

"That is more than a little bit strong," said Jenn.

"Call it what you want, but it is not 'boys will be boys' behavior. I am afraid for both boys, for what could happen to Eli and for what Chapin could do. I don't know how to help either one of them. I want to be a grandmother, not a baby-sitter."

"That is ridiculous, Mom." An exasperated Sammy exploded. "You are their grandmother!"

"I take full responsibility for what has happened." I tried to stay calm. "Chapin was everything in the world I needed after your dad died, but it was supposed to be temporary. I didn't set boundaries on that. In many ways, I used Chapin as a crutch to help me get through each day, and I spoiled him rotten. No wonder he hated the attention that had to be given to a new baby. He had had all my attention for three years. I absolutely doted on him. It's time for a change now. He needs a firmer hand and someone who can help him. That is not me. What I would like is to spend separate time with each boy on the weekends and do grandmotherly things."

I held up my hand when I saw they both were ready to interrupt me again. "I also want the opportunity to start going out with my friends again. It seems like every time I have something planned, your plans interfered— last night, for instance. You didn't come home on time."

"We called you," protested Sammy.

"Yes, but I asked you to come right after work, and you ignored my request completely. This arrangement isn't working for me or the boys any longer. Beginning on Monday, I will come here to watch the boys like, as I used to. I will be glad to interview prospective nannies, if you would like. I don't want to leave you hanging, but I would like this to be resolved by January first."

I could tell they were stunned and struggling with what to say next. Finally, Sammy spoke, after he and Jenn exchanged a look that I couldn't identify. "Mom, I know you are upset right now. We are very sorry that we didn't come home early last night. I am just going to ask you to put your plans on hold until Thanksgiving, which is just next week. We, that is, Jenn and I, want to tell all of you some exciting news, but we can't say anything yet. Mom, you are planning to have us all for Thanksgiving, aren't you?"

I had had Thanksgiving at my house every single year. Jenn's parents came now, and her two brothers and their families. And Laura used to come.

It was a lot of work before and after. I used to enjoy it, but the last couple of years, my heart wasn't in it. It was just too much to keep the boys all day on the Wednesday before, do the grocery shopping, cook, and clean the house after they all went home. I was up most of the night. No one helped. Jenn's mother "just wasn't a cook." That was her excuse. She brought bakery pies, which was fine with me, but certainly that took no effort. I always made Sammy's favorite chocolate pie anyway. Jenn's sisters-in-law worked, and they didn't have time to do anything. The worst part was that no one minded the children. They were all unruly. I was really tired this year.

I looked at them for a few minutes, trying to think about what I wanted to say. "I would like some help this year."

"Well, of course, we will help you," Jenn said impatiently, "just as we always do. My mother will bring pies."

"No," I said. "I need more help than that. I am very tired. So here is what I am asking. I need for everyone to pitch in and bring things, and Jenn, you can coordinate with your family. Your brother's wives can bring side dishes, along with you. The men can bring wine or beer, whatever they want to drink. I need someone to bring juices for the children. I am willing to do the turkey, ham, stuffing, mashed potatoes, gravy, and chocolate pie for Sammy."

"Thanks, Mom," Sammy said gratefully.

"But, but…" Jenn looked truly perplexed. "None of us are cooks. What do you want us to make?"

"I really don't care," I said adamantly. "Thanksgiving is supposed to be family and friends coming together and sharing. Not about one person doing everything. I don't care if everything any one person contributes is store bought. It's up to the rest of you."

"I am not sure how they will all take this. It's the one day we all get to relax and enjoy ourselves," Jenn said sadly.

I held my tongue, but what I wanted to say was that they got plenty of time off and seemed to relax a lot. What I did say was completely shocking to them. "One more thing, If Thanksgiving is at my house, then I will not be available to baby-sit on Wednesday. Both of you still get that day off, don't you?"

Both of them started talking at once, "Mom, we have plans for that day. We can't watch the children. We need you."

"Stop," I said. "Those are my conditions. Things are going to start changing. Now I am going to see Eli and read him a story, as I promised, and then I will be on my way. I will see you both back here on Monday."

# III

When I got home, I felt both exhausted and exhilarated. I felt more energetic than I had felt in years. I decided to call my friend Karen to make a dinner date for tonight. Just a girl's night out.

We went to our favorite restaurant, La Dolce Notte, the best Italian restaurant in all of Baltimore.

After we had been seated and ordered a glass of wine, Karen looked at me and said, "Something is different."

"What do you mean?" I asked, startled.

"Let's face it, Kathryn. I have asked you numerous times over the past few years to go out with me, and it has been a rare occasion when you have been able to. You always have those grandsons of yours day and night. Would you believe this is the very first time that you have called me to go out?"

"It is?" I asked, genuinely surprised.

"It certainly is." She laughed. "So again, what has changed?"

During the course of the dinner, I recounted my recent conversation with Sammy and Jenn, my concerns about each of the boys, and my estrangement with Laura. Karen said absolutely nothing. She just let me pour my heart out until I had no more to say. By that time we were on our third glass of wine and were ordering a sinful dessert.

Finally she pushed her chair back and said, "My God! You finally got some balls!"

"What?" I asked, not understanding her.

"Balls, girl, cojones, and a backbone— you know, that stuff that makes you take that detour from being a doormat to a door."

I laughed. "You're right, but they are mighty little balls right now. I already have some guilt feelings that I am abandoning Eli, in particular. I really do fear for him, because he has no one to stand up for him."

"I agreed with the part about Eli," she said, "but I do think the part about them having a live-in nanny could address that problem in a more neutral way. She would be there all the time as a surrogate parent. I think that is a brilliant idea, and your son can certainly afford it. They have saved a bundle from six years of free baby-sitting."

She was right about Sammy and Jenn's ability to afford a nanny. They made extraordinary salaries for such a young couple. They lived in a huge house that was sparsely furnished, because they just were not interested. They loved high-tech equipment so there was every new technical thing on the market in the house. The boys, of course, had furniture in their rooms and all the material things they could want. They had plenty of toys, and both knew how to use computers. They each already had their own. But the rest of the house had an abandoned feeling. Some of the rooms even had an echo. In the family room, there were two black leather sofas, a huge TV, and one lamp. There was no living room furniture and only an old hand-me-down table and chairs in the dining room. But they never used that room anyway. No pictures on the walls or accessories of any kind around. And the house was a mess. Dishes piled in the kitchen. Boxes of leftover pizza or whatever else they had picked up for dinners would sometimes sit on the counters for days. No real food in the refrigerator. Clothes were strewn from one room to another. You didn't know what was clean or dirty.

That was the reason I'd decided early on to baby-sit at my house. I couldn't stand the chaos in their house, and I couldn't find anything, despite the fact that there wasn't much in any room. They had also started asking me to put a load of laundry in or start dinner or some other kind of household chore. That was where I had put my foot down and decided I would not be their housekeeper in addition to the child-care chores. Now I would be going back into that whirlwind, but with a purpose. A nanny. Whoever that person was needed to see what she was getting into.

"Yes," I agreed. "They will be able to afford the best help that is available. One problem I can already foresee is that they will be resistant. For some reason, they want only me to keep the children, and it's not a money thing."

"Tiny balls." Karen started laughing. "Forgive me for being so blunt. Of course they want you. They couldn't abuse anyone else as they do you. From what you have said—and from what I have observed in all these years—they totally ignore your needs and requests."

Try as I might, I could not disagree with Karen. She was so right. No one else would put up with them. I was even more convinced a live-in person was the right direction. "There is one more thing that I haven't told you. Sammy asked me to put my new plans on hold because they have some kind of big surprise announcement they want to make on Thanksgiving, which he said would make a big difference. I wonder if one of them is being transferred."

Karen said, "I don't know why it feels foreboding to me. It may be good news for them but not so good for you."

"Well, if they move away, I would definitely worry about Eli more than I do now. At least with him here, I can keep my eye on him. That is a whole new worry."

"OK," Karen protested. "Don't start worrying needlessly. You are moving in the right direction, and you will know their plans soon enough. Let's have one more cup of coffee and start planning all the fun things we will be able to do together beginning in January, when you have some freedom."

# IV

Thanksgiving dinner that year would not have been featured in any magazine. True to my word, I stuck with exactly what I said I would make. Jenn's mother brought her usual tasteless pies. We ran out of wine and had no beer at all. One of the sisters-in-law "forgot" to bring something, and the other one brought some kind of mystery green vegetable for her side dish, which she purchased in a grocery store. There wasn't even cranberry sauce. A first for everyone. Jenn brought one bottle of juice for the kids, which soon ran out, since there were five of them. It was the first year that every single bit of the turkey was eaten at the dinner. I did not have even one slice left over. And no wonder, the pickings were meager! Jenn's father kept saying how much he missed this dish or that dish that I usually made. I just nodded in agreement but stood firm. At one point, Sammy took me aside and asked if there was anything else that I could "whip up" real quickly. When I said no, he just shook his head and walked away, muttering under his breath. He just didn't understand.

Finally, when the disastrous meal was coming to a close, Sammy stood up and clinked on his water glass with his spoon. "I would like to have everyone's attention." He went over and put his arm around Jenn. "We have two announcements. The first is that Jenn is being promoted to a vice president at her firm!" Everyone shouted congratulations. Jenn was beaming.

Not only would she would be the youngest vice president in her company but the first female that they had even had. It was truly a joyous occasion for her. She was a complete career woman and was achieving everything she had set out to do.

"OK, what's the second big thing?" someone shouted out. "How are you going to top that?"

"Well, we aren't trying to top it. Sometimes things just happen in life all at once, and this is just one of those times." Sammy stopped and looked down at Jenn. "Honey, do you want to tell them?"

Jenn's face was flushed, and she seemed a little shy. "Well, the other good news, which was just as totally unexpected, is that we are going to have another baby. She will be born in April!"

The table exploded in cries of delight. Everyone was talking at once. I said nothing. I was absolutely stunned. How could they? I wondered. These two people, who should never have had one child, were bringing a third into the world.

Sammy finally noticed that I had not said one word. "Mom, you are as white as a sheet. Are you OK?"

Jenn's father shouted across the table, "Of course she is. She is just as surprised as we all are and excited about getting a granddaughter!"

Sammy came over to me, knelt down, and took my hand. "See, Mom, I told you that we had a surprise that would make your plans null and void," he said proudly. "All you needed was a little baby to hold in your arms again and take care of."

It was at that very moment that I realized I had raised a complete and utter idiot. He was totally clueless. If I couldn't deal with two children, how did he think I would manage three, one of them a newborn?

I took a moment and looked him straight in the face. Then I looked around the table at all the expectant faces waiting to hear my joyous words about raising Sammy and Jenn's third child.

I took a deep breath and stated calmly, "I am pleased for Sammy and Jenn. And I am very surprised about the baby but not about Jenn achieving this new position. It will be quite a challenge to have a new baby and a new position at the same time."

Sammy interrupted, "So you can see, Mom, we need you more than ever."

I continued talking over Sammy. "But we all need to adjust to new changes in our lives. I told Sammy and Jenn last week that I was resigning from my baby-sitting chores to become a regular grandmother—just like you, Linda." Linda had the grace to look embarrassed at that remark. "I will help them find a live-in nanny to take care of the three children."

"But you can't do that," said both of Jenn's parents at once. "These children, we mean Sammy and Jenn, as well as the little ones, need your help. They can't just rely on someone they don't know. You can't just drop them like a hot potato!"

I refused to become defensive, even though I felt my blood rising. "I am not the only grandparent or parent in the picture," I said. "Maybe I have been too selfish, taking over as I have, and now it's time to give you a chance."

Their protests were immediate and loud and clear. "Well, of course, we can't baby-sit. We are too old. We have bridge, golf, friends, and vacations to go on." And so on and so on. I just let them rant on for a while.

"This new baby," I said, "is a perfect time for me to step back and let Jenn and Sammy start parenting their children, because we don't know how many more they will have. I also am too old anymore. I believe, at sixty-two,

I am three years older than you, Linda, so you can imagine, if you can't keep up with them, what it must be like for me."

Linda said nothing. What was there to say? She knew that I knew my child care had saved her countless hours of being with children she wanted nothing to do with except having a Christmas photo taken once a year.

"Mom, you have been a little down lately, but I know this little baby will cheer you up. Trust me on that," said Sammy.

Trust him? Trust him? This son of mine seemed incapable of hearing anything I said or believing me. He wanted his life in a neat and tidy package and without any effort. How would I get through to him? Out of the blue, these words came tumbling out of my mouth, and for the life of me, I will never know what made me say them." I am very glad the baby is coming in April. It won't interfere with my trip."

Sammy looked amused. "What trip, Mom? You aren't going on any trip."

"Why yes, Sammy," I replied. "I am going on a trip in May."

"Mom, just where you think you are going?" he asked in a voice that one uses with a child.

"I am going to Italy, Sammy, to Italy."

The entire room went dead silent. Sammy and Jenn both looked astonished. No one spoke for what seemed like the longest time.

Finally, Sammy said, "Italy, Mom? You are not going to Italy!"

"Yes, Sammy," I replied sweetly. "To Italy. In May."

# V

**"K**athryn, I can't believe you told them Italy." Karen laughed when I told her later that night about the baby. "I wish I had been a fly on the wall."

"I wish I had a videotape of their faces, because it's all a blur now, but I am very proud of myself and how I handled the situation—the whole day, in fact. Even though I think it will go down in history as the worst Thanksgiving meal ever in my life." I laughed, too.

"Why Italy?" Karen asked.

"I really don't know," I said. "It may have had something to do with our dinner at La Dolce Notte. I haven't enjoyed myself in such a long time. I felt like a burden had been lifted from my shoulders just talking to you about everything."

There was silence on the other end of the phone. "Karen?"

"I'm here, Kathryn, and you know what I'm thinking?" she said excitedly.

"I am scared to ask." I laughed again. This was turning out to be a good day after all.

"I am thinking you are full of brilliant ideas lately. First the nanny and now Italy. Let's go to Italy. You and I. In May. What do you think?"

I was startled. "I really didn't mean it, you know. I just said it to get their attention."

"I know, I know," said Karen, even more excited. "But why not? Let's go to Italy. It's the only way you will be able to really make a change. If you aren't here, Sammy and Jenn will have to deal with things. And we are not getting any younger. We are both sixty-two now. How many more chances will we have to take a wonderful trip together?"

She is right again, I thought. I have to get completely out of the picture. I had never thought of going so far away. Italy. Why not? It's supposed to be a beautiful country.

"Why not, indeed, my dear friend Karen? Let's go to Italy!"

# ANA

# I

It is amazing how freeing it can feel to make a decision or change directions in life, Ana thought. Ever since I told Lena that I would go to Italy with her, my life has felt different somehow. Of course I know it's not my life—I feel changed. I feel more energetic, more alive. I know that I look better. My students, my neighbors, and my colleagues have all complimented me on how well I have been looking lately. Working out in a gym hasn't hurt either.

I decided that since I would be doing a lot of walking in Germany and Italy, I needed to get into better shape. I was certainly thin enough but not really in shape to climb up and down all those hills, so I started going to the university's gym. Faculty has reserved times, so I started going in several times a week to do some strength training, biking, and walking on the treadmill. That's where I met Palmer. Or rather met him again.

I was on the treadmill, watching a news program on TV, when I heard a man say, "Dr. Douglas?"

I turned away from the TV to see a pleasant-looking man, although a bit sweaty, looking at me. "Yes," I responded. "I am Ana Douglas."

"I'm Palmer Addison. I teach in the engineering department. I think I met you and your husband several years ago. I was really sorry about his death. He was a good person."

I couldn't for the life of me remember ever meeting him but I politely responded to his statement. "Yes, Mark was a good person. I have missed him a lot."

Palmer nodded sympathetically and asked. "I don't recall seeing you in here before."

I laughed. "I just started coming. I'm taking a vacation with a friend this spring that will have quite a lot of walking and decided I had better get into some kind of shape."

We chatted about some upcoming events on campus for a few minutes longer, and Palmer left. I wondered why I couldn't remember him. Of course we would have no reason to professionally come into contact with each other. Our two departments had nothing in common except university events, and I didn't attend many of those any longer.

But I did see him frequently at the gym, and we struck up an easy friendship based around superficial university issues. One day in December he asked me if I had ever housed students for the holidays.

"Oh, yes, almost every year that I have been on this faculty," I answered. "It has been a lot of fun." The university encouraged faculty to invite students, who for a myriad of reasons stayed on campus during the holidays, to stay in their homes. Mark and I had done it every year from the first, and I continued it, except for the Christmas after his death. I blessed those students in the years since his death, because they helped me get through the holidays. I let them take over decorating and do whatever they wished to do. The house always looked amazing, and I think, because they all knew about Mark, they wanted to make it special for me. I have been eternally grateful and very touched.

"Have you also invited students to your house?" I asked.

"I never have in the past," he said. "My wife—or I should say my ex-wife—was opposed to it entirely. She felt it was an invasion of privacy. But I am thinking about putting my name on the list this year. I wonder, if you have a few minutes, if you can tell me how it worked for you. To tell you the truth, I want to do it, but I am a little apprehensive."

We agreed to meet at the coffee shop across the street after our workout so that I could tell him about my experience.

I began as soon as we settled into our coffee and muffins. "Mark and I decided right away that we would not have mixed sexes, and we decided on girls rather than boys. I did break that rule once for a brother and sister, but girls have worked out well. Now having said that, we also learned that we had to establish a few ground rules for what worked for us, and once we did that, things have been really wonderful."

"Would you mind telling me what the rules were?" Palmer asked.

"Put these in the 'learn as you go' category, but rule one was no boyfriends spending the night. Rule two was that this is a home, not a party scene. They were guests in our house, and we expected our home to be treated respectfully. We also asked that they clean up after themselves, keep their rooms neat, help with meals—not paying for them but preparation, setting the table, cleanup afterward, etc. Their cell phones and music were also issues that we had to address and a curfew time for coming in at night."

"Wow," said an amazed Palmer. "I would have never thought of all that."

I laughed. "Well, remember, I said that we learned from experience. We had to tweak the rules a bit at times. But mainly, the kids were great, and we never had any real problems. I think they were happy not to have to stay in a hotel while the dorms were closed. I have had some students for all of their four years, which is the biggest help, because they help me steer the newcomers in the right direction."

"What did you do for the actual holiday?"

"They usually arrived the day after final exams. After all the kids settled into their bed spaces and had a tour of the house, we brought them into our family room for a meeting about expectations. Mark had a great sense of humor, so even though they knew he was serious about the rules, there was always a lot of laughter. It was based around being in a house with all females and the hormone thing, and they had to give him a break. They loved him." I suddenly stopped. The memory was almost overwhelming.

"Hey," said Palmer, "I'm sorry. This has to be hard for you—remembering your husband like this."

"Yes, it is, even after six years. My best friend tells me I'm stuck, and I think she is right."

"You know what they say," responded Palmer. "There is no time period for grief."

"Thanks for being a good ear. It's true; I am stuck and need to move on. But, listen, I want to tell you about Christmas with the kids. We always had a little gift for each person; usually a humorous book or food basket for their dorm rooms. The repeat kids were easier, because we had a sense of their personalities after awhile. The students that I taught were the easiest of all."

"No wonder they wanted to come back."

"This is the best part," I said. "We didn't decorate until after they arrived. After Mark's little chat about rules, we invited them to help us decorate. We would put all the room and tree decorations in the middle of the room and talk about a plan to make the house look beautiful. I served them hot cider and lots of junky snacks. We played cheesy Christmas music and had the best time. I always made a simple casserole ahead of time so that dinner was easy—salad, bread, and dessert. On Christmas Eve, my good friend's mother had us all over for a huge Italian dinner. By then, the kids were part of the family and felt at ease. We would always go to Mass with the Capellos and the girls who wanted to come would go with us, and the one who didn't just went back home. We didn't make a big deal out of it.

"Mark used to do the coolest thing. I stopped doing it after he died, but the kids loved it and sometimes the repeat kids have continued it. He took pictures all throughout the holidays and presented each of them a little photo album when they were leaving so that they would have a true holiday memory."

"I am not sure I could do anything half as well as that," said Palmer, looking a little anxious. "How many students did you have each year?"

"We started with one, but that was awkward, we found, so the next year, it became two then three. It's actually better with more, believe it or not. I usually have four or five girls now. We had six the year we had the brother. That was the Christmas before Mark died, and that was the best ever."

"What made you do it again—I mean, without Mark?" asked Palmer.

"I wasn't going to do it, but two of the girls who had been with us in the past asked me in September, right after classes started, if I was going to have students stay at my house that Christmas. If I was, could they put their names in right away? I was really touched that they wanted to and told them so."

"'Dr. Douglas,' they said simply. 'We miss you.' How could I not? And truthfully, it has been good for me. I would have pulled down the shades, closed the curtains, not put up one twinkle light, and stayed in bed, if it weren't for the girls. Knowing they have no place to go during the holidays is the one thing that makes me do it. They have brought me laughter, tears, and joy beyond measure in these past five years."

"So it sounds like you are all set to do it again this year," he said.

"I have five girls lined up, and two are repeaters. And you know what? I think I will be in better spirits this year. I am actually looking forward to it, rather than just doing it."

"Can I call on you for advice—how to structure it and so forth?" asked Palmer.

"Sure, anytime," I replied. "I bet there are students whom you have taught who would like to stay with you. Ask around. Just drop it casually in class one day and see what happens."

"That is a great idea. I think I will. I'll let you know what happens."

We said good-bye and went our separate ways. I didn't see Palmer at the gym for almost a week. One night he showed up with a bandaged wrist.

"Oh my God," I said. "What happened?"

"I fell off my bike." He laughed.

"Here?"

"No, my real bike. Just goofing around. I toppled over and twisted my wrist. It's fine, really."

"Are you sure?" I asked.

"Really, it's good. The bandage is coming off this week. Guess what? I have four students staying with me for the holidays."

"No!" I exclaimed. "You went all out."

"I did what you suggested. Told two classes that I was opening my house during the holidays for students. I had all four students before I could even put my name on the host list. I was so surprised to have immediate results, I couldn't turn anyone down." He laughed. "It feels good. These are good kids, and I'm looking forward to it. I still need your help, however."

"Just let me know what I can do," I said.

Palmer and I got into a habit of having coffee after our gym days, making remarks each time about how we were undermining the intent of the workout by having some kind of pastry. Palmer was easy to talk to, and we soon got into some pretty intense discussions about the university, students today versus ten years ago, our career goals, politics, and whatever else came up. We learned early on that we were fairly opposite on just about every issue, and that in itself was funny. Nonetheless, it was enjoyable for me, and it seemed natural that we started going together or meeting at university events, which soon was followed by going out to an occasional movie or dinner. I never once thought of these outings as a date. Palmer was a colleague, and he never pushed the relationship further. He was still pretty wounded by his marriage breaking up, but we were becoming good friends.

Just before Christmas break, we were out having dinner at Mama's Cucina in Baltimore's Little Italy, when who should walk in but Lena with one of the Berretti boys. Angelo Berretti had been in love with Lena since way back when. The look on her face when she saw me with Palmer was one of shock, amazement, and why didn't you tell me. I had never mentioned Palmer to her, because I just considered him a good friend from work. I actually never thought about it. She came over, and introductions were made all around, and then she and Angelo went off to another table, where she kept her eye on me the entire time. I knew I would be getting a call later that night.

I wasn't wrong, so when the phone rang just before midnight, I answered, "Hi, Lena."

"Don't 'hi, Lena' me," she said. "Who was that fabulous man, and why haven't you told me about him? I can't believe you are dating, and you haven't said one single word. When did we stop being best friends? You haven't been out for six years, and now you have a movie star." On and on she went for least ten minutes, until she finally realized that I had not said one word.

"Ana, are you listening to me?" she asked, exasperated.

"That's all I can do, Lena. I can't get a word in edgewise."

"OK, I will shut up, and you had better tell me everything."

"First of all, Palmer and I aren't dating."

"What do you call sitting in a restaurant, laughing, and having a good time?" Lena interrupted.

"I thought you were just going to listen."

"OK, OK. Get back to it."

"I met Palmer at the university gym, and we started talking about university issues and events, and it has led to a friendship. That's all. He is trying to get over a broken marriage. His ex sounds like quite a doozy, but that's another story. Tonight, we were planning a joint party for the students who are spending the holidays with us. It's his first time, and he is nervous about it."

"Wow," she said. "He is one good-looking man. What does he teach?"

I had never really paid a lot of attention to Palmer's looks, but she was right, he really was good-looking. He was a couple of years younger than me.

He'd just turned forty and was having some pangs about it, but he was in great physical shape. I knew that from the gym.

"He teaches in the engineering department. Anyway, Lena," I said. "I am nowhere near ready for any kind of relationship, and Palmer isn't really interested either."

"Really?" she asked speculatively. "How long has he been divorced?"

"I think he and his wife separated more than three years ago, but the settlement seemed to have turned pretty nasty, so the actual divorce just came through recently. In fact, Palmer said it was the best birthday present he could have gotten."

"Listen," I said suddenly. "You are good at this stuff. We thought of having a scavenger hunt with the kids, but we are short one female. I have five students this year, and he will have four, so we thought we would randomly pair them up with a crazy list and send them off into town to find things and then come back for a lasagna supper—that's why we were at Mama Cucina's tonight. They are going to make us two big pans of lasagna and their specialty brownies. We are going to do stupid prizes for the winners and losers. Why don't you and Sara come and be the extra females? That boy will get a female and a half."

"Oh, I don't know about that..."

"Remember, Lena, you owe me one, since I am going to Italy with you just two months after I get back from Germany. Not that this may repay that debt entirely, but it will make a dent. And you know Sara will love it. She has always loved my students during the holidays."

"Oh, OK," she said reluctantly. "At least Sara will have fun. Maybe Mama will throw in some other kind of dessert."

It was a good Christmas. Bittersweet in some respects. Mark would have loved having a big party for both the boys and girls, and it was a great success. I felt happier than I had for years. The girls had made my house look like a fairy forest. There were greens and twinkling lights and candles everywhere. Even the boys were awestruck. We took mountains of pictures for keepsakes. Sara was enchanted by all of the students, and she was a big hit, since her team won the scavenger hunt. She really did her part in finding odd things. The others laughingly called foul and said it was not fair, because Sara was a ringer. That had to be explained to her, and she glowed all night.

Lena and Palmer. Palmer and Lena. Something happened with them. I still can't exactly put my finger on it, but Lena was more vulnerable than I had seen her since before Sara was born. There was definitely an attraction between the two of them. No, it was more than that. More like electricity. The air fairly crackled around them, but Lena brushed it off when I talked with her the next day.

"He is a nice guy, Ana," she said. "But you can tell he is a wounded warrior. He is not ready for a relationship. Anyone can see that."

"Really," I said unconvincingly. "How can you tell?"

"Oh, I can tell," she responded. "There is a certain attitude…you know, like a 'keep your distance' thing."

"Really," I said again. "Well, you may be right." I had no intention of drawing this out, because I could tell that Lena was interested. If I appeared to know this, she would back off, and I happened to think this could be a good match. "But he is a good man and he has been a good friend to me. If you think there is anything he could help you with around my house while I am gone, I am sure he would be available. He has offered to do whatever I need."

I saw a spark in her eyes. "I'll keep that in mind, just in case."

Palmer, on the other hand, was all questions the next time we went out for coffee. My mind was jumbled with a million things that I needed to do before my research trip to Tubingen. I was really just half listening, because I was leaving in two weeks, at the end of January.

He had just asked me something, and I had not heard a thing.

"I'm sorry, Palmer," I said, distracted. "I missed that. This trip to Germany is driving me nuts." Why in the world I thought going there in the winter was a good idea was beyond me. Now the reality of it all was hitting home, and I didn't want to go. "Repeat, please, what you just said, and I promise to pay attention."

"No, no, it wasn't that important. Just wondering about Lena's daughter Sara. Where is her father?"

"Ah, the great mystery of this century. I have been friends with Lena since we were children. We have told each other absolutely everything throughout the years, but even I don't know who he is. She says he was a big mistake, but Sara was worth it. That's all I know, and we never talk about it."

"So it's a touchy subject. Sara is a great kid," Palmer said with a smile.

"We just don't go there—about the father, I mean. I figure one day she will tell me, but I think something happened. She toughened up after that. I can tell you two things. Sara is a wonderful child and my goddaughter. I love her with all my heart. The second thing is that Lena is a heartbreaker. No man has broken through that Berlin Wall since then. There have been many men who have wanted to marry her, but as soon as they get serious, Lena drops them. All she ever says is that she doesn't need that problem in her life."

Palmer's only comment: "I wonder if she would go out with me while you are gone…maybe have coffee with me here."

"I don't know, but it's worth a try, I think. Just keep in mind what I said about Lena, Palmer. She breaks hearts faster than a speeding bullet, and you have been through a lot in the past three years."

"You've got that right," he said with a determined expression. "But I am not looking to get married again, and it sounds like she isn't either, so we are just talking about coffee, nothing more."

"Yeah, yeah, that's what they all say." I laughed, and Palmer joined in. We parted ways, agreeing to meet at least one more time before I flew to Tubingen. He even offered to take me to Dulles, but Lena and Sara were driving me there.

# II

Oh, my God, I thought. I am really crazy. Tubingen was the most charming little city, but in February it was gray and snowy. I was already freezing. I had arrived with no problems, and since I was a visiting professor on sabbatical, I was entitled to housing. I was met at the Frankfurt airport by a university representative who really took care of me. I had two apartments to choose from. One was larger, more modern, and probably had better heat, but the one I chose was closer to the Altstadt and in the center of town, where all the shops and restaurants were. I thought it would be more convenient, but it meant at least a mile walk to the university's library. And that was a very cold walk. I couldn't help, however, appreciating the beauty of this little town only twenty miles or so from Stuttgart.

Two of my former students were on an international exchange program in Tubingen, and we had made arrangements to meet. The great thing about kids is that they know everything and soon told me all the places I needed to go to shop, eat, and be entertained, and how to use public transportation. I could even take the local bus to downtown Stuttgart. My rusty German was improving, since that's what I mainly spoke. More than ever, I missed Mark. He was fluent in German and would have loved being over here.

A few days after settling into my little German apartment, I heard a knock at my door. I was in the tiny kitchen making coffee I had just purchased, and the aroma was wafting through the rooms. I was looking forward to a nice hot cup and a piece of the cake I had also bought on my grocery trip. More than once I had reminded myself that these cute little shops with tantalizing goodies could really make a girl fat.

When I opened the door, there stood a very tall man who asked, "Frau Doktor Douglas?"

"Ja."

He pulled out a badge and introduced himself as Inspektor Theodore Volker from the Stuttgart Polizei.

I was stunned and apprehensive. What could the German police want from me? Had I already violated some ordinance? I invited him in.

"Sprechen Sie Deutsch?" he asked.

This is not the time to practice German, I thought. "Nein, nur ein bisschen." A mighty little bit.

"Then we speak English," he said in flawless Oxford English.

I had found that many Germans spoke English. Almost all young people could speak very good English, and most shopkeepers had a working knowledge of the language, especially in tourist and military areas. Theodore Volker spoke excellent English and had relatives living in New York. He spent a lot of time in the United States, I learned later, working with American police and FBI on terrorism issues.

Inspektor Volker explained that the German police monitored the visits of foreigners as a matter of national security and asked me to explain the details of my visit, how long I would be staying, and many other questions.

Since it seemed that this was going to take some time, I asked him if he wanted some coffee and cake. To my surprise, he accepted. The questions also took on a personal nature, including my marital status, children, and extended family. He seemed surprised that I was a widow but made no comments.

I noticed that he had very intense brown eyes, not hard, as one might expect of the police, but interested. He seemed intelligent and nonthreatening. I found myself relaxing as we drank our coffee and ate the pastry. I thought he must be a really good cop, trapping many unaware criminals with this demeanor. He noticed that I was cold and got up, went over to the thermostat, and jiggled something. Soon it felt warmer. For the first time, I saw his humor.

"Americans like much heat," he said with a little smile.

"Ja, I am not used to this cold weather yet," I responded. "I wasn't sure how to make that thing work. Thank you for your help." I felt at ease with him. He motioned me over to the thermostat and gave me an instant lesson. I had never seen such a tall German before. He was well over six feet tall. He caught me staring at him.

"Frau Doktor?" he inquired.

I was embarrassed, and therefore every German word I knew was immediately erased from my brain. I struggled and made a gesture for tall, "Sie sind dick," and immediately remembered that meant fat or thick and turned deep red. "Nein, nein, grosse, grosse." We both laughed because there was nothing fat about him. I apologized in my best German, and he took his leave after thanking me for the cake and coffee.

Several days later, I was sitting in a café warming up with coffee and an apple pastry when I heard a voice say, "Frau Doktor?" I knew before looking up it was Inspektor Volker. He had a very distinctive and somewhat seductive voice.

"Inspektor Volker, wie geht's es ihnen?" I asked. "Bitte, sitzen..."

I had research material spread all over the table, and he looked curious.

"Bitte, sitzen," I said again.

"Auf Deutsch odor English?" he asked.

"English, please, my German is not good." He told me that he thought I was improving, which was true, and offered to speak both to help me learn. Off we went, speaking in German and English until it became too frustrating for me, and he switched to English only. Inspektor Volker was a very interesting man, as it turned out, and I was enjoying his company. It was easy to forget that he was a policeman. Later that night, I wondered if the meeting was as accidental as it seemed or just a way of checking up on me. I didn't think I was giving off any vibes that might be construed as terrorist. Little did I know then that terrorism was his specialty.

Over the next several days, we ran into each other often. I found out Inspektor Volker lived in Tubingen, not Stuttgart. In fact, he lived just across the marktplatz, behind the old city hall. That was only a few streets over from my apartment. Whenever I ran into him, we exchanged pleasantries but had no further conversation until I had my students over for dinner.

The girls asked if they could bring their boyfriends. One of the boys was American from another university out west, but the other one was a German student named Konrad Richter. He was an opinionated young man and talked constantly about politics. He was very charismatic, and my former student was enraptured. She hung on every word he said. I was glad when they left, because I found him tiresome. The next evening I had a surprise visit from Inspektor Volker.

There were no pleasantries on this visit. He got right to the point. "Konrad Richter was here last night."

Completely taken aback that he would know this, I could only agree. "Why, yes, he was—with one of my former students."

"Bitte, what is her name?" he asked in a tone that suddenly worried me.

"Why do you need to know this? Are you spying on me?" I demanded.

Avoiding the question, he said, "Konrad Richter belongs to the Aryan Jungen, a neo-Nazi organization that has ties to many other organizations we are following. Please let me know what he was doing visiting an American university professor?"

I felt sick. "Oh God, how did Katie get mixed up with someone like him?"

"Katie?" Inspector Volker said.

"Katie—her last name is Willis—is a good girl, just innocent. I will talk to her. Is she in trouble?" I was really worried. This felt like Nazi Germany.

"No, madam. I will talk to her. And what is your connection to Konrad Richter, Frau Doktor?"

I was getting a little angry, even though I was also frightened. Inspektor Volker was dead-on serious.

"Inspektor Volker, I met this young man for the first time last night. I immediately did not like him, if that makes any difference to you. There is no connection." And because I was angry, I said sarcastically, "Do you have a list of people I should not see or talk to while I am in your country? That would helpful for me. I certainly am not looking for trouble with the Deutsche polizei!"

For several minutes neither one of us spoke. We just stared at each other, I knew that my face must be beet red because of the anger I felt, but

I did not back off. He finally broke the silence. He came over to me, put a hand on each shoulder, and looked into my eyes. I couldn't move. I was mesmerized.

Then he said very softly, "Please have dinner with me on Friday."

"What?" I was stunned. This was the very last thing I had expected.

He repeated his invitation in English this time. "I will take you somewhere wonderful, Frau Doctor."

"Dinner?" I said, amazed. "You want to take me out for dinner? But why?"

He shrugged his shoulders, threw his hands up in the air, and walked away. Then he turned around, came back to me, and held my arms close to him. "Because I like you, Frau Doktor," he said simply. "I like you. Will you agree to go with me?"

I will never know what made me accept. I think I was so surprised that I couldn't refuse. "Ja, thank you. But there are three conditions."

"Conditions?" he asked, confused.

"Ja, if I am going out to dinner with you, you must stop calling me Frau Doktor and call me Ana, OK?"

"Ana," he said softly, savoring my name. "And the other two conditions—what are they?"

"I want to be with you when you talk with Katie—" He started to interrupt, but I held up my hand to stop him. "She is innocent, and you will intimidate her—for all I know she might be in love with this Konrad. And I know her better than you. She is just another American student to you. Agreed?"

He said nothing for a moment. "And the last condition?"

I knew Germans were much more formal than Americans, so this was a big request, but in this moment that was so very strange to me, I suddenly felt more empowered. "I would like permission to call you by your first name."

He looked at me and started laughing. "Theo. My name is Theo." And with that, he took his leave.

What just happened here? I thought after he had left. My mood had gone from being scared to angry to astounded, but even I had to admit something had changed in me in the past few minutes. I was attracted to him. I couldn't believe that I was admitting it to myself. I had not thought about a man in the six years since Mark had died. Not one thought. Not even about Palmer Addison, who was so good-looking. I think there had been other men, who might have been interested in me, but I was so shut down, no one could penetrate my own Berlin Wall. I giggled. Even the Berlin Wall eventually fell. It just took the right combination of forces. Is that what happened? Something in the universe came together?

This man, Theo Volker, was like no one I had ever met before. He was physically big, but gentle. I had just witnessed that he could be stern, as well. I liked his looks. His short dark hair was beginning to gray a little on the sides, but it was full and wavy. He had a neatly trimmed mustache, which was also graying, but it made him more handsome. He appeared to be in his late forties. Oh, God, I thought, is he married? I should have asked him.

Is this a date? I wondered. It doesn't count. I will be gone in a month and will never see him again. I thought about Mark. Somehow, I didn't feel like I was cheating on him, because this wasn't real, like it would be in America. I decided that this dinner would mean no more than the times I had gone out with Palmer. How wrong that assumption turned out to be.

# III

I made arrangements for Katie to meet me at my apartment before the dinner with Theo. Theo was there when she arrived. She immediately looked worried, but I tried to put her at ease.

"Katie thanks for coming on such short notice. Please sit. Inspektor Volker has some concerns about Konrad Richter and wants to talk to you about him for a few minutes."

To my surprise, Theo took a seat across the room. He was much less intimidating sitting down. "Fraulein Willis, can we speak in German? Or do you prefer English?" He was leaning forward and spoke softly.

Katie seemed a little less apprehensive and responded in German. Her command of the language was excellent. "Why do you want to know about Konrad?"

"Fraulein, I know about Konrad Richter—all I need to know. What I need answered is your involvement with him and his group, the Neo-Aryan Jungen. Do you know this organization?"

"Oh, sure," she said, more relaxed. "Konrad is the president of the club. They have rallies with students and parties and stuff like that. It's cool. Lots of food and beer. Sorry, Dr. Douglas, but beer is not like beer in the States. Everyone drinks it here. It's no big deal."

I decided to let that one pass for now and not interrupt Theo's conversation with her.

"Fraulein, the Neo-Aryan Jungen is a Nazi organization. Do you know about the Jews and what happened to them in World War Two?"

"Well, I know what we had to read in the history books in America, and Dr. Douglas took all of her classes to the Holocaust Museum in Washington…"

Theo gave me an approving look.

"But," she said, looking at me, "I am not sure anymore all of that is true."

"Katie!" I exclaimed, surprised, but Theo continued talking.

"Why not, Fraulein, what has made you change your mind? Have you ever been to a concentration camp?" Theo's tone had changed to one of great restraint, but it was still soft.

"As a matter of fact, I have—right after I got over here. My friend and I went up to Munich one weekend and decided to go over to Dachau."

"So you saw the real thing, but now you don't believe. What was it, Fraulein, or should I say who was it, that changed your mind? Could it have been Herr Richter?"

Katie shifted uncomfortably in her seat but spoke defiantly. "Konrad said the camps are to make money from tourists and to make Germany look bad. He said religious groups outside of Germany have set these places up. He said the proof is that German history books have almost nothing about these events."

Theo stood up and then sat back down. He was upset, I could see that. "Herr Richter is right about one thing, Fraulein, some Germans want to forget that horrendous time, and there is very little in our history books about that time, but I can assure you that what you learned in America is true." He then dropped a bombshell that I was totally unprepared for. "You see, Fraulein, I am Jewish. Almost my entire family was burned up in incinerators like the ones you saw in Dachau. But for my family, it was Buchenwald. Katie visibly paled. "I am so sorry, Inspektor. How awful!"

"Now, Fraulein," Theo regained his composure. "Here is what you need to know. Herr Richter's group, the Neo-Aryan Jungen, is under surveillance in this country and throughout Europe. Interpol is involved. Do you know Interpol?"

Katie nodded. "I have heard of it."

"What is important for you to decide is if you want to continue to be a part of this group and be with Herr Richter. If you do decide to stay with this group, you, too, will be under surveillance, here in Europe and in America. We consider groups like this dangerous." And with that, Theo pulled from a manila envelope eight-by-ten photograph of Katie, Konrad, and other young people at parties and rallies. He passed them over to her.

"Are you arresting me?" Katie asked in a scared voice.

"Nein. Please understand that there are many organizations looking at groups like Herr Richter's group. Some of them are dangerous also. You need to be aware of your safety. Understand, we Jews will never let happen to us again what happened in World War Two. There are radical Jewish groups, as well. This is very deep water for you to be swimming in, Fraulein, and there are many sharks after your blood. Do you understand?"

Although Katie nodded that she did understand, it was clear that she had not grasped the full extent of what Theo was telling her, and he knew that. "Fraulein Willis, has Herr Richter asked you to do things for him, like delivering packages or envelopes to his friends?"

"One time he did, but it was a school project. A friend needed to review it."

"Konrad Richter is not enrolled in the University of Tubingen or any other university in Germany. His sole purpose for being here is to rally against Jews. Have you not noticed his rhetoric?"

Katie was wide-eyed and silent.

"Fraulein," Theo said more kindly, "he is using you. It's a ploy he has used over and over. He looks for young, naïve girls, mainly Americans, to do his dirty work. That way, he stays clean, and they get caught. When they get caught, they get deported—or worse, they end up in German prisons, which are not very nice, and they stay a long time. I assure you that prisons in Germany are not like prisons in America. You would have no rights, and your embassy would not be able to help you."

"I don't believe Konrad would do that. You saw him, Dr. Douglas. He is nothing like Inspektor Volker says," Katie said wildly, looking around.

"Katie, I didn't like Konrad. I told Inspektor Volker that. Although he said nothing specific about Jews when he was here, he said plenty of other things that spewed hate. Mine was a gut reaction—I just didn't like him."

Katie started crying. "What should I do?"

"Stay away from him and his group," said Theo standing up. "Fraulein Willis today was a friendly conversation. If there is a next time, it will not be pleasant for you."

He started to leave. I called, "Theo…" But he waved me off. He left, and I didn't see him again until we went out to dinner. I had a million questions for him.

"Dr. Douglas, what should I do? I'm scared," asked Katie.

"My best advice to you, Katie, is to take this seriously and get as far away from Konrad as possible. I am only over here a few more weeks. You will be totally alone then. Make friends with Inspektor Volker. He is not someone you want as an adversary. I would trust what Inspektor Volker says about Konrad and his group. You should also be worried about your own safety. Konrad could be setting you up."

Although she looked worried and scared, I could see that Katie was not altogether convinced that Konrad Richter could be that bad. "I will talk to Konrad, Dr. Douglas. I know that he loves me and that he wouldn't hurt me."

"Katie, Inspektor Volker said that your Konrad has used a lot of American girls in the past, and they have gotten into deep trouble. Please break this off now." I gave her a hug as she was leaving. "Be careful, Katie. Listen to what Inspektor Volker just said. He did you and me a big favor by talking to you here instead of the police station. That would have been an interrogation. The Germans are serious about these Nazi organizations. Remember, this isn't America. They don't consider student rallies as kids' stuff."

"Don't worry, Dr. Douglas," Katie replied as walked out the door. "I am sure there won't be a problem."

I hoped that she was right.

# IV

I didn't see or hear from Theo again until he picked me up for our date. I had brought two dressy outfits with me, because I had been told that I would be expected to attend university social events as a visiting professor. One was a black knit two-piece, and the other was forest-green velvet. I decided on the velvet because it was warmer, and it had always been one of my favorite dresses. It had a high neck and long sleeves, and it was fitted through the bodice and waist with a full skirt. Thank goodness there had been no more snow, and I could wear my dress pumps instead of boots. I also decided to get my hair done at one of the hair salons near the marktplatz. I really liked the way it had been styled—very European and swingy. Because I had been indulging in a pastry almost every day, my dress really fit me. That is to say, it was probably three pastries away from not fitting me.

It all paid off. When Theo saw me, he gave me a long appreciative look and said slowly, "Sehr schoen, sehr schoen!" I did actually feel quite beautiful tonight. All the uphill walking, as well as just being outside, had given me high color, and I looked healthy and rosy.

Theo looked wonderful. He had on a dark suit, white shirt, and red silk tie. He was very handsome and dressed more English than German. I think he could have been somewhat of a clotheshorse. He always looked dapper, and he wore his clothes well and comfortably. The dark suit made his eyes look deeper and more mysterious. There was a lot to this man, I thought as we drove toward Stuttgart.

Theo took me to a beautiful restaurant called Chossons on the outskirts of the city limits. It sat back from the road, surrounded by trees adorned with thousands of twinkling lights. The car was valet parked, and Theo was greeted warmly by every staff member. We were led right to a table in a corner of the room, which provided privacy but afforded us the ability to see everything. Chossons was the most romantic restaurant that I had ever been in. Floor-to-ceiling windows were dressed in damask draperies, tied back so that you could see the twinkling lights outside. In between the windows were large, ornate mirrors, in which the entire room could be viewed from any angle. A huge chandelier, in the center of the room, was surrounded by smaller ones on the periphery. The tables gleamed in white linen cloths, heavy silver cutlery, and gold-rimmed china. There were several sparkling wine glasses at each place setting. The restaurant dated back to the belle époque period and was stunning. I was speechless. Theo laughed when he saw the look on my face.

"It is beautiful, no?"

"It is the most beautiful place I think I have ever been," I said simply.

"The room pales in comparison to the food. Wait and see." He laughed again.

Theo ordered the dinner and the wines. The staff anticipated him, and we were brought a wonderful little sample appetizer of shrimp and scallops almost immediately. That was followed by a rich oxtail soup, a simply dressed green salad, and then beautifully presented beef tenderloin with little potatoes and several different vegetables. A delicious béarnaise sauce accompanied the meat. When I thought I could eat no more, an incredible chocolate tart with raspberries was served to complete our meal. Truffles were offered on a silver platter with our coffee.

"Theo, not only is this the most beautiful restaurant in the world, but I have just had the most delicious meal in my entire life. If I never eat again, this will satisfy me forever!"

"Ja, I agree. It is the best. I wanted to bring you here, Ana, and your appreciation of this restaurant and the food makes me very happy." There was almost a sad look in his eyes when he said this, but it quickly passed. I didn't know how to respond.

I felt so comfortable with this man. I had only known him two weeks, and tonight I had seen a side of him that was vulnerable and open. During dinner, I asked him if he would answer a personal question.

He put down his fork and gave me his full attention. "What is it?"

"I am wondering how someone who is Jewish could be a police person in Germany. You lost family during the war, and Tubingen has a history of anti-Semitism."

"Ja, he said, "I lost many relatives, but not my mother, and there in lies my story." He was quiet for several minutes and looked at me directly, apparently deciding whether or not he wanted to tell me.

"I was born in Berlin during the Russian occupation. The city, as you know, was divided into four sections, one of which was controlled by the Russians. My family had always lived in Berlin. My grandparents were wealthy and had a large home. My mother was educated in Switzerland but returned to Germany just before the borders closed. She became trapped, but everyone believed she was still in Switzerland. She was my grandparents' only child. I heard that the house had a lot of hiding places, and she was never seen. When the Nazis came into power, they took over the house, and my grandparents were taken away. The Nazis also believed my mother was still in Switzerland. My mother's old nurse, who still lived in the house and cooked for the Nazis, knew if my mother was ever found, they would take her away. So she asked if she could bring her 'granddaughter' in to help in the kitchen because of her age. I am told my mother was very beautiful, and she caught the eye of one of the soldiers. Although she attempted to stay out of their way, she had to help the old nurse cook, clean, and serve the Nazis. By then, the war was ending, and the Russians were entering the city. The Nazi soldier, one night, saw his chance and attempted to rape my mother. A Russian officer intervened and killed the Nazi."

He went on. "Russian was one of several languages that my mother knew, and this officer saw to it that she got a job as a translator for the Russians. My mother was only seventeen at the time, but she saw it as her only chance to survive. They worked closely together and became involved. She told me that she loved him deeply and that he was a good man, but she never told him that she was a Jew. She didn't trust anyone to know that.

"When she was twenty-four, she became pregnant with me. The Russian was married and had children in the Soviet Union, but his wife would never come to Berlin to live, so my mother and he lived as husband and wife for several years. When I was born, he was delighted that I was a boy, because his other children were girls and had grown up. My mother knew that he could never marry her. When he got orders to return home, he wanted to take me back to Russia. He told my mother that I would have a better life with his family than I would with a single mother in a war-torn country. My mother became scared that he would kidnap me, and even though she loved him, she fled one night back here to Stuttgart. The original owner of this restaurant was her cousin, who had not survived the war, but little by little, the few remaining members of my family came back to Stuttgart and were able to get this restaurant up and running again. This is where my mother worked when I was a young child."

That explained so much to me—where his height came from, and why he was treated like royalty in this restaurant. But I still wondered why he had chosen police work. "What made you decide to become a police officer? You could have certainly had a very comfortable life working here." My arm swept around the room.

"Ja, that is true," he said somberly, "but the few Jews who came back to this area decided that they would be strong again and vowed that there would always be a Jewish presence in Stuttgart. They vowed that they would never be caught unaware ever again. I grew up with that being drilled into my head. This restaurant became an important center for the returning Jews and all kinds of important people. Where else could you hear all the most significant rumors but a restaurant that diplomats, presidents, kings, and political heads would come to? Look around, Ana. All the waiters are Jews, and they are all related to one another and to me!

"And where else could a person keep his finger on the pulse of society? In a police department. European police departments are different from American ones. I know the political temperature of Europe. It is far better to be in the same house as your enemy than outside of it. Jews are everywhere now. Before the war, we were in science, in academia, in music, in banking, and in business, but we were not so much in police work or the military."

I was stunned by this, and it suddenly occurred to me that Theo was not just a regular police officer. "Theo, you are much more than just a policeman, aren't you?"

"Ana, please. We are out to enjoy a good dinner, are we not? Have more wine. Enough serious talk. I want to know about you and your research."

"Just one more question, Theo. Why are you living in Tubingen? Isn't there a lot of anti-Semitism?"

"You are a very perceptive woman," he said. "Ja, many people here are Jew haters but again, it is better to live in the midst and keep your eyes and ears open than to avoid. That is how I learn about the Konrad Richters."

"I want to thank you for being so kind to Katie Willis. I hope she heard what you said. I know she left my apartment scared."

"Good," he said. "She needs to be aware of what she is doing. It is not a child's game. Americans are very naïve, Ana. One day, I think, America will have a very bad thing happen. But enough, enough. Let's enjoy our dinner."

On the way back to Tubingen, Theo asked if I would come to his apartment. He wanted to show me something, but he would not say what. I was in such a happy mood; I saw no reason not to. It had been the most amazing evening. I had been dazzled, but I did not know then that the best was yet to come.

Theo's apartment was located on a street called Judangasse in the old Jewish part of town, just down from the beautiful Rathaus, the city hall. The enormous clock on the Rathaus was chiming 11:30 as we drove along the narrow streets. There is a word in German that is not easily translatable, gemutlichkeit, which loosely means cozy or comfortable but really has to do more with the feeling rather than the actuality. Theo's apartment instantly brought that word to mind when he opened the door. To the right was a small kitchen that seemed, at first glance, well-equipped, and beyond that was a dining area. It was the living-room area on the left that caught my attention. It was in a U shape, with the middle wall all windows, now curtained shut, and the other two walls filled with bookshelves from floor to ceiling. In front of one book-filled wall was a large sofa in a brownish paisley print, with a coffee table and two overstuffed chairs of the same print forming a conversation area. Directly opposite was the other wall of books but with an area carved out for a TV. There seemed to be interesting objects of various sorts interspersed between or on top of the books and photos in frames. The lamps in the room gave off a warm, rosy glow. The whole effect was cozy and open.

As soon as we entered, a huge white German shepherd dog with glacier-blue eyes came out to meet Theo. "Stille, Schnee, Stille," he said, and the dog, Snow, immediately lay down. "Put your hand out to meet him," Theo said. Theo had found him as puppy, starving in an alley, five years before and had brought him home. I learned later that Schnee had been trained at the police academy. He was not just a pet.

"Is Schnee the special something you wanted to show me?" I asked.

"Nein." He laughed as he affectionately rubbed the dog under his chin. "He is special, but there is something else." He went over to a cabinet built into the wall of shelves that housed his TV and took out a bottle of brandy and two glasses. He poured a drink for each of us and, as he handed me my glass, he got Schnee's leash and said that he would be right back. I took the opportunity to look around while he was out. There were several photos of a beautiful young girl at different ages scattered all over the bookcase. Theo returned as I was holding one.

"That is my daughter, Mimi—Marion, after my grandmother who died in Buchenwald."

She is beautiful," I said. "Where does she live?"

"She studies in Heidelberg and lives with her mother. We divorced when Mimi was nine."

He had turned on some soft music. It sounded like Mozart, but I wasn't sure. He came over and took my hand. "Stand here until I tell you to turn around."

I was facing the dining room. Theo turned off the lamps in the room, and I heard him open the curtains behind me. "Now, turn around." The sight was stunning. There was a full moon, and the light that reflected off it flooded the room. The moon was high over the back of the Rathaus, which was silhouetted by trees and other buildings surrounding the marktplatz.

"Oh my," I said. There were no words to describe how it looked. It was a beautiful sight to end an incredible evening. Theo came up behind me and put his hands on my shoulders. "It is beautiful, no?"

"Ja, it is so amazing," I said softly. He turned me around and put his hand on my chin, tilted it up, and very gently kissed me. "You are very beautiful, Ana. Very beautiful." And then he kissed me again with more urgency. I couldn't help but respond. The entire evening had been like a fairy tale. I was attracted to this man. I couldn't explain it, but I wanted to be with him. It had been a long time since I had been with a man. I never thought I would have these feelings again.

I could sense Theo's attraction to me. "Stay with me tonight," he whispered. "Bitte, stay with me." He drew me tighter into his arms and kissed me again. I couldn't move, and I did not want to move. "Ana, come." He took me into his bedroom and pulled me toward the window, which was a duplicate of the one in the living room. He opened the curtains, and the moonlight crisscrossed the bed. He started unzipping my dress. "Ana, OK?" I nodded yes. Before he went further, he took off his shirt and tie and laid them on a chair. Bit by bit, our clothes came off as if we had all the time in the world.

He was gentle and skilled. He touched and appreciated every part of me, and I loved the way he felt. I gave myself to him with abandon. Over and over I heard him use words of endearment, my Ana, beautiful Ana, or just Ana, Ana, Ana. I had never thought of German as a particularly romantic language, but tonight it was. We both behaved liked two emotionally and physically starved people.

When the faintest ray of morning light crept into the room, I knew I needed to leave. My apartment was just three blocks away on the other side of the marktplatz. I started to get up, but Theo pulled me back to his warm body. "I will walk you home," he said sleepily, "but not yet."

Later, at my door, Theo asked if he could see me that night. I could not deny him. I spent the morning thinking about the night before. I had slept with Theo and strangely felt no guilt about it at all. I could not understand myself. I knew I still loved Mark, but there was something about Theo that had touched me to my core. And it had slipped up on me. I was totally unprepared for what had happened. I still didn't know how it happened, but I knew that I couldn't stop it. I also knew that I didn't want to stop it.

I felt restless and decided to get out of my apartment and walk. Fortunately, it was Sunday, and there was no urgency to rush off to the library to do research. I found myself walking leisurely up the hill to the church of Saint George's. I was raised Protestant, but more often than not, I had attended a Catholic church with the Capellos throughout my childhood. My parents were fairly lax in their religious beliefs, so they never protested or even cared where I went.

Mass was long over by the time I arrived in midafternoon, but my plan was to just sit and meditate on what had happened in the past twenty-four hours. I was a jumble of emotions. Within a two-week period I had met a man and slept with him. I also had enjoyed it more than I was willing to admit. After six long years of grieving and missing Mark so much, I had given myself with complete abandon to a man who was virtually a stranger. I had been seduced by him, and it felt good. I would be leaving Germany in three weeks. Would I ever see him again? Would he even want to see me again? Was this just a fling in the moment? It was silly to think that I would ever see him again, once I returned to the States. After all, we lived thousands of miles apart. I couldn't think. I couldn't understand it, and I felt powerless to stop it. My concern was whether I could handle the emotions of it all, or would it end up throwing me for a loop once it was over. I needed Lena to talk to. She would help me put it in perspective. But Lena was too far away, and I didn't know how to write or e-mail what had happened, so I gnawed on it all afternoon.

Theo was intuitive. He took one look at me when he picked me up that night, pulled me close to him, and said "Ana, it will be all right. We are good together, no?" Early on, I had told him about Mark's death, and he had re-marked that I had a haunted look in my eyes; he could see deep sadness in them. "But you have a good spirit. I think you will survive."

Now he looked at me and said, "Ana, I cannot make you forget your husband, but I will try to make you happy now, in the present. Can we just be together for now? You are going to be in my life, if you want to be. Our time together is short. We have to make the most of it." He took my hands and held them close to his chest. "Ana, please trust me. Can you do that? This feels right to me."

I could only nod. I was filled with unexplained emotions, but strangely, I did trust him.

Then he told me that he would have to go to France the next day for the rest of the week. Something had come up. I felt at a loss. With so little time, one week of it would be taken from us. It was good that my research was going well, and I was determined to get the bulk of it done in this next week.

That night was even better than the night before. Theo chased away my doubts, and I believed that he cared for me. How could all of this have happened so suddenly? I asked Theo what had made him ask me out. He thought about it for a few minutes and sat up in bed. "I just knew I wanted you almost from the first. That first day when I came by to look at your papers, there was something about you that appealed to me—more than just your looks. I think it was your sadness. I wanted to make you happy. That's why I took you to Chossons. But I didn't plan on bringing you back to my place. I don't bring people to my home."

"You mean you don't bring women?"

He took his time to answer. "I have been divorced for ten years. There have been a few other women over the years, but none of them have been here except you. Ana, don't take this wrong, but I don't like most Americans. I think they are silly and stupid. I have little respect for Americans, but that is not what I felt for you from the first moment. You made me forget you were American. I liked that you struggled with German. I liked that you joined our way of life and were not demanding like most Americans. I liked your seriousness, but I wanted to see you smile. I like how you care for your students. Most of all, I felt your sympathy for Jews, and that made a difference. I don't know how else to explain it. I don't want or need a woman in my life—it's too dangerous— but I want you." He turned to me. "I want you in my life, Ana, and I hope that you feel the same."

Instinctively, I knew I did. I could not imagine not seeing Theo again.

While Theo was in France, I decided to check on Katie. I knew the best chance of locating her would be at the old wood market, the Holzmarkt, which was a gathering place for students. This market was just several blocks up the hill from my apartment and also the location of Saint George's Collegiate Church. The wide stone steps of the church usually were filled with students hanging out. I was right in my assumption. Katie was near the church sitting outside at a café, but I was discouraged to see that she was sitting at a table with Konrad Richter. He looked up with a smirk as I approached the table.

"Ah, the good professor and Jew lover," he said. I chose to ignore him.

"Hello, Katie," I said. "I was just wondering how you have been, since I haven't seen you for a few days." She looked embarrassed to be caught with Konrad.

"I'm fine, Dr. Douglas. Don't worry about me," she said, not looking at me directly.

"I hope so," I replied. "If you need me, you know where I am." I turned to leave, and Konrad stood up.

"Frau Doktor, she is in good hands, as you can see. Please come to our little rally this Thursday night so that you too can be enlightened." He continued to smirk.

I turned toward him, my anger barely in control, and stated in English, "You are such a waste of humanity, a real garbage dump." Although he understood English fairly well, he didn't get the gist of what I said. As I turned and walked away, I could hear Katie reluctantly translating my statement to him. I was sad about Katie. She was headed for trouble, but there was no more I could do for her. Theo was right about Americans being naïve, but this was just plain dumb.

The time sped by. Our nights were hot and intense but sweet and wonderful, as well. I was smitten. I felt like I was falling in love—I couldn't separate lust and love. This, whatever *this* was, had happened too quickly. On our last night together, Theo gave me a present. When I opened the box, I found inside a beautiful gold necklace with a black onyx heart. The setting was antique. "This is beautiful, Theo. I don't know what to say."

He fastened it on my neck and told me that the black heart was symbolic of the sadness he felt in his heart at my departure. I was touched. Theo had turned out to be extremely romantic. Something I would have never believed of a German policeman. I did not want to leave Tubingen—I had been so happy here—and did not want to return to my lonely house. I couldn't help it, but tears began spilling from my eyes.

"Oh, Ana," Theo said. "Don't cry. This is not the end. I want you to come back." Suddenly he said, "Come back in May to Italy. I have a farmhouse there. Meet me in Italy."

I looked at him blankly. Did I hear that correctly? Italy? In May? "Did you say you had a house in Italy?"

"Ja," he said excitedly. "I will send you the ticket. Will you come, Ana? I will be there for two weeks."

I started laughing. Is this fate? I wondered. How could this be?

"Ana, what is so funny, why are you laughing like that? One minute tears, the next hysterics, hilarity—what is this?"

"Theo, I am already coming to Italy in May." He looked astounded. In all the times we had been together, I had never thought to mention Italy. It had never crossed my mind. I started telling him about my trip.

"It is perfect," he stated. "I will pick you up. My farm is near Montepulciano."

"No!" I exclaimed. "My favorite wine comes from that region. Lena and I always drink montepulciano wine. This is all too coincidental. Sometimes I wonder if you are real, Theo, or if I am just dreaming."

"My darling Ana, this is no dream. We will be together again very soon." We talked and made love for the rest of our last night together. Early in the morning, I got up and dressed. I had to get back to my own apartment to be picked up and taken to the airport in Frankfurt. Theo woke up and started dressing. "Don't get up, Theo," I said. "I can't bear saying good-bye to you." But he insisted on walking me to the marktplatz. We kissed one last time, and I left him standing by the Rathaus. I walked all the way across the platz and turned to look back. He was still standing in the same spot, looking at me. The memory of seeing him standing there on that cold, gray day will be forever etched in my mind. For a moment, I thought I couldn't go, but I blew him a kiss and turned the corner.

I had not e-mailed or written Lena one thing about Theo. I had so much to tell her.

# KATHRYN

**I** never thought I would say this, but I cannot wait to leave," I said to Karen. We were out for our weekly dinner.

"Two more weeks and we are off," she sang gaily. "We are going to have the best time ever. I have to confess that I have held my breath, thinking that you might back out."

"Why in the world would you ever think that?" I demanded.

"Well, I think we both can agree that things haven't been smooth in Sammy and Jenn world since you quit your baby-sitting job with them. I can't believe you haven't gone back."

"If you only knew how close I have come, more than once. But I knew if I caved one time, that would be it, and Karen, even I know that it has been the best thing in the world for me to have gotten out from under that situation. I just keep hoping Sammy and Jenn will step up to the plate and start becoming parents. Three children now, and they are still the world's worst!" I lamented.

"Well, maybe not the worst," Karen said, "but they sure don't seem to be changing much. How many nannies are we up to now?'

"I lost count, but I think four or five. Oh, you will love this. I have burned my last bridge with Linda. She called last week demanding—not even asking, but demanding—that I start taking care of the kids again—a real guilt thing. How could I abandon those little children, what kind of grandmother was I, how selfish I was, and who did I think I was to be going to Italy, of all places, when my son and his family needed me, and on and on and on."

"You are kidding." Karen was outraged. She had never liked Linda. "She had some nerve calling you selfish—she has never once changed one of their diapers!"

"Well, actually, I think she did, and that's why she called. Jenn evidently fired another nanny, and she called her mother for help. She must have really laid it on, because Linda has a million excuses never to be in the same room with the children. I am not even sure she has ever held the baby. Anyway, she spent a day with them, and it must have killed her, because she called me that same night."

"What did you say to her?" Karen laughed. "I wished that I had been there."

"Well, at first, I was so astounded that she was so out of control that I couldn't say anything, but then I got angry. I mean really pissed off. I told her that in six years, those children never knew they had another grandmother, and she had never lifted a finger to help out. I told her she had no right to speak to me at all. I had paid my dues, and now it was her turn. I also said she defined the word selfish, and then I hung up."

"Wow! She needed that," said Karen. "She is a bitch if there ever was one."

"Fifteen minutes later, who should call but Sammy. 'Mom, what did you say to Linda? She called Jenn and said you were terrible to her and said horrible things. Jenn is very upset. Now the baby is crying. What is going on?' I tell you, Karen, I was just completely fed up and still am."

"So now what?"

"Things are a bit strained. I told Sammy that I really didn't know what he was talking about, and that I thought Linda may have been a bit tired after her first experience of being with her grandchildren. I was very sarcastic, but Sammy missed it, because, really, Karen, I raised an idiot, an absolute idiot, and he married another idiot. Somehow, it was my fault that Brooke was crying and that there was no one to baby-sit the next day, because Linda was just too upset by what I had said to come back. As if she ever planned to. I think she would rather live in Saudi Arabia covered in a burqa for the rest of her life than go back over to that zoo!"

Karen howled. "Nah, she would never cover up her hair."

"I decided that that tiresome conversation with Sammy was one that I'd had too many times in the past, and there was no need to continue it. I said that someone needed to pick up Brooke so that she would stop crying. And to kiss Chapin and Eli good night for me. Then I hung up."

"No, you didn't! Two hang-ups in one night. That is priceless! I am impressed at your progress."

"Believe me; I have moments of immense guilt when I see those boys. I can't even think about Brooke, but they have had great nannies, and either Sammy or Jenn sabotages them every time. By the time the boys have adjusted halfway to one person, she is gone. It's a shame. I was hoping that since Brooke was a girl, she might bring out a real nurturing instinct in Jenn, but, as you know, she was back at work in two weeks. Two weeks! I am sticking to my guns. I get one boy one weekend and the other the next, and we do things— just the two of us together—and that has been great fun. Even with Chapin. Although he demands a lot of attention and gets it in a negative way, he really does need it the most. Eli is a delight. It's not fair, but I just adore that child."

"How are they with Brooke?"

"Chapin hates her, even more than he did Eli when he was born. He is starving for attention from Jenn or Sammy. Now there is another one taking what little time they give the children, and he just can't stand it. I don't trust him with the baby, and I have warned the nannies to watch him around her. She is a precious baby. Eli loves her to death. He wants to hold her. He is so sweet. He sings to her. Even though she is just five weeks old, I think she is responding to him."

"Do you think Chapin would actually harm her?" Karen asked, shocked.

"I really do. He is so out of control. He doesn't hit Eli anymore though, not since I enrolled Eli in that martial arts class and he flipped Chapin on his butt one day. That was another bone of contention between Sammy and me. He actually called me to complain about how mean Eli was to Chapin. Can you believe it? As many times as Chapin has hit and bitten Eli. It was the best thing in the world for Eli's confidence and safety to know that he can defend himself. He's becoming very skilled in martial arts. He is small and quick. His instructor said that he's a natural."

"And does Chapin like his art classes?"

"Yes, he does. I always felt that he needed to do something creative to help him channel his anger better. He loves painting. The teacher tells the kids to just put down the colors they want on the canvas and let them go where they want to—free form. Chapin's started out being all black or all red, but now he is actually giving his work some thought. I'm trying positive rewards on him. He needs a good physical outlet, so I told him the first time he goes two weeks without being mean to Eli, I would enroll him in gymnastics. He is excited about that. I made a chart up for Eli to keep in his room, and he marks all the days that Chapin has been nice. He hasn't made four consecutive days yet, but I think he is trying harder. The sad thing is that neither Jenn nor Sammy ever asks them about their days with me—what they do. Nothing. They just aren't interested."

"It is very sad," Karen agreed. "To change the subject, what have you bought to take on our trip? I am so excited, I can't sleep at night."

We spent the next hour talking about our trip. I was also getting more excited about it. I had prepared the boys that I would be gone and had made arrangements for them to continue their classes while I was away. I knew better than to count on Sammy or Jenn. I was so tired of them and their lifestyle that I just wanted time away. Later that night, as I was preparing for bed, I reflected on the past five months. The positive things were that I felt that my relationship with Chapin and Eli was stronger than ever. The individual time that I spent with them was precious to me and to them. I was beginning to see glimpses of the sweet Chapin I once knew. In time, I would build a relationship with Brooke. The other most positive change in my life was that I was regaining a life. I had started gardening again and seeing old friends. Karen and I got together often for dinner. We had talked about starting a dinner group for women our age when we got back from Italy. I felt more excited about life in general than I had in a long time.

The negatives were, of course, all centered on Sammy and his family. How could it continue to get worse? It seemed their family life meant nothing to either him or Jenn. I still couldn't get over her going back to work two weeks after Brooke's birth when she didn't have to. Her company would have set up all the necessary technology for her right in the house, but she said the children would be distracting. They weren't even trying to make things work with a nanny. They needed a nanny themselves! Now there is a future occupation: nannies for inept adults.

Oh, well, I thought, I can't let this get to me. They have got to sort it out, and I have to make sure that I don't get sucked into guilt. No matter what Sammy says, my life is not over. Not by a long shot!

The best thing to come out of the last five months has been the change in my relationship with Laura. She didn't believe that I would stick to my guns, and she has been so supportive. Now we talk weekly, and I try not to have too many stories about the "stuff" that goes on with Sammy. The most amazing thing was how much Chapin took to Laura when she was home at Christmas. It was endearing. I wished that she lived closer. I think she could make a real difference in his life. I couldn't believe she came home. I think she wanted to see for herself what was going on.

I was still interviewing nannies and keeping the children in December. I took them to the airport to pick up their aunt Laura. I had them make welcome-home cards for her, and they each got to pick out a rose to give her. They didn't remember her at all. She looked so beautiful when she got off the plane that we all thought she was a movie star.

She gave both boys a big hug and kisses and told them how much she loved the roses and cards. Then she said that she had something special for them in her luggage. "Who is the strongest? I need strong boys to help me." They both jumped for joy. She had them look for her luggage, which had a big fake daisy tied on it so it would be easily identified on the carousel. "I will need both of you to help. Now remember, there is a present for each of you, so you must be gentle with it."

What a knack she had with them. They never worked better together than the week she was here. They decorated the tree without fighting or arguing. She made cookies with them. She took them on short shopping trips and had them look for specific items. Over and over she rewarded their good behavior. Of course there were some incidents, but she sat them down and talked about it. Chapin couldn't get enough of her.

"Laura, you really don't know what a great effect you are having on these children," I said one day after they had left. "If only Sammy and Jenn would give them the kind of attention that you do. You are a natural with them."

"They are really cute but totally exhausting. I don't know how you have done it all these years, Mom."

"I love them so much," I replied, "and I know that I can't handle them— well, handle Chapin—any longer. They are exhausting, it's true. More than that, I have started resenting Sammy and Jenn. It is way past time to step away. They are all too dependent on me."

"I think you mean they take advantage of you."

"Well, yes," I said sadly, "but I realize that I let it happen. I just haven't been very skilled at getting out from under all of this. I am so grateful that you are here to help me choose a nanny."

"Tell me again why Sammy and Jenn aren't doing this," Laura said, perplexed.

"The simplest way of putting it is that they aren't interested, and they don't believe I won't continue keeping the children. They think I am going through a little phase. I actually heard Jenn telling Linda that! That was the last straw for me. I am more than ever determined that things will change."

"Good for you, Mom! I am really proud of you and excited that you and Karen are going to take this trip," she said, smiling.

"Oh, well, that trip is another thing. I am not sure about that. Karen is the one who really wants to go. For me, it's just an excuse."

"It doesn't matter. It's perfect, and you need a break. Trust me, you will love Italy. It is the most wonderful place I have ever been, and I would go back in a heartbeat."

We had many good conversations during that week. It felt as if her time with me was over in a minute. Then she was gone again, but not without a promise that I would visit her. "There is someone I want you to meet," she said at the airport.

# II

Two days before our big trip, Karen's daughter, Mariah, called. "Kathryn, mother asked me to call you. She is here in Bay Memorial Hospital."

"What? Is she all right? What happened?"

"Her appendix burst, that's what happened. It just happened all of a sudden. She called me last night and said she was having tremendous pains in her side and needed to go to the hospital. I called 911, and they brought her in. She had surgery as soon as they could get an operating room. She doing fine now—well, she's in some pain—but her doctor said she will recover with no complications. "

"I am on my way over. What room is she in?"

"No, don't come over until later. She's asleep right now, but she does want to see you tonight. She is worried about the trip."

"The trip? Oh my God, I had forgotten about our trip. She is not going to be able to go now."

"No, she will be in the hospital for a few days and then will come to my house to recuperate, but the last thing she said before she went into surgery was to call you."

"No problem, we will just cancel and go another time," I replied.

"That is exactly what mother said you would say. And that is exactly what she does not want you to do," Mariah responded.

"But I can't possibly go now," I said. "Who would I get at the last minute?"

"Mother wants you to go on without her."

"I can't go by myself," I said as patiently as I could to someone who didn't seem to understand the situation.

"Of course you can, Kathryn. It's a tour. There will be loads of people on it. Don't reject this outright. Mother is so concerned about you that I am afraid it will interfere with her recovery," said a worried Mariah.

"Mariah, don't worry about this. When I see your mother later tonight, I will make her understand that it is OK that we don't go right now. There will be other times," I said.

Actually, I think I felt a little relieved, because I wasn't at all sure that I wanted to go anyway.

But I didn't make Karen understand. As weak as she felt, she made me promise that I would go. Her argument made a lot of sense. "I can get all my money back from the tour and the airlines, because my surgery was an emergency. You will lose every cent if you don't go. I couldn't live with myself knowing that I was the reason that you lost all that money. Your must promise me that you will go on to Italy. Promise me, Kathryn."

I felt at a loss. I didn't want to go by myself. It was a foreign country. I didn't know one other person on the tour, and I would be a single woman. A fifth wheel. But I promised her that I would go.

My stomach was in a knot, as it had been for the past two days, when I arrived at the airport. I had not traveled anywhere for eight years. The last time I went on a vacation was with Gary, two years before he died, and that was just to Cape May, New Jersey. Italy was a long way off. I wasn't prepared for electronic tickets and couldn't get the machine to work. A nice man with a little girl helped me out. I hated the long wait in the airport. I couldn't eat anything. I couldn't focus on reading the book that I had brought along. I knew that I was in for a miserable three and a half weeks. At one point I thought that I had lost my boarding pass and panicked, but I found it stuck in the book that I couldn't read. Everyone seemed to have someone to talk to but me. Walking around would have helped, but I was afraid I would miss an important announcement over the intercom system, so I only strayed to the restroom when absolutely necessary.

I thought about how much Eli cried and cried when I left. Sammy and the boys took me to the airport. I was surprised, but Sammy insisted. Chapin was excited that I was flying, and Eli was as miserable as I was. Chapin thought I was going to where Aunt Laura lived and wanted to go with me. I promised both boys that I would bring them something very special back and would send them each a postcard. I made them drop me off at the door, because I was just too nervous and anxious to cope with them.

Finally, I heard the call to board the plane. I took a deep breath and hoped that I might fall asleep once we became airborne. My seat was in the middle of three across. Karen and I had planned that she would have an aisle seat and then we could switch off. Now I would be stuck in the middle for the entire trip.

A woman about my age took the window seat, and a man who looked to be in his forties took the aisle. He apparently was with a man just across the aisle from him. My initial impression was that they were very pleasant. By the time we took off, I found out that both of my seatmates and the man across the aisle were on the same tour to Italy! I was astounded. I had sat in the airport for over three hours, worried sick, and in fifteen minutes on the plane, I had already met three people—very nice people—who would be on this same tour. I am such a fool, I thought.

Nan Coulous was also a widow and had never had children. She had always wanted to go to Italy and was very excited about it, as well as very chatty. I liked her instantly. She was as comfortable as an old shoe and had a unique way of putting others at ease. She had retired from a government job in December, and this trip was a retirement gift to herself. She confessed that she had been at loose ends and was looking around for a part-time job working with children. She had started doing volunteer work with a social service agency but realized that supplementing her income might be more beneficial. She wasn't sure how she wanted to do that yet, but she knew that children had to be involved. "I love their energy and creativity. It will keep me going. And I never want to see another government form again in my life." She laughed.

I confessed to her how nervous I had been and that I was glad that there was another single woman on the trip. Janson Sheffield, my other seatmate, interrupted and said that he thought there were several other single women on this tour. He and his partner, William Amerson, had talked with a couple of them.

The called themselves Jan and Wills. They took a trip every year to Europe or somewhere outside the United States. This was their second trip to Italy, and they told me they adored it. They loved the hill towns and fantasized about owning a home there one day. Both worked as lawyers in the Department of Justice and had a town house in the city.

I told them a bit about my last six years, and they were sympathetic. They said I was absolutely doing the right thing to come on the trip for every reason. We all were going to have the best time together. I felt relaxed and completely included. I started looking forward to the next few weeks. Jan and Wills filled Nan and me in on many of the things that we would be seeing, but best of all, they said, was the food. "Italian food is the most delicious food on the planet," said Wills.

Jan said that he wouldn't be surprised if almost the entire tour group was on this plane, since Dulles was the point of departure. He pointed out two sisters, who were in their seventies whom he had met, but said he already felt they were tedious. Wills did an imitation of one of them, and we all laughed. Jan and Wills were so much fun, and I was already having a good time. Poor Karen. She would be having a ball if she were here. Jan and Wills were her kind of people.

# III

By the time we landed at Leonardo da Vinci Airport in Rome, I had learned ten words in Italian from "the boys," one of which I think was pretty naughty. I felt like these three people were old friends. We knew almost everything about one another after nine hours together.

A young Italian woman holding up a sign for our tour met us when we deplaned. She made everything as simple as pie, and we soon had our luggage and were on a bus headed for Sorrento and the Amalfi coast for the next three days. We would then return to Rome, stopping in Pompeii on the way back.

As we stood waiting to board the bus, I took the opportunity to look at the tour group. It seemed very diverse. There were several couples, but there were also some groupings that I would not have anticipated. There were the two older sisters Jan had warned me about; a group of four that had an older woman, two younger women, who were probably sisters, and a little girl who looked like she was between nine and eleven; and to my surprise, the nice man who had helped me with my ticket and his little girl. Where was her mother? I wondered. There also seemed to be several pairings of women who were without husbands. I was the most surprised that two children were on this tour, because school wasn't out yet. I estimated that there were about thirty of us. We all looked totally exhausted.

Our tour director told us that she would ride with us to Sorrento and would be with us off and on throughout the trip, but we would be picking up a different tour leader when we returned to Rome. There would be a welcome reception for the group that night at 7:00, followed by dinner in the hotel. She kept up a running commentary the entire way, but I think most of us dozed off. It was warm on the sunny bus, and the night on the plane had provided little, if any, comfortable sleep. Jan told me to nudge him if he snored.

We arrived at our hotel in midafternoon. Although I felt as if I could sleep until morning, I asked Nan if she was interested in walking into town to the main piazza, not only for the exercise but to keep me up. She was, and off we went. Both of us were a little hungry and managed to buy a slice of pizza and a coke with euros without too much trouble. We had exchanged quite a bit of information about ourselves on the plane and were becoming fast friends. In the course of our window shopping, we recognized others from the bus and nodded to them. It was comforting being to be in a foreign country and see familiar faces.

The reception that night was fun and broke the ice. There was unlimited wine, cheeses of various sorts, breads, and olives. The two little girls seemed to have found one another although the smaller of the two seemed very shy. At our first dinner, I found myself separated from Nan and at a table with a Dr. Aaron Ledermann and his wife Sylvia, the two sisters, Ida Jane and Mary Louise Dawkins, and Phil and Margaret Shells, who were celebrating their fortieth anniversary with this trip. Dr. Ledermann dominated the conversation at the table by talking about all the trips that he and his wife had been on over the years. He seemed to be an expert on every topic, but his wife said virtually nothing. She had the most enormous diamond on her finger that I had ever seen in my life. The two sisters were a hoot and complete opposites. Ida Jane complained about everything: the wines, the food, her bed, the plane ride (I agreed with her on that one), and the weather. She had not slept a bit the entire way to Sorrento. She also said the bus driver drove too fast around the curves, and she couldn't understand half of what our Italian tour director, Giuliana, was saying. We should have an American, not an Italian, talking to us. Mary Louise had slept like a log, according to her sister and had drunk too much wine at the reception, and Ida Jane just knew that she was going to be sick. Mary Louise smiled and stated that she was having a perfectly wonderful time. Between Ida Jane and Dr. Ledermann, as he preferred to be called, no one else could get a word in edgewise. Phil Shells sat to my left, and we were able to have a little side conversation every now and then. The food was delicious, and I went off to bed very pleased about my first day in Italy.

I woke up the next morning feeling refreshed but missing Karen more than ever. It would have been so much fun to rehash the people that I had met so far on the tour. I had the most amazing view of the harbor from my room, and it was high enough up to see down the street that ran beside our hotel. The older woman and one of the younger women of the foursome were walking back up the hill. Where had they been so early in the morning? Maybe just a walk for health purposes. They looked up and saw me and waved with big smiles. I decided that I would try to find them for breakfast or lunch today. I was feeling a bit more adventurous.

Neva Capello was her name and she was seventy-five years old. Her daughter, Lena, and granddaughter, Sara, and Lena's best friend, Ana, had come together on the trip. Neva's children had promised that they would bring her to Italy one day. Her plans were to depart the trip in Umbria to visit relatives and rejoin the tour in Florence. She had gone to Mass early this morning and was on her way back when I saw her and Lena. She was thrilled to be in Italy. I learned that Neva's entire group spoke Italian, because they always spoke it at home in Baltimore. We only lived about an hour from one another. They were a delightful family and obviously had a lot of affection for each other. The "girls," who were in their forties, I found out, were often mistaken for sisters. One of them was a widow—I assumed she was Sara's mother. Neva was just thirteen years older than me, and we got along famously.

Jan and Wills were also having a great time. They already knew the best shops on Capri and what they wanted to buy and look at. They steered me right away to the lemon soap and perfume factory. It was heavenly, but the best thing on the whole island was a delicious lemon drink over ice. The little girls, Sara and Nikki, introduced me to that. Nikki's father was Victor Ansera. He seemed to be constantly on his cell phone or laptop. He was divorced, the only single man on the tour, and had promised Nikki that he would bring her to Italy, because she had studied ancient Rome in school and wanted to see Roman statues. She appeared painfully shy, and my heart went out to her. She was glad to let Sara make all of the decisions.

Nan had met two other single women with the tour, Ginny and Meredith. They were in their fifties and had left their husbands at home. "We wouldn't have had any fun with them. They're sticks in the mud," one of them said. The other said, "They are absolutely relieved that we didn't insist they come." The four of us had lunch together and got to know one another a little better. This trip was a shopping paradise for Ginny and Meredith. They knew exactly what Italian products they wanted to buy in each city we were stopping in. They had done a lot of research for this, and it was a marathon to be conquered. I needed to introduce them to Jan and Wills. From their point of view, cathedrals and historical sites were to be endured, and they hoped they wouldn't take too long on any given day.

By the time we got back to Rome, I felt as if I had known half of the people on the trip most of my life. We shared a lot and laughed a lot. Positano, farther around on the Amalfi coast was breathtaking. Pompeii made me sad—all those people who had burned up. Their civilization was eye-opening and impressive. We spent some time in a cameo factory en route to Rome, and I bought both Karen and me little rings. I wanted her to have some part of what was turning out to be the best thing I had ever done.

We picked up a new tour guide, Francesca Botti, in Sorrento before we headed north. What a delight she was, and she liked Americans. I judged that she must be in her midforties. She was of medium build with short, wavy, dark hair and flashing brown eyes. She had a great sense of humor and was very flexible. She was attentive to the needs of the group and was willing to give extra time for shopping, lunches, or breaks. Francesca always had a local sweet treat for our bus rides in the afternoons and was especially good to little Sara and Nikki. She seems to know everyone in every city and was a real asset on our trip.

The four days in Rome were fun with the little girls. Nikki Ansera was so excited to see the Coliseum and Forum. She knew a lot because of her school project, and we were all impressed. Even her father got off the phone long enough to appreciate her knowledge. Neva Capello cried when she first saw Saint Peter's Cathedral. It had been her lifelong dream to visit the Vatican. She bought a rosary at the Vatican gift shop and had it blessed by the Holy Father. We had all been touched by her quiet devotion. Ginny and Meredith wasted no time in visiting all the historical sites. They spent two full days shopping and bought boots and some clothes. They were waiting for Florence—the big shopping mecca in the sky, they said.

Our mealtime groups had fallen into two loose cliques that rotated easily. The tables seem to be made up Victor, Nikki, Sara (the two girls had become inseparable), Lena, Ana, Neva, Nan, Wills, Jan, Meredith, Ginny, and the Shells. Since we sat at tables for eight, by default, often as not, we would get the Ledermanns and the Dawkins sisters. We all liked Mary Louise, but Ida Jane was difficult. Our lunches and dinners together soon felt like a family of friends. We were very comfortable with one another.

In Rome, Lena spent time during part of each day learning new Italian hair and makeup techniques for her salons in Baltimore. She was quite a businesswoman and was often seen talking with Victor. One day she came back, after spending the morning in training, and offered the opportunity for three women to get their hair and makeup styled the Italian way in one of the major salons in Rome. It was part of her training. I surprised myself by volunteering with Ana. Ginny and Meredith were torn between giving up shopping or having a makeover. It seemed that Mary Louise was interested but was held back by Ida Jane's comments of it being silly foolishness and not what they had paid for. In the end, Margaret Shell asked if she could do it. What a fabulous time we had. I loved my new look. My blonde hair was lightened and feathered. It had a distinctive European look. Ana was smashing. She was given red highlights in her brown hair, which made her hazel eyes stand out all the more. Her makeup was subtle but rich. Her shoulder-length hair had a swingy, flirty style. Little Sara's first impression was exactly what we all must have been thinking. "Auntie Ana, you are beautiful!" Even Margaret's husband whistled when he saw her. Jan and Wills complained that the men should be given equal opportunity, but Lena countered by saying she wouldn't tamper with perfection. That got a huge laugh.

Ana and I sat together when we left Rome as we journeyed to the hill towns. We were astounded to find out how much we had in common. There was exactly a twenty-year age difference. She was forty-two and I was sixty-two. We both had been widows for six years. Our husbands had died without warning—Gary of a heart attack and Ana's husband the victim of a hit and run. We shared how devastated and numb we felt by the deaths. We both felt that we had let life slide by us in the past six years. We found out that we lived within one hour of each other. She was such an accomplished young woman, much like my daughter. They were almost the same age, although it seemed to me that Ana was more like a contemporary of mine. We both laughed when we discovered that we had to be talked into coming on this trip and how much we were enjoying it.

"I really think that I am moving past my grief now," Ana told me. "I literally moved through each day like a zombie for six years. Nothing had any meaning for me until recently."

"Did something happen?"

"Yes," she said radiant. "I met a man in Germany this past winter. I am scared to death that this is just a fling, and my heart will be broken, but I have to chance it. I will see him again in a few days. I will leave the tour to spend two weeks with him at his farm here in Italy. I have a lot of anxiety.

It's been almost two months since I last saw him, and I'm so anxious that he won't feel the same. Our time together in Germany was very intense, and it happened so fast."

"Have you kept in touch?" I asked.

"Yes, we e-mail several times a week, and Theo has even called me three times—that works out to roughly once a month. Sometimes a week will go by, and I don't hear from him, which provokes my anxiety on two levels. One, that something has happened to him—I think he works for Interpol, but he won't say definitely—and the other, that he has lost interest."

"It sounds like he is very interested in keeping the relationship going. Are the e-mails and calls personal?"

"Very!" She blushed. "Kathryn, it all feels so strange to me. I had never thought of being with another man after Mark died. It had never crossed my mind. I loved Mark so much. I have missed him every day…well, until I met Theo, and there is some guilt there. Mark was my best friend. Whenever I came home in a foul mood, he could always make me laugh, and we just had the best time together. I thought that we would be together forever. We had been trying to start a family."

"Ana, I am sorry that you became a widow at such a young age. At least I was older. Here's my best advice. I think you should just relax and enjoy this gift of time with someone that you obviously care about. I don't think you have one thing to worry about."

"That is exactly what Lena said. But you know, Kathryn, it was almost surreal, my time in Germany and with Theo. It came out of nowhere, and I guess that is why I don't trust it. I also feel too vulnerable to evaluate it in its proper light. It felt almost like living in a parallel universe, if that makes any sense."

"I'm not sure that it does," I answered honestly.

"It's kind of like how the time in a foreign country or the time you have on vacation is not your real life, so it doesn't count. Does that make sense? Like now, this is not our real life, this trip."

"I wish it were my real life." I laughed again. "But I do get what you are saying."

"I think that's why the two weeks with Theo this time, over here, will either make or break the relationship. I have to confess, I can't wait to see him!"

"I really hope that it works out for you. When will you leave the tour?"

"I am leaving in Florence. Theo will pick me up on our last day there. He has promised to take me to Venice, because I really did want to see that city, so I think we will go there just before I leave to return home."

"Yes, I am looking forward to seeing Venice, as well," I admitted. "This has been the most extraordinary trip for me. I have loved every single minute. Italy is a wonderful country. I think I am in love with a country, if that is possible. I wish that I spoke Italian."

"You can always take lessons," Ana replied. "Although I spoke some German when I went to Tubingen, I was very rusty. I have spent the past few weeks being tutored in German to surprise Theo. His English is excellent, but I would like to speak better German."

"I am amazed," I replied. "You say that so lightly, as if it is nothing to learn a foreign language."

"Well, don't forget that I am highly motivated." She laughed. But turning more serious, she asked, "Is there someone special in your life, Kathryn? Do you date?"

"Oh my gosh, no," I said, astounded. "There is absolutely no one. I doubt that there will ever be anyone else in my life. I can't imagine dating at my age."

"Why not?" Ana asked. "You are a very beautiful woman and very likable. You have made friends with everyone on the trip. I have seen Italian men look at you."

"You have?"

"You bet." She laughed again. "They were giving you the once-over."

"I doubt that," I replied. "Men tend to like young women. Look at Victor; he is highly interested in your Lena."

"Oh no. That is a business relationship. He couldn't believe how successful Lena is, and he crunched some numbers for her. He is helping her think about a new direction for her third salon. I think he is in love with his laptop and cell phone."

"But he is so handsome," I retorted, "and Lena is very beautiful and bubbly. She sparkles."

"Lena," she said mischievously, "is interested in a colleague of mine, Palmer Addison. She hasn't admitted that to me, but I can tell. I have known her a long time, and she asks loads of questions about him. They saw each other frequently when I was in Germany. Palmer told me, not Lena. That's how I know it's serious—because Lena isn't talking about it. I know for a fact that she has sent him at least four postcards since we have been in Italy. I tease her about him all the time, and she says nothing, so that is the real clue. Actually I think she and Palmer would make a good pair. He is a terrific man."

"Ana," I said suddenly. "I hope you will keep in touch with me when we return to the States. We live so close by."

"I would like that very much."

The rest of our trip to Orvieto was just as pleasant. I liked Ana and felt a kinship with all that she had been through. Jan and Wills joined us. They were the social butterflies of the group and always had something to say to make us laugh.

# III

I knew after one day in Orvieto that I would have to return to this city. We took a little cable car up to the top of the mountain, where our hotel was located, and the view was magnificent. But it was the city itself that I loved. After three days, we had been to Perugia, where we all bought chocolate, Assisi, Gubbio, Todi, Spello, and Spoleto. Neva and Sara left the tour in Todi to meet the Capello relatives and would rejoin us in Florence. Nikki was so sad to see Sara leave that they took her with them. We couldn't believe Victor would let her go, but she cried so much that he relented. I didn't know what she would do when we went home. Tomorrow, we would leave for Siena and then on to Florence. I decided to spend my last day in Orvieto just walking around.

I was sitting in the Piazza del Duoma staring at the beautiful twelfth-century Gothic cathedral when Francesca Botti happened upon me.

"Ciao, Kathryn! Are you enjoying Orvieto?"

"Ciao, Franacesca," I said dreamily. "That is my only Italian word, you know."

She laughed. Francesca was always warm and hospitable. She made an effort to spend time with everyone on the tour, and many of us had gotten to know her well.

"I love this city, and I don't want to leave," I said. "It really has gotten to me."

"Si," responded Francesca." Orvieto is a magical city, just like Assisi and Perugia."

"I like Orvieto better than the other hill towns that we have seen. I really love the narrow cobblestoned streets and the way the town is laid out. It seems friendlier and has a more hometown atmosphere than the others, even though I know that it is a tourist town. I would really like to come back and spend more time here."

Francesca looked at me speculatively. "Don't forget, you haven't seen Siena yet. Or Florence. Pisa is also a nice little town, as well as Lucca."

"I know there is a lot more to see, but I love how Orvieto sits so high up on this mountain. It's like Assisi, in that it looks enchanting from a distance, but it is the character the town has that I like. I feel, in a strange way, at home here."

"Well, you have been here four nights now." Francesca laughed again.

"I can't explain it well, but I really feel sad to be leaving."

"Really, Kathryn? You do seem to feel strongly about being here."

"Yes, I really do, Francesca. I love Italy. I am so surprised at how much I love the entire country, but it's this place,"—my arm swept around the piazza—"this town, that speaks to me. It is whispering to me, 'stay…stay.'"

"Why don't you plan to come back? There is a language school here. You could come back and study Italian. They have two-week classes with four hours of study each morning. You get to meet with the people of the town and speak Italian. You can arrange private tutoring in the afternoons, as well."

"Study Italian?" I responded. "I would love to learn your beautiful language, but I think I am too old."

"Oh no, Kathryn, we are never too old to learn. The school has young and older people here from all over the world. You would meet many interesting people. The classes are small—ten or fifteen people only—that is how you would learn."

"Where would I live?" I inquired.

"The school has some rooms in hotels around the town, or if you wanted to stay longer, you could rent a flat—an apartment."

"An apartment in Orvieto, what fun that would be! Maybe I could talk my friend Karen into coming. No, I think I would want to be by myself."

"Come with me, Kathryn," Francesca said, standing up and putting her arm through mine. "Let me show you where the school is and where some apartments are. We still have time before dinner."

I was so excited. I thought, I really want to do this. For the next hour, Francesca gave me the "other" tour of Orvieto: the back streets. She showed me the language school, Lingua Si, which was established in 1998. It was located in front of the remains of the Etruscan Temple of Belvedere and the park of the Fortezza di Albornoz.

"There is also a small garden for the students to use," she pointed out.

We continued to walk around the town, which she told me had a population of about twenty-three thousand inhabitants. I was surprised there were so many people living on top of the mountain.

"It is easy to live in some of the hill towns now. Orvieto has the funicular and attracts tourists, who have kept it alive. It is a thousand meters up here, so there had to be a way to bring people up, or the town would have died. Now it is known for its arts and crafts, as you know from all the smart shops on Corso Cavon and Via del Duomo-leather, woods, metals, lace, and pottery. There are also the underground caves and Etruscan museums and ruins. The people in Orvieto make a good living and have stayed here. More important, the young people come back. The teatro is very lively also," said Francesca. "There is always some kind of concert playing here. Orvieto attracts people almost all year long."

"There, look." She pointed out apartments above shops on the two main streets. "These are very nice and modern. You would be surprised."

I was enchanted.

"Kathryn, if you are still interested at the end of the tour, after you have been to Siena and Firenze, talk to me again. I can help you. I live not far from Assisi and will help you make arrangements. Orvieto is just a little over an hour by train from Roma and two hours from Firenze. We talk again, no?"

"Si!" I laughed, but I didn't think I would change my mind. I had not felt so excited about something in years. I was determined to make it happen. I would return to this charming city on this lovely hill.

# ANA

I

Lena and I were having a ball in Italy. She flirted with every Italian man who could still breathe, and they all fell in love with her. More than once I said, just like Neva, "Angelena Teresa!" She had more salons lined up to visit in Florence. We were determined to get Mary Louise Dawkins into one of them. Lena was going to offer the same makeover proposal to the tour group, and she enlisted Jan and Wills to help us with Mary Louise. She was a doll. What would she have been like without Ida Jane on her back every day?

It seemed that Mary Louise was engaged at one time, but her beau was not deemed suitable by the family for some mysterious reason, so she broke it off. She had lived in the family home with Ida Jane ever since. Ida Jane continued her constant litany of complaints about everything. I guess the best thing that happened to the group is that the "foreign food" went bad on Ida Jane's stomach, and she had to lie down in her room on three occasions so far. That was a gift to the group and the lottery for Mary Louise! She had so much fun with us. A plan was devised to plant in Ida Jane's head the notion that the food in Florence was making everyone sick, hoping that she would succumb, leaving Mary Louise free for a day at the salon without guilt.

Wills was put in charge of carrying it out, because he was a master of manipulation. We actively sought out the Dawkins sisters at our dinner table rather than our usual attempts to avoid them. "Ida Jane," Wills said the first night in Florence, "you are looking a little peaked tonight. I hope your tummy is going to be a little stronger than mine."

"I am?" said a worried Ida Jane. "This food is going to kill me before I get back home, I swear it is."

"I know what you mean." Wills winked at us. "I plan to drink as much wine as possible tonight to kill the germs. Can I pour you a tad?"

"Well, I don't know. You know Mary Louise and I don't indulge. It's a sin," she said piously, forgetting that Mary Louise had indulged every single night.

"I totally agree," said a very serious Wills, who had shipped cases of wine back to the States. "But I have found a little wine has helped my stomach disorders quite a bit. I think it's the only way I have gotten through. Some of us are a bit more delicate than others."

"That is very true," Ida Jane agreed. "I haven't had one good day here. I don't know why I agreed to come on this foolish trip. It has just wasted a lot of money."

"They say," Wills said smoothly, "that the food in Florence is especially hard on the digestive system."

"No!" Ida Jane exclaimed.

"Yes, and if I may be just a bit indelicate"—he leaned over and stage-whispered—"they say it's the uh…I just have to say it, forgive me, please. They say it's the manure that is used as fertilizer." And with that, he poured a little wine in her glass. "Please, just for your health's sake, drink just a little."

We all watched, trying hard not to laugh. It was really a little mean, but she had just been so tiresome.

"Give it just a few minutes," Wills said. "I think you will feel the germs dying as your stomach, if I may be so indelicate again, starts to feel warmer."

Had the woman never had alcohol? The sad thing was that I could see Ida Jane responding to Wills's attention. I bet no one had ever been solicitous to her before.

"Now how are you feeling?" Wills asked.

"Why, I do believe that it is working," Ida Jane said in wonder. "Mary Louise, you need to take a little of that wine. It's medicinal."

"Maybe just a tad more," said Wills as her poured her a glassful and filled up Mary Louise's glass. "I think you will find that this will ease your digestive disorders in no time."

"Why, thank you very kindly," she replied. "Be careful, Mary Louise, you don't want to drink this too fast. It will go to your head!"

And with that comment, we all laughed. We just couldn't help it. Jan jumped in and said, "I think you mean, Ida Jane, to your stomach…to your stomach."

"Just take sips, Ida Jane," Wills cautioned. "Here, eat some bread with it. I think that is safe and maybe a little soup, but I would skip the rest of the dinner."

"You are very kind," she smiled slightly. We were astonished. That was the first glimpse of a smile that we had seen on her face the entire trip.

"Not at all," Wills said. "We travelers have to take care of each other. Here, just another little sip." He held her glass up to her mouth.

She will be ready to marry him by tomorrow, I thought. Wills kept her glass full, sip by sip, and in no time at all, she was just plain drunk, and that was funny. Mary Louise, on the other hand, was having the time of her life. She knew what was going on. There was no doubt about that. She even said at one point, "Wills, I believe my sister might require another sip of that wine to help her stomach distress."

By the evening's end, which was short for Ida Jane, she'd had almost no food but a whole lot of wine and was completely drunk. Mary Louise had been invited to accompany Lena to a salon day and was very excited about it. "Of course, I will only go if Ida Jane doesn't require my company tomorrow."

"Without saying," agreed Lena, laughing.

Nan Coulous stated that she had not had a thing done to her hair in years and would love one of those "Eyetalian" upsweeps. We all laughed, but Lena thanked her for volunteering. "I will make sure Mary Louise comes with me," Nan said. She had become the caretaker of the group and attended to everyone's needs.

Meredith and Ginny were also invited again but said they had no time for hair. There were just too many shops that needed their attention in between the cultural tours. We all thought they were finally getting into the swing of the arts when we went to the Academia to see Michelangelo's magnificent David. Neither one of them said one word for the longest time, then Meredith burst out with, "He is just one burning hunk of love, isn't he, Ginny? I could go for a man like that." Wills and Jan laughed for hours.

Meredith and Ginny were professional shoppers. They told us or took us personally to every leather or jewelry shop of worth in the entire city. They were on first-name basis with all the jewelers along the Ponte Vecchio before we left. They also gave me a helping hand. I had mentioned that I wanted to buy a male friend something special, and they took me to this little shop where they had seen exquisite cuff links. They were perfect.

Because of Ginny and Meredith, we all got caught up in the shopping fever. I bought a handbag, a beautiful green scarf, two belts, and a beautiful gold necklace. I bought both Nikki and Sara necklaces with little gold crosses as a souvenir of Florence and our trip together to Italy. I wanted to get Neva something special. She had been such a stabilizing force in my life, not only in my childhood, but particularly after Mark's death. I had been looking in every city for something unusual and meaningful for her. It was Ginny and Meredith who actually saw it and told me I had to come with them. It was the perfect gift—the absolute perfect gift. Neva's spiritual devotion was never in doubt. She had been to Mass every single day in every single city we had been in. Sometimes it meant that she had to get up early enough for a 5:00 a.m. Mass, but she went.

The gift was a twenty-four-carat-gold square Renaissance picture of the Madonna and child. It was just one inch high but perfect in every little detail. Neva could set it on her bedside table where she would see it each morning when she woke up and every night before turning out the light. I loved it and knew that she would, too. The jeweler put it in a little red velvet box inside a little green velvet drawstring pouch. I would save it for Christmas.

For Lena, I found a pair of beautiful earrings, which I would also save for Christmas and, on the same shopping excursion, I found a little pair of earrings for Sara. The jeweler also wrapped these beautifully in little boxes inscribed in gold: Ponte Vecchio, Florence, Italy. I couldn't resist getting Lena and me identical, delicate gold chain-link bracelets, which I would give her right away. We were as close as blood sisters, and this would be our symbol.

Neva and the girls rejoined us. Neva had had a wonderful time with her relatives, and they had loved Sara and Nikki. I didn't think Nikki would ever forget this trip any more than we would, but I had a feeling that her life experiences, thus far, had not been happy ones. She and her mother lived about an hour from Baltimore. Victor lived closer to DC, where he worked. Victor had already promised Lena that he would be in touch to help her with financial decisions for the salons when we returned home, and he would bring Nikki on his custodial weekends. The girls were ecstatic.

Florence was one of the most beautiful cities that I had ever visited. We were there for three days, and it felt good to have the time to explore on our own. I loved walking the streets, looking at the architecture, and visiting the churches. Francesca had been wise to limit the cultural visits and give the group ample free time. She always had good suggestions for everyone's needs, whether it was a particular museum, garden, or special event. She had steered Ginny and Meredith to the best shops with the best prices.

We had been warned about the gypsies and getting our pockets picked. It had already happened to two people on the tour. This would be my last city with the group. Theo would be picking me up in two days, when the rest of the group left to go north to Venice. I was sad to say good-bye to my new friends but anxious to see Theo again. The time was almost here.

Mary Louise came back from the Florentine salon looking at least ten years younger. She must have been very beautiful at one time and had remained lovely as she aged. Now she was striking. Lena had explained that much of her clientele was made up of older women, and she needed to learn the best techniques for this population. Mary Louise could have been her poster girl. We all made much over her at dinner that night. Wills, quite wisely, put all of his attention toward Ida Jane, which led to no hard feelings all around. In fact, it seemed that Ida Jane was growing fond of wine... for medicinal purposes only. She reported that her stomach had never felt better.

Nan was also glowing from her new hairstyle. The boys, Jan and Wills, were always gallant with the women and asked if they could escort the two new movie stars to dinner. They both blushed but looked pleased. Most of the women on our trip were going home looking far better than they did when they arrived, thanks to Lena, who gave all the women who asked advice on their hair. More than once, she cut someone's hair on the spot, and it made all the difference.

# II

We were staying in the elegant Hotel Savoy. Its central location made it easy to walk to most of the sights, but it was also a good location for the walks that I liked to take before dinner each night. I had gotten in the habit of resting for about an hour in the afternoon, after which I would shower and change for dinner. I loved how the sky changed the colors of the city as the sun was going down and would go out for a short stroll. It was the second night of our tour in Florence, and as I was walking slowly across the piazza from our hotel, I heard my name.

I turned to look behind me but the setting sun shone so brightly in my eyes, I could not see who was calling me. I watched a figure hurrying across the piazza. As he got closer, I looked in disbelief. "Theo," I said, more to myself than out loud.

He came up to me. "Is it really you? I can't believe it," I said.

"Ja, Ja, it is me. Ana, I could not wait any longer. I wanted to see you. I took a room at the Savoy."

He looked more handsome than I remembered. He was tan now, probably from working on the farm. He had on brown linen slacks and a long-sleeved ivory-colored linen shirt. He looked European—cool and sophisticated. He held me at arm's length and looked at me. "You are as beautiful as I remembered." He then pulled me close to him and kissed me deeply.

The men in the coffee shop on the piazza whistled and cheered. Other onlookers clapped. I was only slightly embarrassed, because Theo felt so good. He kissed me again. "Ana, Italy agrees with you. You are very, very beautiful."

I knew that I looked better than I had in years. I had filled out, which meant that I had gained some of my weight back, and I also had a touch of sun on my skin. The color was becoming and complimented my new hair color. I was wearing a sundress that I had bought in Capri. It was aquamarine with black trim around the bodice. It had a black jacket with aquamarine on the cap sleeves, but I had left that in my room at the hotel. I was wearing black espadrilles, which were not great for walking, but I was only out for a little stroll. Around my neck was the black onyx heart that Theo had given me in Tubingen.

He gently picked up the heart and looked at it and then me. "I will have to give you a gold heart while we are here. My heart is not so black now."

"I have worn it every day since you put it on me," I said simply. I was overwhelmed to see him again and was not prepared for all the emotions that tumbled inside of me. I had been so anxious about Theo for so long, and with one kiss, weeks of anxiety evaporated. Nothing else mattered to me but my feelings for him now. The way he looked at me and the way he held me told me that this man cared for me deeply.

"Let's walk for a bit," I said. "I am so shocked to see you that I can't think straight."

Theo laughed. "It was impulsive, but I was working on my farm this morning, thinking about you and how close you were. I couldn't do anything right, so I just decided that I needed to come to Florence and be with you sooner. Is it OK, Ana? That I came early?" Theo looked worried.

"I can't begin to tell you how happy I am to see you. I have been on pins and needles." I smiled up at him.

"What are pins and needles?" he said, perplexed. There were some things I just couldn't translate for him.

"It just means I wanted to see you also. So very much." I looked at him. "I have missed you, Theo. Every single day since I left Tubingen, I have missed you."

He squeezed my arm and gave me another hug, then another kiss that was more serious. "I have missed you too, Liebchen."

"Will you have dinner with our group tonight?" I asked. "I want you to meet Neva, Lena, and Sara, and so many more people."

"Ja." He laughed. Theo began to look more relaxed. I had never seen him like this in Tubingen. "But tomorrow night, we dine alone. I have some-place special to take you."

"I promised the girls that I would go to Pisa with them tomorrow. Will you come with us? We will be back long before dinnertime."

"Ja, of course, if the tour director will let me."

I need not have worried. When Theo saw Francesca across the room, he asked, "Is that Francesca Botti over there?"

Francesca heard her name and looked up, astonished. "Theo? Theo Volker? Where did you come from, amico?"

Do these people know everyone who lives in Europe? It turned out that Theo had known Francesca and her family from childhood, when they vacationed in Italy. They had been to each other's weddings and knew each other's children and spouses.

125

"I am here for Ana. She is coming to my farm," replied Theo.

Francesca knew that I was leaving the tour in Florence to visit a friend for two weeks, but I had never mentioned much else about it to her. Francesca looked at me and then back to Theo with instant insight. "Ah, Ana. Si, Ana. That is very good. You must tell me how you met."

Francesca normally did not sit with the guests for dinner. She sat with Aldo, our bus driver, plotting the next day's adventures, and sometimes one or two of the hotel staff would join them. They were all old friends and spent their dinners laughing and drinking wine late into the evening. Francesca was very popular with hotel staffs, tour managers, restaurant owners, and vendors along the way.

Tonight, she joined our table, made up of Neva, Lena, Sara, Nikki, Theo, and me. I wanted Theo to get to know my "family." Aldo joined us for the first course but then went off to visit with his old cronies. Theo had made the rounds during cocktail time and met some of the other people on the trip who had come to mean so much to me. He charmed the ladies with his old-world courtliness, even Ida Jane, as much as she could be charmed. She was starting out the evening with a "small" wine just to settle her stomach before dinner. Wills had now been charged with weaning her off alcohol, since she had developed a great fondness for it in such a short time.

We spoke mainly Italian at dinner. Theo was shocked to hear me speak this language so well. I had never gone into detail about my friendship with the Capellos, because it had just not come up while I lived in Germany. I had a good working knowledge of Italian and never gave it a thought. The Capellos spoke a mixture of both Italian and English at home, and I just picked it up easily as a child, the same way that little Nikki had picked up a remarkable amount on this trip. It was just natural. Even Lena and I often spoke a mixture of both languages.

"Ana, you continue to surprise me," Theo said.

"Ana speaks excellent Italian," said Francesca. "I have never had a group in which so many people could speak some Italian. Nikki has learned much in these short weeks. Eh, bambina?" She fondly put her hand under Nikki's beaming face. "Si, bambina, parli italiano?"

Nikki giggled and responded simply with a si. This painfully shy child had changed overnight. Victor could not get over it. Neva had taken her under her wing like a mother hen and had given her the nurturing this little girl so needed. Sara had become her older sister. Nikki had been incorporated into the Capello family just as I had been.

Emotionally, I was rendered nearly mute having Theo at the table with my friends, and I contributed little to the conversation. I took his hand under the table and squeezed it. It was interesting watching him interact with everyone. He was masterful at bringing out the best in everyone. The little girls could only giggle and watch him, wide-eyed. I felt like them. The most interesting thing that I observed was that he revealed very little about himself but got a lot out of everyone else. He must be a great detective. Everyone soon knew that he worked for the police in Germany and that we had met in Tubingen, but not much else of a personal nature, except that he was divorced and had a daughter.

Francesca had kept in touch with Theo's daughter, Mimi, over the years. Mimi had studied in Italy at one point and lived with Francesca's family, and she was obviously very fond of her. It seemed that Theo's and Francesca's daughters had gotten into some kind of trouble as teenagers, nothing serious, but it caused Theo to drive to Italy to have a serious talk with his daughter. Francesca laughed heartily as she told that story. They seemed to have many good memories together and were good friends.

It was a fun evening, and I was proud to have Theo with me. He fit in beautifully and seemed at ease with everyone. His friendship with Francesca, whom we all liked so much, created a positive entrée. I could tell that Neva and Lena were sizing him up to determine if he was good enough for me, and I couldn't wait to hear their reports later in the evening.

Theo and I decided to take another walk after dinner. He asked me if I would move into his room for the next two nights, and I couldn't say no. I wanted to be with him. "I like your Italian family, Ana. You see we have much in common, no?"

"Do we, Theo?" I looked at him inquiringly.

"Absolutely! This is fated…that we would be together. I am convinced."

"Really?" I said teasingly. "How does fate come into this picture?"

"Well, Ana…everything." And he made sweeping gestures around the piazza.

"You mean being in Italy?" I was perplexed.

"Ja, this part of it but so much more." Theo sounded convinced.

"I'm not sure that I see it as you do, Theo, but I have to say that you feel like a gift to me."

"A gift? Now I do not understand," said Theo, laughing again.

We went into a little bar and ordered a drink to continue our conversation.

"Yes, a gift." I started to explain. "I had no desire to go to Germany, but I knew that I had to do the research there for my book. I dreaded it. I didn't want to go in the winter. I knew that trying to speak German would be a struggle after so many years. I didn't want to speak it again. I spent no time before I left refreshing my vocabulary. I went to Germany as if I were in a daydream. Then Lena threw in the clinker about me coming here to Italy with them. She made me feel guilty for not wanting to do this with her family, after all they had done for me. All I could think of was trying to get through one thing so that I could do another thing that I did not want to do. It all seemed like such a burden to me."

"Ana, you never said a word about that in Tubingen."

"Well, no, because I was still in the middle of all of those feelings when I met you."

"And I was a gift?" he asked.

"Not at first!" I laughed. "You were intimidating, and you made me angry when I thought you were following me. It was just the last thing I needed. And then you were so mean to Katie at first. I had just about had enough of you and Germany!"

"I never knew this. I did not follow you, by the way. I just looked for ways that I could...that I could encounter you."

"But why?" I asked. "You told me once that you didn't even like Americans. We were silly and naïve, I think you said."

"There was something about you, Ana, from the first that made me look again. You were tiny and sad. You looked so lost. I think I wanted to protect you."

"I was lost in darkness. Lost in the past. That's where the gift part comes in, Theo. You showed me light again. Remember the night you first took me to your apartment and opened the curtains to that big full moon?"

"Ah, yes, indeed I do remember...so often." He smiled fondly and took my hands.

"I started opening up that night. Maybe it was luna madness or something, but that night changed me. You changed me, Theo."

Theo was quiet for the longest time as he looked me directly in the face. "Ana, you were a gift for me also. I wasn't supposed to be in Tubingen during the time that you were there. I was supposed to be on assignment in Croatia, but it was called off at the last second. I was angry about that. I wasn't happy to be sent to interview an American professor, a routine assignment that I had done many times. Americans can be arrogant and demanding, and you were none of those. I was surprised."

I just sat and listened to Theo. I needed to hear him say all of this, because I had been so anxious about seeing him again. I needed to quell my anxieties and to know this was the right thing.

"When it was time for you to leave, I was more upset than I could believe possible. I have let no woman mean anything to me for a long time, and there you were in my life and then going away. I had always been the one to walk away. I had to think of a way to get you back to Germany, or at least to Europe. That's when I came up with the idea of you coming to my farmhouse here in Italy. I did not know what to make of you laughing about that, until you told me you were already coming to Italy in May. Is that not fate?"

"I honestly don't know, Theo. What I do know is that I am glad we met, and I am glad that I came to Italy. This has been fabulous, and I feel changed. I feel happy, and I have not felt happy in a long time. I have been very anxious to see you again. I mean I wanted to see you again, but I have felt anxiety."

"No! But why?" asked Theo.

"So much happened between us in such a short time, I didn't know if it was real or just in the moment. I didn't know if I could trust what happened in Tubingen between us to sustain itself here in Italy. Theo, a part of me was scared that you might not even show up."

"I am astounded, Ana, that you would think that." Theo looked shocked. "I promise that I will be honest with you. How do Americans say this? I am not a man on the make. Do you believe me, Ana?"

"I do, Theo. I really do." And I did. That first kiss Theo had given me on the piazza outside the Savoy Hotel had quelled all my fears. Watching him with Lena and Neva assured me what a good man he was. Hearing about his childhood from Francesca told me that Theo was a man I wanted in my life. "I just needed to see you again and look into your face. I am sure that I want to be with you."

Theo stood up and put some euros on the table. "Come, Ana. Let's go back."

# III

Later that night, as I was packing my things to move into Theo's room, Lena spoke to me.

"I hope that you are using protection," she said seriously.

"What?" I said. "Are you kidding? I am almost forty-three years old."

"You know what they call forty-three-year-old women who don't use protection?"

"What?"

"Mothers!"

"Oh, come on, Lena," I said, laughing.

"I mean it, Ana. You could get pregnant, you know. It's not too late."

"Honest to God, Lena, the things you come up with."

"Theo is great. I really like him, and I am glad that you met, but Ana, have you thought about this? Didn't you tell me that Theo is almost fifty? And you are no spring chicken. Do you want a baby? And do you want a baby who will be raised continents away from its father? Believe me; I know what it is like to raise a child on your own."

"Truthfully, I have been a little dazed in that department. I never considered that I might get pregnant. But since I am no spring chicken, maybe I don't have to worry."

"Ana, I am very serious."

"I know you are and thank you. I should be thinking better."

"OK, now that the mother/daughter talk is over"—she lightened up—"I hope you plan to throw the nun's underwear away."

"The nun's underwear? What are you talking about?" I asked puzzled.

"You know that white cotton stuff you bought over here—the granny undies? Get rid of it. Wear the lingerie that we bought in Capri. It's sexy and beautiful. It will blow Theo away."

I blushed. "OK, OK. You are just full of good advice tonight."

The Capri underwear was a big hit with Theo. "Wow!" was all he said.

I showered again and changed before I went to his room. It was beautiful and different from the rooms that the tour group had. Those rooms were very nice, but Theo's was elegant and had a sitting room. It was like a honeymoon suite.

"Would you like a drink?" he asked. There was a full-size bar in a console.

"Not if you want me awake."

He came over to me and took my face into his hands. "Ana" was all he said before he kissed me. I was swept away, emotionally and literally. Theo picked me up and took me to the massive bed. It had already been turned down by the maid and there was chocolate on the pillows.

I took mine off, looked at Theo shyly, and said, "I'll eat it later."

There are just some nights that you never forget. The first night that we were together in Tubingen would always be one of those, and so would this one. Everything about it was right. The room was beautiful, the bed was deluxe, the place was the romantic Savoy Hotel in Florence, and then, there was Theo. He was unbelievable. How does a man like this come into your life? He truly was a gift. And I was starting to believe him that we were fated to be together.

I wished I had not promised the girls that I would go to Pisa with them. It would have been nice to have stayed in Florence and spent a lazy day with Theo, walking around this beautiful town together. Theo was a good sport and did all the touristy things. I bought each girl a little souvenir leaning tower, and they were delighted. We got back to the city by midafternoon, and I was ready for a nap. Theo, however, was not a nap person.

"How can you go to sleep, Ana, in this beautiful place?" he asked.

"I think the tour is beginning to take its toll. It has been a long two weeks, more than two weeks, and moving from one city to another so much is exhausting. Don't misunderstand me, Theo, I love Italy, and this has been my favorite city, but a one-hour rest will do wonders for me."

I coaxed him over to the bed. "Come over here and let me rub your back. It will be very relaxing, and then later we can take a little stroll and have some coffee. OK?"

"OK, Ana, but I will set the alarm and in one hour, we get up."

Sometimes Theo could be so…well, German.

To my amazement, Theo fell sound asleep. He was out like a light. He probably has been working hard on his farm and didn't realize how tired he was, I thought. I curled up beside him, and soon I was also in a deep sleep. It seemed like a minute had passed when the infernal alarm clock went off.

"Wake up, Ana," I heard Theo saying from afar. "You don't want to sleep the day away."

"What do you think you have been doing?"

"I was just lying here waiting for you to wake up. I promised you an hour."

"Theo, you were dead asleep! You were more tired than I was," I said indignantly.

"Ja, I admit it," he said. "I was tired, but this is our last night here. Let's get dressed because I want to take you someplace special. Ana, we have to hurry so just put something on fast and wear walking shoes, not those sandal things. We will come back to shower and say good-bye to your friends, and then we will go out for dinner."

I really wasn't in the mood to do this but got up and got dressed. I had not gotten much sleep last night, and as good as it was, I was paying for it now.

"We will walk," said Theo. "It will take about twenty minutes, but we have to hurry." He grabbed two large waters from the bar refrigerator.

What he didn't tell me was that it was all uphill. I was grumpy, hot, and sweaty during the walk. I didn't say much of anything, and neither did Theo. Halfway up, I realized the area looked familiar. We were on our way to the Piazzale Michelangiolo. This famous terraced area gave a brilliant panoramic view of the city of Florence and the Arno valley. There was a replica of Michelangelo's David in the center, and the terrace was usually covered with tourists and tour buses.

"Theo, Francesca brought us up to this piazzale on the first day that we were in Florence," I said a little irritated. Why didn't he ask me if I had seen it? We could have driven up here in the morning before we left the city, I thought.

"Ja, ja, I know. I asked her that, but we are not going to the Piazzale Michelangiolo." Theo took my hand. "It is not far now, but we will have to climb just a little bit higher. Take my arm and lean on me."

We reached the top of the piazzale and the view was breathtaking. Visitors could see all of the white buildings with red roofs surrounding the beautiful duomo, Santa Marie del Fiore. The sun was beginning to set as we reached the terrace.

"Just up the hill a bit to the church of San Miniato al Monte. It will be far less crowded and offers an even better view," Theo said excitedly. The green-and-white Romanesque facade of the church stood before us as we went through the gates and up the steps. San Miniato stood atop one of the highest points in Florence, and Theo was right. There were few people around, and the view was spectacular.

"Listen, Ana. Listen. We got here just in time. Come, let's go in."

From inside the church, I could hear the Benedictine monks chanting. "Is that a Gregorian chant?" I asked Theo.

"Ja, every evening at five o'clock they sing vespers in Gregorian chant. I wanted you to hear it."

Theo never ceased to amaze me. This Jewish man had brought me to a Catholic church to hear monks sing! We sat in the back of the beautiful, cool church. Neither one of us said a word. The church had even fewer people inside, and we were almost alone as the haunting chant filled the church. After several minutes, I was overpowered by a sense of letting go. I felt a spiritual release. Theo sat in the church with his eyes closed, giving way to the music as he held my hand. I let go of his hand and knelt in prayer. I did not realize that tears were streaming down my face. I thought of Mark and our life together. How good it had been. I thought of my last six years and how sad and alone I had felt. I knew that the past would forevermore remain behind me. I was ready for whatever my future held in store. I felt Mark's presence in that church and I said my final good-bye to him. In a strange way, I felt this was a sign from Mark that I could let go of him and start living my life again. He seemed to be telling me that I should not have guilt or sadness any longer. Peace filled my heart. I slipped back into the pew with Theo and took his hand.

"Ana, you are crying." Theo noticed, concerned. He handed me his handkerchief.

"I am fine, Theo. Really. Thank you for bringing me here. This is just what I needed."

We left the church when vespers ended. I felt drained, but a sweet contentment had filled me. We started our walk down to the terrace and stopped for a moment to look at the view. Lights had been turned on around the city, and it had a different, more dramatic look as twilight began.

"I will never forget this," I said to Theo. "I felt something happened inside of me in the church. I was totally unprepared for it, and it took me by surprise. This was meant to be. I don't think I am capable of explaining it to you just yet, but deep inside of me, I feel that I was given a sign tonight."

"Ana, I don't know what to say." Theo drew me close to him. "Are you sure you are OK?"

"I really am. I promise." And I was.

# IV

We said our good-byes to the group before they had their dinner together. I had met many wonderful people on this trip. I had become so fond of the Dawkins sisters, even Ida Jane. Jan and Wills were funny and had kept me laughing. Meredith and Ginny had helped me find all the right things to take home and give as gifts. Nan Coulous was one of the sweetest women I had ever met, next to Neva. Nikki Ansera was a little doll and had developed an adorable personality. There were several couples on the trip with whom I had had wonderful conversations.

Francesca had been interesting and enlightening. I loved her view of America and Americans, and I appreciated the time she had taken with each one of us. She had become more like a friend, and now that I knew that she and Theo were friends, I felt like I would see her again. Sara cried when she said good-bye to me and told me it had been the most fun ever. Lena kissed me and said to use protection. Neva kissed me and said Theo was a good man. They told me to call them the minute I got back home. My most heart-felt good-bye was to Kathryn. We had become close on this trip. Although she was old enough to be my mother, she seemed more like a contemporary in many respects. I admired her spunk and determination to change her life. Whereas my life seems to be changing almost accidentally, hers was deliberate. We vowed to stay in touch, and I knew that I would see her again.

Our last night in Florence was bittersweet. I was sad to be leaving the tour, and I was emotionally drained from my church experience, but I was excited to be with Theo. He told me that he was going to take me to a restaurant called La Terza that was equal to Chossen's in Germany. I had a dressier black cotton sundress that crisscrossed in the back and had a sweetheart neckline, which I wore with the black espadrilles. I took the little black jacket that went with my aquamarine dress, just in case there was air conditioning in the restaurant. I wore my onyx and gold necklaces.

Theo had on a long-sleeved white shirt with khaki pants and a black jacket. He looked both casual and dressed up. I caught a glimpse in a mirror of the two of us walking out of the lobby and thought how good we looked together. As if we belonged to each other. We walked hand in hand to the restaurant, taking our time, enjoying the beauty of Florence at night.

La Terza was, as Theo had promised, quite beautiful inside. It was old-world and elegant, but somehow brighter and lighter than Chossens. True to form, there was several staff that knew and welcomed Theo. There was no menu for us. Our dinner had been prearranged by Theo, and the courses unfolded like a flower, one incredibly delicious dish after another. And Theo kept his word; it was an unforgettable dinner.

By the time we got back to the Savoy, it was almost midnight, and I was exhausted. It had been a long, long day with many twists and turns. I had changed into a beautiful pink gown that I had bought in Capri and got in bed to wait for Theo. I fell instantly and deeply asleep. The next thing I knew, it was morning, and brilliant sunlight was streaming in our room.

Theo was up and dressed and had ordered room service. "What time is it?" I said, confused.

"It is after eight." Theo laughed. "You were…sleeping beauty," he said, searching for the right words.

"I can't believe I fell asleep last night. Yesterday was just too full for me."

"Nein, don't apologize. We have two more weeks together, and today, the drive to my farmhouse is a little over two hours. We will stop along the way and get provisions. I have no food there, so come have breakfast, and we will be on our way."

I had been in Italy more than two weeks, traveling from place to place as a tourist. Now I was going to be living in a house in the countryside for another two weeks. My anxieties started cropping up again in the pit of my stomach, but with each passing mile—or kilometer, I should say—I felt myself relaxing. This was due to Theo's constant chatter and holding my hand and looking so happy to be with me.

# V

Theo had cautioned me that his farmhouse was primitive. He had bought it three years before, and it was a work in progress. I could tell that he really loved it and the work that he was doing on it.

"I am taking my time, Ana. I want it to be perfect, so it will take awhile to get it there. I try to do two or three major projects each year, so that when I retire in the next ten years, it will be all done and paid for. I can't wait for you to see it. The only other woman who has been here is Mimi."

I was touched and had to admit that Theo really cared about me. I didn't know why I couldn't accept it. There was no reason not to.

The drive from Florence was enchanting and peaceful, and I felt more excited the closer we got to Montepulciano. I had mentally prepared myself for a little house not much more than a shack, but I was more than charmed by my first impression of Theo's house when we drove up the driveway.

"Oh my!" was all I could say when I first saw it. It was a real home, and perhaps it did look a little rustic, but it was quite beautiful, and I could also see in an instant that it needed a woman's touch.

Theo's house, which lay between Pienza and Montepulciano, was a long, rectangular, two-story building. There were codes that prevented him from adding onto it, but he could build up, and that was what he had done. He had doubled the square footage in doing so. The golden Tuscan exterior had floor-to-ceiling windows flanking French doors in the center of the building. The upper floor also had long windows. My immediate impression was that it needed landscaping and pots of colorful flowers, which would enhance the overall look of the outside. But I could see its potential and liked the looks of the simple building.

Theo was overjoyed at my initial reaction. "Come, Ana, leave your luggage. Let me show you around." He took my hand and opened the French doors.

The interior was whitewashed, with dark open beams running across the ceiling. There were identical long windows and French doors on the opposite wall. On one end was a rudimentary kitchen, and on the opposite end was the bedroom separated by the living area with a double-sided fireplace. Theo had little furniture—one sofa against a wall and a couple of chairs. There was some kind of buffet and a little table with chairs at the kitchen end. The floor was a terra-cotta tile that ran the length of the building.

"Theo, I was unprepared for how lovely this would be. I had visualized a building falling down in disrepair and was prepared to camp out."

"Camp out?" Theo looked puzzled.

"Yes." I laughed. "Like sleeping outside in a tent and cooking over a little fire."

"You mean like your Boy Scouts?" He laughed with me. "Nein, Ana, I would have never brought you to a house like that. I hope you will be comfortable here. I have made many improvements. Let me tell you about them, and then we will eat. I am hungry."

I was impressed by how substantial the house was. It also looked calm and serene. On closer inspection, I saw that Theo had spent time renovating his bedroom, which had a large bed and armoire. The bed was covered in fine-quality linens and faced the fireplace. The bathroom was a complete surprise. It was just off the bedroom and was spacious and modern. It had double sinks, a steam shower, and a large soaking tub that could not have looked more inviting.

"What do you think, Ana?" Theo looked like he needed my approval.

"I am stunned. I thought there would be no toilet facilities. You have done an amazing amount of work in just three years. It is a paradise."

"Ja, I have worked hard, but I love this house. Come, let me show you upstairs."

The stairs were close to the kitchen area and opened onto four rooms. The middle two rooms looked down onto the first floor. Over Theo's bedroom was another bedroom with a small bed and dresser. It also had fine-quality linens. There was another well-equipped bathroom adjacent. "This is Mimi's room," he said simply. "The room over the kitchen will eventually become my office. One of the other two will be a library. I will have to build bookshelves. And the fourth room, I am not sure yet."

The house was spacious and cool, even in the midday heat. It was light filled, but something was missing. Theo said it. "It needs a woman's touch. I have been so busy with structural things, I haven't thought of how to make it look nice."

"But Theo," I said. "Your apartment in Tubingen is very charming. In time, those things will happen."

"Nein, for some reason, I can't find what I want to make it right. Will you help me, Ana, while you are here?"

I was flattered. "Of course, Theo, that will be fun for me, but I haven't done much decorating in the past few years. I am a bit rusty at it."

"We will look together so that in two weeks' time, it will have a much different appearance."

We went out the second set of French doors to the back of the house. To my complete amazement, there was a pool with a built-in barbecue. I must have look shocked, because Theo laughed and stated, "I have always wanted a pool, and I like your American-style cookout. I want my retirement home to have everything, and I actually had the pool put in before I could live in the house. I am in the process of putting lights around the pool so that at night, I can swim."

The back of the house looked over the valley. In the near distance, I could see the medieval town of Montepulciano. Theo had said that we would go to the market square to the antiques fair, which was held once a month. He wanted me to help him look for more furniture.

We were having lunch when I heard barking. "That is Schnee," said Theo. I could see through one of the long windows an old pickup truck, with Schnee in the back. Theo introduced me to Luigi Caponi, who had helped, along with a myriad of his relatives, in rebuilding the farm. Luigi acted as a general groundskeeper when Theo was back in Germany, as well as supervising the remodeling.

"Buon giorno, signora." He tipped his hat at me and then told Theo that the table and chairs would be delivered in the next week.

When I looked puzzled, Theo said that he had had a long table and six chairs built for outside dining near the pool, Tuscan style. "It's too hot in the summer to eat inside." He was right. Even the first of June was proving to be very humid inside the house during midday. Fortunately, it cooled off at night.

Schnee was delighted to be reunited with his master, but I could see how much Luigi enjoyed him. The house was somewhat isolated, and Schnee was a good watch dog.

The days sped by. We fell into an affectionate, easy life. I couldn't believe that I had worried about this. Each day was perfect. Every morning, we would rise early, go for a walk first thing, come back, and have breakfast. Theo would work on one or another house project by himself or with Luigi, and I would make a list of things that needed to be bought at the market. Midmorning, we would set out for one of the towns in the vicinity to shop. Oftentimes we would have lunch before returning. Pienza and Montepulciano were the two largest towns around.

I was falling in love with the area. The countryside, the quaint little towns, the charming Italian shopkeepers, and the food.

Pienza was a little jewel. It was a beautiful Renaissance city, one of the heritage towns, and was the best-planned town of its period. Of course it was on a hill, but it was unique in its trapezoid-shaped main piazza defined by four buildings. Visitors could stroll on top of its medieval walls. It was a town famous for pecorino cheese, shoes, and ceramics. Theo took me to a wonderful restaurant there, La Buca delle Fate.

Montepulciano was larger and set on a higher hill, which had a long, steep, winding street, the Corso, which took one to the top to the Piazza Grande, the main square. The facade of the town hall resembled Florence's Palazzo Vecchio. Montepulciano had many wine shops and was famous for its Nobile wines. The long climb to the top was broken up by these and other shops where we would often stop and look and then buy products on our way down.

There were other wonderful little towns and villages around. Montalcino was famous for its red wine, Brunello, which could be ordered in the wine bar in a medieval fortress. Near by was the small village of Sant'Albino known for its thermal spas and curative waters. Every day, we went to a village somewhere and bought bread, wine, cheeses, fruits, and vegetables.

Midafternoon was spent resting, swimming, and reading. It was a simple life with no stress, and I loved it. After the table and chairs were delivered, we ate our evening meals under the trees and spoke of our future. We listened to music that drifted from the house via Theo's CD player. He had a tiny little TV, but we did not watch it often.

One day on our early morning walk, I thought I heard something crying. We looked all around, but it was Schnee that found the source of the noise. He started barking and then picked up something in his mouth.

"Bring it here, Schnee!" shouted Theo.

It turned out to be a little calico kitten, just a few weeks old. It was hungry and scared.

"Oh my goodness, are there more of them? How did such a little thing get all the way out here in the middle of nowhere?" I asked. Schnee dropped the kitten, and I picked it up.

"We must go back and find some food for it," I said.

Theo looked at me and said warningly, "Ana, I do not like cats."

"Well, Theo, are you suggesting that we just leave the little thing out here to die?" I asked.

He didn't say anything. I searched but did not see other kittens.

"I just don't understand how this tiny thing, all alone, could have gotten out here," I said again.

"My guess is that an owl had it in its beak and for some reason dropped it."

"What are we going to do with it?" I said to Theo, looking him directly in the eyes.

I think he knew his answer would make a significant difference to me, and he answered carefully, "You can take it back and feed it, but I want it to go. I do not want a cat."

"Maybe Luigi can help us find a home for it," I said. But there was no home to be found for the kitten. Luigi said he knew of no one who wanted another cat. We asked all shopkeepers in the villages, and the answer was always the same: there are enough cats around.

That's how Cara came to live at the farmhouse. Schnee was taught to be good to the kitten that was shameless in attacking him. Luigi softened the blow with Theo and said it was a good thing to have a cat around to keep the mice away. Theo grudgingly gave his consent, and Cara became known as Ana's cat. I was delighted by her.

As my days at the farm were coming to an end, I stood outside one late afternoon waiting for Theo to fix a light around the pool that had been giving him trouble. Cara was lying on top of the table sleeping, and Schnee was underneath it. The sun was starting to set, and the valley had deep shadows and golden lights. Theo was dripping in sweat and needed a shower. I watched him trying to figure out the problem. It hit me like a thunderbolt out of nowhere that I loved this life, and I loved Theo. I loved Theo. I had never said it, even to myself. Here was this big, wonderful Jewish man who thought it was important to take me to a Catholic church to experience Gregorian chants. Although I had only known him a few months, I knew that I would love this man as much as I had loved Mark. It was a different, more mature love, but it was just as deep.

I must have been staring as if in a daze, because Theo was suddenly in front of me. "Ana, are you OK? You are just standing there with the oddest expression on your face." Theo looked worried.

"No, Theo, I am fine," I answered quietly. "I just realized how much I love being here and how happy I am with you. It has been a long time since I have felt this happy and content." I felt shy about telling him that I was in love with him. I knew that he cared for me, but to what extent? He had never told me that he loved me.

"Ana, my beautiful Ana. What will I do when you are gone?" Theo pulled me toward him, forgetting that he was dirty and dripping in sweat. "I haven't allowed myself to think about my life without you." He looked anguished.

"I will see you in July when you visit your aunt and uncle in New York. It's just five weeks from now," I said lightly, but I knew it would take nothing for me to break down.

"It's not enough." He growled. "Oh my God, Ana. Look what I have done to you."

I looked down. I had streaks of wet dirt on my shirt. "It's OK, Theo. It will wash." I reached up and pulled his face down to me and kissed him. "Thank you for coming into my life." I pulled away and turned to go back into the house to change.

Theo grabbed my arm. "No, thank you for being in mine. I didn't think a woman like you existed. Ana, don't be scared, but I think I am falling in love with you. I know it's too soon to say that, but I feel it." He pulled me close to him again, and on that hot June day in Montepulciano, Italy, as we stood together, I knew a new life had begun for me.

# KATHRYN

# I

The flight back was horrible. There were delays on top of delays, and the final straw was a storm on the East Coast that was right behind us, so the pilot had to divert to a safe field in New York, where we sat on the ground for five hours until we could fly back down to Baltimore. I had never felt more exhausted. It was two thirty in the morning before I went to bed, after being up almost thirty straight hours.

I was dead asleep but kept hearing a pounding and ringing. What was that? Groggily, I woke up and realized it was my front door. I put on my robe and made my way downstairs. When I opened the door, there stood Sammy with Brooke in his arms and Eli and Chapin rushing in.

"Grandma, Grandma, what did you bring us?" they both shouted.

"Mom, you look awful," said Sammy as he pecked me on the check.

I was in a sleep-induced stupor and could hardly take in what was happening. The boys were asking me over and over about their presents, and Sammy was talking over them.

"_____emergency. Jenn had an early meeting, and I need to be at work right now." He was chattering. "Boys, be quiet! I need to give your grandmother some instructions."

"Sammy, what are you saying?" I asked, not really hearing anything.

"Mom" he started again. "Boys, be quiet and sit down right now! Mom, there is an emergency. We need you to take care of the kids today. Jenn is at a meeting, and I need to leave right now."

He started handing me the baby and her paraphernalia. "Chapin needs to be at school by eight thirty and Eli by nine, so you need to get dressed."

"Grandma, I'm hungry," whined Eli.

"You boys haven't had breakfast?" I asked.

"Mom, there hasn't been time. I barely made it over here. Here, take Brooke. I need to leave."

I was furious, tired, and very cranky. "Sammy, where is the nanny?"

"She quit last week, Mom. I will explain later, but I really have to get going." He started backing out the door.

I grabbed his arm. "Sammy, I just got home and have had no sleep. I can't do this. I am worn out. Call Linda. And what about their own mother. Why can't she do it?"

"Linda won't baby-sit anymore. She has done it a couple of times, both she and Larry. Jenn___well, you know, she has a lot of responsibilities. She was gone by seven this morning to a meeting."

"So without any warning whatsoever, you were just going to drop them off here my first day back?" I was really angry. Nothing, absolutely nothing had changed.

"No, Sammy, I am not taking Brooke. I am not baby-sitting today. I am not taking the boys to school. I am not making breakfast for anyone. There is no food in the house, anyway. Did it ever occur to you that I would need to go out and buy groceries today? You need to gather up everyone and leave. I am going back to bed."

I looked at the boys and gave each one a kiss. "Grandma will see you later this week with your presents." With that, I walked back up the steps.

Sammy stood at the bottom, yelling up to me, "Mom, what do you think I am supposed to do? I have to go to work!"

I turned around and looked at him. "I really don't know, Sammy, but your children obviously need some food. Why don't you call your wife? She is an executive. She might know what you should do."

I locked my bedroom door until I heard them leave. How dare he, I thought. He never asked me one word about my trip, or how I was, or said that he had missed me. I have been gone for three and a half weeks.

Although dead tired, I couldn't go back to sleep. I was too mad. I wondered what had happened to the last nanny I had set up for them a month ago.

I tried to call Jenn, but her secretary stated that she was not available. "But I am her mother-in-law," I told the girl.

"Sorry, Mrs. Wynham, she asked not to be disturbed, but I will let her know that you called."

Then I called Linda and Larry. Linda was not the least bit cordial when she heard my voice. I told her the story but hit a brick wall. "I don't know anything about the situation," was all she would say. Then she dismissed me. "I have to go now. Have a hair appointment." And she hung up.

I refused to answer my phone when I saw Sammy's number on caller ID. I was still too angry to talk to him. I had planned to go over on the weekend and give the kids their presents, but I needed to cool off.

Four days later, I was thinking about some work I wanted to have done in my house when I heard the door bell ring. It was about six thirty which, I thought, was an odd time for someone to be dropping by. I had just finished eating a light dinner. When I opened the door, there stood Sammy. I could tell that he had just come from work.

"Mom, can I come in?" He looked awful.

"Is something wrong, Sammy?" I asked, ushering him in. We went into the kitchen, where he took a seat at the table. "What's wrong, Sammy? Has something happened to one of the children?" I was now becoming a little frantic.

"Everything has gone to hell," he said, putting his head in his hands. He looked up at her with tears in his eyes, "Mom, my whole life is going down the tubes. I don't know what to do anymore."

I sat down beside him. "Tell me what has happened, Sammy. Did something happen today?"

"Yes, something did happen today, but that's not the whole thing. I was given a final warning that I would be fired if I missed more time at work. So much has happened in the past two months…well, even farther back than that that." And then he started sobbing. "How did it get like this? Jenn and I were so happy when we got married, and now she doesn't even speak to me. Sometimes she doesn't come home for days. I don't know where she is."

I was shocked. "Sammy, how long has this been going on? What about the boys and Brooke?"

"I paid a neighbor a lot of money to take care of them today. They are fine right now, but I have to get home. Mom, Jenn has had nothing to do with Brooke since she was born. I bet she hasn't held her two times in the last month. While you were gone, Chapin bit Brooke, and the bite became infected. I took her to the doctor, and he was so angry that we had allowed this to happen, he threatened to call social services to have her removed from our home. He said if anything like this occurred again, he would not hesitate. This was the final warning. He has seen the bruises on Eli in the past and commented on them. I tried to call Jenn at work, and she wouldn't return the call. That was the first night that she didn't come home."

"My God, Sammy."

"You were right, Mom. Chapin is completely out of control. He has been expelled from school because of his bullying and biting. I have a meeting with the school board this week. He has been home every day for the past two weeks, and that is when he bit Brooke. He blames Brooke for Jenn leaving him. Eli is terrified of what Chapin will do to both him and Brooke. I found him hiding in a closet one day with the baby in his arms."

"Have you said anything to Linda and Larry about Jenn, about the kids?"

"I did call Linda, when Jenn didn't come home the first night. She was there, but Linda would not put her on the phone. Linda said that Jenn needed some time away from all the pressures at home. She wasn't concerned. Anytime that I have tried to talk to Linda, she has said that Jenn is going through a rough patch and just needs some time. Talking to Linda is like talking to a recording, and Larry doesn't say anything. I called Linda after Brooke had been bitten, and her only comment was that I should take her to the doctor. She is a dead end, Mom. I can't count on their help at all." He started crying again.

"Sammy, what happened to the last nanny?" I asked.

"Jenn fired her in a fit of anger one day. She told her that all she did was complain, and it was her job to take care of things with the kids. The woman, I don't even remember her name, just looked at Jenn and walked out. The agency won't send anyone else to our house. They told me it was our family, not the nannies, and that we had such a bad reputation, no one would come to our home for any amount of money."

"Dear God."

"Mom, I have to get home and get the kids. I don't know if Jenn will show up or not tonight. I am not counting on it. I don't know what to do. How do I straighten out this mess? How do I get my family back together? Where do I start?"

"I don't know, Sammy, but I will come with you tonight so that we can talk some more. You go on ahead, and I will be right over. Do you have food for the children?"

"No, I was going to stop and get them a pizza on the way. I have to get some formula, diapers, milk, and some other stuff, so I really have to get going."

"Sammy, I will stop and get all those things. I'll look for something for dinner. Go on and go. Tell the children that I am coming over in a little while. Just spend some time with them. I'll be over soon." He looked so relieved.

"Thanks, Mom. I didn't know where else to go. I know that Jenn and I have taken advantage of you in the past. I am sorry. I was wrong to just come by the other day with all of them, but I knew if I called, you would refuse. It was really horrible of me. I am at my wit's end. I want you back in our lives, not as a baby-sitter but as my mom and the children's grandmother. The children need you as a grandmother, not a nanny. Linda and Larry are worthless."

I kissed him good-bye and looked around my house for something nutritious I could take over for a dinner with the children. I got their presents from Italy and went off to the store to get baby things.

Sammy's house was more of shambles than ever. The kitchen was stacked high with dirty dishes. There were clothes, newspapers, toys, and general debris scattered everywhere. It looked like a train wreck.

But the boys were excited that I was there. "Grandma, Grandma," they shouted. Eli hung onto me. "Grandma, I missed you. I love you. Can I go home with you tonight?"

"Not tonight, Eli, but I have to talk to you and Chapin about our days together. We have to get back on schedule. OK?"

"Grandma, where is my present?" Chapin demanded.

"Chapin, a present is a gift that you give to someone you love and think will appreciate it. I am not hearing that from you. Can you speak to me more respectfully?"

"No, I want it now!" he screamed.

"Chapin, that attitude will not get you a present. When you calm down, pick up your toys in this room. When you can come back and talk to me nicely, then I will give you the present."

"I hate you, Grandma. No one loves me!" Chapin ran off to his room.

"Eli, could you please take your toys to your room while Grandma is clearing a spot for us to eat in the kitchen?"

Sammy had finished feeding Brooke, and she was going to sleep in his arms. "Here, let me hold her for a minute." I said. She was a beautiful baby.

She looked just like Jenn with her little rosebud mouth and fair hair. I didn't see anything of Sammy in her yet.

Sammy looked exhausted. "Honey, why don't you sit on the sofa for a few minutes and just rest. I will put Brooke to bed." He looked grateful. I think my son was finally growing up. Maybe these crises in his life would be the things to make that happen. He was acting responsibly for the first time in a long time. It was Jenn I was most worried about now.

I changed the baby's sheets and put her down. She had a sweet little music box in the room, which I turned on so that she could hear lullabies. I went to Chapin's room, where he was playing with his trucks. He was pushing them as hard as he could into the wall, where they would crash.

"Chapin," I called. "Come give your grandmother a hug and kiss. I know you don't hate me, and I know that you are hungry."

He looked up at me so troubled. We must get this child under control, I thought. "Come on, Chapin, I need a hug and kiss from you." He came over and hugged me and said, "Mommy hates me, Grandma."

"No, she doesn't, Chapin. She is just sad and sick right now, but she will get better. You'll see." I hope that is true, I thought.

"Brooke made her sick and mad. I hate Brooke!"

"No, Chapin. It wasn't Brooke, but she did get sick right after Brooke was born, so I see why you think that. Do you think you can help me in the kitchen a little bit?" He nodded. "Grandma, are you going to give me my present tonight?"

"I sure am. Right after we eat and clean up the dishes. OK?"

The boys were relatively well behaved during dinner. Their manners were atrocious, but that would take time and a lot of reminding. All the things that I had taught them had been forgotten. The kitchen cleaning was such a big job that we only did part of it.

The Italian games and toys were a big hit. I told them that I had a couple of surprises left for them at my house when they came to visit. It was enough for this night. It seemed obvious that Jenn wasn't coming home. After the boys went to bed, Sammy and I resumed our discussion about what needed to happen next.

"Mom, this was the most peaceful night that I have had in two months. Thank you for coming over."

This was the second thank you that I had from Sammy in one evening. I wasn't sure when the last time was that either he or Jenn had thanked me. "Sammy, you seem ready to change things around here."

"Things have got to change, Mom. This can't go on. I am on the verge of losing my job. Jenn has gone. Chapin is out of control and out of school. Eli is terrified of everything, and poor Brooke doesn't have a mother at all."

"Well, it seems obvious to me, Sammy that you need to take a leave of absence from your job. Don't you have a lot of sick and vacation days?"

"The last thing I can do is take more time off, Mom. That's one of the problems," he said, agitated.

I continued, "I think Jenn has postpartum depression, and she needs to see a doctor. She needs medication to help her get through this, and you need the time to start making changes. You may have to enlist her boss to help you. I bet she is not doing her best at work right now."

Sammy looked at me. "You could be right. Jenn mentioned something about an error she made at work and she blamed all the noise and confusion at home as the reason. Is postpartum depression the reason she hasn't wanted to hold or love Brooke?"

"I am sure of it, Sammy. I suggest that you go in to work tomorrow and be honest with your boss about the rough time you're having. Ask for a month's leave of absence to get thing under control. All he can do is say no, and if that happens, we can reassess. If you are willing to do that, I will come for the next few days until we can find a sitter again. If you are not willing to talk with your boss, there is not much I can do to help you, Sammy. You have three children who need at least one parent in their corner."

"I know that, Mom," he said sadly.

"Why don't you go to bed and get some sleep. I will wait here and feed Brooke again later and then go home. I will be back the first thing tomorrow morning."

# II

The next few days were hectic but the children responded to two adults who were trying to stabilize their lives. It was really one step forward and several steps backward, but at least Sammy and I could see some progress. His boss gave him thirty days off but stated that they would talk before he would take him back. His job was not guaranteed on return. Jenn had been gone for nearly ten days, and the boys kept asking where she was and when was she coming home. All we could do was distract them and keep them busy.

Chapin was very happy to have both his father and me giving him full-time attention at home. He did not want to go to school. Sammy's interview with the school board was not promising. He was told that Chapin's behavior was not conducive to a regular classroom, but special education classes were an option. After much discussion and wrangling with school counselors and psychologists, Sammy arranged for home-schooling for the rest of the summer so that Chapin could keep up. This was to buy some time. I had convinced Sammy to look into smaller, private schools that offered more creativity, but Chapin needed better discipline and socialization skills before he could go back into a classroom.

I hired a cleaning team to come in to thoroughly clean the house. I knew I could not do it alone, and I did not want to do it. I could not take over this family, and it would have been easy for Sammy to let me do it. Neither one of us knew if Jenn would ever come back. I had tried to talk with Linda again, but she was still smarting from my last phone conversation with her. She was beyond reason and could not hear that her daughter could be depressed. Her final shot to me was that her daughter was really none of my business, and then she hung up.

"Sammy, you have to get Jenn away from her parents and try to talk to her. I think you should also start thinking about some legal steps to protect you and the children. You have to face reality. If she never comes back, you need to get child support. You are not even sure that you will have a job after this month is up."

"Legal steps?" He was shocked.

"It might be something that would jar Jenn, as well. She has been gone for over two consecutive weeks has not answered your calls, and her parents won't help you. What other recourse do you have?"

"I guess you're right," Sammy said miserably. "I need to do something, but before I see a lawyer, I will go to her office and see if I can talk to her there. I'll do it tomorrow."

That turned out to be a disaster. Jenn had put Sammy and me on a security list, and he could not go to her office. He was hurt and angry but realized then that he needed to have legal counsel.

The children were doing better. Chapin loved his home-school teacher, Mr. Stevens, who taught by many different techniques, including physical activity. This is exactly what that child needs, I thought. Mr. Stevens had a way of insisting on good behavior that Chapin responded to. It also gave me more time with Eli when he came home. He was the saddest little child. His emotions were visible, whereas Chapin's always came out in anger. It was difficult to coax a smile out of Eli these days. He was worried about his mother. He loved Brooke, and she loved him. Her face lit up when he came into the room. I feared that she might have failure to thrive when I first saw her. She seemed so apathetic but now she cooed and gurgled when she was awake. She was a good baby and hardly ever cried.

There were good days and bad days. Sammy was becoming depressed about his marriage as more time passed without hearing from Jenn. Even the legal separation papers, which had been served to her, had not elicited a response. A court hearing was scheduled for the first week in July, and Sammy would ask for full custody and child support. He was told that the court would recommend counseling and mediation to determine if reconciliation was possible. The court would also appoint legal counsel for the children. Some days all of this was more than he could bear.

Permanent child care was the next issue that had to be addressed. I was tired. I had never gotten over my jet lag before I started baby-sitting again. I loved these grandchildren of mine, but I wanted an adult life. I had hardly spoken to or seen Karen. We had one dinner together, but I had been poor company.

"I hope you don't mind my saying this," she remarked, "but you look worse now than before you went to Italy."

"Well, thanks so much," I said tiredly. "But you are right. I was so excited about getting back and telling you about the trip and all the people I met, and now it seems like the distant past. I can't desert Sammy right now because, for the first time in years, he is struggling to do the right things. He is devastated about Jenn. I don't know that he will ever get over her. They were terrible parents, but they did love each other."

"Has he heard anything at all from her?" asked Karen.

"Not one word. Poor Eli. He misses her so much. Brooke doesn't even know who she is. I am afraid that there will never be bonding between the two of them. It is heartbreaking."

"It's a tough situation. How about Sammy's job?" Karen asked.

"That looks bad, too. One of Sammy's co-workers called and told him that they've hired someone new to do his job. His boss has not called yet, but his friend just wanted to give him a heads-up. Strangely, Sammy doesn't seem as concerned about that as he does about losing Jenn. He thinks he can find another job, and he is reevaluating where and how he wants to work. One of the best things to come out of all of this is that Sammy is becoming a good father and likes being at home with the children. The boys adore having him around. Now Chapin has two strong men in his life, and he is doing well. Sammy is taking both of the boys camping this weekend, and I will be taking care of Brooke. She is a sweetheart, but I am tired, Karen. Very tired. I don't want to do this anymore."

"I don't blame you," said Karen sympathetically. "When will you bring in a new nanny?"

"Unfortunately, none of the nanny agencies in town will accept Sammy's applications because of their reputation. They don't want to hear about the changes. They said it's too risky, and they were abused. Abused? Can you imagine? There is a waiting list for nannies, so they can pick and choose whomever they want. Sammy and Jenn were lucky they got so many chances, but now that option has evaporated."

"What are you going to do, Kathryn?"

"I don't know, but I haven't given up yet. What I do know is that with each passing day, I long for Italy. I want to go back. I want to go back to Orvieto. I think if things ever get settled with Sammy, I will go back for a while."

"You're kidding, right?" said a stunned Karen.

"Not one bit. I fell in love with the country and that one city. You wouldn't believe how beautiful it is, Karen. There is a language school in Orvieto that I want to go to. In fact, after Sammy's court date, if possible, I want study Italian at the university here. A conversational summer-school course. That means Sammy and I have to come up with some kind of baby-sitting arrangement. He will eventually have to go to work somewhere."

"My God, you are serious!" Karen laughed with amazement.

"I definitely am. I am going back there, Karen. I need to go sooner rather than later, while I have the courage to do it."

Three days later, at home, I started looking at my pictures from the trip. I really had not had time to look at them or think much about the people I had enjoyed meeting. Sammy told me that he could manage without me and to go home and get some rest. This was the new Sammy. As I happily sifted through the pictures remembering a place, a comment, a person, one person stood out. Nan Coulous. What had she told me? She was retired, never married, no children, but she loved children and was at loose ends. She wanted to work with children. She wanted to work with children who needed help. Well, I certainly knew three children who needed help.

I wondered if she would be interested. We had all exchanged phone numbers and e-mail and home addresses. She lived about thirty minutes from Sammy's house. I decided to call her.

"Nan, this is Kathryn Wynham from the Italian trip. Do you remember me?"

"Well, of course I do! Kathryn, how very nice to hear from you. I've missed seeing everyone that I met over there. You are the first person to be in touch with me," she said cordially.

"I've missed them, as well," I admitted. "Isn't it amazing how close you can get to a group of strangers in such a short time?"

"It really is," she agreed.

"Nan, I have to admit that I am calling you about something entirely different, but I would like to tell you in person. Could we meet for lunch?"

I didn't tell Sammy anything about Nan, because I didn't want to get his hopes up—or mine, for that matter. It turned out to be a wonderful lunch. Nan had impressed me in Italy as a warm, comfortable person. She exuded a calmness that told me she could handle any kind of emergency or crisis. I gave her a brief background on the situation with Sammy and the children. She was very sympathetic. I then asked her the big question.

"Nan, I was wondering if you would be interested in helping us out."

She was very surprised. "How do you see me helping out, Kathryn?"

"My son needs a housekeeper and a nanny, and the children need someone consistent in their lives. There would, of course, be a salary. This is not volunteer work."

"And the mother is out of the picture?"

"For now, she is. I don't know how the future will play out. I have to warn you that the oldest boy, Chapin, is a handful, but he has recently been doing better."

We talked in more detail about how I saw her fitting in. I thought easing her in with me still in the picture would be the best way to do it for all of us. We agreed that she would start out a few hours during the week until the boys got used to her, and then she would take on more responsibility. That is, if she thought it would work for her. It turned out to be a perfect plan. Sammy was delighted that she was willing to help out. He had recently picked up some part-time work with another engineering firm and was feeling more secure about his professional future.

"I will talk to Nan about wages right away, Mom. I am not so worried about how I will manage finances now. Jenn will have to pay child support. My lawyer has assured me of that. She makes more money than I do, so things are looking brighter financially."

The boys didn't notice Nan so much at first. They thought she was Grandma's friend from Italy. Gradually, she started coming without me. Nan was very low-key with the children, and they didn't feel threatened by her as someone taking over for their mother. She made them special treats to eat. They called her Nanny, which we all thought was funny, since they had hated the real nannies. She was competent and organized and ran the house like her government office, but with humor. It had never looked so good and clean. The boys picked up their toys and clothes.

For the first time, the house started looking like a real home. Nan talked Sammy into buying comfortable furniture and lamps so that she could read to the boys. There were carpets on the floor and often flowers in vases. Nan and the children were thriving.

I gradually saw them less and less during the week and got back my personal time. Nan was strict about boundaries. She worked weekdays only and had fixed hours but stated she was willing to renegotiate when Sammy's job hours became regular again. I started taking one of the boys on alternating weekends for grandma time. In many ways, I hoped that Jenn would never come back. The lives of the children had never been better, but I knew that Eli and Chapin missed their mommy every single day. I had not spoken to Linda and Larry again. They had not tried to contact Sammy or see their grandchildren.

The court date arrived. Jenn had not shown up for mediation or the court-appointed counseling. Sammy had decided to take advantage of the counseling, and it was helping him sort through his emotions.

Judge Grayson Tyler was the presiding judge of the juvenile and domestic relations court. Interested parties were asked to meet in his chambers. Jenn was with her parents and her lawyer. Sammy had me and his lawyer.

It was both casual and formal.

Judge Tyler was in his sixties and near retirement. He had heard many cases in his twenty-five years on the bench. His face was sympathetic, but he had a no-nonsense demeanor. I had good feelings about him. After the session was called to order, he recognized both parties.

"Will Mrs. Jennifer Wynham acknowledge herself?" Jenn was dressed in a dark suit and had little makeup on. She had lost a lot of weight and looked pale. Her head was bowed, and she had not made eye contact with Sammy or me when we came into chambers. Linda looked away, as well. Jenn did not say anything to the judge, simply gestured with one hand.

"And will Mr. Samuel Wynham acknowledge himself."

Sammy spoke up in a strong voice. "I am Samuel Wynham, Your Honor."

"I will also need the attorneys and other parties to acknowledge who they are."

Jenn's lawyer introduced herself and directed her hand to Jenn's mother and father as the parents of her client.

Sammy's lawyer did the same.

"Now that we know who the parties are, can we agree that the purpose of this session is to determine custody of the three minor children and child support during this separation agreement?"

Both lawyers agreed with this statement. Jenn's lawyer stood up and stated that his client would waive custody of the children, at this point, in favor of the children's father.

Judge Tyler looked at Jenn. "Is that correct, Mrs. Wynham? You do not want custody in any form of your children?"

Jenn did not look up. She simply nodded her head in agreement.

"Mrs. Wynham, I require that you answer me."

"Yes," she said in a voice that was barely audible.

"Mrs. Wynham, I see that you did not participate in mediation or counseling. Is that correct?"

"Yes." Again in a small voice.

"Mrs. Wynham, have you been sick, or is there a reason that you do not wish custody of your children?"

"No."

Linda spoke up. "Your Honor, my daughter is an executive with one of the most prestigious banks in this city. She has been under a lot of pressure lately and feels that she is not in a good position to care for her children in the immediate future."

"Mrs. Wynham, I need to hear that from you, not your mother."

Linda stood again, but Judge Tyler waved her down. His patience with her had been remarkable, but I could see that it was wearing thin.

"Mrs. Wynham?" But Jenn did not respond.

"Mr. Wynham, could you please fill me in briefly on the state of your marriage and the reasons that you want full custody?"

Sammy cleared his throat. "Your Honor, I believe my wife has post-partum depression that is not being addressed by her parents. Today is the first time that I have set eyes on her in six weeks, and she looks like she has lost twenty pounds. She has made no attempts to call or see the children since she left home. Our daughter will be three months old in a few days, and Jenn has hardly held her since her birth. My wife needs help."

Linda stood up again to speak but the judge told her sternly to sit down. "Please continue, Mr. Wynham."

"My hope is that we can reconcile, but Jenn needs medical help. Look at her, Your Honor. Does she look like someone who can function?"

Jenn's lawyer objected, but the judge took a long look at Jenn and stated that he was ordering her to undergo a psychiatric evaluation. He gave temporary custody of the children to Sammy. He then asked Jenn if she wanted visitation rights, but she shook her head no. This was followed by questions regarding the relationship with the grandparents.

Sammy spoke up. "Your Honor, I could not have made it without my mother. She has gotten me through the past weeks and helped me find a housekeeper and baby-sitter. The children love her, and she gives them quality time."

"I will let you decide, Mr. Wynham, the appropriate arrangements for your mother's visits to her grandchildren." He then turned to Jenn's parents. "And what has your relationship been with your grandchildren?'

Linda jumped up before Larry could say a word. "Your Honor, at this time we have been supporting our daughter."

"What are your wishes for visitation?" Judge Tyler asked.

Again Linda jumped up. "We will continue to support our daughter until the pressures of her work have subsided."

"Mrs. Parker, does that mean that you don't want visitation?" He looked confused.

Linda said, "Not at this time, Your Honor." But to our amazement, Larry spoke for the first time. "Your Honor, if Sammy doesn't mind, I would like to visit the children at his home, at his convenience, maybe once a month. I have missed seeing the boys, and I hardly know my granddaughter."

Linda turned on him, furious. "I don't think that is a good idea, Larry. Not now."

Then Sammy turned to Larry and said kindly, "Your Honor, I am very pleased that my father-in-law would like to visit the boys. They need strong men in their lives, and he is the only grandfather they have. Larry would be welcome anytime he wants to come."

I had never been as proud of Sammy as I was in that moment. I knew that his heart was broken. He believed that the court would have to intervene in their lives. He always thought that Jenn would return home.

We saw tears come into Larry's eyes. The judge again looked at Jenn. "Are you positive, Mrs. Wynham, that you do not want visitation rights?"

Jenn shook her head no. "I then decree that you must pay three thousand dollars per month in child support. Your financial assets support that amount. If you change your mind about visiting your children, you will have to petition the court. Do you understand that?"

She nodded. Linda started to protest the amount of child support but the judge waved her down. "Mrs. Parker, I need for you sit down, or you will be declared in contempt of this court. I have allowed grandparents to be present, but this hearing is for the two parties most involved—the parents. Your daughter has competent legal representation who can better advise her. Mrs. Wynham, I need to make it clear before we adjourn that you must have the psychiatric evaluation. Do you fully understand that? This will have to do with the final judgment on custody, if you and your husband are unable to reconcile and pursue divorce."

Jenn again nodded but said nothing. Linda had her arms around Jenn in a protective gesture.

"I then declare this session over. Please see the bailiff to sign the necessary documents."

Court was over. Sammy attempted to speak with Jenn, but she wouldn't look at him as Linda ushered her out. He and Larry shook hands, and Sammy invited him over that weekend. It was the saddest victory that anyone had ever won. Sammy was more devastated than ever.

# III

Life settled into a routine which seemed, for the first time in a long time, beneficial to the children. All the participating adults in their lives were consistently working together to maintain stability and to give them the love and security that they needed while Jenn was gone. Larry was turning out to be a godsend. The boys were delighted to have him around. They called him Papa, and he truly enjoyed being with them. The most curious thing was watching Larry respond to Nan. He opened up. After years of being married to the Ice Queen, he was introduced to the Earth Mother.

Sammy, true to his word, put no restrictions on Larry's visits. Therefore, he came over several times a week. He relished sitting in the kitchen drinking coffee with Nan and eating her homemade cookies and other treats. He helped around the house, fixing things and shepherding the boys into doing the chores that Nan had developed for them. For a woman who had never had children, she knew instinctively how to make them feel important in a family.

Larry also loved his time with baby Brooke and she loved her grandfather. Every time she saw him, her little eyes would follow him all around the room. It was as if a new man had been born. We were never sure what gave him the courage to speak up in court that day, but we were all glad that he did. He kept us informed on Jenn. She had had the psychiatric evaluation and was found to be depressed. Medication was prescribed, which Linda thought was utter nonsense, but Larry was making sure that she took it. Larry had read somewhere that physical activity was good for depression, so he asked Jenn to walk with him in the evenings around the neighborhood. He used that time to casually talk about his days with the children and show her the many photographs that he had taken of them doing various activities. The boys often made her cards, with Larry and Nan's help, and it was during their walk time that Larry would give them to Jenn. She looked and listened but never said anything.

Because things were going so well, I decided to pursue my dream of going back to Orvieto. I had been in contact with Francesca Botti. I thought going to the language school there was a good idea, and Francesca had sent me brochures. A new two-week Italian class was scheduled to start in September, and I impulsively signed up. I knew that if I put it off, I would never do it. I had enlisted Francesca's help in finding an apartment in Orvieto and the details of getting a train from Rome. It was somewhat daunting, but I was excited.

At dinner with Karen, I tried to explain why it was so important to me. She was having a difficult time understanding.

"I really don't know myself why I need to go back so soon, but I know if I don't do it now, I may never do it, and I will hate myself for not going."

"It's nutty, Kathryn, with all the stuff you have going on in your life right now, to just up and go back to Italy!" Karen said, exasperated.

"I know it! Even I tell myself that I am crazy." I laughed. "And remember how nervous I was to be going over all by myself in May? I was sick with nerves! But now I am so excited that I can hardly stand it. It just feels right somehow."

"But Kathryn—" Karen began.

I interrupted, "There is absolutely nothing you can say to me, Karen that I haven't said to myself. Nothing! Why don't you come with me? It would be so much fun together."

"That's even crazier! Can you see me on some mountaintop trying to speak Italian? I would be a basket case in three days." She laughed. "Maybe you are having a midlife crisis."

"Maybe I am," I agreed. "All I know is that I need to do this and get it out of my system. I have to go back and see what it feels like to actually live in an Italian village. Plus this time, I don't feel like I'm going for all the wrong reasons. I'm not running away. I'm so excited about going back that I can't sleep at night!" I laughed again.

"How long will you stay over there?" Karen asked.

"This is even nuttier, but I am thinking two months."

"Two months!" She exploded. "What in the world will you do there in all that time?"

"Just live like an Italian, I guess. I haven't thought that one out yet. I could take a more advanced Italian class after the first one, but what I really hope is that I will get to know some of the people there."

"God, Kathryn, I am just not taking this all in yet. What about all the work going on in your house?"

"Well, if anything makes sense, it's that I will be gone when all that mess is happening."

When I returned home in May from my trip, I saw my house with fresh eyes. It had become terribly run-down. I had done nothing to it since Gary had died, and all those years of letting the boys run haywire all over it, caused my once lovely home to look shabby and neglected. It had once been the most beautiful and well-cared-for house on our street. Gary loved to garden, and we had flowers in bloom every season. The lawn looked liked green velvet. He had kept it well maintained and in tip-top condition. No more. It needed painting inside and out. The hardwood floors needed refinishing, and much of the furniture needed reupholstering.

With renewed energy, I decided to give it a complete makeover and had an entire team of professionals lined up to get started in August. Karen had promised me that she would oversee the project. Larry also volunteered his services, and I was grateful. Something was going on with him and Linda. I think they were on the verge of separating, and Larry was at loose ends. I had overheard him talking with Nan one day about some problems at home. I had so much on my mind that I didn't pay a lot of attention to their conversation.

In the midst of everything, I decided to enroll in a summer-school conversational Italian class at the university where Ana Douglas taught. I would do a lot better on my own if I knew a little Italian before I went over. The Orvieto language school was an immersion course with people from all over the world, and I felt that I might be intimidated if I knew no Italian. I wanted it to be fun, as well, and I was worried that, at my age, I would be slower than most of the students. I called Ana one night to find out what the university offered and to see how she was. She had become a special and very dear person to me on the trip.

"Kathryn, we have the perfect course for you here at the university. It was designed for American tourists and teaches basic information— how to order food in restaurants, how to shop, how to take a train or other public transportation, how to go to the theater, how to find special sites—just loads of good stuff."

"That is exactly what I need, Ana," I said excitedly. "I really want some vocabulary under my belt before I go over there again. Did I tell you that Francesca is helping me?"

"Really?" said an interested Ana. "It is such a small world. She turned out to be a childhood friend of Theo's."

"How was your visit to Theo's farm and your trip back?"

"There are just no words to describe how wonderful it was," she said. "Kathryn, I am in love with Theo. It hit me out of the blue one day. I tried to talk myself into believing it was just lust, but it's not. I am really head over heels in love with him. I miss him so much, but he is coming to the States this month. I am going to Long Island, New York, to meet his aunt and uncle. His daughter, Mimi, will also be there. I am nervous about meeting all of them."

"Ana, they will love you, don't worry," I reassured her.

"I am not at all sure about that. I think they would rather I were Jewish. And Theo's daughter is very close to her mother, so I don't know how she feels about another woman in her father's life. Families make things so much more complicated."

"Tell me about it!" I laughed. We made arrangements to meet on campus and have lunch.

# IV

Toward the end of July, I was sitting outside of a small café in the shade, studying my Italian lesson for the next day, when I heard someone say my name. "Pardon me, but aren't you Mrs. Wynham?"

I looked up, and there stood Judge Grayson Tyler. "Judge Tyler," I said surprised. "How are you?"

"I am well, thank you. I thought I recognized you. I hope things are going well for your family," he said politely.

"We appreciated your kindness so much in court, Judge Tyler. Please, have a seat. It's much too hot to stand in the sun."

He took the seat across from me and ordered ice tea from the waiter. "I was very impressed by your son, Mrs. Wynham. It is not often that I see such a lack of animosity in separation hearings."

"I was also impressed by my son. He has changed immensely in these past few months. More than you would ever believe. He still harbors the hope that his wife will return home. He loves her as much today as he did before they were married. This whole thing has broken his heart, but at the same time, it has made a man of him."

He looked across the table at my Italian textbook. "Is that Italian that you are studying?"

"I am. I hope some of this is actually sinking in. I'm enjoying my class and very happy that there are many people my age in it. I was afraid it would be filled with college-age kids getting ready for a summer of youth hostels in Italy."

"Do you plan to use it? Are you going to Italy in the near future?"

"Very soon. In fact, just about six weeks from now." I launched into the story of the tour that I had taken in May and my plans for returning to Orvieto. Judge Tyler was an excellent listener and had many questions, which probably came from all of his years on the bench.

"I must say that I am very impressed by the manner in which you are juggling everything in your life—your house renovation, your studies, your family, well, all of it, really."

I laughed. "Believe me, it is quite a change from the past years when all I did was baby-sit. I love my grandchildren, but it wasn't enough. I didn't realize how much they were draining me and how much life I was missing. I am just trying to catch up now. How about you? What do you do in your leisure time?"

It was as if a sad cloud had passed over his face. "I am at loose ends right now. My wife passed away last year, and our house seems like a big empty barn with just me rattling around in it. My children live in New York, California, and Florida. All three want me to move close to them when I retire at the end of the year. I just returned from California, and I don't think that is an option for me, just not too keen on the lifestyle out there.

Too crowded, too many highways, too much of everything. I am going to New York to see my daughter in September and look at some apartments. I do love the city but not the cold weather in the winter. And I really am not too keen on Florida anytime."

"It's certainly none of my business," I said, "but do you feel that you have to live near one of your children?"

"They certainly feel that I need to, and I am feeling a bit more vulnerable without my wife."

"Judge Tyler…"

"Please, could you call me Gray?"

"Only if you call me Kathryn. Gray, I hope I don't sound presumptuous but, based on my own experience, I would tell anyone to take your time and think about what you want to do. Don't let your children dictate your life. It was a huge mistake for me after my husband died."

"That sounds like good advice," he said, standing up. "It has been nice chatting with you, but I need to complete a few errands before court this afternoon. I hope we meet again." With that, Gray Tyler left.

My first impression of him was correct, I thought. He is a very nice man.

It turned out that we did run into each other two more times before I left for Italy. Once in the grocery store and the second time in a bookstore. He invited me out for coffee the second time and we talked for at least two hours. I promised that I would call him when I returned from Italy to tell him about my adventures there.

# V

I arrived at Leonardo da Vinci Airport the first Wednesday in September. It was right after Labor Day and the crowds were beginning to thin a bit in Europe. The Germans, English, and Swedes had completed their summer holidays. Children all over were back in school, so that particular week turned out to be a good one to fly.

I had made reservations to stay overnight at a hotel in Rome my first day back in the country, simply because I knew from my previous trip that I would be terribly tired and jet-lagged. I was a little nervous about getting to the train station, buying my ticket for Orvieto, and getting on the right train, and I thought having good night's sleep would go a long way toward making that work out. My hotel was near the Spanish Steps. It was an entirely different feeling not to have an itinerary to follow. I took my time settling into the hotel, ordered a nice breakfast, showered, and went out for a walk.

It was a gorgeous day. The Spanish Steps has the Piazza di Spagna at its base and the Piazza Trinita dei Monte at the top, with 138 steps in between. Not so bad going down but a steep walk when you are tired going back up. Since my hotel was near the Pinco, an elegant park that joined with the grounds of the Villa Borghese, I decided that I would walk there. Much to my surprise and delight, at the far corner of the Pinco was a spectacular view of Rome that we had not seen on our trip in May. I walked for about an hour and then decided to go back to the hotel and take a nap before dinner.

I was nervous about finding a place to have dinner on my own but did not need to worry after all. A group of American ladies, visiting from Missouri, overheard me talking to the hotel concierge about a restaurant in the vicinity, and they invited me to join them. They did not speak one word of Italian and were very impressed at my ability to order not only my dinner, but theirs as well. It was definitely a confidence booster!

The next morning I was up early and made my way to the train station. My adventures in Orvieto were about to begin.

# ANA

# I

was sitting in the terminal of the Baltimore/Washington International
Airport waiting for Theo's plane to arrive. There had been a thirty-minute
delay. That made me very anxious, considering it had only been three weeks
since the attacks on the World Trade Center and the Pentagon. Very few
people were flying these days, so I had gotten an excellent parking place, and
we would be able to get away from the terminal with a minimum of effort.

Theo had called me as soon as he could get through after the attacks.

"Ana, are you OK?" A man's voice awakened me from a fitful sleep.

It took me a minute to realize it was Theo. "Theo, I wish you were here
with me. It's horrible."

He repeated himself. "Are you OK? I have to know that."

"Physically I am, but emotionally, like most of the people in this country, I am in shock. So many people died, Theo. Some people were jumping
out of the towers. You could see their bodies floating by on television. It's
been too horrible to contemplate. Those poor people on the planes."

"Liebchen, I was so worried about you. Have you been all alone?"

"No, not really. I was in class when a student burst in and stated said the Pentagon and the World Trade Center had been hit. Everyone in the university converged on the student buildings, where we watched replays of the attacks on big-screen TVs. Some of my students had relatives who worked at the towers and the Pentagon, so we were trying to help them get information. I did not get home until eleven o'clock tonight and have only been in bed a couple of hours. It's chaotic as hell. It feels like hell."

"Ana, forgive me for waking you, but I had to know that you were safe. I couldn't get through to the States until now."

"You are the one person in the world I wanted to talk to, Theo. I am so glad you called. I love you and hate it that we are so far apart."

"Me too, but this catastrophe will be bringing me to America as soon as we can fly in. I have to go to Washington." My heart leaped. "You are coming here?"

Theo was cryptic. "Ja, soon, but I don't know when yet. It is the only good thing about the whole incident. I will see you soon. Go back to sleep. I will call again in a few days. I love you."

I realized after Theo hung up that I had not asked him why he would be coming to the States. What did this attack have to do with him?

I soon learned that he would not talk about it over the phone. "Liebchen, I will explain when I see you, but not now."

That was three weeks ago, and so much had happened. The school was trying to resume some normalcy, but I knew that, as a teacher, I would have to find the right mix of teaching, listening, and talking. These young people were wounded emotionally, and many had been touched personally. I spent countless hours talking to individual students, and I felt pretty raw myself.

I spent most of my free time with Lena, Neva, and Sara. They were the only family I had nearby and, in truth, they were my real family. We all wanted to be together. Alphonso, Tony, and their families were with us also. We drew together for food, comfort, and prayers. There were many tears, and for the first time, we could not give the children comforting answers. There was no good answer to why this horror had happened.

The attacks were a culmination of a roller-coaster summer beginning with the two weeks that I had spent with Theo in Italy. I left basking in the glow of new love. For the rest of my life, the happiness that I felt with Theo at his farmhouse could never be recreated. It was wonderful to fall in love again in midlife. I think even more so when you aren't thinking about it and never expect it to happen again. It really does hit you like a bolt of lightning, or at least it did me.

Theo came to the States in July to see his aunt and uncle on Long Island. Selma and Hyaim Epstein were survivors of the Holocaust. They had met at Buchenwald concentration camp when they were nineteen and twenty-two years old. Both had siblings who had survived as well, but sadly the rest of their families had starved to death during their years interred in the camp. Selma and Hyaim had been saved because they were young and strong, and they could work. After the camp was liberated, they immigrated to the United States and started working at various jobs just to stay alive. They thought America was the best place on earth, because the soldiers had been so kind to them after World War II. Neither had any desire to go back to Germany or to immigrate to Israel.

Eventually, Hyaim saved enough money to buy a little store in Brooklyn, where he sold furniture and odds and ends. Selma worked with him every day, just as she had at Buchenwald. Their little store grew into furniture only, and over the years it became well known for its quality and good prices. They opened regional branches and became highly successful. They were part of a tight-knit Jewish community in both Brooklyn and Long Island, where they had retired fifteen years before. They generously donated to Jewish causes in the United States and Israel. The biggest regret and sadness in their lives was that they never were able to have children, due to injuries that they had incurred as a result of their imprisonment in Buchenwald.

Theo's mother and Selma had been sisters. Theo's mother chose to stay in Germany after the war and was part of a group of Jews who rebuilt their lives in their hometowns. Selma and her sister saw each other only a few times before Theo's mother died, but those times were special for Selma, as she grew to love Theo and his sister. They had been close since Theo's childhood, and he made it a point to come to America at least once a year to visit them. His sister did not come as often, but she, like Theo, viewed Selma and Hyaim as second parents.

Given all that they had gone through in the Holocaust, it was important to all Jews, wherever they lived, to rebuild Jewish bloodlines. Selma and Hyaim were delighted when Theo married a young Jewish woman whose parents and other relatives could be traced in relationships from the past. They were equally devastated when Theo divorced, and their hope was that he would marry another Jewish woman and have more children.

Theo wanted me to meet Selma and Hyaim, who were so important to him. He planned to fly into BWI, rent a car, spend a week with his aunt and uncle, and then return to Baltimore for a few days with me. At the last minute, he begged me to go with him, and I had no real reason not to. I had a gut feeling that the visit would not turn out well, and I was right.

Selma and Hyaim were unfailingly polite, but I simply did not fit in. We had nothing in common, and I felt more foreign in their home and community than I ever did in Germany or Italy. They could not figure out who I was to Theo or why he had brought me to visit them. Theo had not been overtly Jewish in Tubingen or Montepulciano. If he had ever gone to a synagogue during the time that I was in Germany, I never knew it. He rarely spoke of being Jewish, but I knew that he was proud of his heritage. I also knew that he fought against anti-Semitism as fiercely as any warrior on a battlefield. His fight was different from his aunt and uncle's. They were survivors of the worst event of the twentieth century, and Theo came from a different generation. Their expectation of Theo and his generation was that they were to be the start of a new line who would be protectors of their history. That expectation included not marrying outside of their religion.

Of course, Theo had never mentioned marriage to me, but from their point of view, why was he wasting his time with someone who was not part of the big picture? As bad as this was, things became infinitely worse when Mimi came. That was part of the tradition. Mimi usually came to visit when Theo did. Whereas Selma and Hyiam were polite but distant, Mimi was openly hostile to me, and I don't think it had a thing to do with me being non-Jewish.

Mimi, at nineteen, was stunningly beautiful in an exotic Near East way. She could have been Esther from the Old Testament or a harem princess. She did not particularly look like Theo, except she had long; dark, curly hair and deep brown eyes, but her mother could also have those. She did have his mannerisms, however. She had the same uncanny way of looking a person directly in the eyes and demanding an answer. She would not take no for an answer. She could be, like Theo, intimidating, but she seemed to lack his compassion. As is common to many young people, life was black or white. She was well educated and entirely serious. There was nothing frivolous about her. She dressed dramatically and looked like a model, but she spoke like a political science expert. Not that she was. There were times when we clashed, but she was clever enough not to do it when Theo was around.

I had just taken a swim in Selma and Hyaim's pool when I saw Theo walking toward me with this beautiful woman.

"Ana, this is my daughter, Mimi," he said proudly.

I could see her sizing me up, but she said hello politely, as one would to a maid or the lawn-care man. Then she dismissed me. I was stunned, but more so that Theo had not noticed. Over and over, he attempted to bring me into the conversation, but Mimi would smile vaguely as if it didn't pertain to her and change the subject entirely.

Mimi's boyfriend, Rueben, had accompanied her. He was a sabra, a native-born Israeli, which brought hero status in certain Jewish communities. Rueben understood English well but spoke it haltingly. German and Hebrew were the dominant languages spoken with Theo's family. At one point, Mimi said sarcastically in German that they had better switched to English so that her father's visitor would not feel left out. Theo thought she was being polite. He had not picked up on the sarcasm.

Before Theo could reply, I interrupted, looked Mimi in the face, and said in German, "No, please, continue your conversation. I understand German quite well." Which wasn't true, but she did have the good grace to flush a bright red. Because I had had enough for one night, I said, "I am a little tired, and I know that you want to catch up with one another and not entertain a 'visitor.' I think I will read a little and turn in early."

Theo looked alarmed. "Aren't you feeling well, Ana?"

"Quite well, Theo. I will see you tomorrow." We were sleeping in separate bedrooms in deference to his aunt and uncle, which bothered me at first, but now I was glad. I decided that this was a horrible situation. I would fly back home as soon as I could.

Early the next morning, Theo slipped into my room and got in bed with me. "What is wrong, Ana? You looked upset last night." How could I say what I needed to say to him without being totally offensive? His daughter needed a spanking. She was one of the rudest people I had ever encountered in my life. His aunt and uncle were perplexed that he had brought me to their home. I did not feel wanted or welcome, but these people were Theo's family, and if I wanted to be a part of his life, they would have to be in mine.

So I began, hoping that my carefully chosen words would sound the way I intended them. "Theo, you are such a good man. That's why I love you. You have honored me by bringing me here to meet the people you love the most in the world. They also love you and need to be with you without a stranger in their midst."

"But, Ana…"

I put my finger on his lips. "Hear me out, Theo. They need to be with you alone. Your aunt and uncle, not to mention Mimi, see you seldom. This is your time with them. I am a distraction. I am going to fly back home the day after tomorrow, if I can get a flight out. I want another day here to get to know Mimi better." That was a lie, but I didn't want to give Mimi the satisfaction of thinking that she had run me off. "I need you to make it look like it was planned all along. That way, it won't be awkward. I don't want your aunt and uncle to feel like they have done something to make me feel unwelcomed, which, of course, you know they haven't."

"But, Ana, I want you here with me."

"We will be together when you come back to Baltimore, just the two of us. I will make it up to you, Theo. I can see what you can't. Your family needs you, too. I can wait for you. It is selfish for me to take any time from them. Selma and Hyaim are lovely people, and I respect all that they have gone through and how they have lived their lives since. They are inspirational." That was all true. I did like Selma and Hyiam. They were two dear people.

"What you say makes sense, Ana, but I don't like it."

I pressed my point. "We will have many days together, just the two of us. Your family is entitled to a little time with you."

"What will we tell them?" asked a concerned Theo.

"We will tell them together, and it will look natural. Leave it to me."

I was so relieved that I was leaving that I was very happy and light-hearted that day.

Mimi did her best to get under my skin. We were sitting out by the pool when Mimi suddenly looked at me and said, "You don't know much about Jews, do you, Ana?"

I gazed over at her perfect body in a tiny bikini and said nonchalantly, "Probably just a little more than German schoolchildren learn. I have visited the Holocaust Museum in Washington."

She flushed a bright red and looked daggers at me. German history books since World War II hardly mentioned the systematic elimination of the Jews. Many Germans born in the latter half of the twentieth century were hardly aware of the atrocities that had happened. The generations before them did not speak about it. It was a national shame.

"You know, Ana, my father has many girlfriends." She changed tactics.

I simply smiled and said, "I don't doubt it, Mimi. He is a very good-looking man, isn't he?"

"He doesn't like Americans. He thinks they are stupid."

"I know. He told me that almost the first time we met." I then quoted Theo in his British English. "Americans are naïve and often stupid. Did I sound just like him, Mimi?"

I could tell she didn't know how to respond, because I was not getting defensive. Before more could be said, Theo and Reuben joined us. "What are you talking about?" said Theo pleasantly.

Theo seemed pleased that Mimi and I were having what must have seemed to him a very nice dialogue. "I think we just agreed that you don't like Americans, Theo."

Now it was Theo's turn to blush. "That does not include you, Ana."

I got up, turned to leave, and smiled at him but looked at Mimi. "I know that, Theo."

# II

We all have our blind spots, and Mimi was definitely one of Theo's, as far as I was concerned. But Theo was not oblivious to what went on around him, so when we met again in Baltimore, he mentioned it.

"Ana, what happened at my aunt and uncle's house?" We were having dinner at a little restaurant in the harbor area that specialized in seafood. Good seafood was not something you could readily obtain in Theo's land-locked part of Germany.

"Tell me more about what concerns you," I responded, trying to buy time to figure out where Theo was going with this.

"Something was off," he said, looking at me in a way that demanded honesty.

"Off?" I gave him a puzzled look.

He put down his knife and fork, never taking his eyes off of me. "Come on, Ana, you know what I mean, and you are hedging."

I also put down my knife and fork and looked at him. This time I was direct. "I am not sure what you observed, Theo, so I will only speak for myself. I think I was the thing that made it seem off."

"You? That's ridiculous!"

"Have you ever taken another woman to visit your aunt and uncle?" I asked.

"What does that have to do with anything?" Theo was clearly exasperated.

"Everything, I think, Theo. Have you taken someone else besides me to visit them?"

"No one but Mimi's mother when we were married," he finally replied.

"And how was she received?"

"Wonderfully. They loved Marta. They distantly knew some of her family, who all died in one or another camp."

"And they were very upset when your marriage ended?"

"Well yes, but what does that have to do—"

I interrupted him. "Everything, Theo, everything. Don't you see that in all these intervening years, they have come to some acceptance that you and Marta are no longer together, but there also has been no one else for you. Then, without warning, you show up this year with me, and with no explanation of who I am in your life. And more important, I am not Jewish."

I could see Theo becoming somewhat defensive. "Were you not well treated there, Ana?" Again that direct look that both melted my heart and intimidated me.

"Yes, Theo, they were as polite as they could possibly be. But can you not see this from their point of view? That's what I tried to explain to you when I was there. I could see that. Give me some credit for a tiny bit of intelligence, even if I am an American." I couldn't stop myself from throwing in that last point. This was the closest we had ever come to arguing.

Theo's face reflected a range of emotions, but I could see him visibly take a step back. He reached across the table and took my hand. "Ana, I love you. That is the most important thing to me. It doesn't matter to me that you aren't Jewish. It doesn't matter that you are an American. It is true that I haven't liked Americans, but there is much about this country that I do like. I just wish the people in your country were more observant about the world. Right now, in this minute, those things don't matter to me. You are who I want. Forgive me for insulting you. I know you are intelligent. You do believe me, don't you? You do know how much I love you?"

"I do believe you, Theo." I smiled at him. "You have given me back my life and spirit in these few short months. We are just two individuals who met and were attracted to one another, but your culture and religion demands more from you, don't you think? That is what Selma and Hyaim must see, and perhaps even Mimi. I think they would all be very disappointed to see you end up with someone who is not Jewish."

"Mimi? Where does she come in?" He looked astounded.

"I think Mimi is very much into keeping the Jewish history and traditions alive. She lived in Israel this summer and has a sabra boyfriend. How much stronger could she be? From a historian's point of view and that is what I am, Theo, Mimi embodies the new Judaism. I am sure your entire family is really proud of her."

Theo looked at me thoughtfully. "Some of what you say may be correct, Ana, but my family also wants me to be happy."

"Theo, I wish I could be what your family hopes for you, but I can't change who I am. What happened to Jews during World War Two is appalling and tragic. I can't begin to tell you how much I admire people—like your aunt and uncle—who have rebuilt their lives so successfully after going through what they did, having sustained the loss of entire families. There is no way I can truly understand how they feel, and they know that as well as I do. I will never be able to share that with them."

"Ana…"

"No, Theo, listen to me. I need to say this to you. We have to put this on the table. We are very different in every single way. It is an amazing miracle to me that you came into my life, and it doesn't matter to me if you are Jewish, purple, polka-dotted, or whatever, but it does matter to your family. Very much. I love you, the man, Theo Volker."

"Ana, I had given up thinking there would ever be another woman for me. I did not want one for more than one night." He looked sheepish. "But you got under my skin. Most Americans are arrogant, and you weren't. You looked like nothing could hurt you any further, and I identified with that. I recognized it. Not only from my divorce but from our culture. You have a fighting spirit. You understand injustice. You teach what is right and true without embellishments. You were not afraid of me. You stood up to me. You have compassion. That is what my family needs to know about you."

"How can we make this work, Theo? How can I become a part of your family and not an outsider? I know it will take time, but I can't be thrust upon your family without warning, as I was with Selma, Hyaim, and your daughter. Can we both admit that didn't work?"

"Ja, Ana, I should have given this more thought. I am sorry if it was bad for you."

"Come, Theo. Let's go home. Enough of families for tonight. I am tired of wishing things were different. It is you I need, and we will have to work on the rest. I am in this for the long haul." He didn't understand "long haul," and after much explanation, he finally got it. "Ja, I am in it for the haul also, Ana." Different languages, different meanings, but love is universal. I learned that again that night.

# III

When I returned from Italy, I made a decision to sell my house. I saw it through different eyes, and it symbolized the past to me. It was a good house that Mark and I had had fun remodeling, and although I had done nothing to it in the past six years, it was still well maintained. The real estate agent suggested some landscaping and painting a couple of rooms but said nothing more needed to be done and recommended quite a high selling price. I was astounded, because it would quadruple the price we had paid for it.

The house sold almost immediately to a nice couple with three children. They loved the neighborhood and the style of the house. They told me that there was some kind of "vibe" that they both felt when they went through the first time, and they knew it was the home for them and their growing family. I felt relieved that a sweet, loving family would live in the house where Mark and I had had so many happy times.

In the end, I decided that I did not want another house to maintain and chose a three-bedroom town house. It was rather luxurious, but I wanted the amenities of a pool and gym. It was also gated, which I thought would give me better protection as a single woman. I chose an end unit with a lot of windows, which made it more expensive, but I wanted as much light as possible. I had not realized what a good negotiator I was, and I got several upgrades for no extra cost and a lower price on the unit than had been asked. I was pleased with myself.

I felt as if I was moving into a new time in my life. My book was coming along well and was almost ready to go to print. In light of all that had happened with Theo in the past months, I was energized enough to move the research along faster than I thought possible. I loved working on this project and wanted to write a readable textbook. My goal was to keep the cost low so that it was affordable to students. There had also been, in recent years, an interest in medieval times for, of all things, video games. I was working with one of my students on developing an educational, historical game to be used in elementary schools that was fun and accurate to that period. The game would be based on the research I had obtained for my book. The scenery in the video would look like a medieval German town. Lucky children, I thought. This is the way to learn history.

I was in touch with Theo daily via e-mail, and he called at least once a month on some kind of international phone through Interpol. I'm not sure it was legal, but I was glad to hear his voice. It was difficult to be so far away from him, and I was looking forward to the times when he could come to the States on business. I had found out through the university that there was a year-long visiting professor program, and I could apply for a position at Eberhard-Karls University in Tubingen, where I had done my research. It was too late for this year, but I started an application for the next academic year. There were four other universities in Germany that I could apply to, but I was not interested in them. I wanted to be where Theo was.

I had not mentioned this to Theo. I wanted to see how our relationship developed. Could it survive the distance? How would we feel a year from now? I knew that I loved Theo, but I wasn't sure how this could be maintained. We were making plans for me to visit Italy again next May, but besides the odd, unannounced trips to the States, I never knew when I would see Theo again. I was hoping that this long-distance romance could survive.

Theo hated the hot, humid weather in Baltimore in the summer. It made him irritable, but there were some things he really loved about the Washington area. The Smithsonian was one of those, and we visited all the buildings when he came in July. He also went back to the Holocaust Museum, which I could see was painful for him. "We must never forget, Ana. I make myself go." He also "visited" the FBI and CIA buildings. What he did there, I never knew. "Its better left unsaid" was all that he would say.

When Theo returned from Long Island in July, we spent a few days on the Eastern Shore eating off newspapers in little crab shacks and walking along the beaches. He loved that. "There is so much about America that is good and pure," he said one day as we were poking through little shops on the shore. "Really," I teased. We both were sunburned and happy.

"Ja, it is an amazing country, all in all, but Americans don't really know how endangered they are."

"Endangered?" What was he thinking?

"Ja, you have not been touched in many ways. You live your life thinking nothing could happen to you. And it will, Ana. One day it will." How right he proved to be. "That's why Americans are so happy. You live like simple little children playing in the sand."

"Theo, Americans know that we have a lot of problems—poverty, crime, school dropouts…"

"Ja, ja, ja, but those are internal." He was impatient with me. I didn't get it. "There is a big world out there, Ana that does not like America and spends its time thinking of ways to harm you."

"That's scary, Theo. How good is our defense system compared to Europe's?"

"It's probably ten times better than Europe's, but that is not your problem. Your problem is that your politicians and agencies don't communicate with one another. They are very frustrating."

"I am glad that I don't know the details of this stuff. I don't think I could sleep at night if I did," I commented.

"Ja, you would not sleep at night, believe me." We changed the subject. Theo knew things that I didn't want to know about.

# IV

The arrival of Theo's plane was finally announced. I saw him before he saw me. He had on jeans, a long-sleeved, blue shirt, and a blue blazer. He carried his briefcase. Since he was head and shoulders above most of the passengers, he was easy to spot. He looked good. Theo was one of those people who could actually sleep on a plane, and he looked reasonably rested. The other passengers looked dead on their feet, but Theo seemed full of energy.

I had worn a sleeveless, beige linen blouse over matching pants and tossed a salmon-colored sweater around my shoulders because of the air conditioning in the terminal. Around my neck was the ever-present onyx heart necklace. On my wrist was a delicate gold bracelet that Theo had given me the last night we were together in Milan before I flew back home. I was tan from swimming at the pool at my town house and hoped that I looked as good to Theo as he looked to me.

He broke into a big smile when he saw me. "Ana, Ana, you look beautiful. I have been so worried about you." He held me tightly against him. "I never want to let go of you." He continued to hold me for the longest time. He felt so solid and warm. I never wanted to let go. He tilted my chin up and gave me a deep kiss. "Ana, let's go get my bag and get out of here. I only have a short time with you."

"What do you mean, Theo? I thought we had all day today." I was instantly saddened.

"Something came up. There are some people I have to meet with later this morning, but I am going to try to postpone it to this afternoon." He got on the phone while we were waiting for the baggage to come around. He appeared to be listening more than talking but told the person at the other end that he would see him later.

On the way to my new town house, which Theo would see for the first time, I asked him if he could tell me how his trip to the States was connected with the recent terrorist attacks. He thought about my question for a few minutes. "There are many governments in the world right now that want to prevent another attack here and help America, if America will let us."

"Why wouldn't we be receptive to help, Theo? Those attacks were horrendous."

"Ja. Horrendous. In America, your politicians want instant solutions. How to handle this will take restraint, will take patience. Help could lie in other countries. I don't think America will like the proposals."

"America wants revenge right now, Theo. We are hurting and sad beyond belief. How could this thing happen here?"

"Ah, Ana, such an American remark." Theo sighed. "It was bound to happen. It was just a matter of when. America has been lucky that something this big hasn't happened before. Americans have believed they were untouchable, impenetrable, and stronger than anyone. It is a hard way to find out what all the rest of us have learned over and over." He took my hand and kissed it. "I worry about your safety. I wish you were back in Germany."

"Do you think there will be another attack?" I was frightened.

"Not immediately. Maybe never. I think you are safer than ever right now, but in time, your country will let its guard down, and you will be vulnerable again."

Theo liked my new house and had supported my desire to move when I told him of my plans in June. "Ja, this is good, Ana." He looked around at the grounds. "I like the security gate. It is good for a woman, no?"

"Yes, I feel protected in here, but I wasn't worried so much about my personal safety before. I am pretty cautious, Theo."

I fixed him breakfast and afterward, he pulled me onto his lap and started nibbling on my neck and ear. "Are you still hungry?" I asked playfully.

"Very!" He continued to nibble and kiss me as he unbuttoned my blouse. "Ana," he said in my ear softly. "I have only a little time, but I need you."

We made love, and afterwards Theo dressed to go to his meeting in Washington. "I don't know what time I will be back. It may be very late tonight. I don't know how long I will be here, but I think I will have to fly back to Germany in a couple of days."

So soon. It was too much. I was unprepared for his next remark. "Ana, I have a favor to ask you. I will talk about it later. It is important to me."

"A favor? You know I would do anything for you, Theo. What is it?"

"I need to explain it, and there is no time now. Tomorrow will be soon enough."

So he left me to wonder about the favor. He did not return until after midnight, and jet lag was catching up with him. All he wanted to do was sleep, and I was content to have him next to me in bed. The next morning, Theo was up early, dressed quickly, and was off to Washington before I could get up. I still knew nothing about the favor. The next three days were the same. In late, up early. We had no time to talk. I hardly saw Theo.

On the fifth night after Theo's arrival, he came home around nine o'clock. I was grading papers and wasn't expecting him. He looked dead tired, with fatigue lines around his eyes. He came in and sat in a chair opposite me. "Theo, have you eaten tonight?" I asked.

"I had a sandwich earlier, but I am not as hungry as tired."

I got him a beer out of the refrigerator, and he took a long swallow. "I could make you an omelet. It won't take long."

"Nein, Ana, sit. I need to talk to you. I am leaving tomorrow."

I was stricken. We had spent no time together. "Tomorrow?"

"Ja, but I will be back in about ten days. I want to bring Mimi with me when I return."

Mimi? Why would he bring her here? I thought she was in Israel with her boyfriend, but before I could ask any questions, Theo continued. "Mimi is having a bad time. She and Reuben are no more...as you say here, they broke up."

"They broke up?"

"Ja. She is back in Germany. Ana, she is hurt and angry. To make things worse, Marta just married a man Mimi doesn't like. She doesn't want to go to her mother's house, and she doesn't want to go back to the university."

I couldn't believe his next statement. It took me completely by surprise.

"I want Mimi to come here and stay with you, Ana."

Omigod. He couldn't be serious. It would be like having an attacking viper living with me. "Theo, I don't know what to say." That was true. I was nearly speechless. The last person I wanted to see, much less have sleeping in my house, was Mimi.

"Please, Ana. This is the favor. Mimi doesn't know what she wants right now, and I am worried about her because she is so sad and angry. I trust you with my daughter. I know you will be good to her. She needs time to think and get over this thing with Reuben. And she needs to return to the university in Heidelberg. Marta has married a good man, and Mimi needs time to accept that, but it won't happen in Germany."

How could I deny Theo? I loved him so much. But Mimi here with me? Would this destroy our relationship? I knew Mimi would do everything in her power to rip us apart. How much easier would it be if she were under my roof? I also couldn't believe that Mimi would want to stay with me.

"Theo, has Mimi agreed to come here and stay with me?"

"I haven't talked to her. I had to ask you first, but it would be for just a few months. I would pay her expenses."

A few months? I didn't think I could survive a day with her. "Theo, I don't think Mimi will want to stay with me. She doesn't like me. Wouldn't your aunt and uncle be better for her?"

"Selma and Hyiam are old, Ana. There are no young people about to make her forget. You have the university here and know a lot of people. What makes you think Mimi doesn't like you? That is silly. She likes you fine. Didn't you get along so well this summer?"

Another moment of truth. "No, Theo, we didn't. I don't take it especially personally, because I don't think she would like any woman you're with. She was quite rude to me when you weren't around." And even when you were, I thought, but you just didn't see it.

"Ana, Mimi knows there have been other women in my life since her mother and I divorced."

"Yes, I know. She made a point of telling me that more than once."

Theo looked so tired and dejected; my heart went out to him. "Ja, maybe it is not a good idea." He ran his fingers through his hair. He stood up, walked over to a window, and looked out into the night. "It was too much to ask, Ana. I didn't have anyone else to turn to."

Oh, God. There is no choice. I couldn't stand to see Theo looking like this—disappointed in me, not knowing what to do about Mimi, so alone, and dealing with whatever he was doing in Washington. "I am willing to give it a try on two conditions, and you and Mimi will have to live by both of them, Theo."

His face suddenly lifted, and he looked hopeful. "Anything, Ana. I am desperate."

"If Mimi agrees to come here, I will give it a trial run for a month to see if it will work. She will have to live by the rules that I give all students who stay with me, and she must treat me respectfully and not trash my new house."

"Ana, sweetheart, that goes without saying. She will be a good girl, I swear…"

"Theo, I have had loads of students stay with me over time, but not for months. They have liked me and have wanted to stay in my home, but Mimi and I would be starting out differently, so it is important that she agrees to this. She doesn't have to like me, but she can't be rude to me."

"We will talk it out together when she comes back with me. She will understand what she has to do. I want her to take some classes at the university. Can you help her with that also, Ana?"

"Well, school has started, Theo, but given the unusual circumstances in America now, I might be able to work something out. I will try. Theo, your daughter is not a girl any longer; she is a woman. She has been living with a man in Israel. Life will be different for her here, and she doesn't like Americans any more than you do."

Theo looked sheepish. "I don't hate Americans, but I do hate some American traits. That is true."

I wasn't about to get into those traits again. Not now. I was upset that Mimi might be staying with me and about what this could mean to my relationship with Theo. Yet part of me thought this might be an opportunity for me to know Mimi better. That was a long shot, however. "The other thing, Theo, is that you can't sleep over while Mimi is here. I am old-fashioned when I have kids around."

"You can't be serious, Ana. Really, that is stupid. My daughter knows that I have sex."

We were close to arguing again, and we were both tired and wired. I sensed that this could go badly. I went over to him and put my arms around his neck. "I'm sorry, Theo, and you know this isn't what I want. I will always want to be with you, but I will respect your daughter and not sleep with her father in the same house. Call me a puritanical prude or whatever. I am not that modern. I am not European. I am American, and by the way, Theo, I am proud that I am American." I was near tears by this point.

Theo saw my misery and held me closer. "Ana, I love you. I love your spirit. Thank you for taking my daughter."

I snuggled into him. "I want Mimi to like me, Theo, but I can't force her, and I refuse to be bullied. You do understand that, don't you?"

"I do understand, Ana. Can we go to bed now? I need sleep." And that is just what we did. Sleep.

# V

So Mimi Volker came to live with me. I could see right away that she didn't want this any more than I did. This will be a battle royal, I thought, but I was wrong. Mimi was angry and sullen, but she was civil. Theo must have said a lot to her, because she was on her best behavior. She even thanked me for letting her stay with me. That was a surprise.

I had given Mimi the bottom floor of my town house, which was really a suite. She had her own bedroom, bathroom, and what used to be my den. Mimi was astounded that she was given so much room. "Ana, are you sure you want me to have all this space? The little bedroom upstairs is enough."

"No, no, Mimi, I really want you to be comfortable and feel that this is your home while you are here." She had no answer but a simple thank you. I could tell that she was on guard.

I did have an ulterior motive. I didn't want Mimi so close. I had originally thought that I would move downstairs, but it was my house, and there just seemed to be a psychological advantage of having her on the bottom.

There were clashes. That was inevitable. But Mimi always backed down. She kept her rooms clean and tidy and gave me no reason to say anything to her. Once, late at night, I went to the kitchen to get some water, and I heard her crying downstairs. It put a crack in my armor. Poor girl. She must be heartbroken over Reuben and lonely here. I knew I couldn't let her know that I heard her, because she was so proud and defensive. I had to find a way to get through to her. But how?

I had never told Mimi that I was a widow, and she took it for granted that I had never been married. I assumed that Theo had filled her in on my background. In one of our clashes, she lashed out at me. "Ana, I am sorry to tell you that my father would never fall for a woman who is as old as you and never married. He likes sophisticated women. Women with experience."

I refused to bite. "You may be right, Mimi. You certainly know your father better than I." On the surface, a stranger might believe that Mimi was very courteous to me, but she had a sideways manner of baiting me.

Help came in two forms and without my intervention. The first way was through the Capellos. That should have been no surprise to me. Right away, they invited Mimi to come with me to their house for a Sunday pasta dinner. At first she didn't want to go, but I think she had grown bored enough with me that it was worth it to her to go somewhere different. Mimi had practically grown up in Italy and spoke Italian fluently. She loved Theo's farmhouse. Whatever animosity Mimi had toward me disappeared entirely with the Capellos. Neva gave her a big hug and kiss, the way she did everyone, and Mimi warmed up to her immediately.

Mimi absolutely adored Lena. Lena took one look at Mimi and grabbed her hair. "Have you ever seen anything as glorious as this head of hair? You are gorgeous." Mimi glowed in their compliments. She was a beautiful, young girl whose heart had been broken, and the Capellos' warmth was healing medicine for her. Sara also was enchanted by Mimi, and Mimi, surprisingly, was excellent with children. She told Sara that she would teach her slang words in Italian, which delighted her.

Mimi was interested in the stories of Lena and me as children and began to see me in a different light. She never commented when the topic came up, but I could tell she was curious. It still had not come out that I was a widow, and because I seemed to be moving on, no one spoke about Mark. Mimi learned about him from Katie Willis.

She was my second intervention. The doorbell rang one Saturday soon after Mimi came to live with me, and there stood Katie. A much more subdued and changed Katie.

I was astonished to see her. "Katie!" I reached out, pulled her inside, and gave her a big hug. She clung to me and became teary. "I wondered what had happened to you. When did you come back to the States?"

"Only this week. I am trying to get back into the university, and I need your help."

"Of course," I said. "What kind of problems are you having?"

Before we could go any further, Mimi had wandered upstairs to the kitchen. I introduced Katie to her. "Katie, this is Mimi Volker, who is staying with me for a while. Her home is the Stuttgart Tubingen area."

Katie's eyes became wider. "Volker…Volker? Do you know Inspektor Volker?"

"Yes, he is my father. How would you know him?" Mimi asked.

Katie glanced my way. "Your father helped me immensely. He is the only reason that I am back in the States now …………….and out of prison."

"What?" I exploded. "Come sit in the kitchen, let me get you something to eat and drink, and I want you to start at the beginning." I made tuna sandwiches for the three of us, and Katie began her story.

"Well, the beginning you know, Dr. Douglas. My time with Konrad Richter." She looked over at Mimi. "He is the leader of a neo-Nazi group in Tubingen, and I got involved with him. I fell in love with him, but he was only using me." Mimi looked at her harder and with some sympathy. "Your father and Dr. Douglas warned me about him, but Konrad persuaded me that they were all wrong, so I continued to go out with him."

"What happened?" Mimi interjected before I could.

"Konrad was planning some stuff that I knew nothing about, like bombing some Jewish cemeteries and businesses." Katie looked over at Mimi. "I am so sorry, Mimi, I have nothing against Jewish people, but Konrad didn't tell me what he was doing. I had no idea that he was so cruel and mean. I never saw that side of him until the police caught me carrying some explosive materials. Konrad had nothing on him or in his apartment, so he wasn't arrested. Your father came to talk to me, but there was nothing he could do to keep me out of jail. I didn't even realize that the items in my possession were explosives. I know that sounds lame, but it's true. Your father knew exactly how Konrad had set me up, because he had done it before. He had even warned me about Konrad when Dr. Douglas was in Germany. He did everything he could to keep me from going to jail. He helped my parents at the American embassy and with the appeal, by cutting through all kinds of paperwork, but he couldn't save me from my own stupidity. I would still be there if it wasn't for the terrorist attack here on September eleventh."

Mimi and I spoke at once. "What did the attacks have to do with you getting out of jail? Where is Konrad Richter now?"

Katie looked confused.

"One question at a time," I said. "You go first, Mimi."

"How did you get out of jail? My father has told me that it is really a bad place."

Katie swallowed and was close to tears again.

"Are you OK, Katie? Do you want to talk about it?"

She nodded and continued. "Since I had never been in jail before, I didn't know how bad it would be, but for me, it was awful. I never thought I would be in jail anywhere. It was scarier than I can tell you. I was with some pretty tough women, older and young. Believe it or not, there was another American, from this university, who had gotten mixed up with Konrad a couple of years ago—almost the very same story as mine. We hung out together as much as possible. She had been sentenced to five years and had served two. I had seven over my head. There is no such thing as parole over there." She looked at me and shuddered. "Dr. Douglas, I could still be in jail for another seven years."

"How did you get out?" Mimi asked.

"After the attacks last month, your father, Mimi, went to bat for me and Ann, the other American, and as a goodwill gesture and for a big fine, the German government let both of us out. But we can never return to Germany again in our whole lives. That's OK. I don't ever want to go back."

"What happened to Konrad?" I asked.

"He disappeared. Something he has done before, evidently, but Inspektor Volker said he would be back, just like a sewer rat. Inspektor Volker had been keeping his eye on me, but he was sent somewhere. That's when Konrad made his move, and I got caught. I feel so stupid. I am stupid. Why couldn't

I see what was going on? Your father was right, Mimi. Americans are really naïve, but I was more than that. I was just plain dumb."

Before I could say anything, Mimi looked at Katie and said, "So you learned a lesson, Katie. Don't be so hard on yourself. That is Konrad Richter's profession and others like him—to prey on people. You didn't have a chance. My father will catch him one day, and when he does…" She left the rest unsaid, but we could see things would be very bad for Konrad.

"I hope I know when that happens." Katie had tears coming down her face. "Now, I am expelled from this university because of my bad behavior in Germany and going to prison. That's why I am here, Dr. Douglas. I am so ashamed, but I want to finish my degree here. This would have been my senior year, but now I have a year and a half to make up in order to graduate. I need letters written to the provost about my character. Would you be willing to write one for me?"

"You bet, Katie. You got caught up in a world in Europe that we never dream about in America. I also think the university could do a better job of preparing our students before they go over for an exchange program. We need to alert our students to organizations and people like Konrad Richter, who are waiting to prey on Americans. I had no idea that we had a former student in jail in Germany."

Mimi, who never ceased to surprise me, put an invitation of sorts out to Katie. I think all of the positive statements about her father made her sympathetic to Katie's ordeal. Or maybe it was their shared broken hearts. "I think I could give you some ideas about European thinking if you are interested. Maybe we could hang out sometime."

Katie looked at Mimi gratefully. "I would like that. Most of my friends here—or so-called friends—have dropped me now because of my prison time, but there are a couple of good friends I would like for you to meet. Do you know many people here yet?"

"No, not at all. I am taking a couple of classes, but I will be going back to Germany soon."

"Where are you staying?" I asked Katie.

"I may try to hang out with a girlfriend. I tried to find her, but she is not at her old apartment this year. I'm sure she will turn up."

"Why don't you stay here for a few days while I see what I can do about getting you readmitted to the university? I have an extra bedroom next to mine, and you are welcome to use it. You know all my rules, and if you have forgotten any, Mimi can remind you."

"I would love to stay here. Thank you, Dr. Douglas. I like your new house, but I kind of miss the old one. That holds many good memories for me."

"You have stayed with Ana before?" asked Mimi.

"Oh, yes, several times. At Christmas and other times. You can't imagine how much fun we all had. My father is in the military, and my parents were not always in America at Christmas, when I had to move off campus for a holiday."

"Well, you will have to tell me."

"Wait a minute," I interrupted. "Before you start talking about me, I need to get some work done today, so you will have to do it on your own time. You are welcome to move your stuff in anytime, Katie. I am going to make some calls to set up appointments to talk about your readmission."

"I'll help you," Mimi offered. "And then let's go in town for some coffee, and you can tell me more about Germany…and America."

# VI

That's how the strange friendship began between Mimi Volker and Katie Willis. They gravitated toward one another. One from loneliness and the other from an experience that left her shattered. Not to mention the broken hearts. Within a week, Mimi and Katie had become fast friends. The three of us spoke a mixture of German and English without being aware of it.

I did not learn until weeks later what Katie had actually told Mimi about me, but I detected changes in Mimi's attitude almost immediately. She confronted me one night when Katie was out about my marriage. "Does my father know that you were married before?"

I was so surprised at Mimi's angry outburst that I was struck silent for a moment.

"Well, does he?"

"As a matter of fact, he does, Mimi. He has known for a long time. Your father is a remarkable man, as I'm sure you know, and he did something for me once that was very healing in my grief."

I could see that she didn't know what to do with that statement. I had struggled not to become defensive with Mimi, but she did have an accusatory manner that could really set me on edge.

"You lied to me, Ana. You made me believe that you had never been married. I don't like being treated like a fool."

I lost it. "Then quit acting like a fool, Mimi." I was angry and tired. It had been a long day at work. "You have made many assumptions about me, as well as many snide and sarcastic remarks. Would it make you feel better to know that I am not trying to trap your father into marriage? He is the one who has pursued me. He is the one who invited me to his farmhouse. He is the one who would like to be staying here, but I won't let him. He is the one who thinks it is ridiculous that I have to sneak out like a teenager to a hotel to stay with him when he is in the States."

"Well, why do you do that?"

"Because of you, Mimi, because of you. I am old-fashioned—something your father doesn't understand either. It feels disrespectful to me. I know that you don't want me with your father, and even if you did, I would not let him sleep over with you in the same house. We are not married, and it doesn't feel right. You might believe that I am a prudish American, but my relationship with your father is private and means too much to me to treat it lightly." I was angry, and I was sorry that I had not controlled my temper better but not about what I had said to Mimi. I had let her get away with too many things in the past weeks for Theo's sake, and she just hit me on the wrong night at the wrong time. "I've said enough, Mimi, and I will stop before I say something that I don't mean. I am going to take a nice hot bath and go to bed."

As I turned to leave, Mime spoke up in a softer, pleading voice. "Wait, Ana, I am sorry for what I said. I am sorry about your husband. Katie told me about the circumstances of his death. I just felt like you should have said something to me. Lena has never mentioned your husband, and neither has Sara."

"I think they are just protecting me. That's why they never mention Mark. And they know how much your father means to me."

"How much does he mean to you, Ana?"

I looked at Mimi and decided that she had opened this up, and I wasn't going to hide my feelings any longer. "I love him with all of my heart." I turned, went into my bedroom, and shut the door softly.

What I didn't know was what Katie had told Mimi about the good times she and other students had had at my house and how much she liked me as a teacher. She had told Mimi how Mark and I took students under our wings when things went wrong in their lives. How much we cared for the students we worked with. Mimi was surprised at how often we took strangers into our home and helped them out. It was not the German way. Katie had also gone into detail about Theo's interview with her at my apartment in Germany and how he had tried to warn her.

Mimi's attitude slowly changed, and she was kinder, with fewer snide remarks. She seemed to be healing from her broken heart as well. Because she was so beautiful, she attracted the attention of many young men in her classes. She and Katie went out often on double dates or just met groups of kids at local hangouts. Mimi appeared to be having a good time, but she berated the students she knew about their lack of purpose in life. She was a fierce debater about anything and everything. She could argue the top off a peanut butter jar. Then she met Brandon Walker, who was a little older and a premed student. He had served in the marines and was tough as nails. A match made in debate heaven. They didn't agree on anything. He wasn't Jewish, but I believed that Theo might like him, because he was honest and had integrity. What I liked about him the most was that he could keep Mimi in check.

Life had settled into a fairly pleasant routine with three women in the house. It helped having three separate bathrooms. Katie was staying on through the semester and auditing one class. The reinstatement decision would not happen until January, so she had found a job and was doing some volunteer work in the library on campus. Mimi had also decided that she wanted to work, because two classes did not keep her that busy. Although the girls did not pay rent, and I would not take money from Theo for Mimi, I was pleased that both girls kept the refrigerator and pantry full. Of course they ate most of the food, but it was good all around that they helped out in this way. They also cooked dinner several times a week, for which I thanked them. Both girls worked off their calories at the gym in our town house complex. They were well known and liked by the staff. Katie had gotten some of her confidence and self-esteem back. Her parents would be moving back to the States in a few months, and she was looking forward to taking Mimi to visit them. Mimi and Katie were making plans to get an apartment together next semester, if Katie was reinstated. Mimi had decided that she did not want to move back to Heidelberg to go to school or live with her mother and stepfather. That was a touchy subject which I never brought up. There was also the matter of Brandon, who I believed was playing a major part in her decision to stay here.

Thanksgiving was fast approaching, and I spoke to the girls about how we wanted to celebrate the day. Theo would also be here and had never had an American Thanksgiving. Normally, we would have gone to the Capellos' for a huge dinner, but this year would be different. Neva had fallen and sprained her left wrist badly and could not cook. She was having dinner with Alphonso and his family. Palmer Addison was taking Lena and Sara to Denver to meet his parents. That relationship had taken a decidedly serious turn after 9/11. Lena, still unsure that she could ever have a good relationship, didn't talk about it much, but I could see that she was falling in love with Palmer. He was a good, decent man and would make a good father for Sara. She adored him.

For the first time in years, I would be having Thanksgiving at home, and in my new home, at that. Mimi, Katie, and I had just finished dinner one night when I brought up the subject.

"Girls, you know Thanksgiving is next week…"

"What is Thanksgiving?" Mimi asked. "I wondered when you would be having a religious holiday."

"It's not religious," said Katie. "It's a day we make a huge feast, with turkey and a lot of other food, and give thanks for whatever we are thankful for."

"So, it's just a day to eat?"

"No," said Katie. "Well, yes, and football on television, but there is American history behind why we do this. It's a national holiday. I will tell you about it later, Mimi. Are you going away, Ana?" I had asked Katie to call me Ana, since Mimi did, and we were living together.

"No, not at all," I replied. "That's what I want to talk about. We will be here together, and your dad will be here, Mimi, so I wanted to plan our menu together, because it will be your and Theo's first Thanksgiving. My dining room is not as big in this town house as it was in my old house, but I think we can easily accommodate a couple of other people, if either one of you wants to invite someone. If we did a buffet, we could have a few more, so let's talk about the guest list."

"You want us to help you plan this, Ana?" Mimi seemed very surprised.

"Well, I definitely would appreciate it, Mimi. Both of you live here, and unless you have other plans, it should be a joint decision." What I didn't know was that Mimi would have never been included in planning an adult holiday in Germany. Her mother would not have asked for her opinion. The only thing Mimi had told me about Marta was that she was one of the most beautiful women in the world, and her father would never marry someone unless she was as beautiful. That was said in the early days. There had been no ugly remarks in several weeks. Things had become quite pleasant, and I think Katie was the reason. She was a good buffer. Katie liked me, and Mimi liked Katie, so peace reigned in the house.

I went over the normal Thanksgiving fare: turkey, mashed potatoes, stuffing, gravy, and the like, and then I turned to Mimi. "I think it would be fun to have some German food, Mimi. What do you think would fit in?"

Mimi thought for a minute. "Red cabbage. My father loves it. Would that work?"

"Absolutely, I like it, too. What else?"

"Sweet-and-sour green beans? A cucumber salad?"

"Excellent. Those are great suggestions. Do you know how to make them?" I asked Mimi.

"Ja, so easy. Tante Selma taught me long ago."

"Good. What about you, Katie, what would you like to make or suggest we have?"

Katie had a ready answer. "I can get pies where I work. I know Germans like cheesecake and apple tarts, so I can get those and a pumpkin pie. Is that OK?"

The girls were really into it and decided whom they wanted to invite. It looked like it could be ten of us, so we thought we would put the leaves in the dining room table to see if we could get everyone seated around it. We laughed and laughed, because it would be a tight squeeze, but by putting all the food in the kitchen, it would work.

"Where will my father be staying?" asked Mimi.

I was surprised that she asked this, because he always stayed in a hotel in Washington or one near the town house. "I am not sure yet where he will be staying. One of the two usual places, I assume. Why did you ask, Mimi?"

She had a sly look on her face. "I thought since it was a holiday, he could stay here."

I didn't understand at first. "Here? No, I think he will stay where he normally does."

"No, Ana. I think my father would want to stay here with you." She looked at me directly. "He wants to be with you."

I blushed. "Mimi, your father and I have already worked that out."

"OK, Ana, it's up to you. I don't care." She walked out of the room, but I knew something had changed. She was giving me her approval to be with her father. I was surprised and delighted. Mimi's attitude had really changed toward me. I thought we could be friends after all, but I still wasn't going to sleep with Theo in the same house with his daughter. On that issue, I was definite.

"Ana," Katie said, "maybe Mimi and I could stay in a motel, and you and Inspektor Volker could have some privacy. This is your home, not ours."

"Don't be silly, Katie," I answered. "Theo and I will be fine. Don't give it another thought." But I thought about it. How nice it would be for Theo and me to be together. The times when he had been back had been a strain, and we needed time together. I kept telling myself that things would be different next semester.

Thanksgiving turned out to be a blast. It was a true German American day. Theo loved the food, especially the German dishes that Mimi had prepared. He was very proud that his daughter had contributed to the dinner. Mimi's dishes were a hit with everyone, and she beamed with pleasure. She had invited Brandon Walker and, just as I suspected, he and Theo hit it off. They both rooted for the same football team. There were three other boys and two girls invited, who contributed to a boisterous day.

Before we started eating, I asked if the group minded my giving a prayer for Thanksgiving. Then we went around the table, and each of us named the things we were most grateful for. "It's always been a Thanksgiving tradition at the Capellos' house. I hope you won't mind."

It was very touching. September 11 was mentioned more than once. Katie thanked Theo for helping her get out of prison. Mimi surprised both Theo and me by saying that she was grateful that she had had this chance to live in America at this particular time. There was much to be read into her statement—glad she had had a place to recover from her broken heart, glad that she had met Brandon, glad to be in America as the national spirit was trying to heal—and then she added one more thing. "I am grateful that my father is happy again." She looked at both of us and smiled. I was touched to the core.

When Theo's turn came, he simply looked at me and said, "I am grateful for Ana."

My heart felt full, and I felt my eyes tearing. I was holding his hand under the table and squeezed it.

Then it was my turn. "I don't know if I can say all the things that I am grateful for this year. I am so saddened by the terrorist attacks, but this has been the most wonderful year in many years." I looked at Theo. "Thank you for being the person you are and for being in my life." I leaned over and kissed him. The table erupted in hoots and clapping. After all, they were all young and loved romance. It also broke the heaviness that had come upon the table, and afterward, we had a lighthearted, fun-filled day with a lot of laughter and happiness shared by all.

It was late when Katie and Mimi's friends left. Both girls had been whispering all day and laughing. I wondered what they were up to, but I was too busy to give it a lot of thought. Katie asked us to come into the living room and sit down for a second. Theo had been helping me clean up the remainder of the dessert dishes. When we were seated, Mimi and Katie stood before us with their hands behind their backs like two little schoolgirls.

"What is this?" asked an amused Theo. He had not looked this relaxed since we were in Italy together. "What are you two up to?"

Katie started. "Well, we thought—Mimi and I, that is—that you deserved time together, so we got you a present of sorts. Well, not a real present, but kind of a present—"

Mimi interrupted. In her abrupt, brusque manner she said, "This could go on all night. Katie and I are going to stay with some friends until Sunday so you can have time alone. We won't be here. Father can stay here."

Theo and I were stunned into silence. It was almost like we couldn't comprehend what was being said.

"Well, say something." Katie laughed. "We aren't going to be here. Mimi and I are going to stay at Brandon's place tonight, and then we are going to Emily's the next two nights."

I finally responded weakly, "You don't have to do that."

But Theo had gotten his voice back and was on his feet hugging both girls. "Like hell they don't. This is wonderful. Great idea. I am going to go over to the hotel and check out right now before they change their minds." Everyone laughed, and Theo and the girls prepared to leave.

"Ana, I will be back right away. Wait for me." Theo was as excited as a child. I had not realized how difficult this had been for him.

As the girls were taking off, both made silly remarks about how we should be careful and use protection, laughing hilariously at themselves.

I was suddenly alone in my house for the first time in two months. It felt unnaturally quiet. But then I thought Theo is coming. I decided to set a romantic mood. The house was relatively cleaned up after our feast, but it still looked a little disheveled. I straightened the pillows on the sofa, turned down the lights, and put on some soft music. I found a bottle of champagne in the refrigerator and put it in an ice bucket on a silver tray with two champagne flutes and chocolates. I then went into the bedroom and changed the sheets so that they would be crisp and clean. The bed was turned down and inviting. I lit candles all around. Now for me. I took a nice bubble bath and put on a sexy black nightgown. Just in time. I heard a rapping on the door.

I opened the door. Theo took one look at me and sighed. "Oh, my God, Ana, I have missed you." He pulled me to his chest and held me tightly. "You feel and smell so good. I don't want to let you go…ever." He kissed me deeply and passionately. "I want to…I want to…" But he couldn't stop kissing me to finish his own sentence.

I pulled away. "Theo, we have all night. We have three nights and three days. We don't have to rush. You can even take your coat off."

He laughed. "Ana, I look at you, and I am just like a boy with his first girl. I can hardly wait. He traced his finger along the top of my nightgown. "You are so soft and warm, like Cara."

"Cara?" I said questioningly. "The cat?"

"Ja," he said, never removing his finger as it went deeper. "The damn thing sleeps with me when I go to the farm."

"You let Cara sleep with you now?" I laughed. This man who never wanted a cat now slept with it.

"Enough about the cat. Come with me." He started toward the bedroom but stopped when he got to the door. "You did all of this for me, Ana?" as he took in the candlelit room with the turned-down bed.

"I wanted it to be special. Could you open the champagne, Theo? We deserve a little toast to each other." And our night began. We had had many passionate nights together, but somehow this one felt different, more solid. More than sex. It felt like loving. I could not get enough of Theo. I never wanted him to stop touching and kissing me. He filled me up completely. There was urgency and there was slowness. There was tenderness. There were tears. Mine. "Ana, why do you cry? You always cry."

"It's so hard to explain, Theo. Our lovemaking is almost spiritual to me. You awaken in me the deepest part of my soul. I love you so much." Theo was on his side, propped up on his elbow, playing with my hair with his other hand. He kissed my eyes, then my nose, and finally my lips. "I will always be here, Ana." He touched my breast where my heart was located. "As long as you want me, I will be in here." He took my hand and placed it on his chest. "And you are here for me, forever. You are the love of my life. There will never be another woman for me. Not ever. I love only you."

Theo left the Monday after Thanksgiving to return to Germany. I didn't know when he would come back. He went back to the hotel Sunday night when the girls returned. Mimi teased her father. "He's hot, my father, isn't he, Ana?" Theo looked very uncomfortable. But I laughed. "Yes, Mimi, he is very hot, your father. Very hot." Theo was embarrassed, but all three of us women laughed. The girls said no more, but they were very sweet around me for the next few weeks as we resumed our normal life together. Things had changed between Mimi and me. I could tell she didn't hate me any longer, and I would miss her when she moved out. I also knew that Theo and I would be OK. We would weather this long-distance romance, no matter what happened.

# KATHRYN

I

True to her word, Francesca Botti was waiting for me at the train station in Orvieto. "Buon giorno, Kathryn!" She laughed gaily and hugged me. "Come stai?"

"Excited, nervous, worried, and a little anxious," I said.

"No, no, don't worry. I am here to get you all settled in. You have several days before your classes begin, and I will introduce you to my cousin, Betta, who lives here. She speaks good English. Let's go up to the top and get you into your flat for the next two months."

Francesca had found a wonderful little jewel for me to live in. It was above a well-known restaurant on the Corsa Cavour, where all the upscale shops were located and along the Via del Duomo, which led to the beautiful cathedral. It couldn't have been in a more central location. I was so pleased.

The apartment was small, but it had everything I needed and was flooded with light. There was a large window in the living area from which I could see the top of the cathedral. Along one side of the living room was a tiny galley-type kitchen that had folding doors to close off the area when it was not in use. Near the kitchen was a dining table and two chairs beside a window that looked out on the street behind the Corsa Cavour. Included in this room were a small TV, a sofa, an overstuffed chair, and occasional tables. There was a small bedroom and a bathroom, which, surprisingly, was quite modern. It was a perfect little apartment, and I knew that I would be happy here.

"Oh, Francesca, this is marvelous. Much more than I expected. Who is my landlord?"

"He is the owner of the restaurant downstairs. Come, I will introduce you, and then we will go to the market to get some food for you."

Bernardo Ricucci was the owner of Via Tavola, another surprise. It looked very urban inside, almost New Yorkish in nature. It was sleek with a lot of chrome, mirrors, and black. Yet it had warmth from the flower arrangements and candles on the tables and around the room. I remembered passing by this restaurant when we visited Orvieto with the tour. Bernardo was very friendly and welcomed me with a kiss on both cheeks, in the European manner. "Welcome to Orvieto. I hope that you will be comfortable here and will dine often with us." It smelled delicious, and I realized I was hungry. I told him I might have my first dinner with him. He was delighted. Maria Ricucci, his wife, was not as forthcoming but friendly enough.

Francesca helped me become oriented to the city and walked me to Lingua Si, the language school, which turned out to be only five streets away on the Piazza Cahen. We spent a few minutes walking around the small garden at the school that was for student use. After an hour or so, Francesca bade me farewell, and I was alone in my new apartment.

I was feeling excited but also a bit overwhelmed by my undertaking. Coming to Orvieto was like nothing I had ever done before in my life. It was thrilling, but I had never lived in a foreign country, and the strangeness of it all was beginning to hit me. I had several days before my classes began, and I wasn't sure what I would do with myself. I had only been in Italy a little over twenty-four hours, and I was missing my old familiar life.

I decided that I needed to get out of the apartment and walk up the street to the beautiful thirteenth-century duomo. It was warm in the piazza, which was a perfect place to sit and observe people who walked by. What I had not taken into account was that Orvieto was a small town, and although I didn't know anyone, many people had heard of me through Francesca. It didn't take long before one or another person stopped to say hello and welcome me. Most spoke good English, but I was very happy that I had some Italian vocabulary to respond with. It made a big difference.

By the time classes started the following Monday, Orvieto was feeling more like my home away from home. I had walked from one end of the town to the other. The town was divided into four quarters. It had quite an active passeggiata in the evenings. It seemed as if everyone in the town came out to walk and share with one another the day's happenings. It was a way of strengthening the sense of community in the town. It was also easy to imagine myself back in the twelfth century as I walked through the medieval city at night with the yellow street lights casting a golden hue over the cobblestones. I felt transported back to another time.

With equal amounts of anticipation and apprehension, I arrived at Lingua Si right on time. The small language school was founded in 1998. The method of teaching was immersion, which made sense to me when I saw the mixture of ages and nationalities who would be participating. There was an initial interview to determine the level of placement. Since I knew some Italian, my interviewer wanted to place me in an intermediate beginner's group, but I really wanted to start at their most basic level.

Within an hour, our group had formed. There were five Japanese men, one young French woman, a Canadian woman who looked to be in her midforties, a woman from New Zealand who looked like a sixties American hippie, a beautiful, blonde woman from Sweden, a man from England, two

German businessmen who looked very serious, and me. As we were milling about waiting for the group to be completed, I learned that the Japanese men and the French woman could speak very little English. All of the rest spoke English in varying degrees. The Canadian and Swedish women, as well as the British man, could speak French. Only the Japanese men spoke their native language. If any of the five could speak another language, they never did. It was altogether a very international group.

I was grateful that I had taken my Italian class in the summer. Still, it was confusing, and my brain hurt by the end of the first four-hour session. The staff, however, was wonderful, and the atmosphere was warm and friendly. There was a lot of laughter at mistakes, but it was a serious academic program. The instructors were determined to give students what they needed. We were given assignments and encouraged to speak only Italian in restaurants and shops. Our first assignment was to break into groups and have lunch together.

Before we ended for our first day, our instructor informed us that over the next two weeks, there would be dinners at local restaurants with the teachers, hikes in the countryside, and excursions to neighboring towns, cooking classes, and winery visits. She also informed us that the Teatro Mancinelle, one of the loveliest theaters in all of Italy, had a full agenda of diverse performances during the next two weeks, and we were encouraged to go as often as possible. All of these things were optional, but I liked the ideas presented and looked forward to participating in many of them.

The five women opted to have lunch together the first day. It was fun and gratifying for me to hear the others share their frustration with the immersion method, but we all agreed that there could be no other way with so many nationalities. My classmates complimented me on my Italian and thought I was doing well.

Inga, the Swedish woman, was the first. "Kathryn, you speak Italian already."

"Not really, but I did take a summer class in the States so that I wouldn't be a complete fool," I responded. "I was afraid that my brain was too old to learn a foreign language."

Inga looked amused. "But you are not old, Kathryn, so your brain is not old—it is ready to learn."

I laughed. "My brain forgot to hear that about halfway through our lessons today. I was getting hopelessly muddled."

I found that Inga also lived on the Corsa Cavour also, but at the opposite end. We walked back to our apartments and agreed to meet for dinner that night. It was much easier to talk to one person than four others in a multilanguage environment.

The second morning began with a review of the first day, and the words began to take on a familiar sound. Slowly new vocabulary was introduced, and we role-played scenarios in which to use the language. It really was fun, and I was getting a lot from it. I felt like I was learning and retaining it, as well. When our lessons ended for that day, the British man asked if he could join the ladies at lunch.

"I'm afraid that the Japanese really enjoy being together, and the two German men seem to want to discuss business. Do you mind awfully?" We were delighted to have him, and he was very charming. His name was Robin Tremont.

Robin, as it turned out, wanted to retire in Italy and needed to speak the language better. "I am so bloody tired of wet, cold days that I want to live the remainder of my time blissfully in the sun with good wine and pasta."

"And your wife," asked Inga in Italian. "What does she want?"

"Thank God there is no signora! She went off to find herself some seven to ten years ago. We were completely mismatched. I think she is still looking. Don't ask me to say that in Italian. I haven't a clue."

Robin kept us laughing. I had not paid much attention to him at first, but he really was quite good-looking. Or maybe it was his charm and wit that I found so attractive. He must be near retirement now, I thought. He looks about my age. He had clear blue eyes and dark hair. He looked like he was a little less than six feet tall and was slim. He wore his clothes well in the way that British men are prone to do.

"Do you have children, Robin?" I asked.

"A parcel full." He laughed. "There are four at last count, scattered here and there. There are even a couple of grands-two boys, mischievous little devils, they are. They all came from wife number two. She left when they went to university."

Inga looked shocked. "You have three marriages?" She struggled with that in Italian, but we all understood where she was going with that line of thinking.

"Actually, it was a bit more like four, when all is said and done." He looked a little sheepish.

"Four!" We all exploded at once.

Margie, the New Zealander, said out loud what we all must have been thinking in one form or another. "My God, man! Are you out of your bloody mind?"

"Completely and utterly. There is not a cell left to count on." He looked completely at ease with a table full of women questioning him about his married life. Even Effie, the French girl, was giggling.

"Now ladies, as much as I love discussing my past indiscretions—no, I haven't gone there yet, have I?" His eyes were twinkling. "I think there are things best left unsaid. What we really must talk about is dinner tonight and perhaps the jazz concert at the Teatro. Who is up for that?"

We all nodded in agreement. Robin clearly was a man who enjoyed being with women and taking charge. "Here is what I am thinking: perhaps a small meal in an enoteca. There is an interesting one on Via Valle that I would like to try. We could sample crostini, bruschette, salamis, or cheeses, and then after the concert we could go have a dolce—something sinfully sweet."

I spoke up. "I would like that very much. I haven't had the nerve to go into a wine bar alone. I have tried the Orvieto Classico, and it's delicious."

"Dear girl, we must do that. Your desires will be met!" Robin slapped his hand on the table, and we all laughed again. He really was fun to be with. It was easy to see why four women married him and easy to see why they didn't stay with him. He was definitely a ladies' man. We were making final arrangements to meet one another that evening, when the restaurant owner approached our table with urgency.

"The Americana signora? Who is she?"

"That's me," I said, alarmed.

"Your country is being attacked! Come to see the television. Prego! Prego!"

We all jumped up and ran inside to see a plane flying into the second tower. The sight was beyond our comprehension. "I don't understand," I said. We all stood riveted to the television inside the restaurant, each echoing the others' thoughts. "Dear God. Oh my God! What the bloody hell?" The Italians were just as mesmerized. It was a little after two o'clock in the afternoon in Orvieto but only nine in the morning in New York.

When I heard that the Pentagon had been hit, I broke down. "Kathryn, do you have family, loved ones there?" asked Doreen, the Canadian. She had been unusually quiet.

"No, no, I don't have anyone in either place. I live an hour from the Pentagon. It's just so close to home."

Effie had turned deathly white. "Effie, are you OK?" we asked.

She seemed to have difficulty saying anything but managed to choke out some words which only Doreen seemed to understand. "Her brother, Armand, works in one of the buildings of the World Trade Center."

"Sweet Jesus," swore Margie. "Is there someone she can call or e-mail to find out about his safety? " We can try, but it may be too soon to find out much," said Doreen. "I'll go with her. We will meet everyone back at the enoteca tonight."

"I think I will try to get through to my son, Sammy, at the Internet café. There is one that I have been using just down from my apartment." I prepared to leave. Inga touched my shoulder and said she would walk with me.

Robin turned to us. "Ladies, if there is anything I can do to help, please let me know. Anything." We thanked him and started the short walk back to the Corsa Cavour.

It was a beautiful, sunny, warm day. It seemed surreal that a horrendous event had taken place back in America. Here I walked on top of a mountain, seemingly protected from everything, and back home, the world had turned upside down.

# II

There was a church service in the duomo that night that was beautiful and compelling. The entire town turned out, and there was standing room only in the piazza outside. The American and Italian flags stood together to indicate solidarity. At the end of the service, a small band played "America, the Beautiful," and everyone stood and touched their hearts. Candles were passed around until everyone inside and out had lit theirs. The service ended with a benediction, and people slowly made their way out of the church into the streets. No one wanted to disperse. People stood around speaking softly, hugging, and comforting one another. Most of the group in our class found one another, the Japanese being the exception, and declared a coffee or drink was in order.

After spending a restless night, I entered the classroom the next day, and I was touched all over again. There hung in each room a big American flag, and in our class, a French one for Effie's brother. He was missing, and she had not been able to find out any information. Her family was frantic. She thought she should go back to France, but her family urged her to stay in Orvieto until something was known. The third day of our course was grim, so unlike the first two, but we decided as a group to press on. I was distracted and had a difficult time concentrating. The staff was so kind, and we could tell that the lessons had been modified so that they were easier.

The days passed, and there were many poignant memories. I was grateful that my family in America was safe and that my new Italian family, the entire town of Orvieto, was such a comfort. Almost from the very minute of the attack, tiny American flags appeared in shops and windows all over the city. Italians would stop me in the street to hug me or tell me how sorry they were. Strangers brought me food, flowers, wine, fruit, desserts, as if I were suffering a personal death. I couldn't have been better cared for. It was the end of the week before we found out that Effie's brother had survived.

Robin decided that a celebration was in order and that we must do something special for the weekend. He arranged for all of us who wanted to, to take the train into Florence. Our instructors had some suggestions for nontouristy things to do and good restaurants to dine in. It sounded like just what we needed.

Since I had been in Florence just a few months earlier, the city looked very familiar to me, and I had no trouble navigating around. Just four of us opted to take this trip: Robin, Inga, Effie, and me. French was spoken for Effie's sake, and I marveled at how Europeans could switch back and forth between languages with such fluidity. Everyone seemed to know a smattering of many languages, and they all had traveled extensively. I felt like a rural hick.

I did have one trick up my sleeve, however. Francesca had shown us excellent gold shops when we had visited Florence in May, and I could lead us to the best jewelry stores, where we could bargain for good prices. I wanted to get Karen something really nice because of her help with the renovations on my house. We had been in e-mail contact daily, and she had kept me informed of what was going on. There were many times over the past few days when I wondered if it had been smart to have all the work done while I was away, but when I really thought about it, I was happy not to be there. Karen was tough, and she would bully the contractors in my house as she would in her own. When I returned home, the work should be nearly complete. Just in time for the holidays.

Robin excused himself to go off sightseeing by himself. "Ladies, we will gather before dinner for drinks. Have a happy time. Spend lots of euros and make the merchants smile." In some ways, Robin was the perfect man. He loved women, he was a great companion, he was not opinionated, and he did not cling. How he was as a husband may have been a different story, but in this capacity, he was the right man to have along.

We found wonderful jewelry for ourselves and for others. I had been thinking of Jenn quite a bit in the past week since the attacks, so estranged from her children, and I remembered how much I had loved her as a daughter-in-law when she and Sammy first married. She was sharp, quick-witted, and full of laughter. I had not seen that person in years, probably since Chapin had been born. Looking back, I realized that she may have had some postpartum depression even then, and it had gotten worse with each baby. Left untreated, it culminated with Brooke's birth. Poor girl, I thought. Having children changed women in many ways. Jenn also had the added pressure of her job, not to mention her mother.

I saw the sweetest little gold pin of a mother with a baby and bought it for her on the spot. I decided that I would mail it right away and not wait until I got home to give it to her. I wanted her to know that I was thinking of her. We had not spoken in months. Just thinking about her, Sammy, and the children made me sad. Would they ever put their lives back together? I realized there was nothing I could do about the situation and, for the time being, I just needed to concentrate on my life in Orvieto.

It was a marvelous weekend, and we all returned in a good mood, ready to begin our final week of classes. Frustrating as it could be at times, the immersion method was working. I was learning Italian and felt more confident each day.

I also felt a solid friendship developing with Inga. She was probably in her late thirties or early forties. She was a very successful business woman in Sweden. She reminded me of Ana Douglas. Both women were so accomplished at such a young age. I wondered if my attraction to them was based on my own lost youth. I was aware that I envied their careers and wished I knew what I wanted to do with the rest of my life. I wasn't trained for anything and had never really worked.

I told Inga one day at lunch how much I admired her success so early in her life.

"Kathryn, how will you spend your time when you return to America?"

"You know, Inga, I am just beginning to think about it. I will be busy until the end of the year with the holidays, but after that, I am not sure. I feel at loose ends. Before this year, I had been a homemaker and took care of my husband and children. After he died, I baby-sat my grandchildren."

"So now is time for you," she said sweetly.

"Yes, there will be plenty of time for me, and I wanted that—want that—but I haven't really thought about what I want to do. I feel like I am in the middle of an adventure right now, and maybe that is what I will do—have more adventures."

We both laughed, but Inga turned more serious. "Do you have a man in your life, Kathryn?"

I blushed. "Oh my goodness, no. I haven't even thought of a male friend. I was so busy with my grandchildren that there was no time. And besides, I am a little too old now."

"Kathryn, that is…I don't know…ridiculous. You are so pretty and young. Why would you not want a man in your life again?"

"I guess that I just never thought about it or pursued it. I wouldn't know where to look or even if I want to look." I shrugged my shoulders. "You see, I am hopeless."

"No, no. You are not hopeless, not at all. Maybe you do need more adventures." She looked at me appraisingly. "Have you not noticed how the Italian men look at you?"

"What?" I was stunned. "What men?"

She laughed. "Oh yes, Kathryn. I have seen several men in town looking at you. Even our Robin. I think he sees you as a different sort of woman, maybe, than the ones he married. Men like you, Kathryn. Maybe because you are not interested. Maybe you are a challenge."

I was definitely uncomfortable with this conversation. "Inga, enough! You are making me blush, and don't start with Robin. We are taking a cooking class together in the afternoon."

"Cooking?" Inga laughed. "I wonder what he is cooking up." She laughed again, and we parted ways as we came to our street. I had to rush so that I would not be late for my Italian cuisine class.

It was one of those extracurricular classes offered through the school, and it was taught in a small villa outside of Orvieto. I usually met Robin at the funicular station, and we would ride down together and take a bus to the little town where our instructor lived. The best part of learning to cook was the feast we had afterward, which also included local wines.

On our bus ride, Robin asked me what my plans were after the language classes ended. "I will be staying on in Orvieto another few weeks and will take the intermediate beginner's class the second week of October."

"What in the world will you do in that small town on top of a mountain for all of that time?" He had the most incredulous look on his face.

"You mean in addition to missing all of you?" I laughed. "I have already arranged through the school for a local tutor to help me keep up with the Italian that I have learned in the beginner's group. I want to go back to Florence and spend at least a day in Siena and perhaps Pisa. I have an Italian friend, Francesca, whom I met in May, whom I want to visit. Her cousin Betta lives in Orvieto, and we have had lunch together once, so I am hoping to get together with her again."

Robin interrupted "Enough! And to think that I was worried about you."

"Really, Robin? You were worried about me? Whatever for?"

"I don't know. You seem so…" He was at a loss for words.

"I seem what?" Now I was curious.

"Maybe, vulnerable? I am not sure, but I can't imagine you traipsing around by yourself."

"How sweet of you to think of me, Robin, but really, I am fine. I am sad about the attacks on America, but personally I am fine. Better than I have been for years, actually." It was true. I felt remarkably happy and adventure-some. "I am not really traipsing all around, you know. I am very selective about where I will be going. Inga is staying an additional week, and we will have one day to ourselves before she heads off to other parts of Italy. How about you? Are you back to England right away?"

"Actually, not. I will take a few days to look at possible retirement areas. I am thinking about Tuscany or Umbria, although the Amalfi coast is a pos-sibility. There are some colonies of Brits down there, and I want talk with other retirees—pros and cons and all that, you see."

"Good idea. I would think it would be a big step to move to another country." We had arrived at the house for our cooking lesson. "Robin, I would just like to tell you how much I have enjoyed getting to know you. You have been so much fun. If you ever come to America, please call me." I meant it. Womanizer or not, I liked him.

He gave me an honest look. "You are a very different woman, Kathryn. I shall look you up. I promise." He took my hand as we got off the bus. "Not at all like British women."

I just smiled and decided that I wasn't going to engage in that dialogue.

# III

The second week ended all too soon. There was a little ceremony to mark our graduation from the two-week course in a lovely restaurant, La Polumba, which was just off the Corso Cavon in a little alley. There were many toasts and personal comments, all in Italian. We certainly were not fluent but confident in our attempts. I stood up before we said good night and expressed my extreme gratitude to the group for being supportive after the September 11 attacks and told each one of them that I would never forget them for as long as I lived. We all took pictures together. I had pictures taken of me with the two German men, the five Japanese, the "girls" with Robin, and my instructors. I also had Robin take a picture of Inga and me. I had talked her into coming for a visit to the States with her boyfriend within the next few months.

We had lunch together a final time before she left Orvieto the following Monday. "I feel like so much happened in the past two weeks, and now it is over," she said.

"I know. I feel exactly the same way but more so. I am going to miss all of you very much." I was feeling a little bit teary. This group had meant so much to me.

"I am happy that I am not returning home and going back to work immediately," Inga reflected. "I need time to think about everyone and the school. Kathryn, I hope that your next class will be a happy one for you. Are you missing America? Do you want to go back?"

"Yes and no. I don't feel that my time here is completed. I need to stay longer, but I also wish I could see my family for a short while."

"How are they coping?" Inga asked.

"I think everyone is trying to get their lives back to some kind of normal. Something good has happened from all of this that makes me feel hopeful," I said. "My daughter-in-law seems to be taking more of an interest in the children. She is spending more time with the baby and individual time with the boys. My son has e-mailed me that she doesn't seem as depressed."

"That's wonderful, Kathryn," Inga responded enthusiastically.

"The biggest surprise for me was that I received an e-mail from Jenn thanking me for the little pin that I sent her from Florence. She said that she was touched that I thought of her, and she has been wearing it almost daily. She said that it made her think of herself and Brooke, and I am beginning to have a little more hope about my son and his family now."

"I think maybe it is a good thing that you are not there," said Inga.

"Really, why do you think that?" I was curious, because I also thought it was good.

"It would be easy, I think, for them to depend on you. You are very nurturing, Kathryn. You are like my mother—always taking care of people. But unlike my mother, you are very sexy in a subtle way."

"Why, Inga, what a thing to say." I was taken aback.

"I keep telling you that, Kathryn, and you will not believe me. But I am telling you this before I leave. There is a man out there waiting for you. Keep your eyes open and don't miss him!" She pointed her finger at me in a playful way. "I mean it, Kathryn. You don't know your power!"

Although I laughed with her, I really didn't know what to think about her statements. I had never thought of myself as sexy, and now that I turned sixty-three, I felt that boat had sailed.

"I can see that you still don't believe me, but you don't see what I see. You are slim, good figure, beautiful face, and all the Italian men love your blonde hair. But the important part is that you act like you don't care. I think that is what intrigued our Robin."

"Oh, please! Don't start on Robin again. He is a faded memory now. Off to find some young Italian girl he can retire with on the Amalfi coast or in a Tuscan villa."

We finished our lunch and hugged each other good-bye for now. I knew that we would always stay in touch, and we would see each other again.

# IV

The next day, Tonio Sierra, my Italian tutor, met me at the language school. He was a young man, barely out of his teens, studying at the University of Perugia. He planned to study engineering at MIT in the next year and wanted to perfect his English. He looked like a Renaissance sculpture with a head of curly, black hair and flashing brown eyes. We agreed that we would speak Italian for one hour and English for the next. We were unexpectedly compatible.

When it was Tonio's turn to speak English, he asked, "Signora Wynham, where is your husband?" I thought that was an odd thing for a young man to ask when he should have been full of questions about university life in America.

When I explained that I was a widow with three grandchildren, he then asked why I did not wear black. "In America, Tonio, women do not wear black after the funeral. Sometimes they don't even wear black to the funeral. We have become very lax in our culture." He looked a little shocked. I asked him about his family.

He said they owned a winery, and the entire family lived on the grounds. His grandfather was a widower, and his three aunts were living with his nonno. His parents came home on weekends from Milan. He had two older sisters, one of whom was married and expecting the first grandchild and the other was in a school for architecture in Rome. His mother and father both worked in the winery business. Tonio said he was expected to work in the winery when he finished school, and his brother-in-law was also part of the family business.

The two hours flew by, and we had a good time together exploring each other's culture. Tonio and I worked out a schedule where we would go out into the countryside and other towns to help broaden my Italian vocabulary. We fell into a good routine, and he taught me vocabulary that I would have never learned in school: teenage slang. But besides that, I was learning a less formal Italian and the dialect of the region. By the end of the first week, Tonio had taken me to the university and a museum in Perugia, the Etruscan ruins in Orvieto, the marketplaces in Spello and Spoleto, and several other places of interest. All along the way, everyone knew him. He was like Francesca, I thought. I wondered if all Italians knew one another in the entire region, and I asked him one day.

"No, no, there are many we do not know, Signora Kathryn." By this time I had talked him into being more casual with me. "But remember, my family owns a business, and we must sell our wines all over, plus we have lived in this area for many generations." It was hard for me to explain to Tonio that sometimes people in America did not know their next-door neighbors. "But that is not possible. How could you not know?" I just shrugged. I didn't have the vocabulary in Italian or the desire in English to talk about how distant we had become as a people. One of things that had drawn me to Italy, and especially a small town like Orvieto, was that everyone knew everyone and had for generations.

The second week of being tutored, which was my fourth week in Italy, brought me two unexpected surprises. The first was the return of Robin Tremont.

I had just returned to my apartment after having dinner at Via Tavolo downstairs. I had become friends with Maria and Bernardo Ricucci, although it had taken time for Maria to warm up to me. I think she was threatened a little by a single woman living so independently in Orvieto. I talked about my grandchildren whenever we were together, and I think that broke the ice, plus I paid no attention to Ricardo. I managed to have dinner there two or three nights a week and had become a regular, and in doing so, got to know some of the shopkeepers on the Corso Cavon better.

I was going over vocabulary words from my lesson with Tonio when I heard a knock at my door. This was so unusual that I was startled. "Yes, who is there?" I asked a little timidly.

"Hello, Kathryn, it's Robin here."

"Robin Tremont?"

"Yes, of course," he said confidently.

I opened the door, and there stood Robin with a bottle of wine and a huge smile.

"Robin," I said with a quick hug. "Whatever brings you back to Orvieto?"

"Well," he said as he stepped inside, "I am on my way back to England and thought I would check to see how you are doing."

"How thoughtful of you. But as you can see, I am doing quite well." I was a little skeptical that Robin Tremont would go out of his way to check on me.

"Yes, you do look amazing, Kathryn, but I thought you always have done." His appraising look made me a bit uncomfortable. "Tell me what you have been doing in the past ten days since I last saw you whilst I uncork this bottle." He made himself completely at home as he looked around for a wine corker.

We sat in my small living room as I brought him up-to-date, but I could sense that he wasn't really interested. "I am having an early tutoring session with Tonio tomorrow morning to accommodate his studies in Perugia, so as pleasant as it has been to see you again, Robin, I am afraid that I will have to call it an early evening. Where are you staying? Maybe we could have lunch tomorrow if you are still in town."

"I thought I might like to stay with you tonight, Kathryn," he stated boldly, looking me square in the eye.

"Here?" I said shocked. "But Robin, you can see that I have no extra space for a visitor, and that sofa would hardly accommodate you."

"I don't mind sharing with you, Kathryn. Not in the least. I think we would do quite well together," he said, never taking his eyes off of me.

In an instant I realized that he wanted to sleep with me and, in that same instant, I also realized I didn't know how to handle this situation. There was no way that I was sleeping with Robin Tremont. I needed to get him out of my apartment, and I needed to save face, if I could. I decided to take a humorous approach.

"Robin, you are a cad!" I laughed. "I have my reputation to protect for my next three and a half weeks here, and I will not have the town's priest calling on me dousing me with incense and such because you have stayed over. Think of the scandal! No, it will not do. If you were old and ugly, I might get away with it. But look at you—no, it just won't do. Now, you must leave before I am completely compromised."

Robin was gracious in defeat and probably flattered, because I had made reference to his good looks. He took his leave, but not before he gave me a lingering kiss. "Are you absolutely sure?" he asked.

"I absolutely must be!" I dramatically clutched my heart. He laughed and off he went. I did not know where, and I did not see him again. "More's the pity," I heard him say at the bottom of the steps.

When I was sure that he had left, I came back in and locked my door. I wanted no surprises in the middle of the night. I didn't know what to make of Robin's visit. I had had no man in my life since my husband had died almost seven years ago. I really had not thought of men, but I had to admit that Robin's kiss had stirred something in me that had been dead for a long time. How I wished that Inga were here so that I could talk about this to her. I did plan to e-mail her right away, because I knew that she would be highly amused at Robin's nocturnal visit.

Tonio was right on time the next morning. I met him at the bottom of the hill after riding the funicular down. We were going to a farm that made olive oil. I had been looking forward to this trip, because I planned to buy some oil to take home.

Tonio took one look at me and said, "Signora Kathryn, are you well?"

"Why, yes, Tonio. What made you ask?"

"You look tired, Signora Kathryn, and not so…" He was fumbling for the word in English to indicate what he meant and at the same time trying to be polite.

"I think you mean "chipper." I laughed.

"Chipper," he repeated, confused. There was no way I could translate this in Italian or English that would make any sense, but he seemed to catch on.

"Si, Signora Kathryn, you do not have chipper like other days." I had to laugh. Tonio was the dearest young man. "Don't worry, Tonio, a few hours with you and all my chipper will be back." And it was. What I didn't tell him was that I had tossed and turned all night thinking about Robin's pass. What little I knew of Robin was enough to tell me that he was not interested in any kind of serious relationship. Did he see me as some kind of easy, desperate target? Was he the kind of man who took every opportunity that he saw, or would he look for an opportunity and pave the way? I just didn't know how to make sense of the whole episode. One thing I was sure of was that Robin had gone off on his merry way and would not give his visit and my rejection a second thought.

Despite it all, Tonio and I had an excellent day, and I learned more new vocabulary. Before he left, Tonio told me that he could not tutor me the next day but had arranged for his grandfather to spend the time with me, if I didn't mind. "My grandfather wants to meet you," he said simply.

"Your grandfather? Why?" I was thrown off because I was so comfortable with Tonio and our casual routine.

"I have told him many good things about you, Signora Kathryn, and he wants to meet you for himself. Don't worry. You will like my grandfather. Everyone likes Salvatore Sierra." he said reassuringly. "He will fetch you and take you back to our winery. That will be your lesson tomorrow. How wine is made."

"Fine, Tonio. I look forward to meeting your grandfather." I certainly can manage this for two or three hours tomorrow I thought, and it may help me learn a different way of life in Italy, much like the olive oil farm did today. That is what I am here for, after all. To absorb Italian culture and language. What I would soon find out is that I would also learn about amore in Italy, and that was something that I had not bargained for. Salvatore Sierra was my second surprise.

On the way back to my apartment that afternoon, I stopped at the Internet café and found I had two e-mails waiting for me. The first was from Sammy with some sad news. Judge Grayson Tyler, that lovely man who had been so sympathetic to our family and with whom I had a budding friendship, had perished in the World Trade Center attacks. He had gone to New York to visit his daughter and to look at possible retirement venues. While there, he had arranged to meet several retired attorneys and judges whom he had known in his career for breakfast at a restaurant at the top of one of the towers on September 11. Because they were so high up, they didn't stand a chance. I was immensely saddened by this news. With a heavy heart, I clicked on the second e-mail from Inga.

*Dear Kathryn,*

*Why am I not surprised that Robin visited you? He is a lech, to be sure, but don't un-derestimate yourself. Remember what I said to you. You are a very attractive woman. I am sure that Robin has not had many rejections, so this was good for him. Aside from Robin, open up your heart, Kathryn. There is a lovely man for you to meet. I know this, but I also know that it was not Robin. Cheers! Inga*

I could almost hear her tinkling laughter. I really missed her. Was she right? Should I think about another relationship in my life? What would that be like? I didn't have a clue how to find someone. Karen always seemed to be looking for a new partner. She didn't want to get married again, but she wanted someone in her life for companionship. She had hinted more than once that I would benefit from a relationship, but I had always pooh-poohed those thoughts. I had been too busy in the last few years to have a man in my life. Maybe this lovely man whom Inga referred to had come and gone, and I had missed him entirely. This was ridiculous thinking. I stood up and looked outside my window on the Corso Cavon and watched the late-afternoon shoppers hurry by. Most of the tourists had gone by now, so the town looked normal and less crowded.

As much as I tried, I couldn't shake the memory of Robin's lingering kiss. I had to admit that I'd liked it. It had been years since I had been kissed like that, and it felt good. It would have been easy with Robin—no regrets afterward—but was that what I wanted? No, I knew that. But what did I want? I felt like a can of worms had been opened up, and I couldn't put the lid back on, no matter how hard I tried. I decided to go out and take a walk to clear my head and prepare myself for the next day and meeting Tonio's grandfather.

# V

Salvatore Sierra was like no one I had ever met before in my life. As prearranged, I met him at the bottom of the hill at the funicular station. I saw this gorgeous man leaning on a silver Alfa Romeo Spider. The top was down on the car, and he stood with arms and legs crossed as he scanned the crowd coming down the funicular. Signor Sierra had close-cropped white hair that outlined his tanned olive complexion. He was a little taller than I and very fit. He was wearing jeans and a black cashmere V-neck sweater with a white T-shirt underneath. He had on black boots and sunglasses. He looked like an ad for Ralph Lauren. In fact, he reminded me of Ralph Lauren. The Italian version.

He came forward as I stepped onto the pavement. "Signora Wynham?" he said in perfect Oxford English. I had been worried that I would not be able to communicate with him. "I am Tonio's nonno, his grandfather." He took off his sunglasses, presented his hand, and gave me a big smile. It was a smile that made me instantly comfortable.

"Buon giorno, Signor Sierra. I am very happy to meet you," I replied in my best formal Italian.

"You are speaking excellent italiano," he said.

I laughed. "No, no. I am very happy that you speak English, but we must speak Italian for one hour. It is part of my arrangement with Tonio." I was very glad that I had taken care with my appearance that morning. I had worn a long black skirt with my flat, black Italian boots. Because the days had started getting a little chilly, I had put on a white cable-knit sweater and brought a black shawl. It was casual but appropriate. I was very happy to have the shawl since it seemed the top would stay down on the car.

"How did you know who I was?" I asked Signor Sierra as he led me to his car. He laughed easily and said, "Tonio described you, and we have few blondes in Orvieto. You also look American."

"Americans have a look?" I asked as we settled in.

"Si, certamente!" He laughed. "Americans usually look happy and optimistic. You look like an Americana." He threw up his hands and shrugged.

The car took the curves beautifully, but the speed we were going unnerved me. Tonio drove me like an old lady, which is what I am sure he thought I was, but Signor Sierra drove like he was on a racetrack. It was difficult to talk because of the wind, except when we slowed down in the small villages.

"I will show you my winery, and then we will have lunch with my family before our lesson ends for today. Will that be satisfactory, Signora Wynham? You must call me Salvatore. May I call you Kathryn?"

I was surprised. Italians were so formal. The younger generation less so, especially among themselves, but Salvatore was my age or older, and he was offering me this level of friendship right away.

"I would like that, but I must confess that I am surprised."

"Tonio has told me much about his Signora Kathryn, and I feel that I have known you now for some time. I also visit America two or three times a year, and I like the friendliness of Americans. We are too stiff here. Do you know my winery, Kathryn?" He changed the subject.

"I don't know. No, not your winery per se, but I have drunk much delicious Orvieto wines, so perhaps I have had yours. What is it?"

"It is better that I show you, and we taste, and then you tell me," he said seriously.

"May I ask about your family?" I asked. I knew I had better vocabulary in this area, and I wanted to know what his wife thought about him spending time with another woman. She must be very confident, I thought, if she allows him, as attractive as he is, to drive women around in his little sports car.

"My family is close. My grandfather, Jacopo Sierra, started the business when he was a young man. He inherited the land from an uncle. He was poor but strong and decided the land was good to grow grapes. He did not marry until he was in his fifties, but my nonna was young. They had eight sons and two daughters together."

"Oh my goodness!" I exclaimed.

"Si, Sierra men are fertile." His eyes twinkled.

"And Sierra women."

"Si, si." He laughed. "We are a big famiglia-family. My father was the only son interested in the wine, but the others remained on the land or married and lived nearby. My grandfather wanted room for everyone. He did not want the family divided. He made my father promise. Today, I have three sisters and Tonio living with me."

"Your wife, Salvatore?"

He was quiet for a while. "Nunzia died three years ago."

"I am so very sorry. I can see that you are very sad still about this. Tell me about her."

Salvatore looked at me, surprised. "You want to hear about my wife?"

"Si." she must have been a very special woman."

"She was," he said quietly. "Nunzia was the most beautiful woman in the valley. All the boys were in love with her when we were young. I didn't think I stood a chance. She wanted the excitement of the city, and I knew that I would always live here in the country. I love the grapes and making wine. It was my father who unintentionally brought us together, but that happened years later. My father had decided to expand the house that my grandfather had built. Our winery was beginning to be success-ful, and our family was growing. I had four brothers and three sisters, there were aunts and uncles. My nonno had died but Nonna lived, so we needed a bigger house. My father invited an architect from Florence to come study the land and build a house that would be beautiful and part of the land, as well as large enough for everyone. It became the talk of the area, the Villa Sierra."

I was spellbound as he wove the family story. His father, Carlo Sierra, had a vision for the family and the business. Everyone wanted to work at the winery because it produced a stable income for the impoverished people of the region. As they worked, they carried away stories of the house that was being built for the Sierra family. Nunzia's father had a small grocery store in a nearby town and sold the Sierra wines. He often went on the property to pick up cases for his store. He brought back tales of the beautiful, big house that was being built. He told about the marble floors, the newest fixtures in plumbing, the big kitchen with the latest appliances, the beautiful frescos being painted, and the expensive fur-nishings. Every time he went to the winery, he came back and described some new thing to his family. Nunzia was fascinated and wanted to see it for herself, but her father said it wouldn't be proper to take her, a young girl, to the winery with all the men working there. It wouldn't look good.

So Nunzia decided to take a different tack. She would have herself invited through Salvatore, who she knew liked her, as did all the young men in a fifty-mile radius.

Unfortunately for Nunzia, she had waited too long. Salvatore had been sent to the University of Perugia to study and would go from there to Milano to learn more about running a modern business. Carlo believed in education for his children. Nunzia did not know what to do. How would she ever see this wondrous house? Unexpectedly, she decided to ask her father if she could study at the university. Her father was astounded, because she had never shown any interest in anything academic. She had always been a beautiful child and had grown into a beautiful young woman. He had expected her to marry any day. Not knowing what her intent was, Nunzia's father, who could deny his daughter nothing, was pleased that she was showing an interest in anything besides boys. He enrolled her right away.

Nunzia could hardly wait to find Salvatore, whom she had paid little attention to in the past. Much to her surprise, Salvatore was quite popular with both male and female students and paid little attention to her at the university. She then looked for ways to get into the same courses that Salvatore was taking, but many of them were filled. She was left to take art and architecture classes, which were the heart of the University of Perugia. Although she had no interest in learning about "old stuff," a curious thing happened to Nunzia at the university. She fell in love with architecture and soon forgot that she was at the university to find a way into the Sierra house.

Two years later, while she was waiting for a local bus to take her home to her village after the semester ended, Salvatore came whizzing by in his little car. He recognized her from her father's shop and stopped to ask her if he could drop her off. He was struck by her beauty all over again. Nunzia had changed during her time at the university. She had become a serious student of architecture and told Salvatore that she had applied to several firms to do an apprenticeship the next year. She was hoping to work for the firm of De Lucca in Florence.

"De Lucca? He is building our house. He has been building, remodeling, tearing out—all my life, it seems," Salvatore said. He asked Nunzia if she minded if they stopped at his house first before he took her home, so that he could pick up some documents to be mailed at the post office in the village. The very thing that Nunzia had been wanting for years was about to happen so simply.

When they arrived at the Villa Sierra, it turned out to be fate that the great De Lucca himself was there that day. Salvatore introduced Nunzia to him as a student of architecture. Whether it was her beauty or knowledge that impressed the old man, he invited her to come to Florence and talk to him about an internship in his business. Nunzia was so delighted that she spontaneously kissed Salvatore on the spot for making this happen. Salvatore, who had no idea what would occur that day, told her that she must have dinner with his family that night to celebrate.

"Did you get married soon afterward?" I asked. The story was like a modern fairy tale, and I was enthralled. By then, we were at an elaborate wrought-iron gate that had a large S engraved in the center. There was a stone wall on either side with the word Sierra etched in the sides. Salvatore slowed down and used a remote control to open the gates.

"No," he said. "Nunzia went to work for De Lucca. She became a great architect herself. It took five years before she agreed to marry me, but she did help build this house, and what you will see is Nunzia's style throughout." He looked serious for a moment. "Kathryn, you are the first woman who ever wanted to hear about my wife and how we got married."

"It is a wonderful story, Salvatore. You must miss her very much."

"Si, I do. But today is not for sadness. It is for Italian lessons, no?" He bounced back into his friendly demeanor.

It turned out to be a wonderful morning. Salvatore was very courtly. He often took one of my hands when he wanted to show me something or put his hand on the small of my back to guide me into a building. The winery was a huge operation and employed many people. It was evident how much they liked Salvatore. He was the boss, but he treated each person as an equal and was not above doing the work with them. At one point when a worker was called away, he took a broom and swept away debris. He knew about everyone's children and family and asked about them. I was introduced to many people that day, and I could not keep them all straight. Salvatore treated me like I was the most important visitor to ever come to Sierra Winery.

It was lunchtime. Salvatore invited me to join him and the three sisters who lived in the house. Up to this point, I had only seen the house from a distance. I was looking forward to going inside, and I was not disappointed. The house was the golden color of Tuscan homes and surrounded by cypress trees and beautiful flowers. It sat on top of a small hill with wide steps leading up to the front door. Each step had pots of geraniums and ivy overflowing along the way. There was a circular driveway in front of the house.

The house was magnificent and elegant. Sierra Winery must do quite well, I thought. We entered through two large wooden doors into a reception hall that had marble floors. There was an impressive staircase, and through arches on either side of the foyer were two formal salons. We walked through one of these, a large room painted a lemon yellow, out French doors leading to a terrace. Lunch had been set up at a rectangular table overlooking the pool. The terrace commanded a breathtaking view of the beautiful valley below.

There were three women about my age or a little older sitting at the table. "Come Kathryn, I will present you to my sisters," said Salvatore, gently guiding me toward the table. I was glad that I had dressed more formally, because his sisters did not have on slacks. No one was speaking. All eyes were appraising me and trying to figure out who I was.

Salvatore was the most gracious host. "Kathryn, may I present Giosetta Sierra, my oldest sister, and Bibiana and Carlotta, my younger sisters." All three murmured appropriate replies, but their eyes held questions. "Kathryn is studying our language in Orvieto, and our Tonio is tutoring her." Their eyes immediately softened. I could see that Tonio had captivated all of their hearts.

"Tonio!" said the one called Bibiana. "Are you learning anything from Tonio, Signora Wynham?"

"Tonio is an excellent teacher," I replied. "I am very fortunate to have him." I could see that these aunts doted on their nephew and were pleased that I found him so charming.

All three sisters spoke English, and our lunch conversation was comprised of a mixture of Italian and English, especially when I didn't know a word or phrase. Giosetta, who seemed the most formal, asked, "Why do you study italiano, Signora Wynham?"

When I explained how I had fallen in love with Orvieto and had come back for a longer visit, they—or at least Giosetta-looked skeptical. I found that curious. Why wouldn't everyone fall in love with this area? Salvatore kept up a running dialogue, teasing his sisters and engaging me in the conversation. Carlotta was quiet but pleasant. When lunch was over, and I was leaving with Salvatore to return to my apartment, Giosetta wished me good luck with my next class and a good trip back to America. She was writing me off, knowing that she would never see me again.

Salvatore parked his car at the funicular station and prepared to ride up to Orvieto with me. "Please," I said. "You don't have to do this. I can see how busy you are. I have had a wonderful day that I will never forget."

"No, Kathryn, it is my pleasure." He took my hand and held it as we rode up. "It has been a long time since I have had such a pleasant time. I thank you for being a good listener. Will you come back to Orvieto?"

"I am not sure, but I hope to. I can't imagine never coming here again. It is so beautiful, and the people of Orvieto have been so good to me. I will miss living here when I go home."

As we walked through the streets to my apartment, people came out of their shops to speak to Salvatore. I could see their surprise that I knew him. When we reached my apartment, Maria and Bernardo came out of their restaurant and shook his hand. They invited him in for a glass of wine, and as an afterthought, me as well. I declined, but before Salvatore left me, he turned and asked if he could see me again. I was surprised but said simply, "I would be honored." He kissed me on both cheeks and disappeared into Via Tavolo for a drink.

I had only been home thirty minutes before Francesca Botti excitedly called me. "Kathryn, my cousin Betta called to tell me you were out with Salvatore Sierra. How did you meet Signor Sierra?"

How did Betta know, and why would she call Francesca? "Betta called you, Francesca?"

"Kathryn, do you know who Salvatore Sierra is?"

"Well, I know now that he has a winery," I answered innocently.

"Not just a winery, Kathryn, one of the biggest wineries in all of Italy— and in the world, for that matter. And, Kathryn, he is the most eligible bachelor in all of Italy. There is not a woman in Italy who wouldn't marry Salvatore Sierra, and you were out with him! All of Orvieto knows this by now. All of Tuscany and Umbria knows this by now. Betta said he was holding your hand. Kathryn, why didn't you tell me you knew Signor Sierra?"

I was stupefied. That kind, gentle man was the most eligible bachelor in Italy. "Kathryn, are you there?" asked Francesca.

"I didn't know, Francesca. I just met him today. His nephew, Tonio, is my tutor. I told you I was getting a tutor. I had no idea who Salvatore was."

"Salvatore? You call him Salvatore? You didn't tell me that Tonio Sierra was your tutor."

"His name meant nothing to me. Really. I never heard of Sierra wines until today. Tonio told me his family owned a winery, but I thought nothing of it. I can't believe how dumb I have been."

By now Francesca was laughing hard. "Only you, Kathryn. Every woman in the world would love to have ridden in that little car with Salvatore Sierra, and you go off and don't know who you're with."

"How did you know about the car?" I couldn't believe this. Francesca lived all the way over in Assisi, and she knew all of this.

"Kathryn, this is big. It is the talk of Orvieto."

"Great. This is not what I wanted when I came here—to be gossiped about."

"Not to worry, Kathryn. I am coming over tomorrow, and you will have lunch with Betta and me and tell us everything," responded Francesca.

"There is nothing to tell, Francesca. Salvatore showed me the winery. We had lunch and then I came back to my flat," I said.

"Nothing? That is not nothing. Salvatore Sierra has not been seen with another woman since his wife died, and you were invited to his villa. That is something, Kathryn, not nothing. Ciao for now. See you tomorrow." She hung up, laughing.

Oh, brother. What had I gotten myself into? My little tutoring lesson is the talk of the valley.

# VI

The next morning, Tonio arrived with a twinkle in his eye and an envelope. "This is for you, Signora Kathryn."

"What is it?" I asked.

"Open it and see," he replied gaily. He looked like the cat that had swallowed the canary.

There was a note inside on heavy, cream-colored paper that had been embossed with double esses on the outside. The script was in Italian. I wasn't sure that I was reading it correctly.

Tonio interrupted impatiently. "Mio nonno said he wrote it in Italian as part of the tutoring, and that I should help you if you don't understand. Do you want to read it aloud, Signora Kathryn?"

"Yes, I'd better," I said shakily.

*Dear Kathryn,*

*Your company is very enjoyable. Please come for lunch on Sunday at three o'clock. I would like for you to meet my son and Tonio's mother.*

*Sincerely,*

*Salvatore*

"Is that what it says, Tonio?" I felt perplexed.

"Si,si," he said, excited. "I knew Nonno would like you, Signora Kathryn. I will come fetch you and take you to our house."

"I don't understand, Tonio. It is very kind of your nonno to invite me, but I am not sure why."

"My nonno was very impressed by you, Signora Kathryn. You are not like the Italian women. They want to marry him, but he is still sad about Nonna Nunzia. He has been sad for a long time, and you made him laugh."

"Tonio, I feel so stupid. I did not know how famous Sierra Winery was, and I am afraid that I made a fool out of myself."

"No, Signora Kathryn. Nonno said you were naturale. He likes it that you came here to study Italian."

"Who will be at the lunch?" I asked suspiciously.

"Oh, the famiglia," he said breezily.

"How many people, Tonio?"

"The famiglia, Signora Kathryn—mio padre, mia madre, aunts, uncles, children..." He gestured broadly. "We always have more on Sundays. It is a family tradition."

"I will be an outsider. Why would your nonno want an outsider?" I felt intimidated.

"Signora Kathryn, I explained. Nonno likes you, and Zia Bibi does, too. She said you were good for Nonno."

I felt that I had to go. It felt rude not to, so with reluctance I accepted the invitation.

Betta and Francesca were all abuzz when I arrived for lunch. They could see that I was flustered. It was true that the entire town of Orvieto was looking at me differently, and it was not my imagination. That was bad enough, but now I had to face Sunday lunch.

I knew whatever I said at my lunch today would be all over the entire town within five minutes after we parted ways, but I had to talk to someone. Both Francesca and Betta sat in stunned silence when I told them I had been invited to lunch at the Villa Sierra on Sunday.

Finally Francesca spoke in a solemn voice. "Kathryn, Sunday is family day."

"I know that, Francesca. Tonio told me that the entire big Sierra family would be there. But what does that really mean?" I was exasperated. They were treating this news like it was a visit to a royal family.

Betta spoke up. "It generally is a day when only the family itself gets together. It is considered the biggest honor a family can bestow on you, if you are invited for Sunday."

"Then why would Salvatore invite me? I certainly mean nothing to him or his family. I can't believe this tutoring arrangement that I have with Tonio would be significant to them."

"No, it would not be Tonio," Betta, who was the voice of calmness, replied. "It means that Signor Sierra finds"—she was momentarily at a loss—"it appears to mean that you made a very deep impression on Signor Sierra. He wants his family to know you, Kathryn." She struggled through Italian and English to get this out.

Francesca simply looked at me and shrugged. "He is a man first, Kathryn, not *the* Salvatore Sierra, and you are a beautiful woman who wants nothing from him. You interest him."

"That is so silly!" I said hotly. "I will be back in America in a few weeks. I can't believe that I could hold any interest for him. I can't even speak his language, and from what I have heard, he can have any woman in the world. Why would he be interested in me?"

"Oh, but Kathryn, you are interesting. Not a typical American. Yes, I can see why Signor Sierra would be attracted," said Francesca.

The conversation felt circular to me, so we spoke of other things, but the Sunday lunch kept creeping back in. They were making me feel more apprehensive than ever.

By the time Sunday arrived, I felt ill I was so nervous. I had decided to wear a two-piece white wool dress and the gold necklace that I had bought in Florence. It was at once understated and elegant. I felt as if I had to represent my country. Just before I left to go to the funicular station, I heard a knock on my door. When I opened it, there stood Salvatore.

"Salvatore, I thought Tonio was coming," I said, flustered.

"Si, Tonio is a good boy, but there will be no time for the two of us today, so I came to get you myself. Do you mind, Kathryn?" He looked concerned.

"Of course not. It is very kind of you to invite me and go to so much trouble for a stranger in your country. I am looking forward to meeting your family." What a lie. I was just hoping that I could remember names and not say something ridiculous in English or Italian.

"They are a great family, Kathryn. You will see." Salvatore took my hand and kissed it in the old-fashioned courtly manner that he had. "Thank you for accepting my invitation."

I could see why so many women could be smitten by him. He was rich and good-looking, and he had a mansion and wonderful manners. We went down the steps to walk to the funicular station. Every citizen of Orvieto must have been out on the streets when we emerged. They all knew Salvatore and spoke respectfully to him. He must have shaken fifty hands before we got to his car. And it felt as if every single pair of eyes in town was on me.

Lunch was an experience. There was beautifully presented food in a gorgeous dining room bordered by frescos. The chandelier sparkled. Thank goodness I had dressed well, because all of the women were dressed in couture outfits. Tonio's parents were lovely and teased him constantly. Carlo and Natalia lived in Milan, where the winery office was located. Carlo was the CEO of the firm. Two of his brothers were there with their families. I learned that Salvatore had five children, four sons and a daughter, Lucianna.

Carlo and Natalia loved visiting America and expressed their sorrow over the September 11 attacks. Two of their sons were at universities in America, and their daughter wanted to spend at least one year there as well. They were a little unsettled at the thought of their children being in a country that had been attacked. Tonio wanted to stay at home. He was so doted on by his aunts that it would be hard to determine who would be sadder when he left for MIT.

Salvatore's sister Bibi was very animated and gossipy. She had left her husband for a while, because she had found out that he had a mistress, not for the first time evidently. He had been barred from the Villa Sierra until Bibi was ready to forgive him. Carlotta had become a recent widow, and although pleasant, she remained quiet throughout the afternoon.

The one jarring note was Giosetta. It was evident that she was the reigning female of the household since Nunzia's death, and she was extremely protective of her brother. Unfortunately, she was seated next to me. "Your husband did not come to Italy?" she had asked me at the previous lunch. When I explained that I had been widowed nearly seven years ago, she looked at me and said, "So you are ready to get married again?" When I replied that I had not thought of getting married, her response was, "All women want to be married, that is why God put us here. To get married and have children." Since Giosetta had done neither, I thought that was a strange answer.

At the lunch today, she stated, rather than asked, "You are Catholic, Signora Wynham?"

"No, since the attacks on the United States, I have attended St. Ludovico's Convent, which has an Anglican service in English. It has been very comforting."

"The duomo is the church of my family," Giosetta said smugly. What a snob she is, I thought.

"The duomo is quite a beautiful cathedral. I attended the memorial services there after the attack, but I felt that I needed something smaller, and a service in my own language was not something I expected to find in Orvieto. In every possible way, Orvieto has met my needs."

"But you leave soon, no?" she asked again. Giosetta had asked me that question twice when I had lunch there on Wednesday.

"I have a two-week class beginning tomorrow, and I leave the week after that is over. I will miss Orvieto and all the wonderful people I have met here, but I will be ready to return home. I miss my family."

Giosetta was unrelenting. "Will you come back to Orvieto?"

Was she so threatened by Salvatore's attention to me that she needed me to write in blood that I would never return and would stay away from her brother? Her attitude bordered on hostility.

"I hope to come back one day. How could I not love this area and Orvieto?" I looked at Giosetta when I said this and noticed that she visibly hardened.

Bibi, who had been listening to this conversation, clapped her hands and said, "Brava brava. It is unusual to have an American appreciate our little towns so much. I hope that you will come back, Signora Kathryn, and when you do, please let me know." She threw his sister a triumphant glance. Giosetta said no more, and I decided that I did not need to get involved in the obvious sibling rivalry that seemed to be occurring between these two.

The afternoon finally ended. I was feeling the strain of talking to so many Italians at once and being the outsider in a family setting. Salvatore must have sensed this and asked if I was ready to leave.

"Si, Salvatore. I am tired and need to prepare for my classes tomorrow." I still had not figured out why I had been invited, but I was ready to return to my flat.

Salvatore, once again, walked with me to my apartment over my protests that he was leaving his family too long. "No, no, Kathryn, I see them every week and some every day. They will be there when I return." Holding my hand, he walked me slowly through Orvieto. On Sunday evenings, the town was often crowded with locals, walking and talking with one another. Everyone stopped to speak to Salvatore, and they couldn't help but notice that he was holding my hand. I hoped they understood that this was just his affectionate manner and nothing more.

At my door, I was prepared for the two-cheek kiss, since almost his entire family had given me one, but Salvatore took my face in his hands and looked for a moment before he said "Kathryn, thank you for meeting my family. I know some of them can be daunting, but I am pleased that you came. May I take you to lunch on Wednesday?"

I was so startled by this that I said yes without thinking. "I have classes until noon."

"I will come at one o'clock." And with that, he kissed me softly on the mouth and left.

What does this mean? It means nothing, I thought, nothing. But why is he asking me out again? And that kiss. It was different, not the kind I was expecting—much more affectionate. What am I getting into?

# V

My intermediate class began uneventfully. It was a small class of eight people. Everyone knew a fair amount of Italian, but the first day was a review so that we would all start with a solid base. I was completely at ease. My time with Tonio and living in Orvieto speaking Italian daily had paid off. One of my instructors asked me to move up to the next level, but I declined once again. I didn't feel that confident, and I didn't want that much of a challenge.

There was only one other woman in this group. She appeared to be German or Austrian. The others seemed to be businessmen. I didn't think I would have the same rapport with these classmates as I had in the first class. By the third day, the lessons had gotten more difficult, and I was glad that I had stayed at this level. Assignments included reading the newspaper and making a daily report. This was also the day when I would meet Salvatore again for lunch. I had given him little thought, but I was looking forward to seeing him again.

As before, he came to my apartment to pick me up. "Kathryn, you look lovely." I had made an effort to look more sophisticated and had on a black leather jacket with black jeans and stylish sunglasses. The days were getting cooler, and the nights were very chilly. Italians didn't turn on their heat until the first of November, so dressing warmly was a must.

Salvatore had on a blue cashmere sweater, jeans, and a brown aviator-style jacket. The look suited him. The top was up on his little car. "I am taking you to lunch in Montepulciano today. It is a longer ride, and I don't want you to get cold." he said when he saw me looking at the car.

"That's wonderful. I have wanted to go there. I have a friend who spent some time at a farm near Montepulciano this summer and loved that little town as much as I love Orvieto."

"I think you will like this restaurant, Kathryn, and it is a little out of the way. It will provide privacy," he said.

"That will be nice. I am not used to being so noticed. Of course, I know that you are the person everyone is looking at, but they are wondering what you are doing with me. I am wondering the same thing, Salvatore. You are being exceptionally nice to a foreigner in your country."

"You can thank Tonio." He laughed. "Tonio made me curious about you. I thought at first Tonio was tutoring a young girl. Then I worried that you were an older woman after a young boy…"

"You're kidding!" I was shocked.

"Don't be upset, Kathryn." Salvatore laughed again. "Tonio set me straight. He told me that I should meet you for myself before I made judgments—the very same thing I tell him."

"So my day with you at the winery was planned so that you could meet me?" I was astounded.

"Yes, I confess. It is true. I am shameless. Will you forgive me, Kathryn?" He didn't look one bit ashamed.

"I don't know, Salvatore. I am shocked that you or anyone would think about me like that." I was feeling a little upset but strangely flattered at the same time.

Salvatore took my hand. "I am very sorry, Kathryn. Tonio likes you very much. He has been worried about me since Nunzia died, and he thought you would lift my spirits. And he was right. You have. I am impressed by you, how you left your home to study my language, and how much you love my country. I am impressed by how much you want to learn to speak Italian well. I have never met a woman like you." He was very serious as he spoke.

"OK, Salvatore. I forgive you for now. Let's see how good lunch is." And I smiled at him.

After we had eaten and were enjoying coffee, I mentioned how much I liked the slow pace of life in the little towns like Orvieto and Montepulciano. How refreshing it was to not feel hurried.

"Have you heard of the 'slow cities movement,' Kathryn?" Salvatore asked.

"No, what is that?"

"It started with the restaurant business and people involved in the culinary fields. Our society had become so busy, no one took the time to enjoy wine and meals any longer. They no longer had la dolce vita, the sweet life. Restaurant owners wanted people to eat and drink well and spend time over a good meal. It started with what you call in America 'grass roots' and slowly spread out across our country, particularly outside the large cities. Now it is a committed movement. Orvieto is one of those cities."

"What does it mean, Salvatore?" I was interested. Maybe this was what had drawn me to Orvieto.

"It is simple. Towns have cut down on the noise of traffic and technology. They look for ways to cut pollution and preserve green spaces. They make pedestrian zones and support local produce. They preserve local aesthetic traditions, architecture, crafts, and small shops. You won't find big supermarkets or shopping malls in these towns."

"What a wonderful idea."

"Si, more small towns are adopting these ways. The populations must be under fifty thousand in order to become a slow city." It is a balance between the modern and the traditional to promote good living. More and more people are moving from the large cities to these smaller towns. They are tired of the pressure of big-city life. That is why I live in the country. I love our life here. It is dolce—sweet, charming, and maybe romantic, no?" Salvatore took my hand, turned it palm side up, and kissed it.

"You are a very romantic man, Salvatore," I said. "I do like this movement. I think many Americans would cherish this kind of life. I will try to bring more of the Italian sweet life into my own when I go home."

"Are you ready to leave us, Kathryn?"

"I miss my family, and I need to see how my house is coming along," I had not really told Salvatore much about my family, and I decided to tell him a little about the turmoil.

When I had finished, he looked at me seriously.

"Si, you need to return to your family for now. But will you come back here, Kathryn? I will miss you."

"You will?" I was surprised.

"Very much. May I come see you in America? I will be in New York in December at a trade show for European wines."

"Salvatore, I live a long way from New York. I live near Washington, DC."

"Not so far by aeroplane, no?" his eyes crinkled in an engaging manner.

"If you feel the same in December, I would be happy for you to visit." I didn't know where all this was leading, but I decided to follow Inga's advice and let my heart be open.

"You are skeptical, Kathryn?"

"I am surprised, that's all. Your life is so full here in Italy. I can't imagine that you will remember me when I'm gone." I looked at him and saw surprise on his face.

"No, Kathryn, I will not forget you. I want to see you again, if you will let me. I have been lonely since Nunzia died. There is a hole in my heart." He looked at me earnestly.

"But Salvatore, there are so many women in Italy, so many young, beautiful women who would be happy—"

"No! These women," he sputtered, "these women do not want Salvatore the man, they want Salvatore Sierra the winery owner who would give them an easy life. No! I do not want them. I have stayed clear of them. They are everywhere!" I could see how heated he was on the subject.

I took both of his hands. "Salvatore, not all Italian women are like that. I have met many wonderful women in Italy, but for whatever reason you have; I hope I will see you again. In America you may see me differently."

"People are the same in their heart wherever they live, Kathryn, and you are a good woman. You did not know who I was, and you were so natural with me. You took me as a simple country man and treated me like a king."

"Oh, Salvatore, from the start I knew you were not a simple country man" I blushed. "I just did not know how big you were in Italy. I felt like an idiot when I found out."

"You are not an idiot, Kathryn. You are a charming woman, and I am glad that Tonio made this happen. Come; let us go take a walk before we go back to Orvieto." He took my arm and held it close to his body.

Naturally, every shopkeeper in Montepulciano knew him and there were many greetings. Once again, I was the subject of curiosity.

I was not as focused in the intermediate class, but I did OK. I could have learned much more without the distraction of Salvatore Sierra. I was invited once again to Sunday lunch. Tonio ran around like the original Cupid. "Signora Kathryn, you and Nonno together, so…" He finished the sentence by kissing his fingers. All was not wonderful, however. Giosetta hardly looked at me or spoke. Carlotta remained quiet, as she had been in the past, and Bibi had returned to her home in Milan to give her husband another chance. Natalia and Carlo Sierra were as gracious as ever, but I felt the strain.

Before I left Orvieto, Salvatore took me to a well-known restaurant nearby called Vissani. It was the most wonderful dinner that I had ever had in my life. The restaurant was very charming. The owner knew Salvatore, of course, and the staff doted on him. Despite that, I think the food would have been excellent anyway.

"Kathryn, I am sad that you are leaving. I want you to have the happiest memories of being here so that you will come back. I want you to have happy memories of me."

"That will not be a problem, Salvatore. You have spoiled me rotten in the past two weeks. I have learned no new Italian except words on menus, but I have had a wonderful time with you. I will never forget you or my time in Orvieto. I am sad to be leaving, as well. I feel caught between two worlds, but I need to go home. So much has happened in America, and so much has happened in my family. I am compelled to return. I know that you understand."

"Si, all too well." He looked sad.

"Don't be sad, Salvatore. You will make me cry. I have been feeling so emotional this week. I have said good-bye to Francesca Botti, who was my angel, and so many other good people in Orvieto. My language instructors gave me a party. Did you know Tonio came by to say good-bye?"

I could see that he didn't know.

"Your family has raised a fine young man. He is your image, Salvatore. You will always live in him." I could see his spirits lift.

"Will you change your mind and let me take you to the aeroporto?" he pleaded.

"I can't, Salvatore. I don't think I could leave if you were there." I meant it. This man had captivated me, but I couldn't allow myself to think about how much. I needed the distance to think about all of this.

"That is reason enough to go. I have to let you go, but I will see you again. Soon." He reached into his pocket and brought out a little box. "Kathryn, this is for you from me. Something to remind you of Italy and of our time together."

I opened the box and found an exquisite little gold brooch of a sunflower, the symbol of Italy. "It is beautiful, Salvatore. I will love it always and wear it often. I will think of you each time I put it on. And I will think of this beautiful country that I have grown to love." I felt the tears coming down my face. "You have made me cry. I didn't want to do that."

"You are becoming Italian, Kathryn. You have heart. Let me take you home, and we will have one more walk around Orvieto before you leave." It was late when we stepped out of the funicular station. The streets were quiet and felt medieval. Neither one of us said anything. Salvatore was holding me close to him. We slowly walked through the beautiful cobblestoned streets, past the duomo, the Etruscan ruins, the language school, the shops, and the restaurants that had become so familiar to me. When we finally reached my apartment, I was nearly undone. "Will you be OK, cara?" he said and touched my wet face.

"Yes. I have loved this enchanted place. I will come back someday. This will not be the last time." I looked at Salvatore. "You are a wonderful man. I am so fortunate to have known you."

With that, Salvatore kissed me, touched my cheek, took my hand, kissed it, and walked away. I could see that he could not speak.

The next morning, I was back on the train to Rome, from which I would leave the next day for America. As the plane lifted and flew over the beautiful countryside of Italy, I looked out of the window and mouthed, "Arrivederci, arrivederci." I will come back.

# ANA

# I

I was back in Tubingen for five weeks for the holidays. It felt very familiar, not quite like home, but not so strange and foreign this time. Of course, my relationship with Theo made all the difference.

When I called Theo to tell him that I could come a week sooner, he was thrilled.

"Ana, how did this happen? What about your classes?"

"It just worked out," I said. "There were several buildings on campus that had heating problems that couldn't be resolved during the Thanksgiving holidays, so they had to shut down the buildings sooner. It was a mad scramble to finish the semester, but the students were very happy, except, of course, the ones who have to find somewhere to stay off campus."

"And the girls, what about them?"

"Oh, they are delighted that I am leaving the town house for the two of them—well, three or four of them. I am not sure how many will be there."

"Who else will be there?" Theo asked suspiciously.

"I'm not sure, but don't worry, Theo, it will be girls, some of the kids who have no place to go for the holidays. Katie asked me if a couple of her friends could stay there for Christmas. I gave them the rules, and they promised to obey them. They are good kids, so I am not worried. I also asked Brandon Walker if he would keep an eye on the girls and the house. He is very reliable and mature."

"You are too generous, Ana," Theo warned. "What about Mimi, will she stay, as well?"

"Certainly. Where would she go?" I asked. "The girls are planning joint holiday celebrations to incorporate everyone's needs. I think one of the visiting girls is Jewish. Theo, really, all I care about is that I will be with you."

"Ja, you are right, Ana, that is the most important thing. I can't believe we will have this time together. You know I will be working, don't you?"

"Can you get some time off? I would love to spend Christmas in Montepulciano. Is that possible, Theo? Could we go there for at least a few days?"

"Ja, maybe. I will work on it before you arrive. I love you, Ana. Have a safe flight. I will meet you in Frankfurt."

"I love you, too, Theo. I can't wait to see you again."

That was a week ago, and our reunion had been wonderful. When I got off the plane, the first person I saw was Theo, standing tall above everyone else. He had a bouquet of flowers for me, which got a little crushed when he kissed me.

"Ana, Ana, Ana, Ana. You are really here with me."

Theo looked great. He had worn a tweed sports coat, an impeccable white shirt, gray slacks, and a tie. I looked as if I had been on a plane all night. It was over a hundred miles to Tubingen, and I wondered if I could stay awake until we got to Theo's apartment.

"Come, we will get your bags. I have a hotel for us in Frankfurt. We will go to Tubingen tomorrow."

"Theo, you are absolutely the most wonderful man in the world," I replied gratefully. "I can't wait to take a hot shower and put on clean clothes."

"Ja? I had some other plans for us."

"Umm," I said, holding his hand as we walked down the concourse. "Maybe I will take a little nap, then a little walk, then maybe something to eat…"

"Ja, ja, ja," said Theo, stopping and kissing me again in the middle of the crowded concourse. "That will all come…in good time." And it did, in good time.

The apartment was empty when we arrived the next day. I had been used to Schnee greeting me with joyous barking last winter.

"Where is Schnee?"

"He is at the polizei academy. I will bring him home later. I always take him there when I am gone. He needs to keep his training sharp, and he loves all the attention he gets. I think sometimes he is sad to return home."

"I doubt that." I laughed. Theo loved that dog more than life itself. "Will you bring him back today?"

"Ja, tonight when I return. Will you be all right, Ana? I will be late tonight. I am working on a case that is at a crucial point, and I have to interrogate some people."

"Poor people. I wouldn't want you to interrogate me again." I laughed.

"When did I ever interrogate you, Ana?" Theo looked astonished.

"You don't remember when I came last winter, and you visited my apartment and asked me all kinds of questions in the sternest possible voice?"

"Nein, Ana. That was not interrogation. Those were just questions—an interview. Nothing more."

"As I said, poor people. Whoever they are. Don't worry about me, Theo. I will be perfectly fine. I will go out and get some food. Unpack. Take a hot bath and be waiting for you when you get here."

"That will be lovely—you here waiting for me. But don't go out for food. There is plenty here. Look around."

With a quick kiss and a very snug hug, Theo left. I had never been in his apartment completely alone before. It felt a little odd, as if I was intruding. It was much more personal than his farm in Montepulciano. That was because he was in the process of renovating that house, and it felt new, without memories. On the other hand, this apartment felt very lived in and had Theo's stamp everywhere. It smelled like him. Very masculine. It was very clean and tidy, but of course, it would be, since he had a cleaning lady. Yet it was more than that. It was his books and papers and even the furniture. They all said Theo. I felt his presence everywhere.

I went into the bedroom. Nothing was out of place, yet it looked comfortable and worn just to the right degree. I could be happy here, I thought, but could I be happy in Germany? I hated the weather. Everyday was gray and wet. Damp to the bones. I decided not to judge too quickly and try to have a better attitude.

I was still jet-lagged but not tired enough for a nap. It would be a long time before Theo returned, so I decided to take a little walk and see the town again. I wrapped up warmly and set out for the shops and the university. Everything looked exactly the same. Nothing had changed one bit except for some Christmas lights in some of the shops. They did add a festive flare to the gray landscape. I had to acknowledge that the little town was still very charming and quaint.

I wanted to check with the university about my status as a part-time visiting professor. I thought if I saw someone in person, it would have more impact than a letter, but I was not up to it today. I was just too tired from the trip. However, I could try to make an appointment for the next day or so. The walk to the university's administration building was bitterly cold. The wind swept through the narrow streets. I pulled my scarf around my face and my hat farther down on my head.

The secretary for my contact person, Herr Doktor Weiss, was like a dragon. No, Herr Doktor Weiss had no free time in the next ten days. He was a very busy man. I should have written a letter requesting an appointment before I left the States. Was I staying in Tubingen or passing through? Why didn't I contact that department when I was in Germany last winter? How serious was I about teaching? On and on and on.

I was very frustrated and getting nowhere. I could tell the secretary was enjoying her bureaucratic role quite a lot. Finally, I said that I would be back tomorrow and perhaps she could find an opening in Herr Doktor Weiss's schedule. Until then I would be at Herr Volker's residence.

"Inspektor Theodore Volker?" she asked, amazed.

"Ja, Inspektor Volker." I turned to go when she stopped me.

"Herr Doktor Weiss will want to talk with you, Frau Doktor Douglas. I will find time for you tomorrow afternoon."

"Tomorrow?" She must have been kidding after the runaround that I had just gotten. German bureaucracy at its worst.

"Ja, Herr Doktor Weiss is Herr Volker's cousin. He will see you." She dismissed me as if none of the previous conversation had taken place. Theo's power extended everywhere, it seemed.

"What would be a convenient time?" I inquired, astonished.

"Three o'clock in the afternoon. Don't be late."

On my way back down the hill, I wondered if all Germans were just naturally rude and bureaucratic. Maybe they were just abrupt. Mimi certainly responded to life in this manner. Is there a German gene for this? Then something caught my attention as I approached Saint George's Collegiate Church. There were very few students hanging out on this cold, windy day, but there was a young man talking to a beautiful, blonde student. It was Konrad Richter.! I couldn't believe it! Theo said he had not been seen for months—not since Katie had been locked up. Who was the girl? I wondered if she were American. They both moved off. He had said something that made her laugh, and they soon disappeared into one of the adjoining buildings.

I was so shocked that I couldn't move. He must be up to his old tricks again. I wondered if the blonde girl could be warned about Konrad. I didn't want to see another American in prison because of that sewer rat. I walked across the street in front of the cathedral and looked at the building that the two had gone into. There were some posters on the outside about an upcoming rally. It was for this weekend. I was afraid to go inside, because I did not want Konrad to see me. I went back to the church and entered, just to stand inside, where I was hidden from street view but could see anyone coming out of that building.

I was on the verge of giving up when fifteen minutes later, the girl emerged alone. She started walking down the hill toward the marktplatz, just where I was going. I decided to follow her. She was a fast walker, and I had a difficult time keeping up and not being obvious that I was following her. It was so cold that most people were not paying attention to anyone else out in the wind. They just wanted to get where they were going as quickly as possible. The girl continued to walk fast and went across the marktplatz, past the Rathaus, and down the street past where I would turn off for Theo's apartment. There was no one else on these streets, and it was getting dark, as it did in early afternoons in December. She looked back once. I think she wanted to make sure she wasn't being followed. Then she disappeared in a maze of streets that I was unfamiliar with.

It was strange, I thought. Most university students lived closer to the school and certainly not on this side of town. It was quiet and residential and had none of the attractions that students enjoyed. Who was she? She looked as much German as she did American. Very Aryan looking, the perfect neo-Nazi youth. But my gut told me she was American and not German. There was just something about her.

I couldn't wait for Theo to get home. Despite what he had said about food, I bought some cold cuts at the deli, nice German rolls, and a cheese-cake—Theo's favorite. I had some coffee brewing when he finally walked in at eleven o'clock that night. Theo was not bothered in the least by caffeine and could drink a cup of the strongest brew and fall asleep instantly. Schnee was with him and seemed to remember me after he had sniffed a few times.

"Mein Gott, that smells good!" he said appreciatively.

"Sit down, Theo; I have something to tell you. First eat a little, and then we will talk."

"Nein, first we kiss," he said, pulling me close to him. "And then we kiss again and then again…"

I was so lost in the kisses that I momentarily lost track of my news. "Theo, stop! I have something important to tell you." I pushed him away and into a chair. "Eat something first, because you probably won't eat after I tell you my news, and I know you are tired and hungry."

"OK, OK, I will eat, Ana." He poured himself a cup of coffee and took a long slow sip. "I must admit the sandwich looks good, and I am hungry. You have only been here one day. I can't imagine what is so important."

"I think my news will be of incredible interest to you, but while you are eating, I will take Schnee out for a little walk so that we won't be interrupted."

"You are acting very mysteriously. Will I come home to this every night?"

"I sincerely hope not."

When I returned from my walk with Schnee, Theo was cleaning up the dishes and had made me a cup of tea. "Now, Ana, tell me what is on your very beautiful mind."

I started by telling him about my visit to Dr. Weiss's office, which elicited a chuckle. "Oh, yes, you have now met the very formidable Frau Graece. We are all scared of her, but I think she is in love with my cousin. She has never married and has devoted her life to him."

"You know what would be helpful to me, Theo? A list of all of your relatives whom I might encounter in Germany and Italy. That also includes childhood friends. Do you know you are related to everyone?"

"No, Ana, my darling, not everyone." Theo laughed. "So you got an appointment with Jakob tomorrow? That is good, darling, but if you had told me that you wanted to meet him, I could have saved you so much trouble. Now, it's bedtime?" He looked hopeful.

"No, Theo, not yet. That was not the important part. When I left his office and was walking back here, I saw Konrad Richter."

Theo instantly sat up. "Konrad Richter, are you sure? Absolutely sure?"

"There is no doubt who it was, Theo. I will never forget his slimy little face. He was talking to a very beautiful, blonde girl."

"So he is back! I knew he would turn up here again. Did he see you, Ana?

"No, I'm sure he didn't. It was so cold, I had my scarf over my face and my hat pulled down low." I told Theo about going in the church and then following the girl.

"She disappeared down here?" He seemed surprised.

"Yes, I can show you the last street that I saw her turn down. I was afraid to follow her any farther."

"I will put my men on it tomorrow. We have some undercover polizei who look like students. Some are students, in fact. I am more curious about the girl. She must be Deutsche to live in this district. She is new on the scene with that group. I would have heard of her. We keep close track of that organization, yet even I did not know Konrad Richter was back. This is indeed big news, Ana. I swear to Gott, I will catch him this time." That last statement was said with hatred.

"Come, Theo," I said, taking his hand, "Enough about Konrad Richter tonight. This is our time. Let's not spend it talking about Konrad all night long. I have other plans for you."

Theo softened. "Other plans? What could they be, Ana?"

"Well, let's start with a little massage around your shoulders…"I put my hands on his shoulders and started kneading. "You seem to have a lot of tension here." I pulled him toward the bedroom.

Theo took my hand and kissed it. "I have much tension everywhere, Ana, my love. Are you up to it? Will you take care of all my tension?" He looked me in the eyes, and I melted.

"I will give it my very best shot, Theo. My absolute very best shot. Let's just see where this goes."

He pulled me down on the bed and ran his hands through my hair. "Ana, you are so good for me. I love you, Liebchen."

"I love you, Theo…so much, so very much."

What a night! And I thought I was jet-lagged.

# II

The next day was not quite as cold. The wind wasn't blowing, and the sun had come out in the afternoon. That is always a treat in Germany. Actually, the little town of Tubingen looked quite charming as I walked up the hill to the university. I wanted to elicit Jakob Weiss's help in working at the university next fall, but I kept asking myself if I could actually live in Germany. I didn't know what Theo might think about it, and I didn't know if I really wanted to live here. I was certain that I wanted to be closer to Theo. It had only been a little over two weeks since I had last seen seen him at Thanksgiving, but it felt much longer. My heart was with him, but I wasn't sure it was in Germany.

I brought Frau Graece a bouquet of flowers to thank her for making the appointment. She was surprised and seemed to thaw a little bit. I could tell she was pleased. "This was entirely unnecessary, Frau Doktor Douglas. I only do my job, but danke schoen. They are quite beautiful, and they warm my office on such a cold day."

Jakob Weiss looked like a German professor. He had longish, white hair and dancing brown eyes. His eyebrows were bushy and seemed to be permanently raised in a quizzical position. He had a very generous mustache. And I found him to be gracious and humorous. "So Doktor Douglas, you are the one who gives my cousin, Theodore, hope for the future."

"Sir?" I was taken aback.

"Oh, yes, he is moonstruck, as we say here. Luna madness. I don't know how he pays attention to his job, but he muddles through. Actually, he is quite lethal in his work. I pity the person who crosses him."

I thought that myself. I needed to put the conversation back on a professional level.

"Herr Doktor Weiss, I have applied to teach here next fall, but my application seems to have fallen by the wayside. It appears to be hopelessly caught up in some kind of bureaucratic tangle. I am seeking your help and advice."

"So, I know you are a medieval scholar and are very sympathetic to the Jewish situation, but what makes you want to teach in our little university?" His eyes were twinkling. His English was Oxford.

"Well, quite obviously, Theo. I want to live closer to him. It is as simple as that."

"I believe you have known each other just a few months, is that not correct?"

"Yes, that is correct, and while that is my main reason, there is much research I could do here for another book. The one I wrote last winter will be published in just a few months and is receiving critical acclaim. When I was here previously, Theo helped me see and understand the plight of the Jews in Tubingen, as well as all of Europe over the centuries. I would like to focus on that issue this time and bring it into the postwar era. I can do that research better in Tubingen. But clearly my impetus is Theo."

Jakob Weiss looked at me a long time, and I looked back. I did not flinch.

He finally spoke. "I have no doubt that your new book will have the same critical acclaim as your current one. You are an excellent scholar."

"Have you seen an advance copy of my book?" I was astonished.

"As a matter of fact, I have. Any research done through this university is open for critique, and I was interested, but"—He held up his hand to stop me from speaking—"my main concern is Theodore. We are close and have suffered losses throughout our lives, about some of which, no doubt, Theodore has told you. I know he is quite taken with you. When he talks to me about you, he lights up. I have not ever seen him this way with a woman. Not even Marta, his ex-wife. That was a comfortable arranged marriage that did not work. Marta has always been a beautiful woman, but she was not for Theodore. She did not stimulate him. She was a good German wife and a good Jewish wife. Theodore wanted more. Wants more. I don't know if you are the one for Theodore, but he is caught up with you. I worry about what will happen if you are not the one."

I wasn't sure how to reply to all of this information reeling around in my head, but before I could say anything, Jakob continued. "Theodore has a hard and dangerous job. He has to be alert, or he will be killed. If his heart is broken by you, and that could easily happen, we all would be very worried. But he is an adult, and he has to handle his own life. You know, of course, there have been other women?"

I swallowed and nodded.

"They have meant nothing to him. Nothing. All of us, his friends and relatives, have thrown numerous good women to him, but there were no sparks. He meets you and there is fire, not just sparks. I can tell. We are more like brothers than cousins."

By now there were tears in my eyes. "Herr Doktor Weiss…"

"Please, Jakob," he said kindly.

"Jakob, I love Theo. I never thought I would be in love again. I would have never chosen a man who lives so far away, a man who is in the profession that Theo is in, a man with…a history. I did not want to come to Tubingen last winter. This was the last place on earth that I wanted to come to. It's cold, it's gray, and it's rainy, and I speak German poorly. Theo intimidated me when we first met. Loving him was the last thing on my mind. Loving anyone was the last thing on my mind. I was a dried-up, frozen, pathetic lost soul whom Theo melted. I can't imagine my life without him now."

"Frau Doktor Douglas—Ana, if I may. Would you be coming back to Tubingen for research if it were not for Theo?"

I paused before I spoke. "I am not sure. My time here last year was so colored by my relationship with Theo; I don't think I can separate the two. He has everything to do with my desire to return, but I am excited about the new research, and this is where I would have to do it. Here and at the University of Heidelberg. I have to work in order to do the research. I can't afford to do it on my own."

"We will talk again," said Jakob. "I have another appointment. How much longer will you be here?"

"I leave the third week in January. I have spring semester to teach back in America."

"So, I understand Mimi is with you?" His eyes were twinkling again.

"Yes. That has been a challenge." I smiled.

"Mimi is a good girl. Just headstrong. Marta has been an excellent mother."

We took our leave of each other. Jakob bowed and kissed my hand in the old-world manner. Frau Graece made another appointment for me without any hesitation, but I left feeling unsettled. Nothing about the conversation had been professional. How could Jakob see me as a serious scholar when all we talked about was my love life?

The next few days were uneventful. Theo and I had settled into a comfortable domestic life. I kept telling myself that this wasn't so bad, and if I were working at the university and doing research, I would hardly notice the weather and all the other things that made me uncomfortable about Germany. I couldn't put my finger on what that was, but there was just something I didn't like. I thought that I might want to look into the apartment rental situation on one of my free days, as well. If I did come back, I didn't know if I would have the option of university housing or not, but I knew that I couldn't just move in with Theo. There really wasn't enough space for me to have an office, and I wasn't sure how much Theo would want me staying there on a long-term basis. We had so much to discuss. But I thought that finding my own place and making it feel more like me would go a long way in alleviating my anxiety about Germany. My own cozy little cocoon might offset the unrelenting gray, rainy days.

There was also nothing new on the Konrad Richter front. Theo just said they were keeping their eyes on him. I soon put him out of my mind.

Christmas was getting closer, and I wanted to celebrate it. I decided to take the train to Nuremberg to the Christkindlmarkt, but Theo didn't want me to go alone. We would go together on the weekend. Being Jewish, he had never been, nor did he especially want to go now. There was a smaller one in Stuttgart, but I wanted to see the most ancient one of all in the old medieval city of Nuremberg.

Being with Theo at Christmas would be a good test for us to see how we handled Christian and Jewish holidays. Theo had not said one word to me about Christmas. I thought he must have believed that I would just ignore it this year, since I was with him, but I had never ignored it, even the first Christmas after Mark had died. I didn't do much that year, but I did go to church with the Capellos. We exchanged presents, and I had Christmas dinner with them. I didn't decorate my house, but the next year, I had students with me again, and we went all out, although though my heart wasn't in it.

I knew that I would have to bring this subject up and discuss it with Theo, but I was strangely reluctant. I didn't want to rock the boat. He also had not said one word about Hanukkah, which I knew had already started. I could not believe that Theo did not celebrate any part of this festival of lights. Did he even own a menorah?

I had talked him into taking the train to Nuremberg, just so he would have an opportunity to relax a bit and not fight traffic. I knew he was only doing this for me. He had arranged for us to have a private compartment, which looked just like something out of the movies. I decided I had to take the plunge and open this up.

"Theo, thank you for doing this." I started.

He was reading a book and looked at me, confused. "Doing what, Liebchen?"

"The whole thing--the train, going with me to Nuremberg, and especially taking me to the Christkindlmarkt. I can't wait to see it."

"You are very welcome," he said and returned to his book.

"Theo, is that book something you have to read for work or something you want to read?"

Theo looked up at me once again. We were sitting opposite each other in the compartment, and our knees were just inches apart. He put the book down and looked at me for a few seconds. "What is it, Ana? You have something on your mind."

He is the most intuitive man in the world, I thought. "Yes, I do have something that I'm wondering about, but I'm having trouble talking about it."

He leaned over, took both of my hands in his, and looked me directly in the eyes. "You have my full attention, Liebchen. What is bothering you?"

"Remember one of our first conversations last winter when I asked you why you, a Jew, lived in Germany?"

He frowned slightly. "Ja, I remember it. Why is that important now?"

"I was impressed that you and your relatives believe that a continuing Jewish presence is an important reminder of the Holocaust, but I am confused as to why you do not celebrate significant Jewish events."

"I don't understand, Liebchen. What are you trying to ask me?" Theo looked thoroughly perplexed.

"Theo, aren't we in the midst of Hanukkah?" I asked a little impatiently.

As if a light had gone on, Theo nodded. "Ja, Hanukkah began two days ago."

"Yet you have said nothing. There is no menorah. Do you even own a menorah?"

"Ja, I have my mother's menorah. It was one of the few things she saved and brought with her from Berlin."

"Then why haven't we been lighting candles each night?"

Theo looked unsure of himself. I had never seen this in him before "Ah, Ana…" He stopped, ran his hand through his hair, and then looked at me again. "I wasn't sure what to do. I didn't know if you would be offended, so I have been a coward and have done nothing."

"Oh, Theo, we can't let this happen to us. This is what will destroy us." I felt tears well up. "Don't you think we can celebrate both of our faiths, our beliefs? Isn't our love strong enough for that?"

"Ja, you are right, Ana. We must talk about these things. I have been worried about your Christmas. What is the right thing to do?"

"We must do both. We must find compromises so that we both feel comfortable. When we get back to your apartment, the first thing you must do is bring out your mother's menorah. We will light those candles and celebrate that miracle. I would like to go to church on Christmas Eve, and I would like for us to have a Christmas dinner and exchange presents. Can we do that?"

"Ana, you are so good for me. Come over here and sit beside me. We can make this work—both religions, both faiths." With that, he kissed me tenderly. I felt like a burden had been lifted. I knew there would be other hurdles, but this one was already feeling better.

We waited until it was dark before we went down to the old historic area near the Frauenkirche where the market had been set up. As we entered the market area, we immediately encountered a huge Christmas tree hung with hundreds of bright lights, surrounded by little stalls draped in white lights. There was music and a festive feel in the air. The little shops were selling handmade crafts such as Moravian stars, cuckoo clocks, and nutcrackers. I slipped my arm in Theo's. "This absolutely magical. It is unbelievably enchanted and romantic."

Theo winked. "I am happy for the romantic part. That will come in handy for later."

Theo bought me gluehwein, a hot, spicy red wine that warmed me up as we walked around. "This is really good." I said as I felt the warmth hit my stomach. "I may have to have another one of these."

"You must also try a lebkuchen. It is traditional for this time of the year."

"What is that?" I asked.

"Here, try one." Theo purchased a little bag of honey-gingerbread cookies. We stopped to listen to a choir sing "Silent Night" as we ate. I made several purchases as we went along. I loved the little miniature clocks and got one for Mimi, Katie, Sara, and Nikki. "I can't believe Mimi doesn't have a cuckoo clock," I said to Theo.

"Ana, only tourists buy cuckoo clocks. I don't know one German who owns one." He laughed.

"Then this will bring a little bit of Germany to her in the States," I said. "I hope it won't make Katie sad. I am afraid Germany holds only bitter memories for her. At least she will know that I was thinking about her while I was over here."

"You are too generous, Ana. You spend all your money on others. What about you? Isn't there something that you would like?"

"No, Theo, there is nothing I want for myself. I have this wonderful memory of being with you here, and I will never forget this. It is our first holiday together in Germany, and this is the happiest that I have been over here. This moment. This night. Being with you."

"Really, Ana? You are not happy with me in Tubingen?"

"I love being with you, Theo. I can't explain it, but somehow Germany doesn't hold the same happy memories that Italy did. I don't know why. I think it is the weather. I seem to be here when it is cold, gray, and rainy. Italy was warm and sunny. I am seeking happy times here, and this is definitely one of them."

Right in the middle of the marketplace, Theo turned me around toward him and kissed me deeply. "Ana, before you leave, I hope there will be at least one more magical moment for you."

"Are you planning something, Theo?"

"Vielleicht, Liebchen, vielleicht," he said mysteriously.

Perhaps? What is he up to? I wondered.

# III

True to our words, as soon as we returned to Tubingen, Theo brought out his mother's menorah, and we lit all the candles up-to-date. We celebrated with a glass of gluehwein. "To your mother, Theo. I wished I could have met her."

"Ja, Ana, so do I."

I had also purchased an advent wreath at one of the stalls in Nuremberg, and we lit two candles in preparation for Christmas. "I am feeling very ecumenical these days," I remarked to Theo. "This will work for us, Theo. We will make everything work for us."

Things were working for us. The happiness of our time in Nuremberg lingered into the next week. I loved Theo's apartment, especially the bookcase across the wall in his living room. He was so well-read, and his living room lent itself to curling up with a good book. I was amazed to find books in Italian, German, and English. The view out of the window at the backside of the Rathaus was almost fairy-tale in its beauty. There would be two full moons before I left Tubingen, and I couldn't wait to see the moon lighting the streets and the top of that building again. I had never forgotten that night when Theo turned me around in his darkened apartment to see it for the first time.

As much as I loved Theo's apartment, it was masculine to the bone. I was bringing a little femininity into his world without changing things. There were candles on the tables, and new placemats. I bought fresh flowers every few days, and I was learning to cook German soups and stews. Theo came home at odd times. There were no such things as normal working hours, and he came home hungry. I found having a pot of soup and hearty bread on hand was just what was needed.

"Ana, what will I do when you leave? You are spoiling me."

"I am freezing soups and stews, so all you have to do is thaw something out in the morning before you leave," I remarked one evening.

"You are doing that for me, Ana?" Theo asked gratefully.

"I worry about you, Theo. You don't take care of yourself. Your work is dangerous and stressful. A little soup is the least that I can do."

Truth be told, I was bored. Domestic bliss only took me so far. I needed more. I had met with Jakob twice more and had grown quite fond of him. He had convinced me to start on my new research while I was visiting, and he pointed me in the right direction. I had access to archives that I would have never seen without his help. He was planning to take me to Heidelberg to do some research in the next week.

I was always a little nervous when walking to the university. I was afraid that I might run into Konrad Richter, especially around Saint George's Church, where he used to hang out. But I had seen neither him nor the young, blonde woman again. I knew he had to be somewhere nearby, so I carefully covered up when I was in that area. Fortunately, it rained almost every day and the umbrella helped me remain incognito.

Today, I was hoping that Jakob could assist me in an idea I had for a present for Theo for Christmas. I wanted to get him a framed picture of his mother. Like so many Jews, his family lost their keepsakes in the war, and there were almost no family photos left.

"That may be impossible, Ana," Jakob remarked, "but there are a few photographs around. I don't know if there is any of Ruth. She lived in Berlin most of her adult life before she returned to Stuttgart. I will ask around and see if anyone has anything. How did you come up with this idea?"

"Theo has his mother's menorah, and it made me think that there may be other things of hers around. He has no pictures of her, and I think he would like one to put next to Mimi and his sister, Leah. What about Leah— would she have any pictures?" I had never met Leah, but I knew that Theo felt close to her.

"Perhaps. I will make inquiries and let you know. Now, let's spend time talking about the rebuilding of the Jewish presence after World War Two."

The time sped by, and before I knew it, I was walking back down the hill. The rain had stopped, but it still was a nasty day, and it was getting dark. I hurried by the Holtzmarkt and past Saint George's. Again, I saw no one. I almost started believing that Konrad Richter had been a figment of my imagination.

When I arrived home, Theo was there with the beautiful, blonde girl. She turned out to be an American, Caroline Hagar. "Ana, is this the person you saw with Konrad Richter?"

"Yes," I said.

Caroline had been crying. "Please, Fraulein, don't be afraid. I just need some information." Theo was being gentle with her. Remarkably, he happened to be in the neighborhood where she was living and saw her walking on the street. He stopped her, identified himself, and brought her to the apartment to wait for me.

"Wait, Theo. Let me make some tea or coffee. Which do you prefer?"

"Some tea, please," she said in a frightened voice.

Once she had gotten the tea, Theo said to her again, "As I explained, Fraulein Hagar, I can do this here or down at the polizei station. It is up to you. We may still have to go there, but first, just a few questions. How do you know Konrad Richter?"

She spoke in a weak voice, which got stronger as she told her story. "I came to Tubingen seeking him out. He is responsible for my sister's death."

"Who is your sister, Fraulein?" Theo asked patiently.

"Ann Hagar. She was in jail here but was let out after the attacks in America on September eleventh. She had served two years for a crime against the state, something Konrad Richter put her up to. She did not know what she was doing or that she was carrying around explosives. She thought she was delivering a package to one of his friends. She trusted this Konrad completely. She was in love with him." Caroline's voice was full of hatred.

"Ja, Ann Hagar. Ana, she was the other prisoner who got out with Katie Willis."

"Oh my God. Your sister, Ann, helped my student survive in that prison," I said as I looked at Caroline. "What has happened to her? I know Katie tried to get in touch with her but kept hitting dead ends."

Caroline started to cry. "She killed herself last month. Did you know that she had a miscarriage in that prison?" She looked at Theo, who shook his head no. "She was carrying Konrad's baby, but he only laughed at her when she told him. He told her she was a stupid American bitch. Prison was hard on her. She felt betrayed and alone. When she got out and came home, she was ashamed, and my parents said some harsh things to her. Ann was extremely depressed and couldn't get on with her life. She told me about Katie Willis She realized when they met that she was one of a long line of women whom Konrad had used. She couldn't get over the whole ordeal and hated herself for being so stupid and a disappointment to our parents. She overdosed. In her last letter to our family, she told us that we should just forget that she ever existed. She had ruined her life and theirs."

I reached out to her. "Caroline, I am so sorry. This Konrad is evil. It was not her fault. He seeks out naïve, young girls. He is very seductive. Katie was warned about him, yet he still was able to persuade her to follow his orders."

Caroline sat up straight in the chair. "Yes, I know how evil he is. That is why I am here. I want to kill him for what he did to my sister and to my family. I had planned to kill him, that is, until Inspektor Volker stepped in. He is ruining everything."

"Fraulein, believe me. That is not feasible, and you would end up in jail yourself. Konrad Richter is cunning. But you may be able to work with us to capture him so that he goes to prison himself. Are you willing to do that?" Theo asked.

"I want him dead," she said vehemently. "He killed my sister. He does not deserve to live."

"Ja," said Theo. "I don't disagree with you, but you may be our best hope of bringing him in and staying safe yourself. Sometimes it is much more pleasurable to see someone suffer than just kill them. If you did that, it would just make him a martyr to his cause. Is that what you want? You would look like a jilted girlfriend who got angry. Nein, Fraulein, we can come up with something much better that would in some small way avenge your sister. Isn't that a little more appealing? Believe me, Konrad in prison would be a good thing. German prisons are not like American ones. I am sure your sister told you some of what she went through."

"How do I know that he would suffer?" Caroline asked.

"There are ways that I won't go into right now, but you can believe me, he will be a broken man within a few short weeks of intense interrogation. I can promise you myself, Fraulein. It will give me great pleasure to see him suffer."

Caroline became calmer. "What would I have to do?"

"First you must convince Konrad Richter that you are a Jew hater. We will come up with a plan to trap him. Are you willing to help us?"

"Yes, if you will promise me that you will hurt him."

"Fraulein, ethically I am bound to protect prisoners, but you would be surprised at how many accidents they have."

Theo was quite convincing that Konrad Richter would be treated the way he deserved to be treated. Konrad was not liked by many polizei, who hated the neo-Nazi groups. "Starting tonight, you must never acknowledge that you have seen Ana, or that she is connected to me in any way. Your life will be in danger if you do that. Do you understand that, Fraulein?"

She looked at me. "This is the right thing to do for your sister's sake, Caroline," I said. "Please put your time and energy here into helping the police. You will have a much better outcome."

Theo took her down to the station to begin plotting a strategy to set Konrad up for capture. When he came home later, he seemed more energized than I had seen him in a long time.

"Do you think Caroline can keep her hatred in check, Theo, to help you?"

"I am worried about her. She is, as you Americans say, a loose cannon, but she is the first break that we have had. She wants him as badly as we do. We have assigned a female officer to be with her, someone who is passing as a student. They will be roommates. We can protect Caroline better that way also."

"Do you think Konrad would hurt her?"

"Ja, he would kill her. We know he has killed others, but we haven't been able to prove it yet."

"Maybe you should just send her back to the States."

"Ana, she would just come back. It is better that we work together so that we can keep our eyes on her."

I was worried about the danger Caroline was in, but it wasn't Caroline who needed to fear Konrad. I soon found out it was me.

# IV

A few days later, I took the local bus into Stuttgart to do some shopping at one of the big department stores. I was looking for a particular brand of German cosmetics that I had started using when I was here last winter. I wanted to get several items in this cosmetic line to take back to the States with me. I hoped to talk Lena into selling them in her newest salon, which was going to be a bit more upscale.

I had just purchased a bag full of different things: moisturizers, cleansing creams, eye creams, lip glosses, and a variety of other samplings of this line. The bag was quite heavy, and I wondered if I was crazy trying to tote all of this back on a bus. I was trying to decide if I wanted to have the store ship them to Theo's apartment, when I felt someone close behind me. A voice was whispering in my ear, but I couldn't make out what he was saying. At the same time, two hands were on my shoulders, tugging at my scarf and steering me away from the counter. Out of the corner of my eye I could see, to my horror, that it was Konrad Richter.

"Konrad!"

"Ja, Dr. Douglas. I was on the same bus from Tubingen and have been following you. No doubt you are visiting that Jew schwein Volker. I have decided that a perfect present would be to have his Christian American girl-friend's body delivered to him for Hanukkah. I think that would make the lights go out. Don't you agree, my lovely little professor?"

While he was whispering this to me, it must have seemed to the other customers that we were two lovers having an intimate conversation. Konrad was smiling with his lips to my ear as he steered me to the back of the store. He held me in a death grip. I couldn't breathe or speak, because he was slowly tightening my scarf around my neck. He was so strong that I couldn't get away from him, and my heavy bag of cosmetics was a hindrance, as well.

I felt panicky. This man was going to kill me. Konrad was whispering that it wouldn't be long now. Soon I would be dead. He was gleeful. I had to do something quickly, or it would be too late. No one was paying attention to us.

Suddenly, he steered me into the gift department, and we moved swiftly toward the back door. I knew once he got me outside of the store, any chance I had to save myself would end.

There was a glass shelf filled with crystal figurines and vases in front of me. With all my might and the little energy that was left in me, I swung my heavy bag into the shelf. There was a loud crash as all the crystal objects tumbled to the floor and broke. I later learned that the shelf the bag initially hit had caused the ones under it to break and crash, along with the objects on them. It was like dominoes. There was complete pandemonium.

Out of nowhere, a security guard appeared. I mouthed the words "hilfe mich, hilfe" and then slid to the ground in a faint from lack of oxygen. Konrad tried to get away, but the noise caused the shoppers to surge forward to see what was happening. He was trapped in the crush. Someone recognized him as my "lover," and the guard held him until I could be revived. I woke up confused by what had happened and could not speak because my neck hurt from the attempted strangulation.

The only person I could see was Konrad. I pulled my coat open and heard a gasp from the nearest onlookers. My neck was red, swollen, and beginning to bruise. Another guard leaned down. "Frau, can you speak?"

I could only say "murder." I looked at Konrad, who was denying that he even knew me. I don't know how I did it, but I said, "Call Volker, Interpol." The guard understood that, and then I fainted again. I remember my neck hurting badly and how hot the store was. There were many eyes looking down at me but none with the hatred that filled Konrad Richter's.

I don't know how many hours had passed when I woke up in a hospital room. I knew where I was immediately. Theo was sitting by the bed holding my hand. His head was bent, and his eyes were closed, but I could see that his eyelashes were wet. My other hand had an IV tube in it. I made a sound, but I couldn't talk. My throat hurt too much. Theo jumped at the sound I made and was immediately alert.

"Ana, darling, don't try to speak. You have been given a mild sedative to help your throat heal. It is important that you don't bruise your vocal cords any further. Do you understand me? Just nod your head if you do."

I nodded.

Theo burst into a big smile. "You will be OK, Ana, Liebchen. You will not be able to speak for several days. The doctor will be in tomorrow morning with instructions. You are being kept overnight for observation and to medicate you. I know you are full of questions, so I will tell you all that I know and you can write questions tomorrow if I leave anything out."

I nodded once more.

"The most important thing—besides you being OK—is that Konrad Richter is in jail and will be there a long time. You were very brave, my little darling. He will never hurt anyone again. The store has on videotape the episode with you and Konrad. There is no doubt that he was trying to harm you, and he is being charged with attempted murder. We also have some evidence through Caroline Hagar, so he will be charged with crimes against the state. We have him good and tight. We have seen the last of that little weasel for years to come. I had the pleasure of interrogating him myself earlier this evening. Unfortunately, our Konrad is quite clumsy and has had several falls and accidents since being retained in custody."

I was having difficulty keeping my eyes open. I heard Theo's voice from a distance. "Go to sleep, Ana. I will be with you all night."

I kept dreaming that I was being strangled and that I was running, running but couldn't get away. I was trapped in a circle of people pushing and pulling me. I couldn't speak. I couldn't yell for help. Every time I struggled, I could hear Theo's voice, far away, telling me to be calm. No one could hurt me. I trusted Theo. I knew he wouldn't let anything happen to me.

I heard a voice from a long way away. "Frau Doktor Douglas, can you wake up? Please try, Frau Doktor. Open your eyes. Try harder. Open your eyes. No, no, don't shut them again. Make them stay open. Don't try to speak, Frau Doktor, just open your eyes."

Slowly, I became more cognizant of my surroundings. I heard someone say, "Gut, gut, keep your eyes open, Frau Doktor."

Standing by my bed, taking my pulse, was a doctor. "Can you hear me, Frau Doktor?"

I nodded.

"Frau Doktor, as soon as you can stay awake for an hour and eat a little broth, I will discharge you. I have told Herr Volker that you must try not to speak for five days. Then you can gradually start speaking in a whisper. Your vocal cords were damaged yesterday, and they need time to heal. You must not strain your voice. The nurse is coming to help you bathe and dress."

I felt weak. I could barely sit up and felt like I had been beaten. "Herr Volker has been called and is on his way here to fetch you," the nurse said.

By the time Theo arrived, I had eaten and was dressed, ready to leave. The doctor checked me over once more, and then we left the hospital for home. I was teary and felt weak. Theo looked over at me in the car and took my hand. "Ana, you will be OK. I am staying home with you today, and I have some good news."

I looked at him expectantly. "The capture of Konrad Richter is such big news that my boss is giving me a few days off next week. We will go to Montepulciano for the holidays, just the two of us—and Schnee, of course. I called Luigi this morning to ask him to prepare the farm and buy some provisions."

My heart leaped. I wanted this more than anything, but I was strangely sad. Theo answered that question as well. "You know, Ana, you have been traumatized by the whole event. Expect to be tearful and frightened for the next few days. It is normal for now. There is one other thing. Reporters from the world over want to interview both you and me."

I raised my eyebrows in surprise. Theo laughed. "Ja, the capture of Konrad Richter and the break-up of this one particular neo-Nazi cell is big news, and your courageous action in Hertie's is a major story. Wait until you see the newspapers. I have *Der Spiegel*, the *Washington Post*, the *New York Times*, two Italian papers, and some others that even I can't translate. Can you believe this, Ana? Hollywood is already talking about making a movie of the incident."

I was astounded and didn't think that I could have talked anyway.

"One other thing. My sister, Leah, called. She wants us to come to dinner on Saturday, if you are feeling up to it. I told her that I would let her know. There have been many calls about you since the story broke. Mimi and Katie called, and Jakob, of course. Your friend, Lena. Your parents from Florida."

The more Theo talked and stroked my hand, the less anxious I began to feel. My throat and neck hurt, and it was difficult to swallow, but the doctor had given me a liquid pain reliever to be taken when needed in the first few days. I also needed to drink a lot of fluids and could eat only soups and soft foods.

As we got closer to Theo's apartment building, there seemed to be a crowd of people milling about. Theo muttered a profanity. "They are reporters and photographers, Ana. You are hot news." I shook my head. "Don't worry, I am calling for help." He drove in the opposite direction. I soon could hear sirens in the background and then Theo's phone rang.

The backup cops had cleared the street, and we were able to get in the house. I couldn't wait to get paper and pen so that I could write questions. Theo stopped me. "First things first," he said. He took me in his arms and held me tightly. He felt so warm and secure. "Ana, will you ever forgive me for putting you in such danger?"

I broke away and found the paper. "Never say that again," I wrote. "Konrad Richter was evil. He is out of our lives forever." I wasn't sure about that, but I didn't blame Theo in any way, and I didn't want his guilt over this incident intruding into our relationship. "I love you, Theo. That's what gave me the energy to fight back. I now know why Caroline Hagar wanted to kill Konrad. I felt exactly the same way. Have you talked to her?"

"Ja, this morning before I came to the hospital. She is overwrought and wants to see you as soon as possible."

"I am tired, but I would like to see her today. Is that possible? Can you go get her or have her brought here, Theo?"

"Ja that is not a problem. But are you sure that you want that today?"

I wrote, "I need to reassure her and let her know that it's over. Theo, I have one more major concern."

"What, Liebchen?"

"I must owe the store, Hertie's, a lot of money for breaking all that crystal. I had already paid for the cosmetics, but I remember a lot of crashing glass."

Theo started laughing. "No, Liebchen, you owe the store nothing. Nothing. That wasn't good crystal on those shelves. The fine crystal is not in the open, it's behind a counter. The store has gotten excellent publicity out of all of this. Their security guards were responsible for capturing the notorious Konrad Richter. The guards have gotten bonuses. Hertie's wants to repay *you* for the cosmetics. The cosmetic line wants to give you free samples for a year. That is the least of your worries. Now let's get you back in bed. Are you hungry? I have a refrigerator full of food that people have sent you. Enough soup for ten years. We will take some of it with us to Italy."

I was tired, so I nodded to Theo that bed sounded good. He brought me some tea, and soon I was asleep. Schnee got on the bed beside me, something ordinarily he was not allowed to do, but he snuggled against me and started snoring. Surprisingly, he felt as comfortable to me as Theo. I felt completely protected.

Later in the evening, Theo brought Caroline over with a warning that I could only sit up and communicate with her for fifteen minutes. She was crying when she saw me.

"Dr. Douglas, I am so glad that you are recovering. It was almost like my sister dying again when I heard what that viper tried to do to you. I have never hated someone so much in my life." Tears streamed down her face.

In a shaky hand, I wrote to her, "I understand your hatred, but it is wasted now. Go back home, Caroline. Start your life over for yourself and in memory of your sister. I will be back there at the end of January. I want us to get together and talk about all of this and then put it behind us forever. Your sister would have been proud of you as I am."

"Thank you, Dr. Douglas. I will never forget you or Inspektor Volker, and I will be in touch. I will try to get a flight out in the next few days." With that she leaned over and kissed me on the cheek.

After she left, Theo came back in the bedroom. "Ana, I will never get over your kindness to people, especially the young ones. I left my Mimi with the right person."

I rolled my eyes at him and was soon back to sleep with my arms around my new best friend, Schnee.

# V

I healed quickly, but not being able to talk was a real annoyance. I looked forward to meeting Leah and her family. We were going to celebrate the end of Hanukkah with her. It would be my first real Jewish holiday dinner, and I was excited. Leah and her husband, Rudi, lived north of Stuttgart. They had two sons, Karl and Jonas, who were eight and ten years old.

Theo's mother had married three years after her return to Stuttgart, and Leah was born two years later. Theo was nearly six years older than she. I had only seen one picture of Leah, and it was a bit fuzzy, so I was unprepared for her beauty and how blonde she was. She looked like a true German and not one bit like Theo, who was so tall and darkly handsome.

It was obvious that Leah's sons were crazy about their Uncle Theo. They jumped all over him. He picked each one up easily and carried them under his arms like two lumpy footballs. They were giggling and shrieking until Rudi made them settle down, but that only meant that they sat under Theo's legs until they got the cue from Theo that they could misbehave a little.

Leah was charming, and I liked her instantly. She was a gracious hostess and explained what each food item meant and how to prepare it. But she warned me that she wasn't a hausfrau or a cook. She loved her job as editor of

316

a successful home magazine that highlighted homes of the rich and famous in Europe. Rudi had been born in the Netherlands and was from a small band of Jews from that country. His import business took him back and forth between Germany and the Netherlands several times per month. Both boys looked like Dutch poster children.

It was also apparent how much Leah loved Theo. He was her big brother, and he had protected her throughout their childhood. Her father had become Theo's true father, and they had a happy childhood rebuilding their lives in postwar Germany. Leah told me that the entire family, small as it was, came together as they discovered each other one by one after the war. She did not remember it but had heard all the stories. It was evident that Theo had told Leah and Rudi how much I meant to him. They accepted me as one of the family. The boys asked if they could call me Tanta Ana.

It was a lovely evening in Leah and Rudi's elegant old-world apartment on the top floor of an old estate. It was furnished beautifully with antiques, crystal, and paintings, yet it felt comfortable and warm. Leah promised to come get me before I returned to the States and take me to her office so that I could see the making of her magazine. She wanted to do a piece on Theo's farmhouse in Italy, but he said it wasn't hoity-toity enough for her readers, and he wasn't famous. Leah just laughed and said, "You are now."

Seeing Theo with his sister and nephews gave me a whole other view of him. He had a real family side that I had never seen. Of course he was Mimi's father, but she was an adult, for all practical purposes, and their relationship functioned affectionately at that level. I loved how he was with his nephews, but more than that, he was the head of the family, and he took his role seriously. Being with Theo meant that I would be involved with his family, and it felt comforting to realize how much I liked them, even Mimi, who could be so challenging.

Mimi had called right away when I got home from the hospital, and in her demanding voice, she yelled over the phone, "Ana, you are OK, no?" I knew now that was the way she showed affection. "You should have killed the bastard."

"I tried, Mimi, I really tried," I whispered hoarsely.

"Gut, Ana, my father will take care of him now. Don't worry."

Then Katie got on the phone and cried and cried. Mimi took the phone from her and said "Ana, Katie is glad you are not more hurt, right, Katie? She wishes that you had killed the bastard too, right, Katie?" Then I heard Mimi's muffled voice saying something to Katie. "Ana, I told Katie we would call again when you could talk. We did not call so you could hear Katie cry. We call again." Then she abruptly hung up. That was Mimi. I had to laugh.

Leah was right. Theo was famous now, and so was I. Our stories had been splashed across major newspaper and TV shows. We were besieged by reporters and decided to give three interviews. The German newspaper, *Der Spiegel*, the *Washington Post*, and one German TV show. The rest were put on hold. The German TV show thought it would be more dramatic to interview us while I could only whisper. They had the footage from the department store showing Konrad's attempt to strangle me and the glass shelves crashing. It made for excellent TV. And it was true; Hollywood wanted to do a movie. Theo and I teased each other about who would play our parts, choosing the most virile and beautiful actors we could think of. I had other ideas. I wanted to write a book about the hatred of the neo-Nazi groups and incorporate the roles that girls like Katie and Ann were manipulated into, and finally, how Konrad Richter had been caught.

Although all of this had an element of excitement and drama, I welcomed the time it would be yesterday's news. Things were blown completely out of proportion, which was crazy, because the real story was dramatic enough. There were also too many questions of a personal nature that made me feel uncomfortable, but Theo just shrugged it off.

# VI

I t was with great delight that Theo and I left for Montepulciano on December 23. I was exhausted, and so was he. We couldn't wait to get away from all the hustle and bustle of the investigation and the reporters who kept calling. We would only have four days in Italy, but that didn't matter. Luigi had promised to have the house ready when we got there.

The very first thing I noticed, as we drove on the property, was a sign that said BAUERNHAUS PARADIS--Farmhouse Paradise. The blending of German and Italian. I looked at Theo.

"Is that a good name, Ana?" he asked.

"It's absolutely perfect, Theo. I love it."

The house was all lit up. Theo had called Luigi when we were just an hour away, and he was there to greet us. Luigi was holding Cara, the cat, when we arrived. She was no longer a little kitten but had grown into an enormous fat cat in just seven months. Schnee barked at her, but she held her ground. There was another cat weaving in and out of Luigi's legs. "Where did that cat come from, Luigi?" I asked.

Theo interrupted. "That's Fritz."

"Fritz?" I said.

"Ja," Theo remarked nonchalantly. "Luigi thought Cara needed a friend, since I am away so much." This was the man who hated cats and now owned two of them! I gave Luigi a look that said, I know what you are up to. He laughed and just winked at me. I had long ago decided that Luigi had "planted" Cara in the fields where he knew we walked each morning, hoping that I would take pity on the little kitten. It made me wonder how many more cats would somehow come to live with us.

I was transfixed by the changes inside. Theo had not mentioned all the work that had been done in the past six months. He had only said that he had continued to have workmen in to do various things. He had decided to speed up the remodel. There was a real kitchen, and it was beautiful. Theo liked American kitchens and had modeled this one on kitchens he had seen on various visits. He had chosen a dark-green marble for the countertops but had used a butcher-block top for an island that separated the kitchen from the dining area. The island was enormous and had storage space underneath. There were dark cabinets that ran the length of the white wall, interrupted only by the large window over the stainless steel double sinks. He had purchased a large refrigerator and a six-burner stove.

"Theo, I can't believe this. This kitchen was quite primitive in May, and now it looks like something out of a magazine—Leah's magazine!"

"Do you like it, Ana?"

"This is a dream kitchen. It's beautiful." I opened up the refrigerator and it was fully stocked. I turned to Luigi. "Mille grazie, Luigi." He beamed. There were freshly baked breads on the counter and cold cuts with cheeses in the refrigerator. We had brought some soups with us from Tubingen. Theo had built in a wine cellar that housed Montepulciano wines, as well as wines from other regions. Tomorrow, I was going out to purchase food for our holiday feast. I felt so happy here.

Luigi and his wife had decorated the rooms with green branches and candles, which gave the long room a festive feeling. Luigi bade us buona notte and said he would see us in the morning.

"Come, Ana, there are some other changes." The living-room area looked much the same, with the sofas that I had helped Theo purchase in May. They were now grouped with two comfortable chairs facing the fireplace. The lamps cast soft, inviting light. I thought Theo was taking me into the master bedroom at the opposite end of the house, but he was leading me upstairs.

"I took your suggestion and made this bedroom the master. The view up here is more commanding, but it was the privacy that appealed to me the most."

Theo had moved the huge four-poster bed upstairs, and it was made up in the beautiful linens and the duvet that Theo had purchased before I met him. It looked wonderfully inviting. This room was the same size as the bedroom underneath, but it didn't have the fireplace. It did feel more private, however. There was a modern bathroom just like the one downstairs, but the big surprise was that Theo had built a door into the adjacent room and made half of the room a walk-in closet.

"Oh my God, this is incredible," I whispered. It was cedar lined with a large freestanding mirror on one end, walls of shelves and hanging rods, and a large chest of drawers in the center. Like all the rooms on this level, it had a large window looking out on the valley. Underneath the window was a built-in vanity. I went over to it and sat down.

Theo came up behind me and said, "I had this made for you. All women need a place for their things." On the vanity was a freestanding antique mirror.

"Theo, how would a man know this is the perfect place to put on make-up with the natural light behind it?" Every little detail had been attended to in this combination closet and vanity.

The other half of the room became a small office for Theo. A third room on this level was a guest room, and the fourth room was now a den with a huge sleeper sofa. This room sat over the kitchen and was as large and spacious as the master bedroom on the opposite end. There was a wall lined with bookshelves, which Theo had already started filling up, and a very large flat-screen television. "What a wonderful room, Theo," I said, "It is beginning to look like your flat in Tubingen."

"Ja, I will one day bring all my books from my flat there, and I needed a place for them. I didn't know what to do with the other room up here, so I just left it empty for now. Maybe you can help me, Ana, decide what its use can be."

I smiled at him. "I feel incredibly honored that you paid attention to my suggestions. This house is paradise. Maybe the little room could be a room for Karl and Jonas when they visit."

"Ja." Theo smiled. "They would like to think they had their own room here when they come. We will have to get them beds and let them help decorate."

The former master bedroom downstairs had been designated as Mimi's room. The house was beginning to look settled and lived-in. Although it still needed a few more decorative touches, altogether it was a wonderful house.

"Ana, how are you feeling?" Theo looked concerned.

I was drooping a bit but also felt very lighthearted. Each kilometer we drove out of Germany made me feel happier, and the anxiety I always seemed to have there was gone in this place and this house.

I whispered, "A little tired but very happy to be here. I love this house, and I am looking forward to the next few days of uninterrupted peace and quiet and being with you."

"Ja, I agree. Let's have a little to eat and turn in early. We both could use a good night's rest. And, Ana, liebchen, no more talking. I think your voice is sounding strained. I am going to make you a cup of tea with lemon and honey. OK?"

I nodded and smiled. He was such a wonderful man. "OK, but I want a nice hot bath before I turn in."

Theo looked at me sternly. "I mean it, Ana, no more talking tonight." I could see him scrambling around looking for pen and paper for me.

"So now you write your answers. We will eat, and then I will run the bath water just as you like it. And then off to bed."

There was no desire to argue with him, because it was just what I needed. We quickly ate, and I had the most delicious bath, filled with lovely bath oils that Theo had purchased with me in mind. I climbed into the down-filled bedding and fell almost instantly to sleep. I barely noticed Theo coming to bed but did remember him snuggling up to me. "I love you, Ana" was the last thing I heard before I drifted into nine hours of solid sleep.

We had four blissful, tranquil days in Montepulciano. It was a very different Christmas for me. Theo was respectful of this significant Christian holiday and even accompanied me to church on Christmas Eve. The night was cold but clear, and we could hear the choir singing as we approached the town square. People were gaily greeting one another. Many remembered us from the summer. Luigi and his family were there and greeted us with presents of wine and olive oil. It felt very spiritual in the solemn Old Catholic church. The service was in Latin, which I did not understand. Ironically, Theo actually understood more than I, since his education has been classical, but the beauty and meaning of the service were easily translatable. It was well after two in the morning when we finally tumbled into bed, and we slept late on Christmas morning.

We exchanged gifts after a hearty breakfast of strong coffee—tea, in my case—cheeses, salami, and hard German rolls. We were cooking a huge meal later in the day. Lively Italian opera was playing throughout the entire house. I had not been this happy in years.

Jakob had come through and found two pictures of Theo's mother for me. One with just her profile and the other with Theo and Leah as little children standing beside her. Theo had never seen either picture and was touched beyond words. I had them framed in handsome silver, which set off the black-and-white photographs. Theo looked at them for the longest time and finally spoke. "I have no words to tell you how much this means to me, Ana. No words. I know that Leah has never seen these photos either. How did you come by them?"

"Jakob found them."

"Jakob, of course. Nothing is beyond him. They will travel with me from Tubingen to Montepulciano. I will have them with me always." Then Theo gave me a strange look. "Ana, I just realized that I do not have a picture of you. I must take a picture today."

"Wait, Theo, until I look better."

"You look beautiful, Ana. You always look beautiful to me." So he started taking pictures-lots of them. Me with Schnee, me with the cats, me cooking, sitting, standing, until finally, I said stop. Enough is enough.

My gift from Theo was a bracelet with diamonds, like a tennis bracelet but more delicate. "There is something else that goes with this Ana, but it is not ready yet." I thought it was probably a matching necklace. The bracelet was actually wearable, in a fancy casual way, and I loved how it looked on my wrist. It would look as good with jeans as it would with a cocktail dress.

Our four glorious days ended all too quickly, and I was sad to leave the farmhouse and the town of Montepulciano. It was such an easy, sweet life in the little Italian village. Not just because it was a vacation of sorts, but it just felt right to me. The farmhouse felt more like a home to me than my condo, despite the fact that it was only my second time here. Theo and I were completely compatible. We both could be comfortable curled up on the sofa reading books, watching TV, or listening to music. Snuggling together in bed each night even felt different in the farmhouse. I could live here and be happy forever with Theo, the dog, and the cats, I thought.

Why didn't I have this same feeling in Germany with Theo and Schnee? What was different? I couldn't identify my unease in Tubingen. Partly, I knew that there was nothing of me in Theo's flat. That could be rectified to some degree, but it mainly seemed to be the town itself. That was what kept throwing me for loops. And yet, I knew it wasn't just the town, because it was a charming little town with much to like. I had a good relationship with many of the townsfolk, and Jakob, of course, but it was something else. Something that gnawed at me and made me feel anxious.

# VII

On the way back, Theo informed me that we would be going back to Chossons for a New Year's Eve celebration. He said his cousins went all out, and people made reservations years in advance. It was the most celebrated restaurant in the entire region. That was exciting. I remembered how much I enjoyed my first visit there.

I had brought a red velvet dress with me, which Lena had helped me select. "You will need something warm in Germany, but that doesn't mean that it can't be sexy," she said. The dress had a square, low-cut neckline, long sleeves, and a full, short shirt.

Theo whistled when he saw me in it. "Ana, I don't think I can let you go out in that dress," he said very seriously.

I was nervous. "I have to wear it, Theo. It's the only dressy dress I have with me."

"Ja, but if you wear it, all the men will be looking at you, and I will probably get into fights. Our evening will be ruined."

I started giggling. "You are so silly, Theo. Really, I believed you at first. You need to get dressed."

Theo wore a black tux and looked so handsome. "Now I will have to fight all the women off. Maybe we should just stay in." I said. I was fumbling with my onyx necklace that Theo had given me in Florence. I had already put on my bracelet.

"There is just one more thing you need, Ana." Theo pulled out a long rectangular box that held a delicate diamond necklace to match the bracelet.

"Theo, this is magnificent. I feel like a queen. This is too much. I am just a lowly little professor, and you are spoiling me with all of this jewelry."

He put the necklace around my neck. "No, Ana, you are my queen." He kissed my neck, turned me around, and kissed me deeply. "I never want to let you go. I always want you in my sight. To think that I could have lost you forever. It's unbearable."

"Theo we are so lucky to have found each other." I hugged him tightly. "Are you sure you want to go out tonight?"

"We have to go, Ana. My cousins would never forgive me if we didn't show up. But there is later. Later will be just for us."

I kissed him back and held on to him. I really didn't want to let him go.

"Come, Ana, we will have a good time tonight."

Chossons was even more beautiful than I remembered it, and this time it was dressed for the holidays. It looked like a refined Tavern on the Green. There were swags of greenery on all the ornate gold mirrors. Each table had a lovely holiday centerpiece, and in the center of the room was a large live tree on a tabletop, with a gold star on top. All of Theo's cousins kissed me on the cheek when I entered, as if I was a part of the family. As they escorted us to our table, I saw Leah and Rudi waiting for us. What a wonderful surprise. Leah looked beautiful in a gold cocktail dress, and Rudi was very handsome in his black tux. The both stood as we approached the table.

Leah gave me a kiss on both cheeks. "You look beautiful, Ana, really beautiful."

I could feel myself blushing. "No, you are the beautiful one. All eyes in this room are on you."

Rudi took my hands and gave me the double kiss that Europeans do so well. "Ana, your voice—it's so sexy, so husky. And with your accent—well, this will be quite a night."

Theo jokingly slapped him on the back. "Back off, brother-in-law. She's mine."

Leah looked at me, concerned. "Your voice is healing, isn't it, Ana?"

"Yes," I said as we were getting seated. "It is far better, and my throat hardly hurts any longer. Theo made me write everything in Italy. I barely talked at all."

"Rudi is right, you know." Leah laughed. "Your voice is very sexy at this stage. Maybe it will stay right there."

"I hope not. It's still a nuisance, to some extent, and I do have to give it periods of rest." It was good to have them with us, because I wouldn't be required to talk as much. The conversation was in a mixture of English and German. My German was better and better. At one point, Leah complimented me on how well I was doing.

"Yes, I am very proficient in one particular aspect of German," I replied.

"Oh?" She and Theo replied at once.

"Yes, swear words. Theo has taught me every single thing you can say in German."

"Ana, that is not true," Theo protested.

"I promise that I could do any German sailor justice. Theo has a very colorful vocabulary at times." We all laughed, and Theo had the good grace to agree.

"It's true. I forget sometimes Ana is there. She has heard it all."

The waiter began bringing us our dinner, one course after another.

The food was exceptional, with a flambé ending. The waiters rolled in the flaming desserts all at one time, which resulted in cheers all around. It was a fantastic evening. Leah told me that she had never seen Theo as happy as he was tonight. She was so glad that I had entered his life. I was beginning to feel as much a part of this family as I did the Capellos.

All at once the room went completely dark. I grabbed Theo's hand. "What is happening?"

"Shh," he said. "Just look at the center of the room."

The tree branches, which were hung with real candles at the tips, were being lit one by one. They glowed in the dark and were absolutely magical. Everyone in the room gasped when it was all lit, even those who knew what to expect. It only lasted a few seconds because the tree presented a fire danger, but it was well worth it. I will never forget what it looked like. I thought this must signal the end of the evening, but the soft lights were brought up, Mozart was played softly on the piano, and the room looked romantic and elegant. Theo's cousin Dieter came over and stood at our table. He put his hand on Theo's shoulder. The entire room seemed focused on our table. What now? I wondered.

Dieter turned to look at the room and like a gracious host welcomed everyone who had visited Chossons that evening. He then turned to Theo and introduced him as his cousin, who wanted to say a few words to the room. I was surprised. Theo had said nothing to me about making a speech that night. I looked at Leah, but she just shrugged.

Theo looked a little nervous, which was unusual for him. He was always so confident and poised. He started out by talking about the recent events involving Konrad Richter. Then he turned to me and spoke about my courage and how much I had come to mean to him in the past few months. Everyone in the room was clapping and cheering for us. I had to laugh. I had never seen Germans so lively. Then Theo suddenly dropped to his knees in front of me. What in the world? I thought. He said, "Ana, you know that I love you. I can not imagine going through the rest of my life without you." He pulled a little box out of his tuxedo jacket and opened it up. Inside was a large solitaire diamond ring, which he took out. "Ana, will you marry me?"

The room erupted. People were clapping and yelling, "Sagen ja, sagen ja." Say yes. I was stunned and not prepared for this, but I only had eyes for Theo. When I found my voice, I whispered, "Are you sure, Theo, you want to marry me?"

"With all my heart, Ana. Please say yes."

I kissed him. "There is no one else. Yes, yes, yes. I love you, Theo."

The room went wild. This elegant upscale restaurant with jeweled and fur-draped women and successful men in tuxedos cheered as if they were at a sporting event and then began to crowd us to wish us congratulations. Leah and Rudi knew, of course. They had come to lend Theo moral support. Champagne corks began popping all over as the cousins served their best to all of their patrons. As if it were planned for us, fireworks began going off, and we all moved to the terrace outside to see the display over the city. I had never had an evening like this one. I was so in love, and I knew how lucky I was to have found, at this time in my life, a man like Theo.

It was the wee hours of the morning by the time we got home and in bed. Theo opened the curtain in the bedroom, and there was a full moon shining over the Rathaus, just like the first time I had been here. I held my hand up so that I could see my ring in the moonlight. "It is absolutely beautiful, Theo. Did Leah help you pick it out?"

"Nein, I consulted with her, and she only told me that I couldn't go wrong with a solitaire. Do you really like it, Ana? I wasn't sure."

"I love it, Theo. It is the most gorgeous ring in the world. And I love you. I was completely surprised. I had no idea that you wanted to marry me. I thought you liked things the way they were."

"Ana, I have been thinking about marrying you since the terrorist attacks in America. Life is too short for us to be apart. I know that we have only known each other a few months, but I feel this is right. We should always be together. I can hardly bear it when you are not here. And this thing that happened with Konrad Richter was frightening. I could have lost you, and I don't think I could have recovered. It would have been too much to have found you and lost you in the space of a few months. I know that we have a lot to work out with your career in America and my job here, but we will manage it."

"Do you think we can have a long-distance marriage, Theo?"

"It will be for just a few more years, and then I will retire to Italy. We will have time to talk about what we will do in Italy to make a living. I want to open an antique shop there. But enough of this, Ana. Let's celebrate our engagement."

What is it about making a deeper commitment and the quality of love? I was no different than I had been a few hours before, and neither was Theo, yet our lovemaking felt more intimate and tender in that first morning of the new year. The year I was to become Theo's bride.

# VIII

It had been an eventful three weeks since I had arrived in Tubingen. I had only about two weeks left before returning to the States. The weather had turned very cold, snowy, and icy. Jakob and I had to cancel our trip to Heidelberg twice because of the snow. I was hoping the weather would get better by the end of the week, because the research I could do at the university there would be significant for me, and Jakob could open doors that I would never have access to. I had become very fond of him, and Frau Graece had become almost friendly to me. My engagement to Theo had made her a little more hospitable.

Jakob was pleased that we would marry. "You are just what Theo needs," he told me yet another time.

"How do you think the family will receive a non-Jew? I am worried about that," I asked him one day.

"I think because you and Theo are older, it will not be much of a problem. You are respected because of your work and your sympathy to the Jewish cause. Of course, the incident with Konrad Richter takes you up several notches in everyone's mind. These neo-Nazi groups have bothered us for some time."

"I am slowly beginning to meet more of the family. I really like Leah and Rudi."

"Ja, they are very good people. You know that Leah and Marta have remained good friends throughout all these years?"

Now this was a surprise, and it must have shown.

Jakob nodded. "Ja, Marta and Leah were girlhood friends, even though Leah is a little older. They were in each other's weddings. Our community was very small after the war, so families banded together so that the children would know one another and grow up together. That is how Marta and Theo ended up getting married in the first place. It was a perfect union from everyone's perspective, but I have a feeling that it must have felt to some degree as if they were each marrying a sibling. They loved each other but were not in love with one another. Does that make sense?"

I nodded.

"Ja, I long observed them. There was no passion there. Nothing like I see with you and Theo." His eyes twinkled. "And Marta and her new husband—that is also different. A chance for two people to be happy—well, four people to be happy."

"I am happy, Jakob. Even though Theo and I have not known each other long, I know that we will be happy and make our marriage work. Theo has convinced me of that. Do you think my path will cross Marta's, or do you think the family will take steps to keep us separated? I don't want things to be awkward."

"Eventually, I think, you are bound to meet," Jakob observed.

And he was right. It happened the next day. I was curled up with Schnee on the sofa, reading a book and feeling a little bit bored. I felt as if I was almost back to normal. My throat no longer hurt, and my voice was much stronger.

Theo usually took Schnee to work with him but left him with me this day. The snow was melting some, so I was hoping that in the next day or so, Jakob and I could make our trip to Heidelberg. I heard a knock at the door. Schnee jumped up and ran to the door, barking.

"Stille, Schnee, stille!" I looked out the peephole and saw a woman standing there. She did not look menacing, so I opened the door.

I knew instantly it must be Marta, even though I had never seen a picture of her. She spoke first. "Frau Doktor Douglas?" I nodded. She looked uncomfortable but said, "I am Frau Marta Reiniger, Mimi's mother. Could I speak with you for a few minutes?"

"Please come in." I was bursting with curiosity. Marta could have been Leah's twin sister. They both were blonde and very pretty. Marta was probably just a bit older than me. Mimi had Marta's facial features but Theo's coloring and mannerisms. No wonder she was so good-looking.

"I am having tea. Could I make you some, or would you prefer coffee?" I asked as I took her coat. It was obvious that she had been to Theo's apartment in the past. She gave it a pleased look.

"I would love a cup of coffee, if it isn't too much trouble. I see that you have brought a woman's touch to Theo's very masculine flat. It looks nice," Marta said appreciatively.

"Thank you, please sit." I gestured her over to the table where I had place a slice of apple torte with her coffee. "I must admit that I am curious about the reason you are here. Jakob Weiss told me only yesterday that it would be inevitable that we would meet, but I never thought it would be so soon."

She smiled. "Ja, I called Jakob and asked if he thought you would see me, and he assured me that you would be friendly."

"I have become very fond of Jakob. He is giving me tremendous help on a new research project."

She smiled again. "Ja, Jakob told me that you tackle things head on. It makes me wonder how you and Mimi are getting along."

"Ah, Mimi," I said. "Obviously, you know that she is living with me. I hope you don't mind. I did it as a favor to Theo. Did you come about Mimi?"

Her face and demeanor turned sad. "Ja, Mimi has not spoken to me since I remarried. She is angry with me. I came to enlist your help, Frau Douglas. Frankly, I was very angry at first when Theo took her to America, but now I can see that it was the best thing to do. Thank you for your hospitality to my daughter. I know that she can be difficult."

"Please, call me Ana. I didn't know that Mimi was not in touch with you. I assumed that she was e-mailing or calling you frequently. We have had our problems, and it's only recently that Mimi has softened toward me at all, but that may change for the worse when I return to the States in a few days. Jakob or Leah must have told you that Theo has asked me to marry him."

"Ja. I am glad that Theo is remarrying. It will be good for him. He has been lonely for a long time, and both Jakob and Leah tell me that you are the exact right person for him. He needs a strong woman. Someone who will stand up to him. I have felt guilty that I have found someone who makes me so happy. It is now Theo's turn. That is why I came. I am hoping that when Mimi hears that her father is remarrying, she will give up hoping that we will get back together."

"I am not sure how she will take it. Believe me; I am nervous about telling her and shattering the little truce that we have. I wish Theo was going with me. We decided to call her tonight to let her know before I return. That way she can scream and yell or do whatever before I get back."

Marta laughed out loud at that. "She does have a temper, and she is stubborn. She wants life the way she wants it. Again, thank you for taking her into your home. Theo has told me how good you are with young people."

"We've had our moments, I have to say, but things have settled down nicely. I have one of my former students living with me, and that has helped the relationship issues quite a bit."

"Ja, that girl, Katie Willis, who was in jail here because of Konrad Richter."

"Yes, but you mustn't worry about Katie being a bad influence. She is really a good person."

Marta laughed again. "No, I don't worry about that. It is Mimi who could have the stronger influence, no?"

I nodded.

Marta continued. "I want Mimi to come home and finish her education at the University of Heidelberg. She seems to like America and wants to stay, but she cannot run away, and I think that is what she is doing. She must make her peace with me and my husband."

"How can I help you, Frau Reiniger?"

"Please, you must call me Marta. We will soon have a husband in common." We both laughed. She could be a lot of fun, I thought. Just like Leah. There was something mischievous about her.

"I am not sure how you can help, but Mimi can always go back to America and work or study at another time. We have Selma and Hyiam there to help her in the future. It is the present that she must confront."

She is absolutely right, I thought. Mimi needs to come home and deal with things here. "I am willing to do whatever you want. Let's put our heads together and come up with something."

When Theo came home an hour later, he found his former wife and his future wife laughing and enjoying each other's company so much that tears were running down their faces. There was a confused look on his face when he realized who was in his home.

"Marta?"

She stood, and Theo came over and kissed her on the cheek. "I think all must be OK. The tears seem good, no?"

"Ja, Theo, Ana is helping me with Mimi. She will make a good wife for you. Now I must get home. I have stayed too long." She came over and took my hand and kissed me on both cheeks. "Thank you, Ana. I will see you soon. I think we can be friends. When you come back to Germany, we will go out with Leah for lunch one day. Would you like that?"

"I would like that very much, Marta. I am so glad to have met you."

Theo looked at me, then at the door closing, and then back at me. He shook his head and said, "This is like an American movie." He came over and kissed me. "Ana, do you know that since you have come into my life, I have not had one predictable day?"

I looked at him and laughed. "And I can say the same thing, Theo. Do you think our lives together will always have drama?"

"Maybe," he said, "but I don't want to change it. So will you tell me what Marta wanted?"

I told him about her concerns for Mimi and that I thought she was right.

"Well, did you two come up with a solution?" He looked amused.

"I don't know if it's a solution, but it may be a beginning to reconciling your daughter and her mother."

"So, what is that, Ana?"

"I invited Marta to visit me in America." I looked as Theo's face changed from amusement to complete shock.

"What?"

"Yes, Theo, Marta is coming to America."

# KATHRYN

# I

M y first day back in the States was just like my return in May. I was awakened by loud knocks on my front door. I just know that is not Sammy. If it is, I will kill him on the spot, I thought, as I grabbed my robe. I had had exactly three hours of sleep. I opened the door without asking who it was or looking out the window first. There stood a tall good-looking man who seemed a little impatient.

He took one look at me and said regretfully, "Mrs. Wynham? I am so sorry. I should have called first. I am Brad Bergstrom, the contractor who has been doing all your renovations. I thought I would catch you up on what we have done while you were away and what is left to do. But I can see this is not a good time"

I was dazed and only heard half of what he had said. "Mr. Bergstrom, no, it is not a good time. I have only had three hours of sleep after two flights from hell with children screaming all night long, delays sitting on tarmacs, and every other conceivable thing that could go wrong."

"I apologize. I should have called. Mrs. Wynham, I will come back later—perhaps this afternoon or tomorrow morning."

Not usually a quick thinker, I blurted out impulsively, "Mr. Bergstrom, do you like Italian food?"

He looked completely confused but nodded yes and said he did indeed.

"Come back tomorrow night at eight o'clock, and I will make you dinner. Then we can talk."

Without thinking, I shut the door in his face and went back to bed for another four hours. When I finally dragged myself out of bed, I nearly gagged when I saw myself in the mirror. I looked like an old hag. My hair was sticking up in a million directions, there was no makeup, and I looked like I had been on a wild drunk for days. I wished! Did I just invite that man to dinner? He is probably out getting exorcised right now. I giggled. It doesn't matter, I thought, I am just a customer, and the most important thing is how good the work is and getting paid on time. I will just call Karen and get the lowdown.

Karen came over and brought me dinner that night. After we hugged and kissed, she took a long look at me. "Something is different about you," she said.

"Yes, it's called no sleep of any worth for two days. And it's called old age." I laughed. "What a way to greet me after two months."

"No, that's not what I meant at all. You actually look wonderful. Maybe a little tired, but really good. Something is different. You'd better tell me everything and don't leave out one thing. You met a man, didn't you? That's it—it's a man!" She clapped her hands gleefully.

"Karen, you are such a nut. I went to study Italian, remember?"

"Does that mean that there are no men in Italy, in the Italian class? You are hiding something. I have known you too long."

"I'll tell you everything, and then you can decide if there is a man or not, but first I have to thank you for all the work that has been accomplished in my house. I am astounded. It looks incredible. I thought I would be coming home to a horrible mess, and my house looks brand-new."

Karen beamed like a proud parent. "It has turned out wonderfully well. The kitchen was just finished two days ago. That was a close one." The house had been painted inside and out. All the floors had been refinished. Bookshelves had been redone in the living room. The oriental carpets had been cleaned and laid. New window treatments had been installed, and some of the furniture, which had been sent out for reupholstering, had been returned.

"I still can't believe how much got done."

"The rest of the furniture should be in by the end of next week at the latest, and Brad is contracting with the landscaper to complete that work as we speak."

"I know that I can never ever repay you for all that you have done, Karen, but I did bring you a little present from Florence, which I hope will let you know how fabulous I think you are."

She opened a beautifully wrapped box and was momentarily speechless when she saw the heavy gold necklace that lay inside.

"Well, do you like it?" I asked, amused. I knew she liked it. It was unique, and it looked like her. It was bold and solid gold.

"Oh my God! This must have cost as much as redoing this house. I love it! I freaking love it!" She took it out of the box and put it on. It was gorgeous on her. "Everyone in this little burg will be envying me forever when they see this. I feel like…I don't know what I feel. Rich. I feel rich."

I laughed. "I knew it was for you when I saw it." I had also bought her the earrings and a gold bracelet to match, but I wasn't giving them to her until Christmas. "Come on in the kitchen. Let's have some wine and dinner, and I will tell you about my two months in Orvieto."

I told her everything. Much of it was a repeat, since I had e-mailed her faithfully, but I had not told her about Robin Tremont wanting to sleep with me. We both laughed until we were crying. I also told her about the horror of living outside the United States when we were attacked, and how good the people of Orvieto had been to me. I reiterated my friendship with Inga Johansen, who I hoped would be visiting me in the upcoming months.

"Wow, those were jam-packed weeks," Karen said when I became quiet. "But there is more, isn't there?"

"A little more. I had an Italian tutor, Tonio. I wrote you about what a sweet boy he was."

"Yes, I remember his name. Didn't you visit his family?"

"Yes, Tonio had his grandfather, Salvatore, tutor me one day on some trumped-up reason so that we could meet. He had told his grandfather about the American woman, and Salvatore was curious."

"Salvatore? Well, that sounds kind of sexy. What was he like?"

"Like no one I had ever met before. I felt like a complete fool after I found out who he was. I didn't know it at the time, but he's one the most eligible men in Italy and a very successful businessman who owns a world-renowned winery. He looked very accomplished when I first met him, not a country bumpkin at all. He had on cashmere and aviator glasses and was driving an expensive sports car, so I knew he wasn't just a local yokel, but I did not know the extent of his wealth. I guess I still don't, but he lives in a beautiful villa with servants."

"You saw his house?" Karen asked excitedly.

"Yes, he took me to his winery and explained the wine-making process in Italian. He introduced me to all of his workers and told me about their families. He is the most amazing man, Karen. There were times when he would jump right in and help his employees do whatever as he was explaining things to me. He even swept the floor once! Imagine a CEO in America doing that. Wine making was part of my lesson for the day. Then we had lunch with his three sisters, two of whom live with him at the villa."

"Did you see him again?"

"Yes, several times. He took me to a wonderful restaurant just two nights ago for a farewell dinner."

"So what does all this mean, Kathryn? Are you in love?"

"No, I am definitely not in love. At least, I don't think I am, but it was very nice going out with an attractive man who was attentive. I can't take this seriously. Salvatore and I are literally worlds and lifestyles apart. I think that he is a little bored with country life. I can't imagine what Tonio must have said to him about me to pique his curiosity, but it was enough that he wanted to see for himself what I was like. They came up with this plan that Tonio had to be away, and Salvatore would be my tutor for the day. Since the name Sierra or Sierra Winery meant nothing to me at all, I was expecting some old grandpa type and not looking forward to it one bit. Salvatore knew instantly that I had no idea who he was, and he was delighted. He's so used to being chased by all those Italian women wanting to get married that I must have been refreshing and a little bit humbling, to say the least.

"By the time I got back to Orvieto, it was all over town that I had spent the day with the famous Salvatore Sierra. When I found who he really was,

I was completely embarrassed at my ignorance and that I was being talked about."

"Do you think you will ever hear from him or see him again?"

"I don't know. Certainly not if one of his sisters has anything to do with it. She disliked me from the start. I think she believes that I am just like those Italian women chasing him. I know that she loves her brother and doesn't want him to be hurt anymore, but I pity the woman who moves into that house with her in charge. Make no mistake; she is the commander of that villa!" I laughed at the memory. "Salvatore has my e-mail, and he says that he is coming to New York for a trade show in December, so we will see."

"Well, it definitely put a glow in your cheeks." Karen laughed.

"The other thing, which is far more important, is that Salvatore deeply loved his wife, and I am not sure that another woman could ever really take her place. Even Tonio said he had been sad for the three years since her death. But despite his grief, we did have some lovely moments together, and I will never forget them or Salvatore Sierra. It's part of my entire Italian experience."

Impulsively, I said, "Karen, we must plan a trip for next spring, if you feel up to it. You get to choose—anywhere you want to go, I am game. I can't tell you how stimulating it is to travel."

"Well," said Karen, "I would like some of that 'glow' stuff that you brought back, and I wouldn't mind meeting a rich foreigner, either."

Attempting to change the subject, I replied, "I think the glow you think you see in my cheeks is a fever from being kicked by the kid behind me for hours on end on the plane. Really, Karen, it was the worst plane experience that I have ever had. There were absolutely horrible children on board, and parents who did nothing to make them behave. Think of

Chapin on his worst day and multiply that by a hundred. I feel black-and-blue with bruises."

"You don't look it. I mean it, Kathryn, you really do look wonderful."

"Thanks. I called Lena Capello from my trip last May. Remember I told you about her?"

Karen nodded.

"I begged on bended knee for her to do something with my hair today, and fortunately, she just had a cancellation late this afternoon, so I went to her new shop, Italia, which is very upscale and classy. She is responsible for my new hairstyle, which is probably what makes me look a bit different to you. I loved the way she did it in Florence, and I think she did a great job today. What do you think?"

"I like it a lot. I think I should give that place a try. I am always in the market for something new and different."

Our conversation veered off into general catch-up about things and friends. What I didn't tell Karen was that I wanted my hair to look good when Brad Bergstrom came for dinner. It had been so long since I had felt attracted to someone that I felt embarrassed, but I knew that I wanted to look a lot better than I did this morning, when he caught me looking like a witch. I couldn't help but remember how good-looking he was, and I didn't want him to think I always looked like a crazed old woman. It was silly, I knew, but for some unexplainable reason, I wanted him to see me at my best.

After dinner, I steered the conversation around to Brad. I knew that Karen would know everything. "Karen, I did something so unlike me when Brad Bergstrom came to the door yesterday that I may regret it."

"What in the world did you do?"

347

"I was so dead tired; I couldn't register half of what he was saying. I was really rude, so impulsively, I invited him over for dinner tomorrow night."

"You did what?"

"I wasn't thinking, and now I am having second thoughts, so I need you to tell me some things about this man. I probably will call him in the morning and cancel. Did you and Mr. Bergstrom work well together? Is there anything I should know if he does come for dinner? I was so tired when I opened the door, I didn't get a sense of anything about him. Can you believe that I did that? At some point soon, we will have to get together and discuss everything he has done. I don't even know if he is married or not. Should I invite Mrs. Bergstrom?"

"You don't have to worry about a Mrs. Bergstrom at all." Karen settled in. I knew I would get the complete lowdown. "Evidently there was a bitter divorce about three years ago, and she pretty much cleaned him out financially. He seems to be a little—make that a lot—bitter about women in general. He went bankrupt and had to start over. This was a big job for him, and he has been grateful for the work. I think in the past six months or so, he has turned the corner and is back on his feet. There are a couple of grown daughters, and although they harbor some ill feelings about what their mother did, they are hoping he will reconcile with his ex-wife. Brad let that slip one day, so I don't know much more. We developed a good working relationship eventually, but it took a couple of weeks. I just didn't buy into his moods and remarks about women."

"Boy that was a boatload!" I replied. "Just so we don't get off on a worse foot than we already are, how should I approach him?"

She laughed. "He already has an image of you!"

I sat up in my chair. "What do you mean? We haven't even met officially. It couldn't be worse than what he saw yesterday."

"Yeah, but from his point of view, you are just some rich, spoiled woman who went off on a great vacation in Italy for two months and left your best friend, your sick best friend, to do all your dirty work."

"You're kidding!"

"Nope. I even told him about how Sammy and Jenn took advantage of you for six years, and what a handful Chapin was, but that seemed to go in one ear and out the other. He sees you as just another bored rich woman.

"That's really hot. I've had no social life for six years. I was buried alive."

"I know that," said Karen, "and I told Brad that your life had been more than rough, but he just gestured with his arm, sweeping it around this great room, and said sarcastically that he could see that. Those were in our tension-filled first two weeks. Things calmed down after that."

I was mad now. "Don't you think that it was a little presumptuous of him to think anything about me at all? He doesn't have a clue about me."

"Calm down. I think he is more curious than anything right now. He couldn't get over how you just up and flew to Italy to study Italian. That is just so far out of his world view that he can't comprehend it. He thought you were going to look for a rich husband over there."

I started giggling. "I guess the sight of me this morning put to rest why I didn't find one. I really don't care what he thinks of me. It's none of his business. He just needs to finish the work." But I was lying to Karen. For some reason that nagged at me, I did care. And I was still more than upset that he had this preconceived idea of who I was: a spoiled, rich gold digger, but most of all, someone who took advantage of her friends.

# II

"Grandma, are you coming over to see us today?" Eli, my sweetest baby, was excited that I was back.

"Not today, darling. I have a lot to do, and I am still very tired, but I will be over this weekend. How are you doing? I missed you loads."

"Grandma, Mommy has almost moved back home," he whispered. "Daddy said that Chapin and I have to be good and not get on her nerves. Chapin doesn't hit me anymore, Grandma. Nanny told him big boys who behave like big boys get privileges. That means special treats. She told me that I was born a big boy."

I chuckled. "Nan is so right. You are a big boy and my best boy. I can't wait to see you. Is Mommy still with Grandma Linda?"

"No. She is at work today," Eli answered.

I'd forgotten how literal children are. "Of course she is. Grandma is a dolt. I meant is she still living at Grandma Linda's house."

"No. She and Grandpa moved into a tiny apartment. Nanny said it was a doll's house. But Grandma, it doesn't look like a doll's house. It's just an apartment."

"Eli, you are priceless." I laughed. "Do you get to see Grandpa Larry often?"

"Yes, ma'am. He comes over every day," whispered Eli. "Grandpa Larry likes Nanny, too. He said she was the greatest thing since hot dogs at a baseball game. Isn't that silly, Grandma? Nanny isn't one bit like a hot dog!"

I adored this little fellow. "Eli, is Nan there now?"

"Yup! She wants to talk to you when we are through. Are we through now, Grandma?"

"Yes, sweetie, for now, but I will call you again tomorrow, OK? Tell Chapin I love him, too."

"How about Brooke, Grandma? Do you love Brooke, too?"

"Of course I love Brooke. Give her a big kiss for me. Bye, darling."

"Bye, Grandma. Here's Nanny."

"Welcome back, Kathryn. How was the trip?" Nan asked sweetly.

"It was fabulous. Italy was even better the second time. I can't wait to go again. How are things?"

"I think things are going very well. Jenn and I have worked out a nice schedule that incorporates her being with the children more. She is here most nights now, and if she isn't, she takes Brooke with her to Larry's apartment. You are aware that Larry left Linda, aren't you?"

"Yes, Sammy e-mailed me. How is Linda taking all of this?"

"She is incensed and blames me for being a home wrecker! Can you believe it?"

"Well, she has to put the blame somewhere. She certainly isn't looking at herself. Don't worry about it, Nan. There was never much of a home to wreck, in my opinion."

"Thanks for your support. The other thing that happened was that Larry offered Jenn his spare bedroom. Linda went ballistic, but Jenn was ready to get out from under her mother's domination, and she quietly packed up and left. It's been quite a fireworks show for the past few weeks, but Jenn has come out of it amazingly. She is looking so good. The antidepressant has done wonders for her, and I think it's what gave Jenn the strength to leave Linda's house."

"It almost makes me feel sorry for Linda. She lived vicariously through Jenn's career, and now she has nothing to do. Life must feel somewhat out of control."

"It's a shame that she never developed a relationship with her grandchildren. They don't want anything to do with her. Can you believe that she never wanted Jenn to bring Brooke over for the night?" Nan said. "She told Jenn they were just not equipped for a baby. I think that is the real reason Jenn decided to move in with Larry."

"I can't tell you how impressed I am at all of the changes in Larry. And Nan, you deserve much of the credit—not as a home wrecker, but as a nurturing friend. He needed you as much as the children did."

"I don't know about that, Kathryn. I think Larry had more to him than anyone knew. He was ready for a change, and he was devastated by Jenn's condition, especially when they were in court, and Jenn decided she did not want visitation with the children. He couldn't believe that his own daughter wanted nothing to do with her children. He was particularly upset that she had nothing to do with Brooke, who, by the way, is the apple of his eye. He blamed Linda, even though he understood that Jenn needed medical help. He knew that Linda was not helping Jenn get it. He was angry about the entire situation, and he wanted out."

"Whatever happens between those two is out of our hands, for sure," I said. "But I am still very pleased with the changes in Larry. Give him my love and please tell Sammy that I will stop by sometime over the weekend. I am meeting with Brad Bergstrom, the contractor doing my renovations, tonight to discuss the work on my house and what is left undone. Nan, I can't wait for you to see it. Brad has done wonders, and so has Karen. I'll call soon."

I felt as if I had gotten my family obligations out of the way. Now I could fully concentrate on dinner and looking good. I couldn't process my feelings—expectant maybe, but about what? I had to get a grip. I didn't know this man or anything about him, except he didn't like women much anymore, and he thought I was some kind of rich bitch. He probably wasn't as good-looking as I thought in my sleepy haze, but the least I could do was prepare him a good dinner and keep it low-key.

I had hardly hung up the phone when it rang again.

"Mrs. Wynham, this is Brad Bergstrom. I hope it's not too early to call."

"Good grief, no," I responded. "I normally get up early, but my sleep is still out of kilter. I woke up at three this morning and couldn't go back to sleep."

"I am not sure you remember, but you invited me to dinner tonight, and I don't want to hold you to that."

"Of course I remember, and I hope you will come. We have to talk about the house, and I am just going to make something simple. Wear jeans. It's not fancy, and it's your personal time. The least I can do is feed you."

"No, you don't have to do that," he protested.

"But I want to. Please let me make up for being so rude yesterday. What is a good time for you?"

We settled on a time that would allow him to work until it got dark and then go home and change. I was determined to be as accommodating as possible, and my goal was for him to have a different view of me by evening's end. Why this was so important to me, I still couldn't decide.

When the doorbell rang precisely on the dot of eight o'clock, the man standing there made me realize that sleepy, dazed, or unconscious, I was right—this was a seriously handsome man.

"Hi," I said. "Come on in. It must feel odd to ring the doorbell."

He looked at me, shocked. He should never play poker. I started laughing. "I must have really looked worse than I thought yesterday."

He had the good grace to blush and stammered. "No, no, you looked fine."

"Right," I said. "You mean fine for a house of horrors?"

"I wouldn't exactly say that, but the change tonight is better," he said tactfully. He took a deep sniff. "Something smells delicious."

"I hope so. You are my guinea pig. I went to a cooking school in Italy, and I have never made this dish by myself before."

"Cooking school? I thought Karen said you went over to learn Italian."

"I did. At least I can speak some Italian now. The cooking school was in Italian also, so we will have to see how this translates. Come in the kitchen with me. I'll get you a beer or some wine, and we can talk while I finish up." I decided that we would just eat in the kitchen very informally. I had dressed in a pair of soft jeans and a turtleneck. I didn't want this invitation to seem like anything more than a casual business dinner.

"My pasta is just about ready, so if you don't mind, we will walk through the house after dinner." He sat at the table and watched me cook and prepare our meal. I could see that he was feeling a little uncomfortable.

"I'm excited to use my new kitchen. It has turned out to be more spectacular than I dreamed. I had to read all the directions on my new appliances this afternoon to make sure that I could pull off the simplest meal. I do, however, think it's appropriate that you have the first thing I cook, since you did all the work." I looked over and smiled at him. I could see he was a bit confused, trying to reconcile his image of me as a rich bitch with Betty Homemaker.

"Well, you know, I wasn't doing this work alone. I had a crew of men."

I glanced at him. He seemed to be a little more comfortable.

"Maybe when this is all finished, I can do something for them. If it's not too cold, a cookout, or whatever you think they would like."

He looked astonished. "No one has ever done that for us before. I think anything at all would be welcomed."

It turned out to be a very nice evening, with some awkward silences at times. He was not an easy person to talk with. I decided to keep the conversation light and more about the house renovations than anything personal. Brad began to relax a little. He liked the dinner and had seconds. I think he was actually starved for a decent meal.

After dinner, we walked through the house, looking at all the changes through his builder's eye. He was proud of his work, and the quality of it was excellent.

"I love the bookcases in the living room. My husband and I had talked about doing this when we first bought the house, but with one thing or another—no extra cash, the kids. Then the years passed, and he died. It just never happened. I know he would have really appreciated your carpentry. He did a little woodworking himself, but not on this scale. He would have hated how I let the house get into such a state of disrepair. It's unbelievable to me now that I didn't pay attention to what was happening."

I could tell Brad was proud that his skill level had been noticed.

"The hardwood floors are beautiful and I like having them extended into the kitchen and upstairs. And I can't say enough about the kitchen. It should be in a magazine. I still can't believe all of this was completed in two months," I said.

"I put my entire crew on your house every day for the first month, and that made a difference. And your friend Karen is a slave driver." He sounded modest, but I could see how pleased he was.

"Thank God!" I laughed but then turned serious. "More than you can know, Brad, the renovation of this house is the start of a new life for me— and of course the trips to Italy. But the first one of those was a runaway trip."

He looked confused. "Runaway?"

"Yes, I was escaping my family. Karen and I were supposed to go together, but…you know about her appendix and the surgery?"

He nodded yes.

"Well, I wasn't going to go when she was hospitalized, but she insisted. I was scared to death of going to a foreign country by myself."

"*You* were scared?" He looked skeptical.

"Oh yes, I was such a wreck that I couldn't sleep for at least a week before I left. The day I got on the plane, my stomach was in a total knot."

"I would have never believed it," Brad said.

"Thank goodness I met some people on my tour right away, including wonderful Nan, who is now my son's nanny and housekeeper, and they all helped alleviate my fears." Did I sense a little curiosity about me? "I have changed a great deal over the last few months, and I think they are positive changes in every way. I was so angry and bitter, and really, I was as mad at myself as anything for getting myself in what I thought was a hopeless situation. Running away helped me enormously. I highly recommend it." I laughed and then, without meaning to, I yawned. "Oh my God, how rude! Believe me, it's not you. I am still jet-lagged, and my time is completely off."

"I need to go anyway. I have a big day tomorrow, but one of my guys will be by in the afternoon to discuss the landscaping with you. This has been an interesting evening, and the dinner was delicious. It has been a long time since I had a meal that good."

"I would be willing to practice on you again. I promised Karen that I would make her something that I learned in my school, so the three of us could get together." I thought having a third person would put him more at ease.

But Brad surprised me. "I don't mind being a guinea pig one bit, especially if the food is as good as it was tonight. But if you don't mind, I can tell you more about your house without Karen. She tends to talk a lot—nonstop, if you know what I mean."

I laughed and agreed. "I do indeed. But she's my best friend, so I don't mind. Thanks again for everything, Brad. I can't tell you how much I love my house."

He beamed and said good night. Wow, I thought. I think I pulled that off. I don't think he sees me in the same way. I hoped not, but it was hard to read Brad, and he didn't say much at all about himself. He was very guarded, but at least I could hope that some of the barriers were broken down.

Karen had found Brad for me after I left for Italy. The original contractor I had hired was in a car accident and had to pull out. I wasn't anticipating any of the work getting done until I came back, but Brad's company had done some work for a friend of Karen's and came highly recommended. I left it in her hands, but that meant Brad and I had never met before the work started. No wonder he had a negative image of me.

I still didn't understand what it was about Brad that appealed to me. He was not talkative unless it was about his work, and I had no idea what his interests were or much else about him. And I wondered—if I hadn't had my Italian experiences would I have been open to him. I couldn't deny how attracted I was, but it seemed to be physical only. I guess that's good enough, I thought. I have learned to appreciate more about life in general in the past few months.

# III

I called Ana Douglas a few days after I got back from Orvieto to let her know how much the university Italian lessons had helped me. We arranged to meet for lunch.

She looked as pretty as ever, but I detected an aura of strain surrounding her. "Are you having a good semester this fall?" I asked.

She smiled broadly. "My students are great, as always. My research has moved into a book that will be published soon. It still needs some tweaking, but that part of my life couldn't be better."

"You seem to have other things going on."

"Yes, Theo asked me last month if his daughter, Mimi, could come stay with me for a while because of a broken romance, her mother's remarriage, and the fact that she seems to be falling apart. She refused to return to the University of Heidelberg this year, and Theo and her mother were distraught. You remember my thoughts about Mimi, Kathryn? How rude and sarcastic she was to me during the summer? Believe me, she was the last thing on earth I wanted under my roof, but I couldn't turn Theo down."

"How is it going?" I asked.

"Theo must have had a very stern talk with her because most of the time she is civil, but every now and then that sarcasm she is so good at comes out in the most sideways manner. Basically, we live in the same house and try not to get on each other's nerves. My hope is that she will return to Germany soon. I know for Theo's sake that I am going to have to find a better way of coping with Mimi."

"That's a tough one, Ana, and I don't envy you. Do you talk with Theo often?"

"Fairly often, and of course we e-mail daily. He comes to the States at least monthly because of the attacks, which is good on two fronts. I see him, and he can keep Mimi in check. She is one strong-willed young woman. But enough about me. I want to hear about your life in Orvieto. Don't you think it is amazing for both of us, Kathryn that our lives have changed so much in the past year?"

I couldn't have agreed more. We had a pleasant lunch, catching up on each other's lives and promising to get together soon again. Ana was one of those people from my tour with whom I knew I would always be friends.

I felt that I had missed fall, even though it still was fall technically, but there was a decidedly wintry feel in the air many days. Thanksgiving was looming, and for the first time in the longest time, I was looking forward to preparing a big dinner. I wanted to have the family over. Nan and I planned it together, because she loved to cook, and Larry insisted on some of his favorite dishes that she had made him. Nan had settled into our family as if she had always been there. In every single way, my trip to Italy had been the best thing that had happened to me in years.

Jenn and Sammy were so sweet together. They were taking extra care with each other. In some ways, they reminded me of the way they were when they had been dating. Jenn said that Nan had taught her how to cook a sweet potato casserole, and she wanted to bring that. We decided that from her family, only her father would be there this year. The situation between Larry and Linda and Nan made it awkward for the other siblings to come, which was fine with me. It was time to make a break from them and start new traditions. I had called Laura to see if there was any chance of her coming east, but she was involved in a big film project that was winding down and couldn't come until December. I did ask the boys, Wills and Jan, and they were delighted to accept. They were bringing all the wine. Everyone requested an Italian dish, so I was making light pasta, which I thought could easily complement our heavy American Thanksgiving meal.

Karen was also coming, and I asked her if she thought Brad might accept. "He is an odd guy," she said, "and sometimes I think he might bite my head off, but he doesn't. He really liked that one dinner you prepared, and it seems like his attitude toward you has changed. What did you put in that food that night?"

I was more than pleased. I had deliberately stayed away from him, even though he had stopped by a couple of times, I told him that I was on my way out and would be back in touch. I wanted him to see how homey the house looked with all my pictures and things in the right places, but more important, I wanted him to see how a family can come back together after a rough patch. And finally, I didn't want him to suspect in the slightest that I found him attractive. I decided to take the plunge and call him the next day.

"Brad, this is Kathryn. I hope I am not interrupting too much." It was the Monday before Thanksgiving.

"Not at all. I am just catching up on paperwork. This is not the time of year that we do much on homes. People are too busy for the holidays. Is there a problem?"

"Everything is great with the house. I was wondering, if you have not already made plans, if you would have Thanksgiving dinner with me, my family, Karen, and a couple of friends. I know it seems like the last minute, but we really are just planning it now. My house looks so beautiful; I want to have a big holiday feast here. It will be casual, with kids, beer and wine, and of course, turkey. And, of course, football."

He hesitated before answering. I had caught him off guard. "The invitation is nice, Kathryn, but I thought I would use that day to catch up on everything."

"Oh, I'm so disappointed. I should have called sooner, but that would have only been yesterday. I just got off the phone with two guys I met on my tour. They are partners—you know a couple. Would that bother you?"

He laughed. "My best jobs are from that kind of couple. No, that wouldn't bother me at all. To be honest, Kathryn, I don't think I would be the best company in the world."

"I know it sounds overwhelming, but you know Karen, and my daughter-in-law's father really wants to meet the man who did such good work on my house. This is the first chance that I have had to bring you together, but I certainly don't want to push you. Think about it. If you change your mind, you would be very welcomed. At any rate, happy Thanksgiving. I will call you later. Oh, one last thing, and this is an enticement. There have been requests for an Italian dish from my cooking school. Think about it." Then I hung up.

I didn't think he would come, but on Thanksgiving morning, the phone rang. "Kathryn, this is Brad. Is the invitation still open?"

"Brad, it certainly is. We will eat around four but everyone is gathering from two o'clock on, so come whenever it suits you." I was more than surprised but also very pleased. I had given Brad up as a lost cause.

I think he enjoyed himself. It was hard to tell. Sammy and Larry went out of their way to make him feel comfortable, and I could tell that he really enjoyed talking about the changes that he had made in the house, Karen kind of bugged him, because she would butt in every now and then to give her two cents worth on the subject, but mainly it was the big guys and little guys. Strangely, Chapin was interested in the building process. Brad told him that he would show him how to hammer properly and build a simple little A-frame house. I hoped he wouldn't forget, because I knew Chapin would not.

Wills Amerson and Jan Sheffield were the best kind of guests. They brought the wine and were absolute charmers. Everyone fell in love with them, even the children. They told us that Jan wanted to adopt a child, but Wills was holding back. He thought it would change their lifestyle. It would, but Jan was ready for this kind of commitment. Jan adored Brooke and held her most of the afternoon until she fell asleep. He would make a wonderful father.

Brad seemed most ill at ease when we sat for the actual dinner. He didn't realize that we, too, were regrouping from previous times. It was Nan's first Thanksgiving with us, and it seemed that she and Larry were becoming a couple. Jenn and Sammy weren't altogether back, so there were some awkward moments when Nan, instead of Jenn, had to quiet Brooke when she wouldn't stop crying. It's an ongoing process, I thought. But dinner was good, and there were a lot more good moments than bad ones. I had never seen Larry so happy. He was a completely different man, much more gregarious and attentive to the needs of others. He was especially attentive to Nan. Unkindly perhaps, on Thanksgiving of all days, I had decided that Linda had been a toxin to the entire family, and she was not missed.

Jenn was looking much healthier and was more like her old self. She was wearing the pin that I'd sent her from Florence. It felt almost sacred to her. I said that I hoped that she and Sammy could go to Florence someday, because it was an enchanted city. She smiled shyly and said perhaps that could happen.

Sammy was also much less tense than he used to be. His new business was doing well, and he was turning into a good father. I could tell that he still worried about Jenn and was careful with her. Between him, Nan, and Larry, she was thriving, as was Brooke, whom I had worried so much about, but she was a happy, complacent baby.

My family was definitely on the right track again—or maybe even for the first time. The boys were behaving much better. Chapin had finally developed some manners, which I attributed to Nan. She was truly the fairy godmother of this family. While we were doing last minute things in the kitchen, I tried to thank her again.

"Kathryn, your family has become my family and given new meaning to my life. You know I had no one, and now I have so many. Those darling children are like my own grandchildren." She looked at me horrified. "Oh, I am so sorry. I hope that you don't think that I am trying to take your place."

"Don't be silly, Nan. Those children needed all the grand mothering and love they could get and still do. I was too burned out to be a grand-mother, but now I hope I can forge a new relationship with them. There is more than enough room for both of us." I gave her a hug.

Today would have been complete if Laura had been here. How I miss my daughter, but I think that relationship has become better since I have developed a more independent life. She still can't get over that I went to Italy on a second trip and will continue to study Italian.

"Mother, what will you do with all that Italian?"

"I'm not sure, sugar," I said on the phone one late night. "Maybe I could be a consultant on one of your film projects." There was silence at the other end. "I was kidding, Laura."

"But Mom, you know that is not a bad idea. An American viewpoint of Italian life. What a great documentary."

"Well, if it comes off, I expect to make big bucks!"

She laughed. "I'll see to it. Big, big bucks. After all, I have to look after my future interests as well." It was great for us to be teasing and laughing together again.

Thanksgiving Day was so hectic, I didn't have any real time with Brad, and he left shortly after dessert. He thanked everyone profusely for including him. It was almost embarrassing, but Larry saved the day with some comment about needing more men on these kinds of days. Larry followed through with plans to bring Chapin over for a building lesson. I could have kissed him, and I think I may have.

Karen called the next day. "You could have blown me over with a feather when Brad Bergstrom showed up. I didn't think he was coming. Why didn't you tell me?"

Karen was sharp, and I knew that she would catch on to my ulterior motives, so there had to be some truth in my statement. "After I talked with you about inviting him, I called him, but he turned me down. I had just gotten off the phone with Wills and Jan who, by the way, adore you. You are their kind of woman. Anyway, it just hit me out of the blue that he might be alone on Thanksgiving, and I thought if anyone besides you should have Thanksgiving in my newly refurbished house, it was Brad."

"Umm."

"I was completely shocked when he called this morning to see if the invitation was still open. I had to scramble and put another plate on the table, but I am glad he came. I hate to think of anyone being alone on a holiday."

"He sure kept his eyes on you," Karen finally said.

"Really? I didn't notice. I didn't sit down until midnight. Do you think he is seeing me slightly different than a rich bitch?"

"Do you care?" She was curious.

"I care only because it's not true, and because he thought that I was some kind of silly woman doing nothing with her life which come to think of it, may be true."

"What do you think of his looks?" she asked.

"He is good-looking, but that's wasted if he hates women. A dead end. Are you interested in him?" This ball was going right back in her lap.

"Who me?" she said in a coy voice. "I could have been, but there is a 'do not disturb' sign on his door. It seems permanently shut."

"I guess I can understand how trust could have been broken, given what his wife did to him. You can see how hard he works, and to be financially ruined must have been devastating beyond words."

"That was just half of it. She ran off with a competitor........., someone who is in the building trade. He used to come by their house a lot and was a good friend of Brad's. So it was a double blow."

"How do you find all of this stuff out?" I marveled. "No one deserves to be treated like that. Have you ever seen his wife?"

"Ex-wife. They have been divorced two or three years and separated for a while before that. No, I've never seen her or a picture of her, but I heard that she was a looker. A redhead. Not sure if it's natural, but there are pictures of the daughters in the office, and they have reddish hair. One of them is supposed to be a dead ringer for the wife, Susan. That's her name."

"Karen, have you ever thought of writing a gossip column? Is there anything about anyone you can't find out? How do you know this?"

"Easy. From the guys who work for Brad. They are the worst gossips in the world, and they know everything. They were there when things went down but stayed loyal to Brad and helped him get his business back on firm ground. They said he was a great boss. Some of them took other jobs to hold them over but came back as soon as he could pay them. But here's the latest. Susan wants to come back to Brad. The affair didn't work out, and she is using the daughters as a hook. They want their family back together, but the guys say that Brad was too badly burned. He will never take her back. However, she does seem to hang around the office a lot these days."

"What a sad mess. I wish him the best." We talked about other things and made plans to meet for dinner.

The whole thing with Brad was a lot to think about. I was attracted to him, but besides his looks, I didn't know why. His situation was not one that I wanted to get involved with in any way, shape, or form.

I didn't see or hear from Brad but once, and that was just a perfunctory thank-you call for Thanksgiving dinner. A week later, all thoughts of Brad flew out of my mind when I received a surprise call from Salvatore Sierra, who was in New York for the wine show. He had flown in with two of his sons, Stefano and Carlo, Carlo's wife, Natalia, and Tonio.

# IV

"**K**at-a-ryna." I heard a familiar voice.

"Salvatore, is that really you?" I couldn't believe my ears. I never thought he would call if he came to New York, although he had e-mailed me, with Tonio's help, a couple of times since I had returned to the States. The e-mails had been polite and impersonal.

"Si, Kat-a-ryna. We are in New York. Can you come? I have missed you."

That wonderfully seductive Italian voice. Just hearing it took me back to another time and place. They had been in New York for two days and would be there another week. They were staying at the Plaza, and Salvatore asked if he could get me a room and send his plane to Baltimore to fetch me. Send his plane? What luxury. I was transfixed and wasn't sure how to answer at first. Yes, I wanted to come but not the next day. I needed a day of shopping, and I needed to get my hair done. There was no way I was staying at the Plaza without the appropriate clothes, even if it cost me a fortune.

"Salvatore, are you sure? I really want to see you, but you must give me a little time. Just a day. This is so unexpected."

"No, Kathryn, I told you that I would call when we came to New York, do you not remember? It is not unexpected at all." He sounded surprised.

"Time has a way of changing people's minds, Salvatore," I replied.

"Kathryn, I can assure you that nothing has changed my mind. Orvieto is a lonely place for an old man without you. Please tell me you will come."

"You are not in the least an old man, Salvatore. All those women over there chasing you must keep you young."

"Kathryn, please, I beg you. When can the plane fetch you? Tomorrow or the next day, no more. I have only a few days in this country."

"I will be delighted to see you, Salvatore. More than you know," I answered sincerely.

I was in a tizzy. I called Karen right away. "Your Italian lover is back on the scene and wants to *fetch* you in his private plane?" She went on and on. "I thought there wasn't much to this romance. This sounds pretty serious to me. When are you going? Where are you staying?"

"Karen, please stop and catch your breath. All questions will be answered. I need your help tomorrow to find clothes, accessories, and shoes. Please, please, please tell me you are available."

"Are you kidding? I would miss the Second Coming to go shopping for this."

Off we went the next day for a whirlwind buying trip. Karen knew exactly where to go and what I would need, and she even found a couple of excellent bargains in the mix. By the time I met Salvatore's plane in Baltimore, I looked the part. New coat, cute hat, excellent boots, leather gloves. There was no doubt about it; I looked the best that I had ever looked in my entire life.

Karen drove me out to the hangar to meet the plane. It was quite an adventure, since neither one of us had ever been on a private plane before. I didn't know what to expect. With a minimum of trouble, we found the right hangar, and the minute we rounded the corner, I saw a plane painted in the Sierra Winery colors and logo. I had expected an ordinary-looking plane, but this one seemed to be the latest sleek model.

As we drove in, we were met by an employee who asked if I was Kathryn Wynham. Then he directed Karen to park her car so that she would be ready to drive out. As she got out to hug me good-bye, the door to the plane opened, and Salvatore stood in the opening.

Karen saw him first. "Omigod, tell me that is the Adonis that you have been so casual about." I looked up and saw Salvatore's wonderful Italian face smiling at me. He descended the stairs with his arms open.

"Kat-a-ryna, cara mia!" And with a huge hug, he drew me in. As if I were the only woman in the world, he held me close, taking his time before the kissed me on both cheeks. "Bella, Kat-a-ryna. You are so lovely."

He then turned to Karen. In his flawless Oxford English he introduced himself and graciously welcomed her as if she was the most important person in the world. I could see that Karen was completely won over. I would never hear the end of this. Before I could say a word, he invited her to join us on the plane for a glass of champagne. There was no way she was going to refuse this opportunity, and Salvatore gently guided her up the stairs while he held my arm.

Neither one of us was prepared for the opulent interior. The cabin was cream-colored and dark wood. There were honey-colored soft leather recliners and two large sofas facing each other. Fresh flowers and fruit sat on little tables. In one corner was a computer station and flat-screen TVs placed strategically around the cabin, which allowed all passengers a good viewing position. The floor had a textured gold oriental-style carpet. There were dark, highly glossed cabinets throughout. I could see a stainless-steel galley kitchen. An attendant came out with champagne flutes and nuts.

Salvatore, ever the gallant host, toasted us. "To the two most beautiful women in America." As he was finishing the toast, the pilot joined us and announced that takeoff would be in thirty minutes. Karen, taking the cue, hugged me good-bye and thanking Salvatore profusely.

Salvatore led me to two recliners facing each other. "It is so exciting to see you in America, Kathryn," he said. "I wondered what you would be like in your own country."

"Salvatore, how can you tell so soon? We have just reunited." I was having a little trouble buckling the seat belt. Everything was so high tech; it was difficult to find the buckle. Salvatore reached across to help me, not once interrupting his dialogue.

"People tend to look like their countries, I believe, and you always looked different from Italian women in Orvieto. But here, you look completely Americana."

"As I should!" I laughed. "I have never tried to be anything but American."

"Si, si! That is one of the things that attracted me to you. You are completely natural and completely you." He was holding my hand as we lifted off. We talked easily as we flew; catching up on each other's families. I was a little surprised at how quickly the time passed. Looking back, I can see that it was because of Salvatore's innate graciousness. He knew how to prevent awkward voids. I couldn't help but compare how different he was from Brad.

It was a short flight to New York, where we were met by a driver who drove us to the Plaza. Again, I was as unprepared for my luxurious suite there as I had been when I saw the plane. What an incredible way of life.

"Kathryn, I will let you rest and refresh yourself. We will meet the others for cocktails at seven o'clock. I will come fetch you just before." Salvatore gave me another continental kiss and left me to explore my room.

Karen had helped me find beautiful things. I decided to wear an aqua wool two-piece outfit that brought out the blue in my eyes. It turned out to be the right choice. Italian women, who are not in mourning, tend to wear more color than New Yorkers. I knew I was right when I saw Natalia later that evening. She had on a beautiful red wool dress that complemented her dark hair and eyes. Salvatore looked at me approvingly when he saw me. He met me with yet another kiss on the cheek, and we went down to the bar where the others waited for us.

Before we reached our table, I heard "Signora Kathryn," and there was Tonio, looking splendid in a dark suit and tie. I had never seen him dressed up, and he looked as handsome as an ancient Roman. Tonio gave me a big hug and a continental kiss.

"Tonio, you are the most handsome man in New York!" I laughed. "It is so good to see my tutor again. You will break many New York hearts before you return to Italy, I am sure."

Protests were heard from the other men in the party. Carlos and Natalia greeted me like old friends. Then I met Stefano. I could tell he was speculating about who I was in his father's world. He was, of course, the essence of politeness, as were all the Sierra family members whom I had met, with the exception of Giosetta.

"Signora Kathryn—I must call you that since my entire family does—it is my pleasure to meet the woman who has stolen my nephew's and my father's hearts. I can now see why." Stefano took my hands and looked at me as if I were a young desirable woman. Do all Italian men have this way about them I wondered. No wonder they have the reputation as the world's greatest lovers. I never did figure out what Stefano really thought of me, but he was like his father, very charming. And very handsome. He was the unmarried son and somewhat of a playboy, but Salvatore had told me in Italy that of all of his children, Stefano had the best business sense.

I had a lovely evening with the family and felt completely included. Tonio repeated so many of my tutoring mistakes that we were all in tears of laughter, but it was in fun and not mean spirited. I got the sense that the family, even Stefano, was impressed by my desire to learn Italian and live in Italy for a period of time.

"Do you plan to return to Italy, Signora?" he asked at one point.

"I hope to come back to Orvieto and take another Italian class. I will take literature classes at the university in the winter and spring and then possibly come sometime next fall. I would like to rent my same flat, because it was convenient. I lived right in the heart of the city."

"But Kathryn," said Salvatore. "It was quite small, your flat."

"It was perfect, Salvatore. Just right for me. I loved it."

He had an amazed look on his face. "Americans love vast spaces and you cocoon yourself in a tiny corner."

"Not at all, Salvatore. First of all, it wasn't all that tiny. It was just fine, really! I loved being in the center of town and looking out my window, seeing all the sights. I also loved living over La Tavola. I had many good dinners with the Ricuccis in their restaurant. After all, I moved to Orvieto to be a part of the culture, as well as learn the language."

"Signora Kathryn, what will you do with all this Italian? No one speaks it in America," asked Stefano.

"I know it sounds insane. All of my friends and family certainly think so. They think that I am crazy to learn a language that I won't be speaking or to take off to a country that I have no connection to, and I can't explain it to them. Italy just touches me, Orvieto in particular. I simply fell in love with that little town on top of the mountain."

They were all silent for several moments. No one knew how to respond. Finally, Salvatore said, "Thank you, Kathryn, for loving our country. You have touched our hearts." He leaned over and kissed me on the cheek. Something changed after that conversation. I had said exactly the right thing. Even Stefano seemed to accept me.

The four days in New York with Salvatore were like a romantic fairy tale out of some women's magazine or a movie. I could hardly believe it myself. I spent every waking moment with Salvatore. We went to the trade show the first morning, and it was amazing to see all the wine exhibits. Salvatore was known and respected by all the vintners.

The rest of the time was spent in museums, eating at great restaurants, going to the theater, and walking in Central Park. That was my favorite. It was very cold, but crisp and sunny. We linked arms and walked slowly, talking and laughing. We never ran out of things to say to one another. We spoke in a mixture of Italian and English. I loved the opportunity to speak Italian again.

One morning we were sitting on a bench in Central Park, holding hands and laughing at the pigeons, when a little girl, a toddler about eighteen months old, walked over to us muttering baby talk. I reached out to her, and she walked into my arms. "What is your name, darling?"

Her mother came over to apologize. "Her name is Emma, and I am afraid she is already a big extrovert."

"She is a doll baby," I said, giving her back. After they had walked away, Salvatore reached for my hand. "You are a natural nonna, Kathryn."

"I have three grandchildren, Salvatore, you know that. It's simply practice."

"No, no, you are a natural with bambini."

We had gotten up and started walking back to the hotel. "Many people think Italian women are naturals with children, but they are not. Nunzia loved our children, but she was a career woman. She loved her work just as much. She was good to them, but my sisters were just as much their mothers."

"My daughter-in-law, Jenn, is like your Nunzia. She loves her job and is very successful, but she is not a natural homemaker. I never had a career, Salvatore. Sometimes I think that I missed out on a big aspect of me. Something never developed. Maybe that is why learning Italian means so much."

"I am glad that you took that risk and came back to Italia. You opened up my life, Kathryn," Salvatore replied. "I have missed you. My days are empty again."

He looked so serious that I was momentarily lost for words. "Salvatore, your family, your winery must all keep you busy."

He made a dismissive gesture with his arm. "It's not the same, Kathryn. The thing that is missing is you."

I wasn't sure how to respond. I had missed him also, and my life in Orvieto, and I loved seeing Salvatore again, but that was another life—that life in Italy. I simply smiled at him, and we strolled on in compatible silence.

We walked toward Columbus Circle, where little Christmas tents had been set up. They were strung with twinkling lights and looked festive in the dimming daylight.

Salvatore broke the silence after awhile. "Kathryn, do you think you could live in Italy?"

"You mean always, permanently?" I was taken aback.

"Si."

"I don't know. I've never thought about it. I would miss my children and grandchildren dreadfully, I would think."

Nothing more was said about that. On a different day, we walked in the morning and ended up at Tavern on the Green for lunch. What fun that was. The restaurant was overly decorated for the holidays, but still, it was a treat to see. Although it was crowded with Christmas tourists, Salvatore managed to get us a quiet corner. I had worn a red sweater with a beige suede skirt and tan leather boots. I had a beige coat with a fur collar the same color as my skirt and boots, and just for fun, I had draped a multicolored wool scarf around the coat that picked up the red in my sweater. "Kathryn, you are as beautiful as the tree in this room," Salvatore said admiringly.

Salvatore made me feel beautiful and special. He had a way with women. I had observed this same courtliness with Natalia. He knew how to treat women, and he was a great conversationalist. I didn't know how to respond to this kind of attention, and yet I felt it was genuine. I knew that Salvatore really cared for me and was enjoying our time together as much as I was. Natalia had told me one evening that she had never seen her father-in-law so happy.

I was stunned. Salvatore had so much in his life. There was no doubt that his family meant everything to him and his winery was his world. There wasn't one single thing that he didn't notice. Although he had turned the business over to his sons, he knew exactly what was going on every day. His days were full. How could I mean that much to him? We had had many lovely days together in Italy, but we both knew it wasn't permanent. We lived too far apart. And for that reason, I had kept my emotions in check. I didn't know how I felt about Salvatore, except that I enjoyed his company as much as anyone I had ever known, man or woman.

I also had never had so many compliments in my life. My husband had given them sparingly, and they'd had little meaning, but I knew Salvatore and his family meant them. It was a heady experience. In fact, I was aware that, despite our different languages, different cultures, and different life-styles, Salvatore and I were a good match for each other. We had more in common than either one of us had suspected. We also had a great deal of fun together. He was a wonderful companion. I had not thought of Brad Bergstrom once.

On my last night with the Sierra family, we went to the New York City Opera. They had box seats. I felt like royalty. I had bought a dressy black outfit with a matching coat, which was perfect for this event. Salvatore and his sons wore tuxedos. Natalia had on a low-cut silver dress that made her look like a movie star. I thought we were an outstanding group.

Before we departed, Salvatore dropped by my suite a bit early and apologized, but I was ready. He pulled a little blue box out of his pocket.

"Kathryn, I hope you will permit me to give you this," he said shyly.

I took the box and open it up to find diamond earrings from Tiffany's.

"Oh my," I said, astounded. "They are simply beautiful."

"Please do me the honor of wearing them tonight."

"Salvatore, these are too extravagant. You have already done so much for me."

"Kathryn, I can only tell you that this has been the most wonderful time for me. I have never liked New York before this. You have made it magical."

With that, he took the earrings out of the box and put them in my hand. "Please," he said.

They must have cost a fortune, because they were not small. They were teardrop-shaped, and I remarked on it.

"Think of it as the tears in my heart when I return to Italy, and you are here in America."

What does one say to that kind of statement? "I hope that you will come back soon. I would love for you to visit me in Baltimore."

With that, Salvatore kissed me. Not the continental kind on both cheeks but a real kiss. The kind you don't forget. "Kathryn, you must know how I feel about you."

I was at a loss for words. I stammered "I…you………we…we are very compatible, aren't we?"

"Si, very compatible. I find you a very exciting woman. I am sad that we live so far apart. I have thought of you often in these past weeks, and when I saw you again, a few days ago, I knew that my feelings were true. Kathryn, I am falling in love with you."

I was shocked. "In love?"

"Si, do you not have feelings for me?"

We were standing face-to-face. I pulled back a little. "Of course I do, Salvatore. How could I not? You have swept me off my feet. I have loved being with you and your family. The Sierra family, each and every one of you, are wonderful people."

"But Kathryn, what do you feel for me?"

"I am absolutely enchanted by you, Salvatore. I never thought of being in love again at my age. Or that someone might fall in love with me. I don't know what to think, really."

Salvatore frowned. "I have rushed things. I should have kept my feelings to myself. Do you not think people our age can fall in love?"

I began to tear up. "I don't know. Of course they can. I never thought about it. I thought that part of my life was over. I just thought I was unusually lucky to have met a man like you, like no one I had ever known. I never would have dreamed that you could have been serious about me, about a relationship."

"Don't cry, Kathryn. It's our last night together for a while. Can you promise me that you will think about us being together?"

"Yes, I can do that. Will you promise me that you will give me time? I don't know yet what I really want, but I do know that you mean the world to me, and I want you to be part of my life."

"That will do for now, but Kathryn, I have not been known for my patience," he teased me and smiled.

We did have a wonderful final evening, and I did cry when I returned to the plane. Salvatore did not ride with me back to Baltimore, I think because it was as difficult for him as it was for me to say good-bye. I felt lonely for him, and I felt completely confused.

# V

I was a coward and put my feelings on the back burner. It was only a couple of weeks before Christmas, and I had a lot to do. I had decided to have an open house the Sunday before Christmas and reunite with some of the people from my tour of Italy. Ana Douglas, I learned, had returned to Germany to be with Theo for the holidays, but Lena, Neva, and Sara Capello came. Lena brought a delightful man, Palmer Addison, with her. Victor Ansera and little Nikki came. Nikki had lost her shyness and was a bright-eyed little minx.

I also invited the two sisters, Ida Jane and Mary Louise Dawkins, both of whom accepted immediately. Nan, of course, with Larry and my best boys, Jan and Wills. In addition, Sammy, Jenn, and the children. Karen would be there and was helping me with preparations.

"Are you inviting Brad?" she asked.

"What do you think? I wasn't sure what to do. I didn't know whether he was back with his wife. Maybe I should just let sleeping dogs lie, as they say."

"Well, I can tell you that he is definitely not back with his wife, but it's not because she isn't trying. He seems annoyed as all get-out with her. He even hides from her at work. That's what I am hearing, at least. You know two of his guys are doing some repair work at my house right now."

"In that case, maybe I should. I haven't heard one word from him since Thanksgiving, but I have really not given it much thought since I got back from New York."

"I guess not!" teased Karen. "If I were you, I would have been on that plane back to Italy with that man. In my book, he is a keeper, big-time."

"He is an unbelievable man. I haven't sorted through all of that yet." Of course I had told Karen everything. I had no choice. She demanded it.

"I think after the holidays, you need to sit yourself down and think whether or not you want to take a chance on losing a man like him and then hop on a plane to Italy, pronto!"

I laughed. "Yeah, I think we would all be a little surprised if I did that. I'm not sure I am ready for that yet."

I called Brad at his office the next day and left a message on his answering machine. I did not hear back from him, so I was not expecting him for the open house.

My house looked like something out of a home decor magazine. There were candles in every window and greenery on the staircase and over the mirrors in the dining and living rooms. I had a huge tree in the hallway to greet guests and a smaller one in my family room. Every single room had some kind of Christmas finery. The buffet looked inviting. I had spent several days cooking and baking all of my favorite party foods. Karen could not stop talking about how beautiful the house looked. She was proud of her work on my behalf. Fires were lit in both the living-room and family-room fireplaces and brought a warm glow to the rooms, as well as much needed extra heat on that cold day.

Everyone arrived within thirty minutes of one another and soon fell into a party mood. There was much loud chatter and laughing as old friends greeted one another. The children got along well, with Sara Capello as the ringleader. I noticed that Chapin was very taken with her. I had to laugh at Ida Jane Dawkins. She still complained about everything, but Wills paid her so much attention and gave her so much wine that she soon forgot the essence of the complaints. Karen was right in the thick of it, and it almost seemed as if she had gone with me to Italy.

A little over an hour after the party began, the doorbell rang. I thought everyone was here and couldn't think of who would be missing. When I opened the door I was surprised to see Brad. I hoped that it didn't show. "Brad, welcome. I didn't know if you had gotten my message."

He looked me over for a full minute and smiled appreciatively, "You look............ good, Kathryn. Thanks for inviting me again." I had worn my new two- piece aqua dress—not exactly a Christmas color, but it was a good color for me.

"Thank you, Brad. Please come in. We are all just getting started on the buffet. I will get you something to drink." I wasn't sure what to make of him just showing up, but I was definitely having a reaction. What was it about him that turned me on so? He was sexy. That was it. Just plain sexy. Not charming, like Salvatore, but sexy. I wondered if he knew that. I could hardly keep my eyes off him.

Brad made a beeline for Larry and Sammy. I didn't see much of him because of my hosting chores, but we had a couple of opportunities to exchange small talk, mainly about the house. He had gravitated toward Wills and Jan, who were thinking about some renovations in their home and had loads of questions. I could see that social occasions were not easy for Brad, but just the same, he seemed fairly comfortable.

Brad stayed only a short time. I think he had run out of things to talk about and people to talk to. He tried to avoid Karen. It was easy to see how her personality made him crazy. She talked a lot, loudly, and interrupted often. Impulsively, as he was leaving, I invited him to be with my family on Christmas Eve. I wasn't sure what plans he had, but I thought he might not want to be alone, and I knew he enjoyed Larry and Sammy's company.

"We just have a simple Brunswick stew and salad. The kids run around and drive us nuts about Santa Claus until they go home to bed." I laughed.

He was silent for a second and then stated rather curtly, "I am not sure that I can make that." It almost sounded rude, and I was surprised, because the evening had been fun and lighthearted.

"Well, don't stand on ceremony, if you can come, if you want to come, just come. It's casual and we gather around five thirty, if you change your mind," I said politely.

Brad hesitated for a moment and then said something I was not prepared to hear on this very happy day in my life. "Kathryn, I am sure you mean well, but you need to know that I am not up to this."

I was confused. "Up to what, Brad?"

"A relationship. I am just not interested in being involved with anyone right now."

We were standing in my doorway, and I could see some of the others beginning to gather coats and make their rounds to say good-bye. I was stunned by Brad's comment.

"You think I want a relationship with you?" I sputtered.

"I am sorry, Kathryn." He turned and left.

My shocked turned to anger, but my guests were leaving, and I had to politely wish them a happy holiday. I was seething.

Karen knew instantly something was wrong. "What is it Kathryn? Are you well? You look both feverish and pale."

"I will tell you later," I said through clenched teeth.

After the last person left, she grabbed me and took me in the kitchen, where she had a cup of tea for me. "I don't need tea. I need a strong drink and a gun," I yelled.

"What in the world?" Karen began.

"It's that insufferable prick, Brad Bergstrom. He thinks I'm chasing him. Can you believe that?"

"You're kidding, right?" She was astonished. Of course, she had no idea that I found Brad so attractive. She was blinded by my recent trip to see Salvatore.

I recounted his last few words. "Can you believe the absolute gall of him? Does he think he is so hot that all women are bowled over by him?" I was pacing the kitchen floor.

"Calm down, Kathryn. I haven't seen you this agitated in a long time. What does it matter anyway what he thinks, anyway? You have this great Italian man panting away for you, who whisked you off in his private jet to New York. Does Brad Bergstrom think he could possibly compete with that?"

"You're right, Karen." I stopped pacing and sat down. "From the start, even before Brad knew the first thing about me, he was already making assumptions about who I was. He is absolutely clueless. No wonder his wife left him. Why she wants him back is the question."

"That's easy," said Karen. "She needs someone to take care of her. All the money she took from Brad is long gone."

"They sound like a perfect match to me."

Christmas came and went with no word from Brad. I didn't expect to hear from him, and I didn't. For my part, I never planned to speak to him again. I had had enough. I did hear from Salvatore on Christmas Eve. He wanted to send his jet so that I could spend the New Year in Italy with him. I regretfully declined on trumped-up excuses about baby-sitting for the grandchildren.

I was angry at Brad, and I knew I would be too vulnerable around Salvatore. I had not sorted out my feelings about Salvatore. I wasn't used to having men in my life, and I felt conflicted. I had been very attracted to Brad and felt rejected, but I cared about Salvatore deeply. I knew that I wasn't being fair to Salvatore, because I had let my feelings about Brad dominate my decision. I knew that was really stupid, I never intended to see Brad, and there was no need. My house was completed, and he did an excellent job. I would give him that. I also knew that Salvatore deserved better than he was getting from me. In some respects, I liked my life better when I never thought about men.

# VI

I sat in my bathrobe with my third cup of coffee, looking out my kitchen window at the January snow, which seemed to be getting deeper by the minute. Sometime in the middle of the night, the snow had started, as predicted by the weather forecasters, and for once, they were accurate. At least eighteen inches were predicted to fall, so I knew I need not hurry to do anything. It would be a long luxurious day of indulging myself. I had allowed myself to have an extra hour of sleep, took a leisurely shower upon waking, and then made myself a pot of coffee. For reasons that I could not explain, I had put on light makeup and brushed my hair back into a ponytail. My God, I thought, I can see every little wrinkle with my hair pulled back tight like this. But then, no one will see me today. No one at all. I could just stay in my pajamas all day if I wanted to.

Then I giggled to myself. I didn't think that I'd ever done that in my life. I'd always gotten up, gotten dressed, put on make-up, and styled my hair. But today, I felt very content just to sit here and look out the window and not worry one bit about how I looked.

I thought about how busy my life had been since returning from Italy. I had hardly had time to think about my exciting experience there. Today, my thoughts were drifting back to those two months in Italy and the two months since I had returned. My life had changed so much in the past year and this new year would be the best ever. I just felt it in my old bones. The silly thing was that I didn't feel as old this year as I did at the start of last year. For one thing, I was no longer fighting with Sammy and Jenn, so I didn't feel that tension in my life any longer. I was finally a real grandmother who could visit and enjoy my grandchildren. I felt so blessed.

There was tension of a different kind. It came in two forms: Salvatore Sierra and Brad Bergstrom. Who would have thought at my age that I would even be thinking of a man, much less two of them? Karen said I should just let it rip, whatever that means, but it did keep me a little bit stirred up. Well, a lot actually. I felt as if I had two different lives, the one in Italy and the one here. But they intruded on each other, and that was the problem.

At first I was only faintly aware that someone was knocking on my door until it became louder and louder. Good grief, who would be out on a day like this? The snow must be six or eight inches by now.

I got up and moved quickly in my bathrobe to the front door. To my absolute amazement, there stood Brad Bergstrom. I couldn't say a word.

"Kathryn, I came to apologize." He stood there turning white before my eyes as the snow stuck to him. It had been six weeks since my open house, and I had not seen or heard from him.

"You drove out here in a blizzard to apologize to me?" I was astounded.

"Well, I also wanted to know if the house is holding up in this weather," he said quietly.

We were still standing at the door. I had not invited him in. "If I had had any problems, I would have called you. On my telephone. Do you own a telephone, Mr. Bergstrom?" I said icily.

"Look, Kathryn, could I come in for a second? I do want to check on a couple of things. I can understand you being mad at me. I sorta misread your kindness," he said sheepishly.

Just having him in my house brought back all those angry feelings I had. I didn't want to see him. "Check all you want. I am going upstairs to put on some clothes." With that I left him and returned about thirty minutes later in jeans and a sweater. I deliberately decided not to refresh my makeup or do anything to make myself look more attractive. Why should I? I wasn't interested in him. Yet I had to admit, he still looked good to me.

He was in the kitchen when I came back downstairs, and he had helped himself to a cup of coffee! "I hope you don't mind. I was freezing, and the atmosphere in here isn't exactly warm."

I decided not to take the bait. "Are there any problems in whatever it was you were checking?" I stood behind a kitchen chair as if it were a weapon.

"No, everything we put in or replaced is holding up nicely. I didn't expect any breakdowns, but I wanted to make sure." He put his cup down and looked at me. "I'm lying. That is not why I'm here. I can't get you out of my mind. I was wrong to say what I did. Your friend, Karen straightened me out."

"Karen?"

"Yes, I ran into her at the supermarket a few days ago, and she gave me a piece of her mind—or yours, I'm not sure which. I realized that I had been wrong long before that. I just didn't know how I should approach it. I'm not very good at this, and I have had a hellish three years, but that's neither here nor there. I am sorry. I really am. I should go now."

I had not said one word. Brad moved to put his hat and coat back on.

"Thank you for apologizing. I was hurt and angry, but the thing I want you to remember is this. I do not chase men. I never have, and I never will."

"I realize that now. I just took all the things that had happened and looked at them one way."

"What things?" I said confused.

"The Italian dinner, the Thanksgiving dinner, the party, and then the invitation for Christmas. It all seemed like…well, I know now that I was about as far off as anyone could get. If it's any comfort, I feel like the biggest damned fool in the entire state. Karen told me about your boyfriend. I should have known that a woman like you would have some rich guy in your life."

Damn Karen, I thought, I don't need her spreading rumors about Salvatore. "Again, Mr. Bergstrom, I think you are making assumptions about me based on what you hear, and I don't know why it should make any difference to you at all."

"You're right. I don't know you at all. I need to go now." Brad opened the door and was met by a virtual whiteout. "God, this stuff is coming down," he muttered as he ran toward his truck. It was one of those big trucks that can get through anything, but it wasn't moving anywhere today. The snow was icing up. I watched from the window as Brad tried everything to back out of the driveway but all he was doing was spinning his wheels. Finally, in defeat, he started walking back up my sidewalk.

I opened the door before he could knock again. "I'm stuck," he said.

"I can see that. It seems like you are as good at reading the weather as you are at reading women." I smiled sweetly.

"I don't think sarcasm is necessary, Kathryn. And by the way, when did I become Mr. Bergstrom?" He swept into the foyer.

"When I realized that if I were more professional with you, I would not be misinterpreted. And by the way, I'm not being sarcastic. You might as well make yourself at home. You may be here for a while." I was dismayed. I had looked forward to this quiet day to myself, and now I was stuck with this man who irritated me to no end.

He stood in the living room with his hands on his hips. I was still in the foyer. "Look, Kathryn, I have apologized. I am not a game player, if that's what you are up to. For better or worse, I will be here for a while. Can we just call a truce?"

God, that man was infuriating! "Is that what you think I am doing? Playing some kind of mind game with you? For your information, I did not seek you out today or any day, and I don't take kindly to rudeness. I had no intention of ever being in touch with you again unless something dire happened in the house." I was pretty angry.

"OK, OK, I concede. I am a horse's ass and have behaved worse than that. I'm sorry that you're stuck with me today. I would leave if I could." He spread his hands out in a conciliatory manner but looked uncomfortable.

It was going to be a long day, but I needed to make the best of it. It might not be a bad idea to have a handyman around in case something did happen. It was a nasty storm. "Truce accepted. In fact, if you haven't had breakfast, I will make you something, in case the electricity goes out."

"You don't have to do that."

"Have you eaten?" I asked abruptly. "It's midmorning, and the snow isn't quitting. We both should have something in case it's our last hot meal for a while."

"In that case, breakfast sounds good. What do you have in mind?"

"I can make most anything. What's your pleasure—eggs, pancakes, waffle?"

"Would scrambled eggs and waffles be too much trouble? I'll help cook and clean up."

"In that case, I'll throw in some sausage or bacon."

So began our day together—and a new relationship. Brad turned out to be pretty decent in the kitchen, and he did help clean up. After breakfast, which was delicious, I took inventory to see what was there for the rest of the day and evening. I saw no way that Brad would be leaving before the next day.

Throughout the day, he checked on various pieces of equipment to make sure everything was running efficiently. "Everything is working fine for now. As long as the power stays on, we are in good shape." He had built a fire in both fireplaces for extra warmth. I made cookies. "It's a tradition, cookies and hot chocolate on snowy days," I told him. Just in case the power didn't fail, I had made a vegetable soup and it was simmering in the Crockpot. I had some nice crusty bread in the freezer that I would pull out and warm up and there was always wine…lots of wine.

"You know, Kathryn, you aren't half bad to be around." Brad said at one point in the afternoon. I was curled up on a sofa with a soft throw around me, reading a book.

"That's almost a compliment, isn't it?" I said in disbelief. I decided to take a risk. I had nothing to lose. "Brad, why do you have such a low opinion of me? You don't really know me. I really wasn't chasing you, you know."

He turned red, and his face looked anxious. He ran his fingers through his hair. "That is a loaded question. I don't think I can answer it without making you madder, and so far, today has been pretty nice—well, after the morning episode—so I don't know what to say or how to say it."

That made me sit up. "No, I mean, really. What did I ever do to you?"

"Nothing. You didn't do anything to me. I just didn't think you could be true."

"True?"

"You know, straightforward. I haven't had…Well; you know that I am divorced. Women haven't worked out for me in the past. I have never met an honest woman, one who doesn't want something from me." He looked at me, hoping that I could understand what he was trying to say so badly.

"But I was just a customer. I meant nothing to you"—I corrected myself—"mean nothing to you. So why did you take your attitude out on me?"

"All right, Kathryn, you asked for this. I didn't bring it up; you did. I will admit that I formed some opinions when I was working on this house. You weren't even here. Your friend was doing all of the work. I thought that was pretty shabby right away. You left it all up to her, and to top it off, she had just had surgery a few months before you went back to Italy."

"But—"

"Let me finish….…you wanted to know. I understand what I'm saying will make you angry, but the more I saw Karen, and the more she talked about you having the time of your life in Italy, I thought what a little witch you were. I felt that you had taken advantage of a friend, and I knew how that felt."

"But—"

"Do you want to hear this or not? You started this." He had moved closer.

I nodded. "Might as well get it all out and over with. I won't interrupt again or defend myself." I was getting upset, because it wasn't a fair assessment. I also felt teary, because it was so untrue. Karen wanted to help out. She loved it.

"So when you got back, I wanted to get our initial meeting over with as soon as possible. I was unprepared for what answered the door." He started laughing. "Your hair was sticking up all over the place"—he pointed to various places on my head—"and you never really opened your eyes. You looked like a zombie or something. Then you commanded that I come to dinner the next night and shut the door in my face. I stood there for several minutes wondering what had just hit me. In all of my years in this business, that has never happened before." He was still laughing, but I just sat there not saying one word.

"When I came over the next night, you were like a different person before me. You looked great, and the dinner was excellent. You didn't flirt or anything. I was wondering what your game was."

Good God, I thought, what kind of experiences has he had with women? I still said nothing.

"Then you invited me to Thanksgiving. I wasn't going to come, but then I thought, what the hell, I need to eat. I liked your family a lot. Your son and Larry are good men, and they really wanted to know about the house. I really liked them. They were down-to-earth, and Larry knows about a great deal about building and contract work. You were pretty standoffish, and I thought you were playing your little game. Then there was your Christmas party and then the next invitation. I decided to put an end to it. You know, like nip it in the bud before it really began. I thought I was being pretty upfront. That is, until Karen told me off the other day. So that's my story."

I still didn't say anything. I didn't know what to say.

"Kathryn?" He was sitting on the floor quite close to me by now. "How mad are you?"

I didn't answer him directly. "Brad, I would like to tell you a little story about me. All I ask is that you don't interrupt me or ask questions until I have finished. Agreed?"

He nodded and stood up to poke the fire and then came over and sat beside me on the sofa. So I began from the time Gary died and talked about my baby-sitting years and my time in Italy and how Karen couldn't go with me. I told him about returning to Italy to go to Italian classes, right up to coming back in October. I said nothing about Salvatore.

"That's just about it, Brad. I am a very ordinary woman with a son and a daughter and three grandchildren. I am blessed with good friends and having been left with a little money when my husband died. Italy was a fluke that turned into a passion. Along the way, I met some new friends."

"Including a boyfriend."

"I would not call him a boyfriend, although he means a lot to me." I had not mentioned Salvatore's name. I didn't know what Karen had said to him about Salvatore, but I could only imagine what an extravagant spin she must have put on her story.

He was silent for a few minutes, and then he picked up one of my hands. "There is nothing ordinary about you, Kathryn." Before I knew what was happening, he leaned over and kissed me, first gently and then passionately. "I don't know what it is about you, but you got under my skin the first moment I met you—the one when your hair was sticking out all over."

It was a very sexual kiss. Salvatore had kissed me passionately on several occasions, but this kiss was different. It was exploratory and hinted at more to come. I could stop it or find out where it would lead. The daylight was fading. The room was taking on a deeper hue with light only from the fireplace. Brad had stirred up long forgotten feelings. I wanted him, and so I took the plunge and kissed him back.

"Kathryn, I want more. I want you. I have wanted you for a long time." His hand was moving under my sweater. I felt like a teenage girl with her first grope. I felt warm; no, I felt hot, almost feverish. Before I knew it, we were both nude. He was in rock-solid condition. I guess from all that construction work. I wondered if I looked flabby, but at the moment I didn't care. I just wanted him in me. It had been so long, and it felt good.

Afterward, we just lay there, and neither one of us said anything for a while. Brad broke the ice and said he needed to put another log on. "Kathryn, are you all right? I didn't know this was going to go in this direction. I don't regret it, and I hope that you won't."

I looked up at him and smiled. "No, I don't regret it at all. It was good." He was the sexiest man that I had ever known. What I was thinking—but didn't say—was that I wouldn't mind doing it again. But I didn't have to, as it turned out. The second time was not as frantic. A much slower pace and better. Sex is really better when you are older, I thought. I couldn't believe how easily it had all happened and how much I liked sex with Brad. It had been over seven years, maybe more, since I had had sex. And on a very cold, snowy day in January, it just happened as naturally as something I did all the time. Wow! Wow! Who would have thunk it?

"Kathryn, you really amaze me," Brad said as we were getting dressed.

"How?"

"Most women just want to talk and talk after sex, but you have hardly said five words."

"I don't need to say anything, Brad. I just wanted to savor the experience. You are a good lover, and I appreciate it. That's all." I dressed and we went into the kitchen, where we had our soup, salad, bread, and wine. I felt wonderful. Sex had been a physical release. It had taken tension from my body that had been building for years. There was no way I could explain that to Brad.

The rest of the evening went by very pleasantly. Brad was much more relaxed and told me about his ex-wife, his daughters, and the problems he was having with them. There was a lot of baggage in his life, but that was not my problem. I hoped that we would have sex again. I wasn't looking for a boyfriend, and I had not thought of sex in a long time, but I would welcome it again.

When bedtime came, Brad assumed we would sleep together, but I said no—a lot had happened that day, and I needed to be alone. I put him in the back bedroom downstairs, and I went to my own room upstairs. He didn't understand that at all, but there was nothing he could do about it.

I woke up early, took a quick shower, dressed, and went down to the kitchen to start the coffee. I felt wonderful and was singing when Brad came in the kitchen. "You are very happy this morning," he remarked.

"Yes, I am. Yesterday was nice. I'm glad you came over." I smiled at him shyly.

He gave me a lingering good-morning kiss. "I am glad I did also. I never would have thought things would have turned out as they did, but I'm glad that we have resolved some things. You know, Kathryn, there was always something about you. Like you didn't care—no, I don't mean that you aren't caring, it was more like you didn't care what I thought. No, that's not it either. I don't know what I am trying to say. I just didn't know how to figure you out. All I knew was that I couldn't get you out of my mind, but I didn't want to look at it any deeper. I didn't want anymore females in my life or head."

"OK," I said noncommittally. I was surprised that Brad had given any thought to me but decided just to keep my own attraction to myself for now. I wasn't sure of my own feelings at the moment. Brad left after a bit of a struggle to get his truck out of the ice. He promised to call later.

I was strangely detached from all that had happened between us. But I knew after yesterday that I wanted Brad in my life, and I also wanted Salvatore in my life. I just didn't know how I wanted them to fit in. They were as different as night and day in every possible way. Whatever the answer was would take time. I felt as if I could face the future, no matter what it would bring.

# VII

Brad and I began seeing each other regularly. He would come over once or twice a week, and sometimes more. It was a very comfortable arrangement for me. I had my university class, which I loved, and the lunches with Ana Douglas afterward. I was going out for lunch or dinner with Karen once a week and I had rejoined my garden club. Nan Coulous and I sometimes went out together, and sometimes she and Larry would join Brad and me for dinner at my house. I felt like I was getting my old life back, but so much better. I regularly went to my health club to exercise, and I never felt better. Every now and then I went to Washington to see Wills and Jan. We would have dinner and go out to the theater or a concert. I treasured my new life. Every day was an unexpected joy.

One night after Brad and I had pizza and beer while watching a movie, he remarked casually that it would make things a lot simpler if he moved in with me. He was still living in the one-bedroom apartment that he had moved into after his wife left and he had to sell his house. He had grown to love my house as much as I did and was constantly suggesting new and improved ideas, but mainly my house offered him a comfortable home, something he apparently never had.

I had only been listening with half an ear but picked up on the undercurrents. "How would it make things simpler, Brad?" I turned to look at him.

"Well, you know, I would be here every night and we could eat together, sleep together. It would be more normal than just dating or hanging out."

That was exactly what I did not want again. I loved my new freedom with no responsibility to anyone but myself. "It sounds like being married. How would it be different from marriage, Brad? We both have said that we don't want to get married again." I tried to keep my voice neutral and quizzical.

He stood up and began pacing, which is what he always did when he felt himself cornered. "It would give you more protection to have a man in the house."

"Oh, you mean like a roommate with benefits, as the kids say?"

"No, that's not what I mean." He was beginning to look exasperated.

"I have never felt unsafe in my neighborhood, and I do take precautions. My door is usually locked—"

"Look, Kathryn, you know what I mean. We see each other a lot. Doesn't it make sense to you that we live together?" He sat back down and looked at me.

I kissed him, and as gently as I could, I said, "No, Brad. I don't think it's a good idea for me. I am not at home much anymore, and I am not ready to settle into that kind of domesticity again." He started pulling away, but I kept a firm hold on him.

"I love having you in my life, but we are still new in this relationship, and it is much too soon for us to be talking about living together. You, on the other hand, I think would benefit from moving into a better place. Your business is booming, you work hard, and you need a retreat to come home to every night. You owe it to yourself. I could help you find a place, and I know Karen would love to help you decorate."

"Karen! Are you crazy?" He stood up again with his hands on his hips. "You don't want to live with me?"

I stood up and came over to him. "It's too soon for me, Brad. Can you accept that, and can you accept what we have now?"

"You are the damnedest woman, Kathryn." He pulled me close to him. "You really are. The damnedest woman—way too independent. But that's probably what I like about you, as much as it drives me crazy."

I knew this part of me did drive him crazy, but I also knew that our relationship would fall apart if we moved too quickly. I knew this about myself, and I knew this about Brad, even if he didn't.

At the end of March, Inga Johansen, her boyfriend, Aric, and her mother, Lara, came to visit. I was delighted to see Inga. We hugged and hugged. Lara was near my age and quite pretty. She had fine, blonde hair that hung to her chin in a classic style and Nordic blue eyes that were kind and experienced. I could see immediately where Inga got her looks. Aric was built like a Viking, and I learned that his family had descended from an ancient tribe. His red hair was a giveaway. We all spoke English, the common language.

Because I was in school taking my Italian literature class during the day, the three of them were on their own to sightsee until I got back home in the afternoon. Inga got up early one morning to have breakfast with me and chat, just the two of us. It was like old times.

She started laughing.

"What's so funny, Inga?" I asked.

"I knew it was bound to happen." She smirked.

"What are you talking about?" I asked, perplexed.

"You and a man. I could tell in Orvieto that you would soon meet someone. It was just a matter of time. I don't mean the way you met Signor Sierra, or a Robin Tremont, but someone on your own."

Young people can be so to the point, into people's private business, too blunt. But I wasn't mad at Inga. In fact, I laughed. "You have always been such a nut, Inga."

Brad had joined us for dinner the second night they were here. He turned up wearing a blue blazer, blue shirt, and dark pants. He looked great. He had a way of holding his head to one side and looking at you that was very sexy indeed. He also could be very charming when he wanted to, but I knew that he felt uncomfortable with strangers. But with Inga, there were no strangers, and soon I could see that he was relaxing and talking to Aric about his business.

Inga interrupted at one point and questioned Brad. "Your surname is Swedish, no?"

"Yes, I think so," Brad said, "but I really don't know for sure. We have been in America for so long, we have lost touch with the European side of us."

"You must come to Sweden and look it up," Inga said excitedly. "You and Kathryn can come visit, and you would get the opportunity to see what your roots are."

I looked at Brad and could tell this was the last thing he would want to do. He was a hunting, fishing, and football kind of man. He wasn't into museums or genealogy or anything of that nature. "So what do you think, Brad, about a trip to Sweden? They invented the hot tub, you know." I laughed.

He gave me an electric look. "A hot tub I could go for." We all laughed.

Inga looked at me thoughtfully over our toast and coffee, "I like Brad, Kathryn. I am not sure he is the final one, but I like him. He is very sexy, yes?"

"Yes, I think he's sexy." I smiled, thinking of all of our late nights together. "It doesn't matter whether he is the final one, as you say. It's good for now."

"Yes," said Inga approvingly. "And that is very continental of you, Kathryn. Very. Most American women are too possessive. He will want you more because you aren't strangling him."

"Maybe." I shrugged. "Who knows?"

A month or so later, after a robust evening of lovemaking, I brought the subject up.

"Brad, are you at all interested in going to Sweden?"

He thought for a minute. "No, I don't think so. The whole travel thing doesn't interest me. Just give me a quiet afternoon by a stream and some fish, and I will die happy."

"You know, Karen and I are planning a trip together in June, after I finish my next language course in Orvieto. I will meet her in Florence for a few days, and then we will fly to Paris for a week. Then we'll go on to Sweden to see Inga and Lara. You could meet us in Sweden."

"I'm aware that you are going back to Italy." He said in a flat voice. He had turned over on his stomach and was looking directly at me.

"You don't like it, do you?"

"Damn right I don't and you know why." There was a hint of anger in his voice.

"Salvatore?"

His voice was steely. "Well, how would you feel if I was going off to see another woman?"

"Brad, in the first place, I am going to a language school. In the second place, we both agreed that we would lead independent lives but be sexually monogamous."

"How do I know that you will come back?"

So that was it. I leaned over and kissed him. "Well, you would be one reason, a son and daughter would be another, and three grandchildren would be the third."

He turned back over, and we sat shoulder to shoulder. "I have never asked you this before. I guess I didn't want to know the answer. How much does this man mean to you?"

I was unprepared to answer that, but I knew I had to. I thought for a minute and looked at Brad. "He means a lot. He is a wonderful, special man, and maybe if he were an American and lived here, he would mean more. My home is here, Brad, not Italy."

"Kathryn, where do I fit into this world of yours?" His voice implied some anger.

This was turning more serious than I had given thought to. "You are here with me now. We have been together for four months. You made it very clear to me that you didn't want to get married again. I happen to agree with that. I don't want to get married again either. What has changed?"

"Nothing. No, that's not true," he said, picking up my hand and massaging it. "My feelings for you have changed. I don't know if it's falling in love with you or what, but I know I want to be with you. I appreciate how you don't push. You have given me a long leash. I never thought I would like, much less trust, another woman, but I do trust you, Kathryn. You don't lie. It's a chance I have to take that you will come back."

"It's not one-sided, you know," I said quietly. Brad looked at me quizzically. "I am always waiting for the other shoe to drop—your ex-wife."

"What the hell does Susan have to do with us?"

"Plenty, I think. She wants you back. Your daughters want the two of you back together. They don't want me in your life." Brad had arranged for me to meet his girls for dinner one night at a local restaurant. It was disastrous. They behaved as if I were a fortune hunter and could have taken lessons from Giosetta. Susan had even come to see me once and told me to lay off her husband. My only reply was to state quietly, "I believe you are divorced by your choice." Then I shut the door in her face.

"That's preposterous!" Brad exploded. "I never want to see Susan again, and my daughters will eventually come around."

"Nevertheless," I said, "it is a risk that I take that you will fall in love with your wife again. She is very beautiful and much younger than I."

"You are such a fool, Kathryn," Brad said, kissing me hungrily. "It's that age thing again. Susan is no match for you. I was never as happy with her as I have been with you. You restored my sanity and gave me space. Susan is a pain in the ass."

We had discovered, in the course of getting to know each other, that I was nearly four years older than Brad. Susan was five years younger than he, so I did have some anxiety. Brad teased me often about being with an older woman but always countered it by saying I was the best looking grand-mother on the planet. He was constantly telling me that his guys thought I was "hot."

"Brad, I think we are having growing pains. We just have to trust that what will be, will be. We don't own each other. If what we have is right for us, it will stand the test of time."

He groaned. "You're right. About everything. I know that I am definite-ly growing." And with that, the evening continued along a very nice course.

# VIII

I was all packed and ready to go. Brad had been over earlier to tell me good-bye. I didn't want him to take me to the airport. I have a thing about good-byes.

Before he left to go home, he took my face in his hands and said, "Promise me that you will come back."

"Promise me that you will be waiting," I said half-teasing, half-serious.

There was no doubt that we both cared about one another more than we had said. Was this being in love? I didn't know. I did know that I would miss him if he went back to Susan. Would I be devastated? No, I didn't think so. I could weather it and come out of it OK. I was much stronger than I used to be.

Was marriage an ultimate goal? No, not now, but never? I didn't know. The best thing about my relationship with Brad was that he also gave me space, even when he didn't understand why I wanted to do something. We were still discovering each other. Physically, we were great together, and I liked the way he interacted with my family.

I was excited about returning to Italy. My Italian had improved vastly, and I felt confident in my ability to communicate and get around. I wanted to perfect my accent. I had a little idea brewing in the back of my mind about teaching children Italian. Ana actually planted the seed, because she was thinking about opening up an English school for children in Montepulciano eventually.

We had been having lunch together once a week at the university. What a dear girl she was, and she was so radiant these days. She had gained weight and looked beautiful. Theo would be a good husband for her. I was envious of their love. It was strong and lovely to be around. Ana was a better person than I. She brought Theo's ex-wife back to the States to reconcile with Mimi. I could never see me and Susan having that kind of relationship.

Brad and Salvatore. Two very different men. Two years ago, men were not even a blip on my radar screen, and now there were two of them vying for my attention. I was excited to see Salvatore again. I couldn't wait to catch up on his family. Francesca was another person I couldn't wait to see. I had a whole other life waiting for me across the ocean.

I am content with my life, I thought. It is vibrant and dynamic, and I feel accomplished. I have been enriched by my experiences in Italy and with these two men. The world is just beginning to open up for me, and I have no intention of tying myself down at this point. I want to experience and love it all.

# ANA

# I

eah, Marta, and I flew back to Baltimore together. I was nervous about
Mimi's reaction at seeing her mother again, and Theo was no help. He
thought that it was really a bad idea for Marta to just show up without warning. We had many late-night planning sessions on the best way to do this, but
the only thing agreed on was that Mimi needed to come back to Germany
to finish her university education in Heidelberg. All of us realized that my
involvement could end the delicate truce that Mimi and I had established,
and given Mimi's volatile personality, she could hold it against me for years.

"I will talk to her the next time that I am there," Theo said over and
over. "I will just tell her that she has to come back."

"Theo, that hasn't worked in the past. Why do you think it will work
now?" Marta complained.

"Circumstances have changed. Her heartbreak is over, and she is ready
to move on," Theo replied.

"Don't forget, Theo, Mimi has a new boyfriend, whom she may not
want to leave. She likes her life in America," I retorted.

"Ana, Marta cannot show up at your door with you when you get back. Mimi will eventually come around to her mother, but she will resent you forever. You know my Mimi now. Is that not true?"

He was right, and we all knew it. We felt deadlocked.

It was Marta who thought of using Leah as an intermediary. "Mimi loves and respects Leah. How do you think she would react to seeing her again?"

"Well, ja, she loves Leah, but why would she be going to the States, especially with Ana? None of this makes sense," said Theo.

"Ana, doesn't Mimi know that you are meeting all of Theo's relatives? Don't you e-mail and call Mimi often?" Marta asked.

"Yes, all the time," I answered.

"Well then, can't we just concoct some kind of plausible story that Leah is coming back with Ana but will stay at a hotel for some reason? I will be there with Leah. It removes Ana a bit from the complicity. Mimi will come to the hotel to see Leah, and I will be there."

The idea had merit, and we worked on it. Leah was as skeptical as Theo when it was initially introduced to her but willing to help out because she, too, wanted Mimi to finish her education in Heidelberg and reconcile with Marta. The whole thing was a strain on the family.

"I am willing to do it, but I am not sure it will work at all. One thing I know is that Mimi knows that I love her. I e-mail her at least once per week and often mention seeing Marta in my notes. I agree that Mimi is too old now to continue to have this grudge against Marta for remarrying. It is adolescent in nature. Perhaps I can appeal to her more adult side. Ja, I'll do it."

The plan was tweaked, but we all were nervous. What power Mimi had over us. The best part of the plan was that I became closer to Leah and Marta. We decided that we would not tell Mimi ahead of time that Leah was coming with me, but we all agreed that in e-mails and calls to Mimi, we would talk about her returning to Germany. All but me. We decided that it would be best if I said nothing about her return, and I was glad not to be a part of that. My e-mails spoke about looking forward to seeing Mimi and Katie, and of course, all of the Capellos.

Theo and I had called to tell Mimi of our engagement. She was quiet at first. "I am not surprised," she finally said. We couldn't tell from her voice how she felt about it.

I took the phone from Theo and spoke more rapidly than I intended. "Mimi, you know how much I love your father. I never thought I would remarry—ever. I was too devastated by Mark's death. Your father has given me a new reason to be happy again, but I don't ever want to come between the two of you. He loves you more than me. You are his daughter, his only child."

"Ana, no excuses," Mimi interrupted. "If my father has to remarry, it should be to you."

"Thank you, Mimi," I said quietly. "Here is your father."

"Mimi, it's OK, no? Ana will need your help when she comes back. She is not strong yet and cannot have a lot of tension. The doctor says—"

"Vater," said Mimi, "ja, it is OK. Ana has courage and is smart. I will take good care of her when she comes home. Don't worry."

So we got through that hurdle, with the big one to come. We all wanted to do the right thing for Mimi.

I had told Mimi and Katie not to meet me at the airport. Lena would pick me up. That sounded convincing to them, because they knew how close we were, and it was natural for Lena to do this. Lena did come to get me. I had told her the entire story of the attempt to reunite Mimi with her mother, and Lena recognized what a minefield this was going to be.

I introduced her to Leah and Marta, and then they quickly found a taxi to go to their hotel. Lena hugged me tightly.

"Ana, how are you feeling? How is your throat?"

"I am exhausted, but not because of my ordeal in Germany or the flight. I'm just worrying about how all of this will play out with Mimi."

"I think all of you have underestimated Mimi," she said in the car. "Mimi has grown up a lot in the past few months."

"Yes, but Lena, she has had nothing to do with Marta. She won't write her, e-mail her, or talk to her on the phone. Marta is completely crushed, and all of this is because she remarried to a perfectly nice man."

"How long has it been since she has seen her mother?" Lena asked.

"It must be nearly six months. She has been here five months, and there was a big blowup before she came to the States."

"Well, you can't tell me that she hasn't missed her mother. As much as she loves Theo, she has to have missed her mother," Lena said calmly.

"I hope so. Tomorrow is the big day. Leah is going to call her, and I am going to take her to the hotel to meet her aunt. Only she doesn't know that her mother will be there also."

"Will you stay there?"

"No, I will leave but come back to get her if she wants me to. That is up in the air right now."

"Don't worry so much, Ana. Think of yourself. You have been through a lot and need to rest. My mother sent you chicken soup."

We both started laughing. Neva's answer to all the problems in the world was chicken soup. She had been doing it for years.

Lena went in with me to say hello to the girls. Both greeted me with hugs and kisses.

"Let's see the ring, Ana," Katie shouted. "Omigod, it's a rock!" she said, holding my hand. "Mimi, your dad has good taste."

Mimi took my hand, looked at the ring for a few seconds, and said, "It is very beautiful, Ana. My dad does have good taste, no?"

"Your dad is the most wonderful man in the world, Mimi. I keep telling you that," I said, "but the ring could have been from a bubblegum machine, and I would have loved it."

"No way!" said Katie. "No frigging way! This is a ring."

"Tante Leah suggested it to him, Mimi," I said.

"Tante Leah? You met her?" Mimi's face softened. This girl is homesick, I thought. Maybe this won't be so hard.

"Yes, I met Leah, Rudi, the boys, some of your cousins, and Jakob Weiss. I'll tell you more tomorrow. There is a surprise coming for you. I hope you like it."

"For me a surprise, Ana? What is it?" She looked delighted.

"I absolutely promised I wouldn't tell, and you will know tomorrow."

Lena interrupted, "Girls, no more. Ana has to get rest. There is chicken soup to eat."

Both said, "Neva!" We all laughed.

# II

I didn't sleep well, and it showed the next day.

"Ana, are you OK? You look tired," Katie asked in a concerned voice.

"I'm OK. Just jet-lagged. I will do better today. Where is Mimi this morning?"

"I guess she is still in bed. She hasn't come up for breakfast, but as soon as she smells this coffee, she will be here. She hasn't missed a day yet."

"The two of you have become such good friends, haven't you, Katie?"

"She was my only friend when I came back to the States. It is amazing how she stuck by my side. I think it's because she knew what Konrad was like and about the Jew-hating thing. You know, she was amazed and impressed at how you fought him. She kept saying, 'Ana, fought that bastard. Can you believe it? Ana fought that little Jew hater and won.' She has talked about you every day," Katie said.

Oh, God, I thought. What will she be thinking of me by tonight? "I hope she doesn't hate it that her dad and I are engaged."

"No, I think she doesn't mind, because it's you. Maybe if it were someone else, she wouldn't be too happy."

Just then the phone rang, and I knew it would be Leah. Let the games begin, I thought.

"I'll get it, Katie."

"Ana," said Leah "is Mimi awake?"

"No, but that is no problem. We will get her." I looked at Katie. "This is a call for Mimi. Would you go wake her? It's a surprise, so don't take no for an answer."

"Mimi comes upstairs looking grumpy and disheveled. "Hello?" Tante Leah? Where are you?" I could hear the wonder and delight in her voice. "Ja, Ja. I can do that. I can't wait to see you. Tante Leah, wait a minute, I will ask her. She is sitting here." Mimi covered the phone with her hand and looked at me. "Could you take me to Tante Leah's hotel?" I nodded yes and waited for her to get off the phone.

She was so excited. "What is Tante Leah doing here?"

"I think part of it has to do with her magazine, and part of it has to do with wanting to see you."

Mimi said, "I don't care what the reason is, I can't wait to see her. When do we leave, Ana?"

"Well, if you want to go in your pajamas, we could leave now." I laughed. "But I think more realistically, let's shoot for an hour."

"Ja, I want to look very good for my tante. And Katie, you must go also. I want you to meet my tante."

Uh, oh, I thought. I had not planned on this. "Mimi, maybe you should have some time with Leah first, and then you can introduce her to Katie later."

Katie got the hint. "That's a good idea, Mimi. You haven't seen her for a long time, and I would just be a fifth wheel."

"Whatever," said Mimi breezily? "I am going to get dressed, and Ana, you need to get moving yourself. Are you sure you can drive me?"

"No problem, but I am going to drop you off, and you can call me to come get you and tell me what your plans might be for later."

"Plans?" she asked suspiciously.

"Well, sure, like lunch, dinner, you know. I will be available to be your chauffeur. Just keep it loose."

"Ja, you are right. I can't wait to see her."

I dropped her off at the hotel and then returned home to wait for the fireworks. I waited and waited, but there was no word at all. Finally, around eight that evening, Mimi burst through the door with murder in her eyes.

"Ana, you knew. You knew that meine mutter was there also, and you said nothing. You have betrayed me again. I thought we were starting to be friends."

I looked at Mimi calmly, even though my stomach was in knots. I decided that I had had enough of the drama queen and being bullied. "Yes, I knew about your mother."

"I knew it!" she said triumphantly. "I knew you had something to do with this."

"I cannot believe that you hate your mother so much, Mimi. She seems like a very good woman to me, and she asked me not to say anything. She wanted to see her daughter. I saw nothing wrong in that request. After all, she is your mother, and I can tell that she loves you very much."

"You don't know anything, Ana. Nothing! You don't know what she did to me," Mimi screamed.

"No, I have no idea that she did something to you to make you react like this. Theo never said a word, nor has Leah. How would I know? You never talk about your mother." I remained calm. "What is the problem with the two of you?"

"Meine mutter hates me. She knows how much I dislike Karl, but she married him anyway."

"Has Karl been unkind to you, Mimi? Because I am sure your father would have something to say about that."

"No, no, no. You don't understand anything, Ana. How did you ever get to be a university professor? You have no understanding."

I stood up and looked at her directly. "I do understand one thing, Mimi. I see a spoiled young woman having a temper tantrum, which I will not listen to another minute. Your mother loves you enough to come all the way to America to talk to you, because you won't communicate with her. This is so adolescent. When do you plan to grow up?"

"You are just like Tante Leah. She said the same thing. No one understands me." With that, she stomped down the steps.

Katie came out of her room. "Ana, is something wrong?"

"Only if Mimi wants it to be," I said wearily. "Sit down, I will catch you up so that you can understand why Mimi is behaving the way she is."

After explaining all that I knew, Katie quietly reflected and then said, "I don't understand why her mother's remarriage made her angry. Is the stepfather mean or abusive?"

"Oh, no. Not at all. From what Theo tells me, Karl is a very kind and decent man and has never tried to intrude in the relationship with Mimi and her mother. No, the problem is that Mimi wanted, and probably still hopes, that her parents will remarry. I don't think she ever forgave them for divorcing, but she has taken it out on Marta more than Theo. Theo has indulged Mimi's every wish, like most guilty fathers, and that is now proving to be a disaster."

"Wow! That is crazy! Should I go down and talk to her?"

"No! Let her wallow in her self-pity. I don't think she even knows what she is mad at right now, except no one told her that her mother was here to see her. What a crime! I have to confess, Katie, that I am losing patience. I'm also exhausted, and I am going to bed. I think you should do the same."

# III

Theo called early the next morning. "Ana, Liebchen, how did it go?"

"Just as you predicted, Theo. Mimi threw a fit. I don't know exactly what happened, because I haven't talked to Leah or Marta. I am going to call them later this morning and meet with them. Mimi is as mad as a hornet."

"What? What is hornet?"

I had forgotten how some things didn't translate with Theo. "It's just a saying we have, Theo. Never mind. Think of a volcano spewing hot, toxic lava, and that would be your daughter."

"I will talk to her…"

"No, Theo. Don't. Mimi needs to work this out with her mother, and she doesn't need other people enabling her self-pity."

"Ana, that is not like you," Theo said. "You have been so kind to Mimi. She is just a girl."

"Theo, Mimi is nearly twenty years old. She lived with a man in Israel last spring. I am pretty sure that she is sleeping with Brandon Walker now; that is, if they are still going together."

"Ana, that is beside the point," Theo responded heatedly.

"No, the point, Theo, is that Mimi is not a child, even though she is behaving like one. You and Marta will never remarry, and both of you have the right to be happy. Mimi has had adult relationships. She knows what it is like to be in love. She has to let go of her childish fantasies. She is being cruel to her mother, and I am not willing to stand in line to be the next scapegoat. I am tired, and I have completely lost patience with all of her juvenile drama."

"Ana—"

"Theo, I trust Leah and Marta to work this out. You and I need to step aside and let that happen. I want you to remain in Germany. Do not look for an excuse to come here now and don't call Mimi. It would be the worst thing in the world. I love you. Now go back to work or go home and take Schnee for a long walk. I will stay in touch." I hung up the phone with a renewed determination that Mimi was going to grow up, come hell or high water.

Katie was waiting for me in the kitchen with strong, hot coffee. "Ana, I am worried about Mimi. I think I should go down and talk with her."

"I have a better idea, Katie. I want you to get dressed, because we are going into the city to have lunch with Mimi's aunt and mother. I want you to meet them, and I know that Marta wants to meet you. I have told her what a lovely person you are. They both know about your ordeal with Konrad."

"What about Mimi? Won't she be mad?"

"I would bet money on it. Just call it rescuing Mimi from herself."

I called Leah and arranged for us all to meet at the hotel. We didn't go into it over the phone, but Leah said it had been really bad yesterday when Marta appeared. Mimi had been horrid. She had never seen her niece like that. Lucky her, I thought. I have had a lifetime already of Mimi's bad side.

I did two things before we left. The first was a note to Mimi, stating that we were having lunch with her mother and aunt and she was welcome to join us, and the second was a call to Neva to explain the situation. I did want someone to check on Mimi, and I knew Neva would be the perfect person for a number of reasons. Mimi liked Neva, and Neva would not put up with Mimi's foolishness. Neva also had credibility, with her staunch moral values, and she was practical.

One look at Marta told me that she had had a sleepless night. Her eyes were red, and she looked devastated. Leah looked worried. "Ana, how is Mimi today?"

"I don't know. She wasn't up when we left, or she just deliberately didn't come upstairs. She is pretty angry at me, also. Neva Capello will check on her soon. This is Katie Willis. She speaks excellent German. Far better than I do, so feel free to speak in your native language."

Marta said she didn't think she could go out with us. She felt nauseated.

"That is nerves. Please try, Marta. I want you to at least eat some soup, because it is time for our next plan."

"What plan, Ana? We don't have a next plan," replied Leah.

"I am having a little dinner party tomorrow night to welcome the two of you to America."

"What?" All three said at once.

"Yes, a dinner party, to which I will invite Mimi's closest friends, including her boyfriend, Brandon, and the Capellos—not all of them. Just Neva, Lena, and Sara."

"Ana," Katie said, "I don't think Mimi will come."

"That is entirely up to her, but she will look petty in the eyes of her friends if she doesn't show up at a party to honor her mother and aunt, and we know that Mimi is all about image."

It was the first time that I had seen Marta smile. "Ja, that is true, Ana. Even as a little girl, when Theo and I were together, Mimi always thought of image. She thought we were the perfect family. I think that is why she was so hurt when Theo and I separated."

"Well, it's time for Mimi to learn that families can still be good, even if the configuration is different. So, agreed?" I looked at Leah and Marta, and they reluctantly nodded. "Now let's go get lunch. I am famished."

Lunch went pretty well, all things considered. The story of yesterday unfolded, and it was ugly. Mimi told her mother that she was selfish and that she hated her. She disowned Leah as her aunt. Imagine! How self-indulgent this girl is, I thought. She doesn't deserve this wonderful family.

After lunch, I made Leah and Marta promise me that they would take a nice long walk, get a massage, go shopping, and rest. Katie would pick them up the next day and bring them over. Katie had fallen under Leah's elegant spell. "I am sad that I can never visit Germany again and see your magazine."

"Hmm," said Leah thoughtfully, "I can at least send you copies. You know, Katie, something has occurred to me. Next year, we are opening a branch office in New York. We will need staff members who speak German. Would you be interested?"

"Oh my gosh! Do you mean it? I would love to do that. That is so wonderful. I can't wait to tell Mimi. Oh, I can't tell her. She'll be furious, won't she?" Katie looked dismayed.

"Of course you will share your good news with Mimi," I said. "Her own aunt has offered you a wonderful opportunity. I think it would be good for her to hear your opinions of her family, but don't expect her to be enthusiastic. She will be curious, however. You know how Mimi wants to know everything."

"Ana, you really know Mimi well," replied Leah.

"I have had loads of practice—loads and loads," I answered. "So Katie, we need to go and plan our party. I will need your help, and I want to find out what happened when Neva went over to my house today."

I kissed both women good-bye and told them that I would be in touch.

# IV

I called Neva as soon as I got home. Mimi was nowhere in sight. Katie went downstairs to look for her.

"Neva, "I said, "how was Mimi when you saw her?"

"Ana, she was curled up like a baby on her bed. Tears were streaming down her face. It took me awhile to understand her, because she was speaking German. It took longer before she could talk to me in English or Italian, but she did give me a hug when I went into her room. In fact, she clung to me like a tiny child. Not since Lena came home pregnant have I have seen someone so hurt. Your pain over Mark was different, Ana. Theirs could be rectified, but not yours. Yours was permanent."

"You don't have to explain, Neva, I know what you mean. What happened next?"

"For a long while I just held her and told her that everything would be all right. She kept saying that everyone had turned against her and hated her. I didn't contradict her, because I knew that was useless. She was just like you and Lena used to be as girls, so I knew she had to get it out of her system. After awhile, I told her to go wash her face and come upstairs so that she could eat a bite and tell me why she was so sad, but I made her eat before I let her say another word."

"What did she say?"

"Not a lot, Ana. She is brooding, but I think she is also a little bit ashamed of what she said to her mother and aunt."

"She should be," I replied hotly. "She has been unbelievably cruel to both of them. Her mother is devastated. I hope she is rethinking her entire reaction and is ready to apologize."

"I don't think she is there yet. She feels justified in her anger, especially because she feels that everyone tricked her."

"Honestly, Neva, I don't think I can take much more of this. She is spoiled and selfish. We all walk on eggshells around her. Anything that doesn't go her way can set her off. I wish I had a magic wand to help her handle her emotions better."

"Maybe time will help a little bit. You must rest, Ana, and not let this interfere in your recovery. You have been through a huge ordeal. How can I help you?"

Wonderful, wonderful Neva. She was always there for everyone. "There is something you can do, Neva, and this is a big request." I told her about my planned dinner party and asked if she would help me. She agreed to help me cook the food. I really wasn't feeling up to doing a lot, but Neva jumped right in and started planning everything.

"Don't worry, Ana, it will be fine. I know things will work out. Don't underestimate Mimi. She is a good girl at heart."

I was just about to take a hot bath after talking with Neva when I heard a knock on my bedroom door. "Come in," I called.

A bedraggled-looking Mimi was standing there. "Can I talk to you, Ana?"

"Only if you promise me that you will not scream and yell at me, Mimi. I am truly worn out."

"I am sorry, Ana," she said humbly. "Maybe tomorrow morning would be better?"

"No, let's do it now. Come sit on the bed."

"I don't hate my mother or aunt. You know that, don't you, Ana? I have made a mess of everything, and now they all hate me. Even Katie thinks I'm mean. My aunt offered her a job today. You know that, Ana?"

"Yes, I know that. I was there when Leah thought of the idea. It was completely spontaneous. By the way, I don't think they hate you at all. They love you enough to fly all the way here to talk with you. No one knows what to do with you, Mimi." I was exasperated.

"What should I do, Ana?" Tears were coming down her face. She looked like a little girl.

I took her hand. "Mimi, I think you should call your mother and apologize, and then I think you should go back to the hotel and talk to her. That is the only right thing to do."

"It won't change anything. She will still be married to Karl."

"Of course she will!" I was getting annoyed again, and my patience was shot. "Your father thinks Karl is a very nice man. What do you have against him?"

"You don't understand, Ana. Karl took my mother from me. It was the two of us, always, after father left. When she met Karl, there was no more time for me."

"I'm confused, Mimi. I thought Theo told me that your mother didn't meet Karl until you left for the university."

"Ja, ja that is true."

"You were not there most of the time, yet your mother was supposed to sit at home, alone, until you showed up again?"

"We never had time together again, and father was always gone. That's why I went to Israel."

"Your mother didn't marry Karl until you came back, right?"

"Ja, but—"

"No buts, Mimi. Your father and mother deserve to find happiness. You should be grateful that they have a good relationship and are so caring toward each other. Most divorced people can't stand the sight of each other. And there is no question how much they love you."

"That is just it, Ana!" She stood up and started pacing. "If there had been no Karl"—she looked directly at me—"and no you, Ana, they would have remarried. I am sure of it. They love each other."

"Oh, Mimi. I feel so sorry for you. Your mother and father would have never remarried. Jakob Weiss even said that. They love each other like a brother and sister. You have to let go of these childish notions. All children of divorced parents, especially good and loving parents like you have, want their family back together. It will never happen. Theo loves me, and I love him. I am sure your mother loves her new husband, or she would have never married him. Your mother is wonderful, Mimi. I like her so much, and your aunt. Can't you accept the reality of this situation?"

She said nothing, but she was listening.

"Mimi, I am becoming part of a new family. My family in Germany. Your family. Your aunt and your mother are included, as well as their families and your cousins. I have learned how important it is for families to stay together and remain strong. You know what your ancestors have been through. You have been to Israel. You know this. You are making a choice not to be a part of them. I was an only child, too. My parents loved me, but they loved each other more. It was not until we moved next door to the Capellos that I had a real home and family. I will always love them, no matter what choices they make, even ones that I might disagree with, and they will love me. They took Theo, your father, right into their hearts; because they knew that I loved him, even before I did. That is what families do."

Mimi had stopped crying and was looking at me. She sat down on the bed and took my hand.

"You must learn to trust. Your mother made the right decision for herself, which does not mean that she loves you less. She wants to talk to you. She needs to touch you, and I believe that you need to hug her. You both are overdue. Go call her now, Mimi. Don't think about it. Just go do it."

# V

I never knew what passed between them, but Mimi did call her mother and spent the night at the hotel, Leah phoned to tell me that they were working things out and not to worry. I didn't worry. My jet lag had caught up with me, and I slept for fourteen straight hours.

My dinner party was not what I would call a huge success, but it wasn't all bad either. There definitely was tension, and Mimi was uncharacteristically quiet. Sara kept the chatter going and decided that since I would be living in Germany a great deal more in the future, she would learn German. Children are marvelous at times. Leah took it upon herself to teach Sara the German names of every object that she touched that night and told her that she must come to Germany soon to meet her sons.

Katie also took a leading role in covering awkward moments. I don't know whether it was the job offer she had gotten or she was just being kind, but she spoke German much of the evening. Leah was impressed. All in all, things went better than expected. The dinner was delicious, but I knew it would be. Neva had never made a bad meal.

Leah and Marta left soon after dessert and coffee. Mimi kissed both of them good night and went to her room. She has a lot to think about, I thought. The next day Mimi seemed to be somewhat back to her old self. That is, the old self I had a truce with.

"Ana," she said, "they don't hate me, and we are making up. Tante Leah will call you. She wants all of us to have dinner together before they fly back. Tomorrow, we are going to Lena's new salon, Italia, to get our hair done. You should go also, Ana, so that you will look good."

Yeah, Mimi was getting back to normal. Bless Lena's heart, I thought. She doesn't do hair anymore, because she has too much to do running three shops, but there are rare times when she makes exceptions. I will never be able to repay that family for all they have done for me. It never stops.

"Ana?"

"Yes, Mimi?"

"Meine mutter likes you. She said that you will stand up to father and will make him a good wife, but I want you to promise me one thing, Ana."

"What is that?"

"That you will not have children. You are too old anyway, right, Ana?"

"Get lost, Mimi!" I pointed my finger at her. "It is none of your business what goes on between your father and me. Remember that—always!"

She laughed as she walked away. "OK, Ana, just remember my father is virile, and for a man, he is young, but for you, not so young!"

Things were getting back to normal.

# KATHRYN

# I

"Karen, something is going on with Brad. I have been back from Italy for two days, and I haven't seen or heard from him. I have left him two phone messages and neither has been returned. He stopped e-mailing me about ten days ago. I don't understand. It's like a dark curtain has dropped. He has vanished."

Karen had planned to meet me in Italy, but there had been some changes and we postponed our trip together until autumn. I had been gone for over a month and felt like something bad had happened. I was worried sick.

"Karen?"

"I don't know what to say exactly..."

"Does that mean you know something or you know nothing?"

"I know rumors, and they aren't pretty," she finally said, "and I don't know where to start."

"Just say it, Karen. I'm worried."

"OK, then. His guys—the ones working at my house—told me Susan is back working in the office. She showed up one day with some hard-luck story, and Brad told her she could work there as the office manager for a couple of weeks until he could hire someone else. The other girl left, and Brad was stuck. Susan knows the routine, because she worked as the manager before. The guys say she has been nothing but trouble since the moment she walked in, and Brad is totally unaware of it."

"I don't understand what that has to do with him not being in touch," I said.

"Kathryn, don't be a dolt! Brad dropping out of your life started when Susan came back into his. I would bet my house that she is behind this."

"Are you saying that they are back together? Why hasn't Brad told me himself?"

"No, that is not what I am saying. I don't know. All I know is what the guys have told me, but we both know that she wanted to get back with him. They say she is playing him. She just wants more money."

I was fuming. Why didn't he tell me in person that he wanted to break up? Yet I still couldn't quite believe that. I needed to see it for myself. The next morning I went over to his office. His truck was out in the yard, so I knew he was there, but he wasn't in the office. Susan was. She was examining her newly painted fingernails when I walked in. She looked nervous when she saw me and looked out the back window.

"Brad is not here, Kathryn, and he doesn't want to see you again. Save yourself some humiliation and just drive away. We are back together and happy as two honeymooners." She was gloating.

"I know he's here, Susan. His truck is here. And if he doesn't want to see me, he can tell me himself. I'll wait for him or just go look for him out back."

I started out the door. She seemed jumpy.

"No, wait, Kathryn. Brad has a lot going today. Why don't you write him a quick note? I will give it to him later."

I turned and looked at her. "You don't want me to see Brad, do you, Susan?"

"Don't be ridiculous!" she said. "I think you're wasting your time. Your little fling with my husband is over, and he's back with me now."

"You mean your ex-husband, don't you? The one you left after running off with his friend and taking all his money."

Her face turned as red as her hair. "Get out of here. I told you that you are wasting your time. Brad is through with you."

I could see she was lying, and then it hit me. "You did something with my last e-mails to Brad, didn't you? He never got them. And my phone messages—he didn't get those either. You have been messing with his computer. He doesn't know that, does he, Susan?"

Neither one of us had seen Brad come in the side door, but he had overheard my last remark. "Is that true, Susan?"

"Brad!" we said at the same time.

"Susan?" His voice was steely.

"I have no idea what she's talking about, Brad. She needs to leave. We can discuss this later."

"I don't think so, Susan. Kathryn, I did not get any phone messages from you. The last I heard was the e-mail telling me that you didn't want to see me again."

"What?" I was shocked. "I never e-mailed you any such thing. I wouldn't e-mail something like that. Out of the blue—you think I would just break up with you without talking to you in person?"

A myriad of emotions passed over Brad's face, the least of which was fury. "Susan, get out and never cross my path again. If you come on this property again, I will have you arrested for trespassing. I am through with you. Don't test me on this, Susan. I have had a bellyful of you."

Susan picked up her purse and turned to leave. Her face was flushed. "She is lying, Brad. I have done nothing wrong. I have gone out of my way to help you out in the past two weeks, but I am leaving, and you will be sorry."

She stormed out of the office. Brad and I looked at each other. He looked ashamed. "Kathryn, I…"

I was hurt. I felt wounded. I had thought of nothing else flying home from Italy but seeing Brad again. I couldn't wait. Even now, I wanted nothing more than for him to put his arms around me, hold me tight, and kiss me deeply, but I couldn't shake how easily he had fallen for such a flimsy deception. Without even questioning the false e-mail, he had taken it for truth.

He stepped forward, but I put out my hand to hold him back. "Don't Brad. I'm leaving. Maybe Susan did me a favor. If this relationship is this shaky to you, and you can't tell when something doesn't smell right, then it probably isn't right. I came here to find out what was going on, because I knew that something was wrong—dreadfully wrong. I told you—no, I promised you—that I would come back to you and you didn't believe me."

"Kathryn, don't do this. Susan is poison. Give me a chance."

"Brad, I'm just too hurt right now." In fact, I was beginning to tear up, but I wasn't going to give him the satisfaction of seeing me cry over him. I looked at him and said quietly, "I would have fought for you, Brad. You were worth it to me. I am sorry that I wasn't worth it to you. Please don't call me or come by."

"Kathryn," he yelled as I got in my car. "Don't do this!"

# II

I was devastated. I was surprised at how much it hurt. I didn't want to see Brad again. My trust in him had died. Everywhere I looked in my house there were pieces of him. A shirt, a hat, a tool of some kind, so many little things that had become part of the daily landscape. I gathered them all up when I got home and put them in a box. I drove over to Karen's house and broke down.

"God, she is a bitch on a stick," said Karen after I had told her the entire story.

"I have no right to ask you this, but could you take the box with his stuff to his office tomorrow? I can't face him so soon. One look and I will be a blubbering mess. Make sure he understands that it is over for me. Really over."

"It's not over though, is it, Kathryn?" said Karen quietly. "You love him."

"I was willing to explore that, but not anymore. Between Susan and his daughters, there really never was a chance for a relationship. He is just too easily swayed. They will always be in his life one way or another. Its better that my heart is broken now rather than later."

"Poor baby!" She hugged me. "There is only one remedy for this crappy day, and that is wine—and lots of it."

I had to laugh a little. That was Karen's answer to everything, but it wasn't mine. "No thanks, my good friend. I am going home. I have hardly unpacked, and it feels like my trip to Italy was ten years ago, not a few days ago. This whole thing has almost negated all the good experiences I had there."

"Wait, Kathryn. What about Salvatore?"

Salvatore. Another lifetime. "Another time, Karen. I can't talk about any of that right now."

The days passed. Whatever Karen had said to Brad stuck. He didn't come by or call me. I still missed him. Every part of my house reminded me of him, and I wanted to see him badly. I ached, I hurt so badly. It was like flu in some ways—mental flu. My memories hurt. Everything hurt.

I felt displaced in my own home. Nothing was pleasing to me. I didn't want to do anything. I recognized depression, but I couldn't be bothered. Three weeks had passed, and things just seemed to be getting worse.

Laura called. She knew most of the story and was smart enough to fill in the blanks. "Mom, why don't you come out here for a while? It might help you put a new spin on the situation, a different perspective. At best, it will get you away."

"I am not sure that's the answer." I started.

"Do you have a better plan?"

"No." I had to confess. "But I just don't want to take another long plane trip."

"It's not that bad, and once you get here, it will be very relaxing. I am renting a little place at the beach for a while. You know, until I get my next gig. I think you would like it, and you would be great company for Coco."

"I don't think I am great company even for a dog right now."

"Well, how about this one? It would be nice for me to spend some time with my mother. It's been a long time. We could be two bachelorettes together." Laura had broken up with her long-time boyfriend, but strangely, she didn't seem very upset about it.

I couldn't argue with that one. I had not spent any time alone with Laura for years. She got the short straw every single time.

"Anyway," she said, "I want to discuss that project I mentioned to you some months ago about an American—you, specifically—going to study Italian at the language school. I still think it has potential for a documentary. Are you planning to return to Italy in the future?"

"Just for a quick few days at the end of September, and then Karen and I meet for our trip together. There are no other plans for Italy after that. Everything is on hold for now."

"How about your Italian Prince Charming? What is the status on him?"

"Salvatore. That's on hold also. Everything seems to be at a standstill."

"More reason for a change of scenery."

"Maybe, you're right, Laura. There's no reason not to come out for a couple of weeks."

"Let's make it a tentative month, with renewal options."

I had to laugh. "Is all your language in Hollywood-speak? Will I have to hear that for a month?"

"I'm willing to learn some Italian and eat some pasta. Is it a deal?"

"I think so. But I'm warning you not to expect much from me. I'm too spent."

A week later I was walking through the arrival area at LAX. I heard Laura shout my name, and there she was. My beautiful daughter could hold her own with any movie star walking down the street. Her blonde hair was longer, she was even thinner, and she was stunningly dressed.

"Mom, you are so thin," she said as she hugged me. It was true. I had not been eating.

"I think I could say the same about you," I retorted, "but I must admit you look wonderful, healthy, and very suntanned."

"Oh, that's out of a bottle—or a sprayer is more like it." She laughed. "Just like my hair."

"I like it longer. It looks glamorous and natural at the same time."

"Good, that's what I pay for! It's an image thing. That's what Hollywood is all about."

We chatted easily all the way to her rental house. She was driving a Mercedes convertible, which she was leasing, and soon we drove up to the gated community of Malibu.

"You live in Malibu?"

"Just for the summer. I thought it would be fun. I have the money and good connections now, plus I am actually getting quite a deal on the place." She told me the owner's name. He turned out to be an international star.

The house was a true movie star house. Not huge, although spacious; it was all glass, chrome, stainless steel, and white. There was absolutely no color in any room.

"My God," I said, astonished. "If it snowed out here, you would never find your way from the bathroom to the kitchen!"

Laura laughed. "You are so right, Mom. It's a hoot, isn't it? Here's Coco. She adds a bit of color." Laura's little brown poodle was the only bright spot in the whiteout.

The house sat right on the beach and had decks on two levels. It was spectacular, and I loved it on sight. As sterile as the interior was, the view of the ocean made up for everything. I can heal here, I thought.

The refrigerator was as empty as the house felt. There was nothing in it but water, and there was lots of water. "I'm really not here much, Mom, and I eat out every night." Laura shrugged. "We will go grocery shopping after dinner."

# III

My days in LA took on a life of their own. I felt as if I had landed on another planet: Planet Hollywood. We ate out almost every night in some hot restaurant where Laura was well known by staff and patrons alike. There was never an uninterrupted meal. Someone was always stopping by to discuss a project coming up. Laura had made her mark on this town, it seemed, and she knew how to play the game. I was proud of her and her success but thought she would eventually burn out. Her days were long. Up around nine thirty and not in bed until the wee hours of the morning. Hollywood time.

I usually went to bed as soon as we got home, which was normally midnight, and was up at six for a walk on the beach. Years of habit would not allow me to sleep later. Coco and I were often the only walkers so early in the morning. Actors and their crowd didn't show their faces before noon. It was nice having the beach to myself. Laura was right. I was getting a different perspective on my life, but it had a disturbing element. I felt lost and out of sync. I had no desire to go home, and I didn't want to go back to Italy. And I certainly didn't want to live in Los Angeles. It was too superficial. I talked to Karen every day, but she was not allowed to mention Brad's name to me, ever. I couldn't believe how strongly I felt about his betrayal. I couldn't forgive him, although I knew in my heart that he was probably hurting as well.

I didn't seem to fit anywhere. Oh, I knew the kids loved me and wanted me in their lives. Jenn and Sammy were back on track. The grandchildren were doing well. Larry had divorced Linda, and he and Nan were now a legitimate couple. Nan had transformed our family and become a part of it. Eli and Chapin still wanted me to do things with them, but that would change as they got older. Nothing seemed to have meaning for me any longer. I just couldn't get a handle on anything. My brain seemed to have stopped functioning.

Help came from the most curious direction. Once or twice a week, Coco and I were joined in our early morning walks by a lone runner who nodded in our direction as he sprinted by. From what I could tell, he was a handsome, familiar man in perhaps his early forties. Three weeks into my visit, I came upon him limping down the beach in obvious pain.

"Omigod! Are you badly hurt?"

"I think I twisted my ankle. I ran into a sand hole."

"How can I help? Can I call someone? Our house is just behind you."

He glanced back. "That's Mario Varga's house. I thought he was gone."

"Yes, he is. My daughter is living there for the summer. I am Kathryn Wynham, by the way."

He held out his hand and introduced himself as Jack Scubi. He was in one of the longest running TV shows currently showing. He played a detective.

I had not recognized him until he said his name. "I am a big fan of your show"—which was true—"but I have to admit, I haven't seen the current season. Can I call someone for you?"

He winced and said that if he could limp into the house, he would make some calls. Jack ran in shorts or a bathing suit, so it was easy to see what good shape he was in. I overheard the call and knew that he would not be picked up immediately. I got him some ice, and we elevated his foot. He remained on the phone calling various people—set director, trainers, script-writer—all sorts of people.

In the meantime, I made a pot of coffee and brought him a cup. When he got off the phone, he finally looked at me for the first time. "I'm sorry to impose. I hope I'm not interrupting your day."

"Not at all. I'm a visitor only. My daughter is still asleep, and I am going to fix some scrambled eggs. Would you be interested?"

I was surprised when he said yes, because I had observed that most actors didn't eat. They tasted food, but they never seemed to eat a meal. Laura also did this. She would order dinner, her only meal of the day, and taste a few bites, and that would be it. Most of the meal went back to the kitchen. Great diet plan. I felt like a pig whenever I finished anything.

Jack's foot was propped up, but he was able to sit at the table, where he regaled me with stories of misadventures on the set. He was charming and genuine. He loved being an actor but not the fame. He missed privacy. We were laughing and having a great time when Laura stumbled in the kitchen.

"Mother, what in the devil is going on?" She stopped when she saw Jack. I saw her eyes open in amazement. "Jack Scubi?"

Jack was also amazed. My daughter, I must admit, looked like every man's fantasy. Her long, blonde hair was a mass of tangled curls. She had almost nothing on, and you could see through that.

"Honey," I said gently. "You might want to go put some clothes on."

She looked down, blushed, and beat a hasty retreat. When she returned, her hair was in a ponytail, her face was scrubbed but free of makeup, and she was dressed in jeans and a loose top. She still looked delicious, and I could see that Jack was quite taken with her.

They had never met but knew of one another. Jack was, of course, the bigger name, but they had connections in common. Another Hollywood word. His people knew her people. Before we knew it, Jack's housekeeper had returned from shopping and was knocking at the door. With apologies and promises of getting together with Laura, Jack left.

Laura was so confounded that I had met one of the biggest stars on television that she inadvertently ate two pieces of toast and some scrambled eggs. I felt the best that I had felt in a month. She couldn't stop talking about Jack. "I would do anything to write a screenplay for him," she said. "I actually have one in the works that would be a great match." On and on she went, until I stopped her.

"Why don't we invite him over for dinner in a couple of days?"

"Are you kidding, Mom? You just don't call someone up here and ask them to come over for a bowl of spaghetti. This isn't Baltimore."

"OK. It just looked like he enjoys eating. A novelty in Los Angeles, I think. Actually, he may like spaghetti. His last name sounds Italian."

"Oh, Mom. Get real. You can't do that. He wouldn't eat carbs anyway. Way too fattening."

"OK, how about if I ask him to come over and eat a stick of celery with us. We could split it three ways."

"Very funny, Mom, very, very funny." She left to dress for work.

But what did she know, my very successful Hollywood daughter? Three days later, I saw Jack running gingerly down the beach. He stopped to greet me and Coco.

"How is the ankle?" I asked.

"Better, much better. I am looking out for all the hidden land mines this time." He laughed. "I want to thank you again for taking good care of me."

"No thanks needed. The lovely flowers you sent were a big surprise. We now have some color in the whiteout."

"The whiteout?" Jack looked confused.

"Yes, that's what I call the living room."

He laughed again. "And thanks for breakfast. I mean it when I say it was really delicious."

"It was fun cooking some food for a change and watching someone actually eat it. I miss cooking."

"You can cook for me anytime. My cook—so-called cook—can't make anything that tastes normal. Everything is some fancy concoction. Half the time I don't know what's going in my mouth. I long for meatloaf, and macaroni and cheese. I couldn't eat like that every night, but it would be nice once in a while."

"Give me a night," I said.

"What?"

"If you mean it, and if you will eat it, I will make you a great home-cooked meal."

"Tomorrow night?" he said hopefully.

"It's a deal. I will surprise Laura, but I don't expect her to eat much of it."

Laura was dumbfounded. "I can't believe he is actually coming over here to eat a meal of total fat." But he did, and the dinner was a huge success. Clearly, Laura and Jack hit it off. She didn't dress up for him, but she looked great. Of course with each bite they took, each one of them moaned about the calories and how long it would take to get rid of the extra poundage, but they ate and ate. I was delighted.

It was the most fun I'd had since I had come back from Italy. I suddenly realized that I missed cooking, having people over to my house, and seeing my friends and family. I was homesick. It hit me like a bolt of lightning when I was cleaning up the kitchen. For the first time, this very sterile environment that I had been living in for almost a month seemed warm and human. I had shooed Jack and Laura outside to discuss their various projects, but I could still hear their laughter and chatter, and the house had the lingering odor of something delicious.

I had missed all of that. I realized that I didn't want to sell my house, as I had been thinking. I wanted to go home to it. My airline ticket was open-ended, and I decided that I would leave in a couple of days, as soon as it could be arranged. Suddenly, I felt completely energized. Brad was still a big question mark, but I needed to go home.

# IV

I told Laura the next day. "But Mom, it's too soon. I want you to stay awhile longer."

"Laura, you have a very busy life, and I have gotten all I need from being here. The ocean restored me, and I feel both rested and full of energy. I miss my life in the East."

"Well, we will have to have one big blowout evening on the town before you go," she said.

I really had no desire to go out with Laura to another fancy restaurant and watch her schmooze. "I have a better idea. I would like to fix one final dinner and invite Jack again, if he will come. Something Italian." I put my hand up to stop her argument about the fat factor. "It will be lower cal than last night's dinner, I promise. Would you be willing to call him?"

I could tell that she would love to call Jack on any excuse. "Mom, don't be surprised if he doesn't come. He is really huge out here. I'm sure he will be busy."

Fate intervened, and I saw Jack before Laura could call him. He was running on the beach but stopped to thank me when he saw me. "Kathryn that was the best dinner that I've had in ten years. Anytime in the future… that you want…to cook, call me." He was out of breath from jogging.

"Laura is going to call you today, in fact. I am going home, and I want to make an Italian dinner before I go. I would love for you to come."

He got a faraway look in his eyes. He was a Jersey boy at heart. There was nothing that I could discover about him that said fake, phony, or super-ficial. "When?"

"Thursday night. I am leaving on Friday morning."

He stopped jogging. "That soon."

"I have been here nearly a month, Jack. I need to go home. There are some unresolved problems in my life, and I have been running away from them."

He looked surprised. "You look so calm and confident, Kathryn. I can't imagine you running from anything."

"Well, I am finding out a lot about myself that I didn't realize. It's been a huge help being on another coast and thinking about things. Now I am ready to go back and confront them."

There was a speculative look in his eyes, and he looked on the verge of saying something else but thought the better of it. "Good luck to you. I have a feeling things will turn out well."

"I think so, too. I really do." I waved good-bye as he jogged away. What had I learned about myself? I knew three things that were true. The first was that I was far more emotionally vulnerable than I thought. The second was that I missed Brad more than I ever considered I would, and the third was that I still didn't want to get married. I also knew that I needed to see and talk to Brad again. No matter how things turned out, I needed closure and peace of mind. I also realized that, in the time that I had spent in Malibu, I had thought of Salvatore very little.

I called Karen. "I am flying back home on Friday."

"Finally."

"I plan to call Brad and see if we can talk. What do you think?"

"Am I allowed to mention his name?"

"Yes. Have you seen him? Do you know if Susan is still in his life?"

"He looks like hell, Kathryn. He has missed you, and I bet he has lost ten pounds in the past month. I can tell you emphatically that Susan is not in his life, but I will let him give you the details. There's lot to tell you about that. Some things have happened."

I was curious, but I didn't want to appear that interested, even to Karen. I knew from experience that she didn't keep much to herself. "So you think he will see me?"

"I know that he wants to see you more than anything. I talk to him fairly often because of the work his guys are doing at my place. He knows that he screwed up."

"I think I overreacted a bit. I was especially angry that he had let Susan back into his life, but I guess she will always be in his life one way or the other because of their daughters. I just don't know what to do about that. I think if I could trust Brad about how he feels about her, it would be easier."

"You might find that has changed significantly when you talk to Brad," Karen replied.

"Why do you say that?" I asked.

"I'll let Brad explain it to you. It would be better coming from him. Why don't I pick you up at the airport?"

"No, don't bother. You never know if the plane will arrive on schedule or three hours late. I'll get transportation back home. Please don't say anything to Brad, Karen. I need to figure out things a bit more."

"I'm glad that you're willing to talk to him. He's a good guy, Kathryn, and he loves you."

"I don't know about love. I think that's a bit strong, but I do know that I was more emotionally involved than I thought I was."

I felt happy that I was going home. I missed the little ones and couldn't wait to see them. For all practical purposes, counting my time in Italy, I had been away for over three months. So much had changed.

One positive thing was that my relationship with Laura had become closer during the time I had been in California. I had a feeling that something good was happening between her and Jack. I wondered if two Hollywood types could find a real relationship in that crazy world. I never found out what had happened to the man that Laura had been seeing, but I understood how easily things could go wrong.

Who was I to pass judgment? I had certainly proved to myself that I was no expert in the relationship field.

Our last dinner together was a rousing success. Neither Laura nor Jack said one thing about calories or fat food or carbohydrates. They just ate and ate and laughed and laughed. I was leaving my daughter in good hands.

"Kathryn, your daughter is something, do you know that?" Jack said at one point.

"I do indeed know that, but how did you find out?" I laughed.

"I have committed myself to a project with her—some kind of comedy—when we go on hiatus. Believe me, plenty of people have tried to obligate me to something they are working on but have not succeeded. Your daughter, in the space of two times together, has done just that. I think I need to know what you have put in your food."

We all laughed. "I think it was carbs. Obviously, you both need them." Again we laughed. When dinner was over, both Jack and Laura wanted me to go barhopping with them for a final drink, but I begged off. My excuse was that I was nervous about flying and didn't want to feel sick on the plane, but I really wanted them to be alone together.

I don't think they missed me.

Laura drove me to the airport and hugged me tightly when we said good-bye. "Mom, I will miss you more than you know." She was glowing and looked beautiful. "Jack told me last night that he knew what I would look like when I was twenty years older. He thinks you are the best—and gorgeous to boot."

"I knew I liked him instantly." I laughed. "Please keep thinking of projects for him. We need to keep a man so flattering in our lives."

"I will do my best. I promise. I will do my best." She waved good-bye. I knew she would be all right.

# V

The trip back was uneventful. I spent my time trying to figure out the best way to be in touch with Brad. Should I invite him over to my house, or should I just show up at his apartment and confront the issues? Maybe a neutral place would be better, such as a coffee house. But that was unappealing because of its public nature. Maybe we could meet in a park, where the elements of nature would support us talking rationally.

What did I want to say to him? That was the hardest part, because I was unsure. How could I tell him that Susan couldn't be a part of his life, although I had Salvatore in mine? But I felt that I had been more open about Salvatore than he had been about Susan. I needed to know where she was in his life. Had they slept together? That was the burning question, because if they had, it would be over for me. I had been monogamous in Italy, and I expected the same of Brad. Susan had said they were back together. Was she lying?

I needed to get home to my own house. Maybe there it would come to me.

I didn't have to wrestle with it after all. Brad was at the airport to meet me. Because I was not expecting to be met, I paid no attention to the people standing around as passengers deplaned, but when I heard my name,

I automatically scanned the crowd. I saw him standing apart and was appalled by how sad and miserable he looked. My heart melted. Never heavy, he was thin to the point of gauntness. There were huge dark circles under his eyes. He didn't look like he had eaten or slept in the past month. Even his voice was shaky when he said my name.

"Kathryn."

"Brad." I stood for a moment, not believing that I was actually seeing him. "Brad." I made my way over to him and reached up and touched his face. There were tears in his eyes.

"Kathryn, can you forgive me? I know that I don't deserve it, or you, but I have so much to say to you. Can we talk?"

I nodded. I didn't trust myself to speak, and I couldn't take my eyes off of him. I couldn't get over how awful he looked. It was true grief I was seeing, and it was because of me, of us.

I squeezed his hand. "Yes, I need to talk to you. Let me get my luggage, and then we can go home." I could barely whisper.

Brad nodded and said nothing else. He couldn't speak either. We both were so choked up that neither one of us could trust ourselves to say anything. We drove to my house in virtual silence, but there were tears running down my face.

The lights were on, inside and out, when we drove up. "I stopped by before I drove to the airport," Brad said. "I still have your key."

I still had said almost nothing. My mind was in turmoil. I ached for myself and Brad. When Brad opened the door, I walked into a house full of flowers—tulips, to be exact. From the foyer, I could see vases of red, yellow, pink, and purple tulips all over the living room and even in the study. Brad knew they were my favorite flower.

"Did you do this?" I asked him as I walked over to touch a pedal.

He nodded.

"They are astoundingly beautiful. I feel like I'm in a garden." All at once my emotional dam broke, and I started crying. "Oh, Brad…" He came over and put his arms around me. I could tell he was affected as much as I was.

"Brad, I am so sad and miserable"—he continued to hold me—"I need to get a grip. Could you make us some coffee while I take a quick shower?"

I pulled out of his arms and went upstairs to my bathroom. I needed some time to get myself together. I wasn't prepared for a showdown with Brad. I looked as bad as he did, and as miserable. There was no way this man didn't mean everything to me. But I had to have the truth before we could go on.

I took a shower in the hottest water I could stand and changed into a soft, white top and pants. I felt better. I went back downstairs to the kitchen, where I found Brad. He was drinking a beer.

"I thought we—at least I—needed something stronger than coffee, and this was all you had. I need some liquid courage."

"Beer is good," I said. "I think better than coffee." We were standing apart from each other on opposite sides of the room. "Where do you want to talk?"

He took a big gulp from the bottle and put it down. "Here is as good as anywhere, I guess. Before you say anything, Kathryn, I want you to know that I am deeply sorry. I was wrong. I made an error that is costing me the love of my life." Brad was unflinching. "If you decide to throw me out in the next five minutes, I hope you will let me say a couple of things first." He waited for me to acknowledge him.

"Brad, I…" I sank down onto one of the kitchen chairs.

"Let me finish this, Kathryn, before you say anything. Let me just have my say," he begged.

He brought his bottle over and sat down across from me. "You were right about everything. After you left that day, I was mad as hell. I have never hated anyone as much as I did Susan in that moment. I couldn't believe what she had done, but worst of all, that I was such an ass that I couldn't put two and two together. I read the e-mail that we were finished; you didn't want to see me again. The wording didn't sound like you, but I was devastated. I believed that you would stay with that guy in Italy even before you left."

"Brad—" I started.

"No, Kathryn, let me finish. I have to get this out. I expected to get an e-mail from you kissing me off. From the day you left, I was afraid that you would stay over there and marry that Italian. I was consumed by it. It was all I could think of every day—that you were with him."

"Brad—"

"Kathryn, just hush and listen. I was crazy with jealousy. That was the state that Susan found me in. My secretary had left, because I was so hard to live with. I barked at everyone. The guys knew what was going on, but Annie couldn't work with me, so she up and quit. I don't blame her. I was a real S.O.B. My office was a shambles and getting worse. Susan offered to straighten it out if I would pay her. She was hard up again. I felt like I had no choice. She knew how to manage the office. I was desperate and getting further and further behind in my paperwork. It was supposed to be a temporary arrangement."

"I had stopped getting e-mails from you until the one came—the one Susan wrote—about you leaving me. Susan had been deleting your messages. When you showed up that day, in one sickening moment I knew Susan had something to do with the e-mails. I didn't know how, but I knew she was behind it. I saw you drive up, and I rushed over to see what had happened.

That's when I heard you confront Susan. I saw that look on your face, the hurt and outrage, and I knew you were through with me. Your words about fighting for me—well, they cut me like a knife. I don't deserve you."

I was about to speak again. He held up his hand. "Wait, Kathryn, there's more. I knew we were finished, and I think I could have killed Susan if I had found her, but she disappeared. I was really mad and disgusted at myself for being taken in again by that bitch. I was sick. Really, Kathryn, in my heart. It broke. I broke." He stopped for a moment to get himself back in control.

"I heard from Karen that you had gone to California. She said you were as heartbroken as I was. That gave me a little hope. I wanted it to mean that you still cared about me, but I had nothing I could say to you. I picked up the phone a million times to call you. But what could I say? There was nothing I could do or say to make it right.

"One of those bleak nights, when I held the phone in my hand in my office, I looked at the computer. Something you had said about Susan messing around with it hit me like a ton of bricks. I went into my accounts. Susan knew all the passwords. I had never changed them. I am the dumbest ass who has ever walked the face of the earth. And then it clicked. In the two weeks she had been in my office, she had transferred over five thousand dollars from my business account into her bank account. She did it in thousand-dollar increments, so it wasn't as noticeable as it would have been in a lump sum. That day when you walked in, I lost you, and I almost lost my business—again—and to the same evil woman. I went into a rage.

"I contacted the police the next day. The transfers were easy to see. There was no mistake. She didn't cover her tracks at all. I guess she thought I was too stupid to figure it out, and she was right. You saved my business, Kathryn. I owe you everything, and I have given you nothing but heartache. For what it's worth, I had Susan arrested. The cops found her in DC. She is sitting in jail awaiting trial, because she can't make bond. She is considered a flight risk, so the bond is high. My daughters aren't speaking to me; because I had their mother arrested and won't give her the money for the bail. They have turned out to be chips off the same block, but that's their problem. I am not speaking to them right now until they can see their mother for what she is."

I took a deep breath but didn't speak.

"All I have left to say is that I love you, Kathryn. I never meant to hurt you. I deserve to lose you. It took all of this for me to understand it. I should have trusted you, trusted your word. You always stood by your word. I should have known that you would come back. You promised. I had to get all of this off my chest. I needed to say this to you."

"Don't blame Karen for me being here. I have begged her every day to let me know when you were coming back. I started to come to California, but Karen told me it would be a bad idea. You needed time. I can go now, if you want me to. I have said all I wanted to say."

We both stood up. I was a wreck. I was teary and having a hard time speaking. "Brad, there is so much. So much. I was hurt, and I still hurt. I ache just looking at you. I owe it to you to tell you that I am at fault also. I shouldn't have run away. That was stupid and caused both of us more pain. We both have behaved like love-sick teenagers."

Brad made a move to take me in his arms, but I held up a hand. "I have to ask you one thing. I know this question will anger you, but I should have asked you that day I came out to your office."

"For God's sake, what is it Kathryn?" His voice was full of anguish.

"When Susan came back...it's hard for me to ask this. She told me that you were back together, like honeymooners. Did you sleep with her, Brad?"

He exploded. "Shit! I can't believe you would even ask me that, Kathryn. I hate that woman. I have hated her ever since she left me. I hate her even more now." His face was dangerously red, and he was as mad as I had ever seen him. "How could you think that? How could you ever think that?"

He turned to leave. "No, Kathryn, I never slept with her. Does that do it for you? Is that all you need to ask me?"

"Brad, I had to hear it. I had to hear the words. It's been my worst nightmare that you would go back to her. She said all the right things that day. She gloated. When I realized she was lying, I couldn't get over the fact that she had fooled you, and that you had let her back into your life. I also couldn't believe that you would simply take an e-mail at face value, that you didn't write me back or come see me when I came home. You accepted that message without question, even though it didn't sound right to you. It made me feel like that I meant nothing to you, that the time we had together meant nothing. I realize now that I wrong, but I couldn't see that then. I was just so hurt."

He was at the front door. I looked at all the tulips in the living room and knew I didn't want to lose this man. "Brad, do you think we could start over? Can we find a way of trusting one another? Are we willing to let your ex-wife tear us apart?"

"I don't know, Kathryn." His hand was on the doorknob.

"Am I worth fighting for, Brad?" I grabbed his arm and turned him toward me. "You said you love me. What does that mean to you?" I was teary, but I held firm. "If you really want me in your life, are you going to walk out that door right now and out of my life forever?"

"Goddamn it, Kathryn, you are the most infuriating woman I have ever known."

He took me into his arms and kissed me. "I can't live without you, but goddamn it, I don't know how to live with you."

"Brad, all I ask is that we work on it. I am worn out. Really worn out." I was. I couldn't think, and I could hardly stand up. I really wanted nothing more than to go to bed with him. Not for sex, but just to have him near me. I knew all I had to do was to say the word, but that was not where we should start. I knew that in my head, but my heart sure wanted to go down a different path.

"Will you come back tomorrow night after work? I'll cook dinner. I have some things I need to say to you, some conclusions I came to in Italy about us. Would you come back so I can tell you?"

"Can't you tell me tonight? Now?" he asked. He didn't want to leave.

"No, I'm too tired. I want to tell you tomorrow. I'll see you then. I think we both need some time and rest." I pushed him out of the door before I could change my mind.

I went to sleep in my own bed that night and slept the best that I had slept in a month.

# VI

There were some rough weeks ahead, and there were many times I didn't think we could work it out, starting with the second night back, when Brad came over for dinner.

Ideally, it would have been nice to have eaten out on the terrace, a calm and serene setting, but it was not possible in the warm evening. I wanted to keep our dinner casual, but even the kitchen felt too hot, so that left the dining room, if we were going to be cool. I tried to make it as informal and comfortable as possible. I had made one of Brad's favorite meals: pot roast with all the trimmings and an apple pie for dessert.

Just before he arrived, I changed into a deep-blue cotton blouse and cropped pants outfit. I was tanned from my month in California, and I knew the blue looked good on me. I had just slipped into my silver flip-flops when I heard him call my name.

"Coming, Brad." He was at the foot of the stairs. We both laughed. He had on a blue shirt and khaki pants. We both had worn the same color at other times, and it felt momentarily like old times. "Some things don't change, do they?"

As I reached the bottom step, Brad came over and put his arms around me. We were at eye level. "You look beautiful," he said. He kissed me lightly and then sniffed. "It smells great in here."

"It's just about ready, but we are eating in the dining room, where it's cooler. Can you open some red wine for me? I am also having ice tea. What about you?"

He looked better today—not as strained. "Do you have any beer? I'll start with that and have ice tea when we eat."

We kept the conversation light until we finished dessert. "How about coffee?" I asked.

"No, I think I'll just stick with tea. This was the best meal I've had since before you went to Italy, Kathryn. I don't think there are any leftovers."

"Just enough roast so that you can have a sandwich tomorrow, if you like."

"You don't have to ask twice. These are just a few of the million things I missed about you: good food, leftovers, the way you make a home feel like, well, a home. I told you this before, Kathryn. I never had that with Susan. Even when the kids were little, she wasn't a homemaker, and she was not always a good mother. She wanted to be rich and have someone wait on her." I saw the bitterness in his face, which had hardened at the mention of her name.

I stood up and put my hand out for him to take. "Let's make a deal not to talk about Susan tonight, OK?"

"Deal."

"I think its cool enough now to go sit outside in the glider." It was something we had started doing just before I left for Italy—late evenings sitting in the glider on my terrace, looking at the stars, talking, and holding hands. The weather was a lot nicer in early spring, but the roses were in bloom now, and they smelled heavenly.

"Tomorrow is garden day for me," I remarked as we settled in, holding hands. "There are more weeds than flowers growing out here." I turned to Brad. I could see his face in the glow of the kitchen lights. "I became homesick when I was in Italy this time, and more so in California. This is my way of life, Brad. This is my home. That was one of the conclusions I came to in Italy. I love being there. I love the language, the people, and the culture in Italy, but it isn't home. I could never be more than a visitor in that country. I need to live where I belong. I missed you dreadfully. I missed the kids. Of course, I missed Karen." We both laughed.

"Settle this for me, Kathryn—the Italian guy. What about him?"

"Salvatore is part of the whole thing about Italy. He is not separate. Even if he asked me to marry him, which I don't think would happen, I would still be a visitor—in his house, in his family, and in Orvieto. Besides that, he loves his deceased wife. No woman will ever take her place. The other thing for me is that I am not ready to be married again, and I don't think Salvatore could ever understand that. I plan to tell Salvatore about you when I return to Italy in a couple of months. I think he knows there's someone else. I don't think he will be surprised."

"And now?"

"Nothing has changed in terms of me staying in Italy. This is my home, with or without you. I hope that you will be a part of my life, but I need more from you."

He groaned. "Kathryn, you know I don't like to travel."

"That's not what I mean, Brad. I don't care so much about that. There might be times when I would like to go somewhere with you, but I can accept that travel isn't your thing. However, you can't expect me to stay home for the rest of my life." I felt myself getting heated. "You know that Karen is going to meet me in Stockholm when I leave Italy, so that we can have time with Inga and her mother. Then we are off to Paris and Provence for three weeks."

"I know. I know very well. That's all Karen has been talking about lately. No, Kathryn, I don't like it that you are away for so long, but that is because I miss you. I miss us." He squeezed my hand. "I have had thoughts lately that we should get married. I wish we were married, and then none of this would have happened."

"Are you kidding?" I couldn't believe him. "Do you think marriage instills trust? That almost seems like you are trying to control me, Brad."

"I am," he answered honestly. "I wish that I could put you in one place and know that you would always be there waiting for me when work is over. I know how that sounds, Kathryn, but honest to God, I can't stand the thought that you may walk away someday. I think the more you travel, the greater the chances are that you will meet some-one else—like the Italian guy—and that will be it. I admit it. I am jealous."

"That is absolutely insane, Brad. Do you know that?"

"Yes. A part of me knows it, but I still think that. I'm going to get a beer. Can I bring you something?'

"A glass of wine, please."

He came back with our beverages and remained standing. "Here's the thing, Kathryn. This is what I want. I want to come every night to a clean and orderly house, to a beautiful woman, to a home-cooked meal, to a foot-ball game afterwards. Then to bed with my beautiful wife. I am a simple man. That's all."

"Wow! You have never said that before. I thought you didn't want to get married again."

"It took you being gone to make me realize that. It hit me about two days into your trip. It's not so much that I want to get married. I want to be with you. I like your family. Did you know that Larry, Chapin, Eli, and I went fishing one Saturday?"

"No, no one told me. When was that?"

"Soon after you left. Larry brings Chapin around fairly often. Chapin is good with his hands and likes to build. The guys call him 'Little Jug head.' They are teaching him a world of things, including bad language, which I've had to warn them about. Larry and I have struck up a good friendship. Nan had me over for dinner once."

"I had no idea all of this was going on," I remarked. "I feel so out of it."

"Eli is a good little fisherman, but Chapin can't keep his mouth shut long enough to let a fish bite. We had to bribe him. Your family feels like my family, Kathryn. It's an entire package that I don't want to lose. My daughters are just like their mother—money grubbers. I am ashamed of them and disappointed. I hated the way they treated you."

"Brad, I don't know if I can be what you want me to be, what you need. I am in a different space now in my life. For over thirty years, I was that wife you talked about. Then I was a baby-sitter, and I don't want to do that again. I think it is ludicrous that you think I will meet someone because I am traveling. For the entire seven years after my husband died, I met no one. Not one single man. I wasn't looking for anyone then, and I still am not looking. I am very happy that you came into my life, or at least I was. I hope that we can recapture what we had before I left for Italy. I don't want to be controlled or manipulated."

"Is that what you think I am trying to do? Control you? Manipulate you?" Brad asked heatedly.

"I don't know. I don't want to answer to someone else. I want to get up in the morning and plan my day the way I want it to go. If that sounds selfish, it is. I don't want to be held hostage by a house, a person, or a marriage. I like my freedom." I could feel Brad getting angry.

He stood up. "So what you are saying, Kathryn is that there is no place for me in your life."

"No, Brad. If you had heard one thing I said, you would have heard me say that I want you in my life, that I missed you, that I was miserable without you, and that I was homesick. Didn't you hear that?"

"So you want me on your terms only. Is that it?"

"I know that it sounds like that, but what I want to do is find a compromise, if that is possible, and I don't know what that is yet."

"Bullshit, Kathryn! You can't have it only the way you want it. I also need more from you."

I stood up. "It's late, Brad. You have an early day tomorrow. I don't think we are getting anywhere tonight. Call me when or if you want to talk to me again. For what it's worth, I love you, too."

He didn't say anything for a minute or so. "I'll call you later in the week, Kathryn." He gave me a little kiss and left.

# VII

Every time we got together it seemed to start out well and then go down-
hill. Brad told me in one of our many arguments that if I really loved
him, I should let him move in with me. There was no doubt that his apartment was awful, and he was at my house several times a week. It would have
made sense, but I didn't want him in my space all the time. I liked having my
privacy.

Then there was the sexual tension. We had not slept together since I returned from California. I wanted to, but I didn't want to sleep with someone
who ultimately might not be in my life.

Karen came up with the perfect solution. "Kidnap him and take him
somewhere that he would like—a fishing village or the mountains. It would
do you both good to get out of town."

I did some research on the internet and found a charming little town
on the Eastern shore of Maryland. I called Brad at work. "Can you take off
on Friday?"

"I could, but why?"

"No questions allowed. Be ready at nine o'clock with a suitcase and your fishing gear."

"What?"

"I will pick you up."

"Kathryn, what are you up to? I have a million things to do."

"Are you game, Brad? Will you go with me?"

"Hell, I guess so. Why not? I'll be ready."

I had done my homework. I rented a little cabin and bought some groceries. I planned a happy, relaxing, and casual weekend.

I drove up to his apartment and honked the horn. Brad came out. "Get in," I said.

"Are you going to tell me what this all about?" he asked. I could tell he was a tiny bit excited but trying not to show it.

"Do you have any adventuresome spirit at all, or have you become an old fuddy-duddy?"

"I'm in your hands." He loaded his gear in the car and came around to the driver's side.

"I'm driving," I said. "I have been driving for a very long time—longer than you since I am older—so I think you're in experienced hands."

He shrugged, grinned, and got in. "Yes, ma'am." And he gave me a little salute.

"Are you going to tell me where we are going?" he asked.

"Soon. I will need you to watch for signs. Just relax for now." Not an easy thing for Brad to do when he wasn't in control, but gradually, as we drove along a sleepy two-lane road, I could feel the tension leave him.

"OK, Brad, start looking for a little town called Saint Amelia's Cove. That's where we are going," I said after forty-five minutes. The drive had been beautiful, and we both had been singing off-key to old songs on the radio.

Saint Amelia's Cove was not disappointing. It was a quaint little fishing village with a church, a few shops, and several restaurants. The population was fewer than fifteen hundred people. We found our cabin easily, and my personal fear that it would be too rustic was unfounded. The cottage was as charming as the town, with a water view and shabby-chic décor. It was just the right mixture of masculinity and femininity but not too cutesy. It looked genuine. Brad walked through each room. I could see that he was pleased, but he came out of the bedroom with a frown on his face.

"There has been a little mistake," he said.

"Really?" I thought I had made everything perfectly clear when I made the arrangements.

"There is only bedroom."

I was putting groceries in the refrigerator. "Does it have a king-size bed?"

"Yes, it looks like it's king-size."

"No mistake," I said coming into the room and putting my arm around his waist. "This is what I asked for."

It took a minute for reality to dawn on him. "We both are going to sleep in that bed?"

"Unless you want to sleep on the sofa."

"God, Kathryn, I had given up hoping." He pulled me tighter and kissed me. "I am willing to try it out now and see how it works."

"You or the bed? No, we are going for a walk into town for lunch. You are going to check out the fishing pier, and I plan on reading this afternoon. Then we will see how things work out tonight. OK?"

"I guess I have no choice, do I?"

"Sure you do, bed or sofa. That's your choice." I playfully elbowed him in the side.

The weekend was a great success in more ways than one. Brad fell in love with Saint Amelia's Cove, and we ended up looking at real estate. The town was the perfect place for him to relax in and was just over an hour from his office. He found a little house that was made to order. I had never seen him so excited. It was big enough for him to have a woodshop for all of his projects, but the house needed some major work. Brad was up to it and had already started making plans for renovations before we left town. The little village had exceptional fishing and enough amenities to make it habitable, and it was extremely friendly.

"Do you think when Chapin is a little older; Sammy and Jenn would let him spend a weekend out here with me? Just two guys?"

"I think they would be delighted, and I know Chapin would. That is just the kind of attention he needs. Thank you for thinking of him, Brad." I reached over and touched his face. "This has been the best weekend ever."

Our first night back together had all the right ingredients. It felt fresh and new but familiar and comfortable. It was fun, playful, and tender. Brad showed me a side that I had never seen before—pure happiness. It was contagious. I was happy, too.

"I think we are back. This feels so right to me. I couldn't be more content," I said to him as we were drifting off to sleep.

As the days melted into hot summer weeks, there were fewer rough patches. Brad was consumed by his house and renovations. He was in the height of his building season so there wasn't much time to spare. He had finally found a good office manager, and to my immense surprise, he asked Karen if she would help him stage houses to sell.

"You and Karen working together?" I reacted incredulously.

"Why not?" he said one evening. "She's great at it. Look at your house."

He was right, and Karen was excited about having this new venture in her life. She wouldn't get into the full swing of it until after our trip to Europe. "It actually won't take off until January, because of the holidays so soon after we return, but I am full of creative ideas and hoping to pick up more on our trip."

"Do you think you and Brad will get on each other's nerves?" I asked curiously.

"Of course we will!" She laughed. "But he owes me big-time. I kept him informed about you while you were in California, and he knew that I wanted the two of you back together. I was the only person he had to talk to. God, Kathryn, I don't know what would have happened to Brad if you had not reconciled with him. I've never seen a man so down on himself."

I was starting to feel better about everyone. Laura and Jack were still seeing each other. They had become a hot item in Hollywood, and Laura thought there was a chance that the relationship could sustain itself despite the hype.

Sammy and Jenn were a couple and a family again. The children were happy and had parents who could care for them, with help. Larry was a model grandfather and had blossomed without Linda in his life. Nan continued to be the fairy godmother of this family.

Karen had boosted my excitement about returning to Europe so soon. She couldn't wait to see Paris, and I owed her one—a big one. She had been my friend and confidante in so many ways. She had as much to do with saving the relationship between me and Brad as we did. I owed her the best possible trip to France, with all the enthusiasm that I could muster. I knew it would be fun once we got underway.

Brad looked ten years younger and better than ever. The one remaining thing that was nagging me was a birthday gift for him. I had racked my brain, and it came up empty every time. It finally came to me in a dream. I thought it was the perfect thing, but I was a little worried about Brad's reaction to this gift.

Brad's birthday was just ten days before I left for Italy. It was his sixtieth, so I wanted it to be a big deal. Of course, Brad wanted no fuss made over him at all. He thought a quiet dinner or even another weekend at Saint Amelia's Cove would be enough. I decided to do a cookout at my house and invite his work crew, Karen, and my family. These were all friends whom Brad felt comfortable with. I would keep it low-key and casual, but there would be a big cake with a lot of candles.

The boys were beside themselves, because it was a grown-up party. Brooke was too young to know much of anything, but she looked adorable. Brad's work crew knew my house well from the renovations, and they felt right at home. They also knew Larry because of his friendship with Brad. It was just the right mix of people for Brad to be comfortable with.

We had Japanese lanterns strung all over the garden and twinkling white lights in some of the shrubbery. Balloons and streamers were everywhere. It was festive and fun looking, and soon everyone got in the spirit of the day, ribbing Brad about his new senior status. Uncomfortable with being the center of attention, he nevertheless was a good sport, and I could tell he was having a good time.

Soon it was time for the cake, which the boys help me bring out. They started singing "Happy Birthday," loud and off-key, but were quickly drowned out by the rest of us. Afterward, Brad said he wanted to say a couple of things.

"If this is what being sixty is like, bring it on," he began to a round of hearty cheers. "But I want to thank all of you for being here to celebrate with me. I think the next decade will the best of my life. I can't imagine it without you, Kathryn." He looked directly at me. "You have given my life new meaning."

I went over, gave him a big kiss, and whispered, "I can't imagine my life without you either." He gave me that sexy grin that I loved. Then someone yelled, "We're still here. Remember us? Get a room!" Much laugher followed and several ribald comments that I hoped were over Chapin's and Eli's heads.

Presents followed. There were sweet ones, and practical ones, and censored ones from his co-workers. It was my turn. "I'll be right back. It will take just a few minutes." My present was at a neighbor's house, where I went to retrieve him. I came back into the garden. The boys spotted me first. "Grandma, it's a dog, it's a dog!"

I took him up to Brad. "His name is Brewster, and he needs a new home." Brewster was a rescue black Lab/Great Dane mix, still a puppy, but already weighing seventy pounds at six months. Brewster was wearing a handsome new red collar that had a big red bow attached. He sat at Brad's feet and looked up at him adoringly. I had already fallen in love with this dog.

"Hey, feller," Brad said, reaching down to scratch him under his chin. "You are a big boy. Do you think you will like riding in trucks?" Brewster stood up and wagged his tail. I could see that Brad was totally smitten.

"Is it OK?" I said. "I thought a dog would be nice company for you at the cottage." I was a little anxious, because I didn't know how Brad would feel about a dog.

"He is a great dog, Kathryn. I like him a lot, and I think we will get along just fine."

Little could I have known they would become inseparable. I had already decided that I would keep Brewster if Brad didn't like him, so I felt a mixture of relief and sadness.

My date to leave for Italy was approaching. Brad and Brewster were moving into my house and would stay there while I was gone. They would spend weekends at the cottage, renovating. Brad had given up his apartment and would be living with me for a while until his house at the shore was winterized. My concession to him living with me was that he was welcome whenever the weather was bad or he worked late. Brewster was always welcomed. "I think you like the dog better than me," he grumbled one night.

"Umm, maybe," I said. "But you generally smell better."

I would be leaving for Italy this time at peace with myself. Brad and I were on an even keel. I could see us growing old together. Maybe we would get married one day. I felt confident that our differences could be worked out. Issues around trust and my independent nature lingered, but I felt confident that time and patience would eventually resolve them.

Besides, there were enough weddings going on. Larry and Nan had decided to get married on January first, to start a new year and a new life together. Their small attached house at Sammy's would be completed by then.

Brad was doing the work, and I knew he would get it finished so that he could devote his attention to his own place.

So much had changed in the past two years. Nan would remain in the role of housekeeper nanny for Sammy and Jenn, but with a maid service to assist her. Larry was very protective and did not want her to be overwhelmed in her new life, and he wanted them to have time for themselves. He was a changed man and knew a good thing when he saw it. I couldn't believe that he was the same man who had once been married to Linda. Brad and I often joined them, both at home and out on the town. They made a delightful couple.

Sammy's life also was much happier than it had been in years. I was so proud of my son. He had stepped up to the plate when push came to shove. He had really proven himself to be the man I hoped he would be, and he was the best father imaginable. He loved his new business, and it was booming. Life felt good all the way around. Eli remarked recently that he had two sets of grandparents. Both boys seemed to have forgotten Linda altogether. It was her loss. Brad fit right in, and the boys adored him.

It would be a bittersweet trip back to Italy this fall with Karen. I did not know when or if I would ever return after this time. I would gently say good-bye to Salvatore. He had meant so much to me. I could hardly think of him not being in my life, but I knew that I had to commit to my life in America, and to Brad. I no longer felt that I needed to run away. I was excited about my future, and there was so much to be explored right in my own backyard.

# EPILOGUE

# ANA

I

oday is my wedding day. I am excited beyond belief. Who would have thought two years ago that I would be getting married again? My love for Theo is immeasurable. It is different from my love for Mark. He will always be in my heart. I have not and will not forget you, my dear Mark. You were once the love of my life. I know you would approve of Theo. You would admire his passion for what is right in life. His intuition is solid, and he is so gentle and caring. I know that he will love and protect me all the rest of my life, as I will him.

Theo and I decided to be traditional and spend time apart before the wedding. I have been sequestered in this hotel in Montepulciano for two days and nights with my family and friends. My room overlooks the main piazza, and I can see almost every street from my window on the third floor. The town sparkles in the early morning sunlight on this early fall day. This is the first moment that I have been completely alone as I wait for the wedding to begin. In one hour, I will leave this room with the women in my life: my mother, Mimi, Lena, Neva, Leah, Marta, and of course, Sara and Nikki.

We will walk to the city hall together and meet Theo, my father, Rudi, his sons, and Jakob Weiss, who will come from the opposite direction for our civil ceremony. As we proceed through the city, a medieval band from

Assisi will lead us, playing the lively tunes from those ancient times. There will be no religious ceremony, but we are treating this as a real wedding. The men will wear tuxedos, and I will have on my beautiful, green organza dress. Sara and Nikki are dressed in tea-length buttercup dresses and will throw flower petals from little baskets as we walk. Along the way, our families and friends will join us as we walk through this sweet little town. I am touched to see that many homes and businesses have been decorated with flowers and signs wishing us well.

It seems as if the entire village is involved in our wedding in many ways. Luigi and his family have helped prepare food, much of which has been donated by the merchants whom Theo and I have come to love. I am told that a group from town has decorated the farm to look like a garden. I can't wait to see how beautiful it looks. There will be music from both a quartet and a band. Salvatore Sierra, Kathryn's friend, has sent cases of champagne. There is a running rivalry between him and the other vintners in the area. They, too, have sent all kinds of wine for the wedding. All is in good fun because Signor Sierra is well respected in this region. He will be Kathryn's escort today and her friend, Karen.

I see Kathryn now, down on the piazza, waiting for the bridal party, holding hands and laughing with Salvatore. They are sitting outside a little café, having a morning cappuccino. Kathryn looks so beautiful and young in her pale-blue silk dress. Salvatore and Kathryn are very affectionate with one another. He leans over, kisses her on the neck and says something in her ear, and they both laugh. Salvatore is clearly smitten. Can this man, Brad, compete with him? Kathryn seems to think so, and she is handling the situation well. I know I couldn't do it. Theo is the only man I want in my life.

Kathryn looks breathtaking. She sparkles like a gem. No one would ever guess that she is sixty-four. We met once a week for lunch after her Italian class last semester, and we marveled at how much we have in common, being twenty years apart in age. Initially, our common ground was six years of widowhood with no life to speak of, but now we have our mutual love of Italy, the Italian language, and new relationships in our lives. We both believe that we are just beginning a new chapter in our future. Kathryn is a model of how I want to be when I am older, and she has taught me so much about starting over.

She told me recently that she feels like all the tension has left her life, because many of the issues troubling her have been resolved. "The biggest news," she divulged at one of our lunches, was the marriage of Nan Coulous to her daughter-in-law's father. She would continue to support the family as the housekeeper. The children's grandfather is a sidekick in whatever was needed. The family is thrilled with this solution, especially since Kathryn's daughter-in-law received another promotion.

"What about Brad?" I asked Kathryn. "Does having him in your life ease the tension, as well? And will you see Salvatore again?"

"Brad brings a different kind of tension. He still doesn't entirely trust women, but I think he now realizes that I am not out to get him or manipulate him into marriage. In fact, he is the one who wants to settle down, but I still need space and independence. I think we have worked out a good compromise for now."

"Don't you want to marry again?"

"No, I don't think so, at least not in the immediate future. Brad and I are still working through our differences, and there is a lot of stuff going on with him and his family. It will take time to sort through all of this. I don't like his daughters, and I have already had enough family stress to last me a lifetime. I don't need to have it in my life again. Brad, on the other hand, has been a wonderful addition in my family. He has been great with Chapin, who absolutely adores him. Brad has taught him many little building tricks, and along the way, some discipline in getting a job done well. That has softened my heart in a huge way in this relationship, despite the problems with his daughters and ex-wife. Right now, I don't need anything else from Brad but exactly what we have. There is no reason to hurry into marriage."

"And Salvatore?"

"Ah, Salvatore. Another story. How can you not love a man who adores your every move? He is interesting and cultured. I love being with him. We can talk all day long and never be bored. I think if he lived in America, this would be a far more serious thing. However, the reality is that he lives thousands of miles from me in his family home, which was designed by his beloved late wife, with a sister who guards him like a lioness. No matter how hard Salvatore tried, I would never fit into his family, and his villa would always be Nunzia's home. My love for him would not survive daily life there. I would feel stifled and depressed in a very short time. No, sadly, that's a relationship that is doomed. And in my heart, I am not sure that Salvatore really wants to get married again. I think his love for Nunzia is forever."

I laughed. "Poor Kathryn. What a dilemma—two men who have your heart."

"I am very lucky, and I appreciate both of them. They are both good men."

As if she knows I'm thinking about her, Kathryn looks up and sees me in the window. She points me out to Salvatore, and they both throw me kisses and wave madly. Salvatore makes a celebratory gesture with his arms raised over his head. What a lovely couple they make. I walk back across the room and my thoughts turn to a conversation that I had had with Theo a week ago.

I told him that I wanted to convert to Catholicism. The Catholic Church has been in my life since I moved next door to the Capellos as a child, and I am very fond of the village priest, Father Nickolaus. Theo is fine with it. "Whatever makes you happy, Ana, will make me happy."

My only sadness today is that we are not getting married in a church and having the blessing that it would bestow on our life together. I would love to hear the church bells ring out after our ceremony, echoing throughout the entire town. Father Nickolaus reminded me that the bells always ring at noon, and I might want to plan my day accordingly. So we have. Our ceremony is scheduled for eleven thirty and we should be walking back through town just after noon.

Religion is not an issue in our lives. We both have strong beliefs, and they complement one another, philosophically and spiritually. The blessing of the Church is my personal issue, but Theo says that God brought us together and has already blessed us. I think he is right.

We are going to Israel in two months. Theo has some Interpol business, and I am going to do some research for my next book. Things are going well professionally. Fifteen universities have picked up my first book as a text for their classes. I have been invited to speak at symposiums on medieval Jews and on Jewish life in contemporary Germany. The money that I am making from this will help sustain me until I can find a permanent job in Tubingen. I will be an associate visiting professor this winter, thanks to Jakob's influence, but that is just for one semester. I've decided that I am not going to worry about the future, because I know something will turn up. Theo supports me entirely in my professional endeavors. He has given over his second bedroom in Tubingen as an office for me.

I love our farmhouse here in Italy. I have put twin beds in the extra room upstairs, for the little nephews, but I reminded Theo that Mimi will probably get married one day and have children.

That was earthshaking for him. "Me, an opa?" he said wonderingly.

"It's always a possibility."

Now he is looking at ways to put another little bathroom upstairs. The house is so beautiful, with the best of American and European design. It is our house together. My stamp is on it as much as Theo's.

I return to the window and see Francesca Botti talking with Mimi and Francesca's daughter, Toni. Toni just received a scholarship to American University. Francesca is thrilled, because she secretly wants to move to America. Theo says her life is miserable with her husband, Fredo.

"He has been a brute since we were kids. We warned her about Fredo, and I think he has beaten her, but Francesca is too proud to say anything. He is a drunk—and a mean one, at that. I hope she gets away from him. If Francesca had ever said one word, I would have put that louse in the worst prison in Italy, and she knows that. She has been supporting him for years. He almost never works now."

Maybe I can offer Francesca my town house for a while, and Lena could help her find work. We just have to find a way of offering help without offending her, as if she would be doing us a favor. I know Kathryn would love to have her nearby, and she would be a great support.

Mimi will give Toni good advice about how to adapt to American life. It is too bad, in one respect, that Mimi will back in Heidelberg this fall. Marta was able to convince her to come back, and they have reconciled to some degree. It will be beneficial that both of her parents will be remarried. Whew, she is headstrong and stubborn. It will take a strong, strong man to live with her. I am grateful that we became friends.

There is a knock at my door. Lena enters, looking gorgeous in a fuchsia strapless dress. Her dark curly hair surrounds her head like a cherub's. We both look at each other, my lifelong friend, who has always, always been there for me. I start tearing up and see Lena's eyes becoming wet. We hug each other tightly.

"Don't you dare cry," she warned. "You will ruin your perfect makeup."

I can't help it, and tears start down my face. "Lena, what would I ever have done without you? You will visit me often, won't you?"

She starts dabbing my wet face. "Stop crying, silly, of course I will visit. Sara and Nikki are coming next summer, aren't they? Mama now thinks she will come also.. That will make three visits to the Todi relatives in three years. Don't worry; you will see a lot of us."

"Is it time?" I asked.

"Yep, girl. It's getting-hitched time, and there is a handsome man down there waiting for you. Are you ready?"

Before we can leave, Mimi bursts in, wearing a deep-purple dress. She looks at Lena and me and says in her exasperated, staccato manner, "Tears? Ana, you are marrying my father. What are you crying for? It is time to go. We cannot be late." Sometimes, Mimi can be just as German as her father.

Lena and I laugh and hug again. I even give Mimi a hug. "You are right, Mimi, I am marrying your wonderful father."

I look around my room. I see all kinds of things that have been part of the past two days cluttering the room. They represent my past and present. I am ready, so ready, to marry Theo. It is time to meet my future.

# II

That night at the Savoy Hotel in Florence, I lie in Theo's arms. We are both tired and happy. Theo wanted us to come back to the Savoy for our first night as husband and wife.

"It was the most beautiful wedding in the world." I comment.

"Ja. I will never forget you walking through the streets of Montepulciano to meet me. You were a vision, Ana, enough to make me think of saints."

I laugh. "I think I have just proved that I am no saint."

He chuckles. "Ja, perhaps. But you are right; the day was perfect from start to finish. Luigi and Francesca did a magnificent job getting the food and the house ready for our guests."

"I agree. One of my favorite memories will always be the townspeople, in their doors, clapping and yelling happy thoughts before and after the ceremony. And how they followed behind all the way to the city hall. I will love Father Nickolaus forever for waiting for us to pass the church and then walking over to give us his blessing."

"Ja, Ana that was very special. I was touched that he would include me, a Jew. He is a true man of God."

I continue recapturing the day's highlights. "I was awestruck at how beautiful everything looked when we arrived at the farmhouse. Flowers spilled from every possible place. It looked like a garden that had been in place for years. We must keep it that way—it is the final touch for the house. It needed landscaping to complete all the work that had been done inside."

I continue as Theo lazily strokes me. "The tables were exquisite and the food was delicious. I have never seen so much food in one place before. Do you think every single person in Montepulciano made something?"

"Ja, it's possible." Theo chuckles.

"Theo, our house looked perfect, didn't you think? All the changes that you made are impressive—and our new furniture, the antiques we bought in Todi—I couldn't believe how well everything came together. Everyone seemed to have a good time and really enjoyed themselves. Leah insists that Farmhouse Paradiso will be in a future magazine article.

"Ja, Leah will hound us until we relent and let photographers come in. She took many pictures at the wedding, so maybe she could just use those and leave us be." He changes the subject. "Your friend, Kathryn, and Salvatore Sierra, very serious, no?

"No, I don't think so. Kathryn's heart is in America. I am not sure that she will see Signor Sierra again, and I think he will be heartbroken. She is very serious about another man. But on the other hand, I am not sure she is ready to give up Signor Sierra. I think it is a dilemma, but one she is enjoying."

"You Americans are heartbreakers," Theo jokes. "I think Lena could be the next bride. She let her guard down today."

"That's what Italy does to you," I say playfully. "It's magical. You forget your problems and concerns and allow yourself the freedom to fall in love. Palmer is an excellent choice for her. I know they would be happy together. I hope cupid's dart went straight into her heart today."

"Ana?"

I'm drifting off.

"Don't go to sleep yet, Liebchen. I haven't told you the secret place we are going on our honeymoon."

I had forgotten, and now I'm instantly awake. "Where?" I can't believe that I have not asked about the destination. I knew it was somewhere in Italy, but that is all Theo would tell me. He wanted it to be a total surprise.

"This is a truly enchanted place. I always said if I ever married again, this is where I would go."

"I'm completely awake. Tell me."

"Lake Como. We will stay at the Villa d'Este. The hotel is the ultimate in luxury, and the lake is the most beautiful place that I have ever been. I can't wait for us to be there together. I will also take you over to Bellagio for dinner and shopping. It is a charming little town, and I know you will fall in love with it. But it's the Villa d'Este that I can't wait for you to see."

"It could be a shack, and I would love it. I love you, Theo. I knew you would choose the perfect place for us." I kiss him hungrily.

"Mmm," he says with a low growl. "I love you, too, Ana. We may be too tired for our honeymoon tomorrow."

With that, our prehoneymoon continued.

Made in the USA
Charleston, SC
07 June 2014